ROGER SANDRI

THE DEN OF STONE

THE BLOOD KEY

Cover art by Giulietta Zawadzki.
Cover design by MiblArt.com
Editing by River Ari

Published by Roger Sandri
@roger_sandri_wordslinger on Instagram

To all those Rainny days

that made me pick up the pencil

and write.

Thank you.

Also thanks to you, reader, for taking a chance on my debut tale. This is a dark story. You should be forewarned about some of the content contained within. My main goal is to entertain and I have no desire to bring up past traumas. Potential triggering content includes violence, language, sexual content, nudity, sexual assault, loss of loved ones, alcohol abuse, forced captivity, and claustrophobia.

PROLOGUE

September 24, 2013

The winged gargoyle watched from the shadows deep beneath tall pines as two small shapes loped toward him. A figure the size of an average human in a dingy hoodie and jeans followed. Smoke began to rise from the roof of the sprawling mansion behind them. The beast's elongated jaw twisted into the best smile it could manage.

"Is it done, Havardr?" the gargoyle asked as they escaped the dim light of the rising sun and entered the forest shade.

The minion gargoyle Havardr pushed back his hood and nodded, holding out his clawed hand. A small stone nestled in his palm. Edthgar leaned closer. His glowing eyes flared bright crimson at the sight of the ancient carvings in the stone.

Two gremlins hopped about their feet. One piped, "Yes, Lord Edthgar. May we have our reward now?"

Havardr tucked the rune back into his pockets as Edthgar turned to the gremlins. *"It was freedom you wished for after this mission, correct?"*

The two gremlins nodded eagerly until Edthgar's large fingers wrapped around their spindly bodies. Their tiny claws jabbed his stone skin to no effect.

"Havardr, grant their wish."

The minion gargoyle withdrew a copper dagger from his pocket. The gremlins squealed in Edthgar's crushing grasp.

Havardr plunged his dagger into the top of each of their heads.

The two small creatures stilled and Edthgar let out a low, grating laugh. Blood coated his granite claws as he watched Havardr wipe the dagger's blade clean on a tree trunk.

"Dinner?" Edthgar asked, holding out one of the gremlin corpses.

Havardr shook his head. Edthgar stuffed the gremlin into his jaws and crunched.

The minion gargoyle tucked the dagger back into his hoodie pocket and watched the first flames emerge from the mansion windows.

Edthgar swallowed the chewed gremlin whole and said, *"We must make haste before the sun rises too brightly. I'll toss the other one into the waves where none of his brethren will see."*

Havardr's dark eyes returned to Edthgar. He raised his hood again before climbing between his master's wings. They took off into the remaining clouds as the mansion's alarm system began blaring.

1

Courtney muttered under her breath as the anti-lock brakes shook her Pontiac. Her car stopped inches short of the minivan backing out of a driveway in front of her. Her hand slammed the horn once she caught her breath. "Watch what the fuck you're doing, numb nuts," she yelled, wishing the careless van driver could hear her.

Courtney accelerated slowly, dictated by the crawling minivan. The frown on her face faded some as she tapped the steering wheel to Iron Maiden's "Fear of the Dark." The heavier rhythm guitar at intro's end perked the final frown vestiges into a devious smirk. *I should've stuck with it instead of selling my guitar.*

The van braked hard as she let her disinterested mind wander. Courtney skidded to a halt inches from the van's bumper again. A raccoon waddled across the road, so she couldn't blame the van driver this time. She did anyway, uttering curses under her breath.

Courtney glanced at her watch as the van leisurely accelerated. 9:38 p.m. Thirty-five minutes gone since she'd left the parking lot at work; not long until she'd pull in the driveway to Uncle Hank's mansion. In five years living with her uncle on the outskirts of

Drake's Landing, only twice had anyone slowed her drive up Overlook Road on a weeknight. Even the weekend cruisers avoided this street, twisty and smooth with only two houses on nine miles of asphalt, which was part of why she liked it.

The van turned left, descending towards Sir Francis Drake Boulevard. Courtney opened the throttle and zoomed up the wooded hill. The Pacific breeze whipped into her open window and through her wavy shoulder-length rusty red hair. She loved driving fast whenever possible, which had been a rarity growing up in San Francisco.

The road was lined by heavy coyote brush with scattered pines in the first half mile, but firs took over further up. Shortly before the Mays mansion, the tree cover thickened enough to cast dark shadows across the entire road surface on the brightest sunny days. Trees surrounded the house and insulated it from the rest of the world. Courtney loved the serenity the forest provided from the rest of small-town northern California.

The satellite radio signal broke up before it snuffed out completely. Signal loss always happened as she rounded the final corner before the driveway, but it didn't bother her since some Def Leppard song was playing; she wasn't fond of them. Courtney never knew if thick branches disrupted the signal or if her uncle possessed some sort of device interfering with it and her few friends' cell phones. She liked to think Dear Old Unc figured out a way to steal satellite TV.

The two stone gargoyle statues on either side of the driveway came into view as she rounded the corner. They never failed to give her the creeps, even after five years. Hank told her they provided an intimidation factor before seeing the house—and deterred Jehovah's Witnesses and politicians.

Courtney flicked her car around the gentle turn up the wide and twisty driveway. Her Pontiac passed beneath the intertwined branches of two trees forming a natural arch as the pavement straightened, ending in a circle big enough for several full-sized cars in front of the house. An old metal street lamp she always wondered how Hank got a hold of stood in the grassy island in the middle of the circle, lighting up her uncle's SUV and a large sedan in front of it.

Her brakes screeched as she parked behind Hank's old Blazer. He made his living restoring and modifying antique vehicles, and the immaculate finish showed his attention to detail to potential customers.

She stuffed her keys in her leather purse, climbed out of her Pontiac, and walked past the house entrance to have a look at the unknown car. A winged 'B' adorned the trunk lid. The car shone in dark metallic green, not black like she first thought. Its wheels gleamed in the dim lighting from the antique street lamp, as did the hood ornament. "I knew you had some rich friends, Unc, but someone who drives a Bentley Mulsanne? I'm impressed," she said to herself as she stared at the blunt mesh grill.

Curious about the owner, she hurried to the mansion's wooden steps. Her friend Andrea called it menacing, with three floors and cut granite construction. The house had Victorian influence with a mansard roof and a tower on one side rising above the main portion of the house as a fourth level. Arched windows rounded the tower, which was topped with an onion dome. She teased Hank sometimes about taking the phrase 'a man's home is his castle' too literally when he'd designed the place.

Courtney stopped at the aged oak door and reached for the iron ring in the center of the door to announce her presence. The door creaked inward. She stepped into the foyer.

Off with the work shit.

She set her glasses and purse on the small table by the door and yanked off her blue polo, chucking it in the corner of the open closet as she kicked off her sneakers and pushed them under the table. The chain strap on her Harley purse jangled as she slung it back over her shoulder.

"Much better." Courtney removed her belt and tossed it over her shoulder, then grabbed her glasses and headed to the stairs at the end of the hall.

Her uncle called out as she passed the kitchen. "Courtney, do you mind coming in here? I have a guest I'd like you to meet."

Let's get this over with. I'll meet the rich prick in my tank top. Hope the pencil-necked geek is intimidated by these abs.

A tall man in a tailored black suit stood next to the marble-topped island in the center of the kitchen. The first thing she noticed were his piercing blue eyes. He had short, wavy black hair, and his strong jaw was coated with a thick layer of stubble. Late twenties or early thirties, but he exuded an air of confidence suggesting he might be older. Uncle Hank generally only worked for people he liked since retirement, so this man likely earned whatever fortune it took to buy the Bentley out front, despite his youthful appearance. Something didn't click, though, and she regarded his outstretched hand with a raised eyebrow.

"My name is Ivan Trebeschkov, and I am pleased to finally have the opportunity to meet you," the man said with a noticeable Russian accent, though every word was clear.

She shook his hand, and his grip was firm but gentle. The thought crossed her mind he could crush the bones in her hand if he wanted to. Her gaze drifted to the copper ring on his finger with a large ruby on it, then over the carefully stitched suit. Ivan seemed precise, perhaps to a fault, despite what the stubble on his chin suggested.

"Courtney Mays. Pleased to meet you, too. I love the Bentley."

He held her hand in his palm to kiss the back of it, then spoke again. "Thank you. Your uncle has told me much about you, such as how you aided him with the restoration of my 1932 Cadillac. It is most embarrassing to have not become acquainted sooner, though I wish it were under better circumstances. You see, my mansion outside of San Rafael succumbed to a fire earlier this morning while I was away attending to business, and I am in need of a place to stay in the area so I can deal with my insurance. I asked your uncle if I may store one of my vehicles here, and he extended the offer for me to stay as well. Long story short, I may be residing here for a few weeks, dependent upon the swiftness of my insurance. I hope you do not mind?"

"Uh, not at all. As long as I don't have to give up my room."

"Fear not. I am staying in the storage room above the garage. I shall not interfere with your routine. I have lived in far less accommodating conditions in the past, so there is no concern," Ivan said.

Courtney nodded. "Speaking of the garage, do you mind if I take a peek at that Caddy? It'd be nice to have a nostalgia trip."

"I am afraid that is impossible, as the Cadillac appears to be a total loss due to the fire. My most prized vehicle survived. I had it outside of my garage because I intended to go for a drive in celebration of a successful deal. It is a 1930 Bugatti Type 37. I can show that one to you if you would like."

"I'd love to, but I should talk to Unc first. I'll meet you in the garage."

"We have a deal, Miss Mays," Ivan said, nodding towards her as if to tip his nonexistent hat before exiting the kitchen.

Courtney turned to her uncle. "Wealthy Russian businessman friends who aren't decrepit? You're full of surprises."

Hank rubbed his chin through his full gray beard as he said, "I'm sorry I couldn't get a hold of you at work. Ivan called about half an hour after you left. If you'd get a cell phone like I keep asking, I could've at least sent a text."

"I like being hard to reach. Besides, if it's enough of an emergency you have Andrea's number. You could text her and have her tell me."

"I'd much rather be able to get a hold of you than the ditz queen. No offense. But anyways, how was work?" Hank asked.

"Sucked. And yeah, I know Andrea isn't the smartest, but she's always there for me. I hate even carrying my purse around, so why would I want to lug around and pay a mint for some damn phone that's smarter than I am, and never use it aside from the two times a year you'd call me with something I'll find out when I get home anyway?"

"Maybe to humor your poor old uncle?"

"Unc, you sure as hell aren't poor. Your taste in hairstyles may be, but you're not."

"It's been this way since 1976. Don't fix what's not broken."

"Exactly, and me not wanting a cell phone is perfectly reasonable, not broken. I'm going to look at Ivan's car now, then call Luke, and I'll be back to talk more, okay?" she said as she walked to the doorway.

"I'll be here when you come back." Hank sipped his green tea.

"You better be, or I'll track you down."

Courtney headed down the short hallway. Often she wondered what possessed her uncle to choose slate gray for the walls, though she loved the thick hunter green carpet. The medieval-style lanterns hanging from the ceiling struck her as strange, too, especially since they contained modern compact fluorescent bulbs. Then again, Uncle Hank made no excuses for his eccentricity. There were no family pictures on the walls, aside from one of her standing next to the finished Cadillac. Numerous framed photographs of his favorite restoration projects lined the walls instead.

An empty picture frame hung at the end of the hall. This was reserved for Hank's pride and joy, the 1941 Willys sedan he rescued from a junkyard in the Arizona desert—his first project car after his medical discharge brought him home from the Vietnam War. The frame would remain empty until he was satisfied with the car, which probably meant as long as he lived.

Courtney dropped off her purse and belt by the wrought-iron spiral staircase, then turned right at the end of the hall to head toward the heavy door to the garage, which had a shaded window for when Hank welded. The door sealed like a freezer, preventing any potential gas leaks or fires from escaping into the rest of the mansion.

Courtney opened the heavy door and looked over the perpetually unfinished Willys parked closest to the interior of the two-bay garage workshop. Massive tool boxes lined the walls, with matching burnt metallic orange paint like the old sedan, and chrome handles to match the car's modern wheels and glistening chrome trim. Her mind drifted to the tuned V8 under the hood and her dreams of seeing how many tires she'd destroy if she ever got to drive the thing.

She sighed and looked away, knowing Hank would change everything about it after a few months. It hurt to think about since she thought the current state of the car was perfect. Green was her favorite color, but in her opinion nothing complemented the curvy Willys better than this shade of orange in all its metal-flaked glory.

What she saw when she glanced away was equally breathtaking. The old Bugatti sat beside the Willys, but the shocking part was the contrasting appearances of the cars. The open-air Bugatti wore a heavily faded British racing green paint job and the brown leather seats were severely worn. The dull chrome bits were pitted and scratched. A couple of spokes were missing from the wire wheels, and the small fenders were covered in dings and dents. The car looked as if it spent years driving through gravel pits, then wound up locked away for decades in some forgotten barn.

"What do you think?" Ivan asked, standing in the corner by the staircase to the upstairs storage room.

"It'll be impressive once it's restored."

Ivan shook his head and said, "No restoration is necessary. I have done what maintenance is necessary to keep her running as perfectly as new, as well as free of structural damage. This car has been in my family since she left the factory. The blemishes tell the stories of her past, just as surely as the exhaust note speaks of her intentions."

"I see." Courtney stared at a large ding in the left front fender, reminiscing about Hank teaching her to shape new fenders on the Caddy.

He noticed and walked over, placing his hand on the spot. "This is from when I let my love, Anatalia, drive her for the first time. All these marks have a tale behind them, and I can tell you of all of them. They are battle scars, some of which are cautionary tales, and others tell of great and honorable deeds. Over eighty years, this car has been through hell and back. It would be shameful to take that history away with a restoration," he said as he shook his head.

"If you don't mind my asking, where is Anatalia?"

"She passed away quite some time ago," he said quietly, looking away.

"I'm so sorry. How did it happen?"

"That is a story for another day. Come now, have a seat." He beckoned her towards the driver's side.

Courtney gingerly climbed in so she wouldn't mar the finish any more than it already was or nudge the shifter on the roadster's side. It crossed her mind how odd it must feel to drive a right-hand drive vehicle on American roads as she settled into the worn seat. The thought of Ivan's departed love and his unwillingness to share details about what transpired crept into mind. She wondered what he was thinking as a smile crossed his face. Her eyes darted over the gauges to avoid looking into his icy gaze.

"Do you know how to drive a standard?" he asked.

"No. I've tried to talk Unc or Luke into teaching me, but nothing yet."

"I have never had the opportunity to drive an automatic shifting vehicle. Perhaps we shall both be presented with the chance in the coming days."

"Maybe we will. But wait, the Bentley isn't an automatic? I thought all Mulsannes were," she wondered aloud, staring at the Bugatti's bare aluminum dash.

"It is a standard, and quite possibly the only one in existence. It is amazing what one will do for someone who possesses the financial wherewithal to purchase the entire company merely with the intent of liquidating the position of the individual who said no," he mused.

"Sounds fun. Would you have done that?" she asked, contemplating what his statement said about his morals. Every word he spoke added more questions than answers.

"No. However, it can be quite fun to flaunt money in that manner without having to spend it at all. If they said no after my threat, I simply would have bought something else instead to maintain the disguise of an affluent snob who wants to be chauffeured." Ivan paused. "Now, I do not mean to change the subject, but may I inquire as to who this Luke you mentioned is?"

Courtney blushed. "Luke Stillman. He's my boyfriend. He works in a used auto parts store in Inverness."

"Ah, yes. Goldman Auto Parts is one of the nicest stores in the Point Reyes area. I have been there a few times. They have a talent for finding parts for rare and unusual vehicles. Goldman is the only place in this area I was able to acquire parts for my Volvo PV544. It is quite a rugged little automobile, and I am glad I had it shipped to my Romanian mansion months ago. I would have been heartbroken if that car had been lost."

Courtney laughed. "Luke has some old '70s Volvo wagon he won't give up on. He's kind of scruffy with uncontrollable hair under a ratty old Sharks hat."

"Yes, I have met him. Your boyfriend shares much blame for my obsession in keeping another faithful automotive companion on the road."

Courtney thought of the call she had to make to Luke, and tried to block out Ivan's unnerving speech patterns and mannerisms. "I should get going. I need to call Luke to let him know I got tomorrow off from work, and maybe warn him we've got a house guest so he doesn't drool on the Bentley when he picks me up."

"I would not want to delay you. Enjoy." Ivan gave her his hand to help her out of the Bugatti.

"Thank you," she said, walking past the Willys to the open door.

Ivan nodded and knelt down to rub the dented fender. At the doorway she looked back again at the conundrum of Ivan Trebeschkov. Whatever troubled her about him hid within a dense fog, so she tried to ignore the ridiculous conspiracy theories darting out from every corner of her mind.

She walked to the staircase, glancing back at the door's small window. Courtney grabbed her things and hurried up one spiral to the second floor, passing the laundry room on her way to her bedroom.

It was sparsely decorated, with a hardwood floor like the kitchen and storage room. Half the floor was empty, serving as space for her workouts using the mats tucked behind the headboard. A rack containing dumbbell weights stood in the corner. On the wall hung a pull-up bar, while the opposite door hid behind a shelf full of worn fantasy books and DVDs. The wall at the front of the house was dominated by a large window shrouded in emerald green curtains.

Her purse and belt dropped on the bed's dark green sheets, and she grabbed the cordless phone from the stained wood nightstand beside the bed. Phone in hand, she departed the room and headed up the staircase.

The third floor was Hank's domain, with his room and office. She only ever set foot on the third floor if Hank was sick and needed help with something. The office always made her curious, but not enough to betray her uncle's wishes. That mystery never bothered her as much as Ivan's strangeness.

She climbed the stairs to the tower she loved so much. Arched windows gave a serene view of the trees around the mansion and backyard. As she dialed Luke's number, she gazed at the grassy clearing behind the house. A small artificial pond connected to a natural stream formed a border to the clearing. The outside light over the rear patio reflected in the rippling water, which moved in concert with the trees as they swayed in the gentle breeze.

On the other end, the phone rang once, twice. Courtney watched a squirrel jump into the bird feeder at the edge of the trees. The phone rang a third time and a fourth before she heard the click of the answering machine. "You have reached Luke Stillman. Please leave a message after the beep, unless you're a telemarketer. If that's you, just hang up because I don't want to buy your crap or vote for you."

Courtney snickered every time she heard this, and the end of her laugh always ended up at the very start of her message. She must sound like a dork, though Luke never mentioned it. Perhaps everyone reacted the same way to his answering machine, or maybe he was especially tolerant of awkward message openings.

"Hey Luke, it's Court. Just thought I'd let you know I managed to swap off of work tomorrow, so I'll be free for anything you want to do. Let me know if six sounds good. Later."

She pushed the button on the phone and set it down on the tower's wraparound wood bench to watch the squirrel in the dimly lit feeder. It dashed out and scampered across the grass to a distant tree. Something large rustled in the brush near the feeder, but she couldn't see what it was. Tule Elk, maybe?

An odd growl emanated from the forest. It was anything but deer-like. The growl sent a chill down her spine and made her reach for the phone to head back downstairs.

Courtney darted into her room and grumbled to herself, "Idiot. Scared of a growl. Some tough martial artist you are."

Even if it was a cougar, it couldn't get in the house. She put the phone on its base and set her glasses down next to it, then shook her head as she sat on the bed. *What next, worry more about Richie McSoviet? Oh, work out. Yeah, that.*

She walked to the desk to turn the computer on. A special playlist always accompanied her routine to help her time it. Her eyes fell upon the picture of her and Hank at the famous Point Reyes Station. He'd taken her there as a high school graduation present and she'd framed the photograph. It might have been the happiest moment so far of her life, as John Carpenter's *The Fog* was one of her favorite movies and the lighthouse played a prominent part in the film. It was just one of the many times throughout her childhood and adolescence she'd wished she lived with Hank rather than her parents. Two months later, on her eighteenth birthday, a particularly bad argument with her father had transpired. That night she'd called Hank and packed everything she owned.

The memory reminded her of her promise to Hank to continue their conversation. She hurried down to the hallway, intending to creep to the kitchen.

She loved sneaking up on her uncle, even if it felt childish sometimes. Her gymnastics and martial arts training made her agile and stealthy. He usually sat on a high stool facing the window above the sink, which made the task easier.

She tiptoed into the kitchen to find Hank facing the doorway.

"If you're going to sneak up on me, don't tell me you'll be back," Hank suggested, still sipping slowly at his tea.

Courtney rolled her eyes. "So, what were we talking about before?"

"Your day, your stubbornness in the cell phone department, our guest. Feel free to add anything you want," Hank reminded her.

"Don't change anything about the Willys. It's perfect the way it is."

"Not to me. What do you think about that Bugatti?"

"Not bad. Ivan sure is sentimental, and a bit odd. I prefer cars with a roof."

Hank smiled and said, "You wouldn't be saying that if you drove it. Those old roadsters are the epitome of man and machine being one. It takes a lot of effort to drive, but it's more rewarding because of it. Maybe Ivan will let you drive it someday and you'll see for yourself."

"Unc, you won't even let me drive your truck. What makes you think he'll let me drive an old family heirloom?"

"As you said, he's very sentimental. He tends to like sharing the things he enjoys. He's also a very patient man, far more than I am."

"For someone who shares so much he sure knows how to be mysterious. Besides, I'll need to learn how to drive a standard first." Courtney sighed.

"That's exactly why we're going to look at a cheap car for you tomorrow before lunch, if it doesn't interfere with your plans with Luke. I found a dark green Jeep you might like."

"You've got to be shitting me!"

Hank scowled.

"Come on Unc, I'm twenty-three. I might not know what I'm doing with my life, but being a proper lady ain't it. I think I can swear every once in a while."

"It's the 'every once in a while' part we have differing opinions on."

"Just like your hair."

"We're onto that again? Really? I may have to rethink this whole Jeep thing."

Courtney stayed quiet until Hank spoke again.

"Very smart, Cricket."

"I always wonder why you picked that nickname instead of grasshopper."

"You're chirpy. Sometimes annoyingly so, sometimes enchantingly so. You're also much easier on the eyes than David Carradine. Therefore, you're Cricket. We've been over this countless times," Hank prodded, amused.

"It never gets old, though. Thanks for the compliment. I'm glad I'm better looking than a dead guy," Courtney joked.

"You're very welcome."

Courtney grabbed a water bottle as she said, "I could never talk to my dad for long. He'd always go total dweeb mode like how I needed to be better academically if I had any hope of being a nurse, when I wanted no part of medicine. He was fuming when I didn't get into Columbia, and even more when he realized I was relieved to not have to go to med school. What a tool."

"Now, now, this is my little brother we're talking about here. Our parents thought he was the good one. I was the screw-up who volunteered to go to 'Nam just to get away from them."

"Unc, you're a little strange, but it's a good strange. You're not a total douche. How many times has he called you since I moved in?" she asked.

"Once. The day after."

"And what did he say?"

"He accused me of brainwashing his little girl, and said the next time we saw each other would be at one or the others' funeral," Hank said quietly.

"For being such a brilliant doctor he's a total moron. Could see I hated hospitals but kept pushing anyway. How can two brothers be so different? You get people's personalities. To him, people are just organs and if you're a square peg who doesn't want to try to fit in a round hole it means you have a disorder. It's why I always wished you were my father, why I knew I had to call you when I needed out. You're so thoughtful with everything—like not just a Jeep but a green one."

"For being so great by your description, I have to wonder why I could never keep a good lady my age interested."

"Thank goodness. My mom was enough. I don't know if I could handle a stepmom."

Hank smiled and looked down at his near-empty mug of tea. He glanced back up at her without saying anything.

"No more arguing? Where's the fun in that?" Courtney teased.

Hank shrugged. "Discretion is the better part of valor. I wasn't quite your age when I got out of the army hospital and came home from 'Nam, thinking I'd get a hero's welcome. Getting spit on before I was off the plane wasn't what I expected, and if my arm hadn't been in a sling I probably would've started a fight. For a while after, I pushed every argument, thinking I knew everything from my time in the jungle. It's a family trait, always having to be right and fighting to prove it. But things happened and my outlook changed. I settled down and learned when to fight or not. You will, too, someday. I just hope it's not from what I went through."

Courtney took a sip of water. "Are you ever going to tell me what happened?"

"Hopefully I never have to. It's better left unsaid unless it happens to you. Ivan would tell you the same."

"So you've told Creepy Commie and won't tell me? I see how it is," Courtney said. "Time to get my workout in, I guess." She put the cap back on the water bottle and stormed out of the kitchen.

"Goodnight, Courtney," Hank yelled.

She didn't acknowledge hearing him. Her breathing echoed in the stairwell though her steps were silent. She paused at the second floor hallway. "Fucking secrets. Bullshit." Courtney headed up to the tower again.

The outside lights were still on, so she leaned on the windowsill and watched the trees sway in the breeze to clear her mind. Her friend Andrea teased her about duality, being both the most impatient person she knew and the closest to zen. Courtney had no desire to be a zen master; she just enjoyed calm. The jokes continued no matter how many times Courtney explained, since as best friends since daycare, Andrea knew all the buttons to push. Their birthdates were days apart; though each was an only child, they may as well have been twin sisters.

Courtney's mind drifted from her best friend back to the bone-chilling growl earlier and she knocked over the water bottle. It bounced off her knee and landed softly in the gray carpet lining the tower, snapping her back to reality.

She checked her watch as she bent down to pick up the water. *Eleven already? Damn, time flies up here.* She left the tower and hustled down the steps to her room.

"Let's get some frustration out," Courtney muttered as she entered the open doorway. She changed out of work khakis and into her favorite shorts. Next came the mats. She covered the floor as they unfolded, and fussed to arrange them perfectly.

Once the mats were set, she reawakened the computer. While waiting on the slow desktop she opened the clasp of her necklace, a silver Celtic knot-work heart Hank gave for her sixteenth birthday. By the time she was done fumbling with the clasp and placing the necklace beside the computer, the login screen popped up. She typed in her password and the waiting game began again, so she fetched her dumbbells from the corner and placed them on either side of the mats where she would do her stretches.

The computer played its little welcome sound and she opened her workout playlist. It started slow, beginning with a recording of a local blues guitarist to time her stretches. As the first notes flowed from the speakers, she lay on the mat and grabbed the dumbbells. Courtney attributed her ability to beat Luke at arm wrestling to this part of her regimen. Afterward came leg and core stretches, accompanied by the last few minutes of the long blues track and Chris Isaak's "Heart-Shaped World," one of Luke's favorites.

Courtney sprang to her feet as Iron Maiden's "Trooper" started and the martial arts part of the routine began. An imagined opponent bore the brunt of her punches, along with a few kicks. The kicks supplanted punches a couple of songs later with an occasional flip thrown in. Once Metallica's "Whiplash" began, so did the acrobatic portion of the workout. The penultimate flip came at the song's finale, ending with her hands on the bar for pull-ups. She dismounted from the bar and landed on the mat with her final flip. Upon landing, she faced upwards with her eyes closed and arms above her head like in the gymnastics competitions that were one of her few good school memories.

Clapping came from just beyond her open door and made her jump. She turned to see Ivan grinning. He enjoyed the show if his enthusiastic clapping was any indication.

"How long were you watching?" she asked, blushing as she took on a defensive stance.

"Your uncle suggested I make my way up here once he heard the music begin, and I arrived shortly before you finished stretching. I must say, you exhibit a focus and determination which is most uncommon amongst appliance salespersons. Your uncle said watching your routine would provide greater insight as to your personality than any conversation could, and his statement has been proven true," Ivan complimented.

"Focus and determination that's most, um, whatever the rest was.... Thank you, I think? Luke only tells me I look super-hot doing this." More questions about Ivan's character rushed to mind. He was analyzing her personality just as she was trying to analyze his, which spooked her, since she suspected she was barely scratching the surface of the enigma before her.

"He is most certainly correct as well. I hope he realizes what a lucky man he is."

"I remind him constantly," Courtney said, staring at the mats instead of Ivan.

"I am certain you do. Now, I must be turning in for the night. You have a wonderful night, Miss Mays," Ivan said as he tipped his nonexistent hat again and left the doorway.

"You too." Courtney walked over to the bed as she watched Ivan leave. One part of her wanted to trust this man immediately, yet another part expected to discover he was a murderous cyborg sent to reap vengeance for the bully she'd forced to eat an earthworm in middle school.

Getting on with her normal post-workout cleanup helped drive away her psychoanalysis of Ivan. Once the mats and weights were put away she walked to the computer to shut it down. A system update message appeared; she scowled at the screen and picked up her work clothes.

"You'd better be done updating before I'm out of the shower." Courtney hissed at the computer as she exited the room with her dirty clothes in hand.

She grabbed a towel and one of her bathrobes from the laundry before heading to the bathroom. The bathroom door swung out to the point where it could hit the storage room door. With Ivan staying there she'd have to be careful not to smack his door.

It occurred to her she didn't have the bathroom to herself anymore, and she swore under her breath. Her work polo was still downstairs, too. The damn thing could stay there.

She'd had concerns about other friends of her uncle's in the past, which wound up allayed over time, so perhaps Ivan would prove to be the same. Hank had decent taste in friends aside from that crusty old Brit, Alec.

Maybe she had reason to worry a little bit. Alec struck her from day one as the typical dirty old man, and she'd caught him gawking at her in tight outfits in the past, or when she'd wandered downstairs in her underwear without realizing there was a guest. Even he never watched her workout.

Hank sent Ivan up, though. He would never send someone shady to watch her. She trusted her uncle completely, despite the secrets he withheld from her. Her concerns faded somewhat as far as Ivan being a pervert. The troubling mystery remained, though, so she resolved to stay wary.

She shut the door behind herself and locked it, in case Ivan didn't think before wandering in to use the bathroom, and she took a moment to scowl at her eyeliner in the mirror. It always wound up being a bit overdone, so she'd taken to wearing dark lipstick to match, along with black nail polish. The look went well with her metal band T-shirts she favored outside of work. Her breath fogged the glass as she brushed a sweat-soaked strand of hair away from her jade green eyes.

Courtney checked her watch and took it off. 12:23 a.m. *Eh, guess I'll be in bed after one.*

The knob squeaked as she turned on the water so it could warm up before she stepped inside. A Cranberries tune she'd loved since she was a kid crossed her mind, but as she hummed the instrumental intro, she thought of Ivan. *No more singing in the shower for a little while—not that I'm any good. Guess it's just me and my thoughts about secrets and mysteries.*

She couldn't hear it while she undressed, but the thing out in the trees growled again as it stared up at the storage room window. Mysteries threatened to be blown wide open.

2

ourtney jerked awake and sat up in bed. She rubbed her eyes, looking to the digital display on her alarm clock. 4:17 a.m. *Three hours' sleep? What the fuck. Whatever woke me up better be damn important.*

Uncle Hank wouldn't be awake this early. She doubted Ivan would be either, since he went to bed shortly before her. Then again, she harbored plenty of doubts about the man.

A metallic clank came from the kitchen. Was a burglar in the house or might Ivan be up to some sort of nefarious misdeeds? Another thump came from below and Courtney threw back her sheets. Her heartbeat hastened as her feet hit the floor.

The green glow of the clock lent a little illumination to the nightstand, reflecting on the glossy finish of her large flashlight. She grabbed it, covering the beam with her fingers so sparse light spilled through in case the potential burglar had a getaway driver outside—only enough illumination to find her glasses on the nightstand and get around her room silently so she could grab a shirt.

Courtney tiptoed to the closet and pulled out one of the worn flannel shirts she liked to wear whenever she helped Hank with a car restoration. The flannel was a bit oversized, and the cuffs stayed unbuttoned, so she had no trouble fitting the sleeves over the flashlight with it against her arm to cover the beam.

Grab the flip-flops? Nah, they'd make noise I don't need. Suck it up, buttercup. Cold steps are nothing compared to what'll happen if this burglar hears you coming.

Some other sound came from below as she slipped into the hall. Almost like... a growl. *Just your imagination. Forget about what you heard in the tower.*

Courtney's heart accelerated as she moved down the moonlit hall. She switched off the flashlight since the moon provided enough illumination. It clicked louder than expected, and she mouthed her favorite four-letter word.

You're just paranoid because of the tower. It's no louder than it's ever been. No burglar would've heard.

Her reassurance failed again, but she believed the part about paranoia. Courtney held the flashlight like a club in case someone did hear the *click* and came up to say, "hi." She wondered if her thunderous pulse was audible. Her steps stayed silent on the metal steps as she descended, but as she focused on stealth and forced away the thoughts of her heart, the chill from the metal pierced. *Don't race for the comfort of the carpet. Don't race for the comfort of the carpet. Sneak.*

Her mind turned instead to the dryness in her throat and mouth. If there wasn't a burglar, a water bottle from the kitchen was in order. A small rumble came from her stomach. *Dammit, not you, too. Keep quiet. Don't go into whale song and give me away.*

She turned so her back was against the opposite wall as she exited the staircase. A random sequence of thumps and bumps came from the kitchen: sounds of a struggle. A solid thump with a metallic ring followed. Hank's stool? There was another thud, like one of those exaggerated smacks from old movies.

More metallic sounds rang out, followed by a voice speaking softly in Russian.

Ivan. I knew there was something weird about that smug bastard.

She rounded the corner, keeping her back to the wall as she tiptoed to the kitchen. Light spilled from the doorway into the hall, so Courtney crouched, hoping the scene in the kitchen was on the opposite side of the island so she could sneak in unseen. Her heart pounded. The flashlight shook in her profusely sweating hands. The mystery beyond the open door scared her, yet part of her relished the chance to use her martial arts on a real target, and picturing Ivan helped wash away the fear.

Bullies and anger had marred her school years, and she'd turned to martial arts to keep the anger under control. However, being skilled with her fists made things more dangerous if she succumbed to an outburst of rage. The thought of a high kick to wipe away the smirk she pictured on Ivan's face quirked the corner of her mouth upwards. Her hands ceased shaking.

Courtney spun through the doorway, still in a crouch, and stopped with her back to the island. A figure stood on the opposite side, and it looked like Ivan from her quick glimpse. He pushed down on something, presumably the burglar, though the grunt it made was weird. *What the fuck is he doing?*

She scooted along the edge of the island to peek around, but paused at a gurgling sound. *Maybe I should run upstairs and pretend I didn't hear anything. Snuggle up under those blankets and forget this.*

Yeah, right.

Her heart jackhammered against her sternum as she leaned her head back against the island, eyes shut tight.

What if it's Unc on the floor? Courtney raised the flashlight and poked her head around the corner.

Her free hand covered her mouth to stifle a gasp at what lay on the floor. The thing resembled the statues at the end of the driveway. It lacked wings but had a short beak in place of a nose and mouth like the statues, if statues leaked blood from their lips.

Are they called lips on a beak? Wait, seriously? There's a monster on the fucking floor and you're going into semantics of lips and beaks? This is insanity.

Moist, greenish-gray scales covered most of what was visible of the body. The torso, shoulders, and head had tougher patches of dark reddish-brown resembling an armadillo's hide. Elongated claws tipped the fingers of its reptilian hands, weakly grasping at Ivan's leg. What struck her were the creature's eyes. They were yellow like a hawk, and conveyed a sentience that recognized and feared its imminent death.

Ivan thrust the tip of a sword into the creature's throat. He twisted the blade and the gurgling ceased. Blood geysered from the wound. A brief sound of suction followed as Ivan tugged the point free. The thing's head flopped onto its side and the dying creature's eyes aimed straight at Courtney. It blinked a final time and stilled.

She ducked back around the island, closed her eyes, and tried to block out the image of the corpse's grotesque face. Head down, she drew her knees to her chest and hugged the flashlight as if it were her childhood teddy bear. No sound escaped her mouth. Her heart found another gear as it tried to burst from her chest and flee without her.

"Have no fear, Courtney. This beast has taken a final breath and shall no longer befoul our realm with its presence," Ivan said.

Courtney turned around the corner of the island again, keeping her eyes high to avoid the sight of the monster. Her voice was high and fast. "How did you know I was here? And more important, what the hell is that thing and what is it doing in the kitchen?"

"I saw your uncle in the doorway, looking down. It was quite easy to analyze the expression on his face. I can also assure you this gargoyle was not making itself a sandwich," Ivan said as he looked down at her and sighed.

She glanced back to the doorway. Her uncle stood over her. Hank wore a hardened expression that accentuated the fine wrinkles of his brow and the corners of his eyes. *Damn, Unc, who knew you could sneak so well? I never heard you behind me.*

He spoke in a quiet voice. "I guess you'll be getting your explanation shortly. Ivan and I will clean up this mess first. You stay right there and be patient."

Courtney nodded and stood. She forced herself to watch as they cleaned up the dead thing and the fluids it leaked.

Ivan wiped the blood off his blade on the thing's thick upper arm before setting the sword onto the granite-topped island. He wrapped paper towels around the throat of his slain opponent, then draped more towels over the shoulder of his crisp white dress shirt. He picked up the dead body with ease, throwing it over his shoulder like an empty duffle bag and walking out.

"That blood is going to be a real bitch to clean up. Are you sure you want me to just stand here? Or, um, maybe look into a funny farm because there's no way this can be real? I must be dreaming, or Andrea was smoking something more than her usual cigarette in the parking lot after work and the secondhand smoke fucked me up. What in the actual fuck is this shit?" Courtney said, staring at the blood puddle.

"It's real, Cricket. You're not crazy—well, not this kind of crazy. We have a special solution which reacts chemically with gargoyle blood and makes it wipe up effortlessly every time." Hank reached into the cabinet under the sink. He held up an unlabeled bottle of what appeared to be orange dish liquid, then squirted some into the puddle of blood.

She'd wondered what the stuff was for years. "Every time? You make this sound like it happens a lot."

"Well, it hasn't in the past decade, but it used to. I'll explain in a moment, Cricket," Hank said, directing her attention to the orange liquid mixing with the blood. It all turned into a clear substance with the consistency of water.

Courtney picked up the roll of paper towels Ivan left on the island and tore off a few. Her hands shook, and she dropped the towels into the puddle while trying to hand them to Hank.

He grabbed her wrist as she reached for them. "No. Don't touch the blood. If it gets on your skin, it'll be absorbed and they'll come for you too," he warned.

A cold, wet sensation seeped under her toes as he finished his warning. She looked down to see the puddle's edge flow around her bare foot.

"Unc, it's touching me," she squeaked, staring down.

"Then it's already begun," he said in a grim tone. Hank released her hand and allowed her to wipe up the puddle. She tossed the soaked towels at the trash receptacle hidden in the cabinet. They hit the side of the bin and fell to the floor; she walked over to drop them in with shaking hands.

Yeah, the flip-flops will make extra noise. Fuck. Now you're in for it, dumbass. What the fuck is going to happen now?

"So what exactly am I in for?" she asked.

"They're gargoyles," Hank explained. "They were once prominent, driven back into hiding most recently during medieval times. They hid in Eastern Europe and were stirred up around the time of the Russian Revolution and the end of World War I. The first to reemerge were in the vicinity of St. Petersburg, and since then they've had a slight resurgence and moved worldwide, though they still stick to the shadows. Anyone who crosses paths with them and is unlucky enough to absorb their blood is marked. They seek those people out for vengeance. There is a pocket of activity in this area, and we think they may be hiding out in some sort of underground cavern created by the San Andreas Fault."

"That still doesn't explain what one was doing in our kitchen, or what Ivan is doing with a sword. Does he think he's the Highlander or something? He's got the wrong accent for—wait, never mind, they had a French guy play Connor MacLeod."

"I'll probably let him explain the sword, but both of us absorbed gargoyle blood. So every once in a while we have to deal with this. Sometimes it's much worse, but it's been a long time since they posed a real threat. It's a deadly thing to be wrapped up in, though."

"So you guys have to kill monsters or be killed? How does that stay secret? I mean, there's YouTube and shit. There's bound to be videos out there, like Sasquatch stuff, right?"

"Ivan is very wealthy, as you know, and wealthy people tend to have friends in very high places. Places like the FBI, CIA, KGB, NSA, MI6, you name it. Those are the kinds of places specializing in secrets. Have you ever heard of Volkodav Securities?"

"Yeah, they're huge. They make guns, explosives, ammo, tanks, security systems, all sorts of goodies. Why? What's that got to do with monsters creeping into our kitchen?"

"That's one of Ivan's companies. Knowing him personally is how I managed to get so many nice security features in this house for free. Of course, it's also how he knows the codes that go with the system. Letting the gargoyle in made it easier to kill since it couldn't hide. One solitary gargoyle couldn't get in on its own; it'd take a massive war party to break through the doors, and we'd have plenty of warning. That's why it's been peaceful here for five years despite monsters prowling about. They had no interest in you because you hadn't absorbed blood. It wasn't worth revealing themselves to get at me."

"I know it should bother me that there's been monsters around for years and Ivan let that thing in the house, but I guess I can see fighting it in familiar territory. I'm more interested in how you got wrapped up in this. What happened?" Courtney leaned against the island to wipe the liquid off of her toes. She groaned as the cleaner also wiped away the black sharpie on her nails.

Good thing I was going to get some real polish on there, I guess. Heh, so silly. Gargoyles are going to hunt me and I'm more pissed about nail polish.

She turned back to Hank as he suppressed a laugh at her scowl and began his tale.

"Before I bought my old shop, I was just a mechanic there. I was working alone late one night in '74. I was still in my mid-twenties, but I was the most trusted mechanic they had so I got all the tough custom jobs. I was rebuilding and beefing up the transmission for a hot rod '59 Buick when I heard strange voices outside. I grabbed a tire iron and headed out. Behind the shop, I found a gargoyle standing over a man. It was clearly going to kill him, so I bashed its head in. In the process, blood splashed on me."

"That is when I stood up to thank your uncle," Ivan said as he reentered the kitchen. "I also told him of what lay ahead in his future, much as he is telling you."

"Surely you mean your father, Ivan," Courtney protested. "You couldn't have been born yet, let alone an adult. You don't look much more than thirty."

Ivan smirked. "You are much too kind. I know you noticed this ring on my finger. It is imbued with the blood of the winged gargoyle Alphaesto, and grants immortality to whomever wears it. I acquired it in the Carpathian Mountains of Romania in 1938, from the hidden tomb of an old Sumerian king named Dugdamme. It is a long story, perhaps best saved for another day when you can process it, instead of having to add a history lesson to the fresh knowledge of gargoyles, magic, and immortality."

Hank added, "And if I'd known he was immortal before I 'saved' his life, I could've avoided this whole mess."

Courtney raised an eyebrow as she looked at the copper ring with its large red stone. "No simple piece of jewelry can make someone immortal. It's not possible."

"Conventional wisdom also states gargoyles do not exist, yet you see they do. Your eyes will be opened to many wondrous things in the future, least among them the fact I was born on July 17 of 1908. Perhaps all this would be easier to accept if it came from someone you have known for more than seven hours. I shall return to my quarters to clean my sword and leave any further information to your uncle. Let me simply say first that this gargoyle came for me, and I am truly sorry it has resulted in someone so young and lovely as you becoming entangled in this situation, Miss Mays." Ivan exited the kitchen again, still holding the sword.

Hank took Courtney's hand. "Come up to my office."

They headed to the third floor. As they passed Hank's bedroom and approached the office, Courtney's heart raced. In five years, she'd never seen the office door open. She didn't know if she should fear what lay within or be thrilled at the mystery ending.

As Hank reached for the door knob, she swallowed hard and cursed herself for forgetting water.

Courtney shrank back as the door cracked open, half expecting a gargoyle to lunge out. Instead, she saw a large flat-screen monitor against each window, facing outwards as if projecting images to the outside world. Between the two faux windows stood a computer monitor about ten feet wide and a lavish cherry desk of equal length. A rack close to the door contained several swords while the shelves below the far window were filled with books.

A large glass gun case stood by the opposite wall, filled with pistols, assault rifles, machine guns, and cases of ammunition. Courtney stared at the arsenal with her mouth open, though she knew little about guns aside from the fact they went *bang bang*. Another opaque cabinet stood next to the gun case. More bookshelves lined the rest of the wall to the end of the room, which was hidden by a row of filing cabinets. A large table filled the center of the room like in war movies. It was empty aside from a disassembled gun.

Hank led her to his desk and plucked a picture from the corner. He handed it to Courtney, smiling. Two men stood facing each other with crossed swords. One she recognized as her uncle in his late twenties, sans beard. The other was clearly Ivan, appearing exactly as he did five minutes ago. She stared at the picture, dumbfounded. It proved his immortality, as hard as it was for her to believe. At least now she understood the feeling he harbored secrets. She handed it back to Hank without a word, staring at the photo as he set it back down.

"You should see some of his pictures. There's one of him with Boris Karloff. He was hunting monsters and stumbled onto the set of one of Karloff's movies, and almost gutted him. I'll let him tell you that one someday; it's much funnier with his accent."

"I'm sure." Courtney pointed to the massive screen. "What's this for?" She gazed in wonder at a satellite image of the Point Reyes area. Numerous dots of different colors were strewn about the screen.

"This is our monster tracking map. The green dots are gargoyles, and the white dots are those of us who have absorbed their blood," Hank explained.

"I was hoping it was the other way around. I only see six white dots, and hundreds of the green ones. What about the others, like that purple one right next to us?"

"The purple one is Ivan. Normally purple would signify undead, but his immortality makes the computer see him as such. Blue are amphibious creatures, though not all are detectable. Orange signifies lycanthropes, which you know better as werewolves. Brown is for Sasquatch. Red is for demons. Grey is for aliens, though we don't worry about them; they're up to the government and usually harmless. Yellow signifies anything else that doesn't fit into those categories. There are also gremlins in the area, but this can't pick them up because of their small size."

"In less than fifteen minutes I found out all kinds of monsters and aliens exist, even though I've been told for twenty-three years they don't. It should be overwhelming like when I saw the ugly fucker on the kitchen floor, but all I can think now is when I get to use one of those," Courtney said, pointing to the sword rack.

One sword in particular drew her attention. The blade was made of darker steel than the others. It was utilitarian in appearance aside from a few decorative bits. She thought of Vikings, but that didn't seem quite right. The markings on the blade were something she couldn't place. A small emerald was embedded in the center of the cross guard. Blackened leather of modern origins wrapped the handle, which was large enough to accommodate both of her hands. The blade wasn't long enough to look unwieldy. The pommel was a plain circular piece of steel, and matched the coloration of the blade.

Hank grabbed the sword carefully by the cross guard and held it out to her handle first. She took it and looked closer at the ancient markings on the blade, marveling at how balanced it felt. It wasn't as heavy as she'd expected; she twirled it easily with a flick of her wrist. The edges of the blade had dings, showing it wasn't some ceremonial sword. This weapon was well-used in the past. She thought of Ivan's Bugatti showing its battle scars, and pondered the weapon's history.

"That was the sword of the ancient Sumerian king Ivan told you about. The guardian Ivan defeated used it, and made him promise it'd be cared for. It was an honor when Ivan gave me it, and today I give it to you. It predates the Roman Empire by well over a thousand years. It might be the oldest steel sword in existence. Steel was ancient knowledge before it was rediscovered, and only known to a select few. Ivan never shared every detail about the sword—just that potent magic was used to forge it in an era when steel was technologically impossible."

Courtney couldn't contain her smile. She kept looking over the markings. "That's fucking old."

Hank gave her the typical scowl that accompanied her swearing.

"Remember, Unc, I'm twenty-three. I'm an adult. I'm entitled to drop an F-bomb now and then, especially when I'm excited."

"I'm very aware you're an adult now. Sometimes I can't help thinking of you as the shy girl I took to the lighthouse, not the beautiful young woman with a bad habit of walking around in lingerie when I have guests," Hank said with a sigh.

"I can't help being hot, Unc."

"That doesn't mean you have to flaunt it."

"I meant temperature hot. At least now I know it's because there's a fancy computer above my room. It puts out some heat," Courtney said as she pointed the sword at the radar.

"Ah. You still nearly gave old Winfield a heart attack."

"Come on, knowing the old fart he probably enjoyed it and pretended to be horrified so he wouldn't offend you."

Rather than responding, Hank grabbed the sword's scabbard from the rack. He handed it to Courtney. "You'll need this as well, and we should find a gun for you since it'll be easier to conceal. I'd recommend keeping the sword close whenever possible. I know it won't be possible at work or in public, but whenever practical."

"I'll keep it under my pillow, but fuck guns. You know I hate the things. By the way, about aliens...." Courtney said.

"Yes?" Hank pushed his glasses up his nose.

"Have you ever seen one?"

"No, but I'll bet that some well-known celebrities are aliens." Hank chuckled.

Courtney laughed, then asked, "Why do you think so?"

Hank ran his finger over his lips like a zipper.

Courtney laughed again and said, "I hope I can get back to sleep now."

"It can't be that disturbing finding out monsters exist and want to kill you, or hearing vague alien conspiracy theories."

"No, I'm actually kind of excited now. How many girls get to own a sword, kick monster ass, and know an immortal Russian? Besides, the History Channel has so many alien conspiracy theories I think I'm desensitized to some of the ridiculous stuff. Luke watches it all the time because of the ancient civilizations, so I might have to flaunt this thing," Courtney said, grinning at the sword.

"Not many girls, and I hate to burst your bubble, but we need to focus more on Ivan training you to protect yourself from gargoyles than learning to drive a standard, so no Jeep. I'm sorry, but it's pointless to buy that and have you unable to defend yourself. Plus, while I'm not telling you not to show Luke the sword, keep the gargoyles a secret. Attribute it to our house guest needing a younger sparring partner."

"It's okay. A sword is a damn good consolation prize. Thanks, Unc. Somehow the idea of killing monsters or being killed is easier knowing you've got my back."

"Don't get too mushy on me now. I'm the favorite uncle, nothing more. I'm off to bed now, so goodnight, Cricket."

"Goodnight, Unc," Courtney chirped.

She hurried down the cold steps to her room and dropped off the flashlight, then headed back to the kitchen for the water she'd forgotten. Courtney set the sword on the island.

She tiptoed around the spot where the gargoyle blood spilled, though the floor looked perfectly clean. The refrigerator lit the kitchen when she opened the door. Her stomach rumbled again as she spotted the pizza box from dinner a couple nights ago.

Hell yes.

She pulled out the box and scowled at the two slices inside. Her eyes drifted to the Heineken bottles.

"Don't mind if I do. Sorry, water." She grabbed one of the beers, sat on the floor with the open pizza box beside her, and wrenched off the bottle cap. *A little sleep aid could help as long as Immortal McFuckface doesn't open the door for any other monsters. I'm way too excited to sleep right now.*

She took a long gulp of beer, sighed, and grabbed the first slice of pizza as she stretched her legs. The blood was already in her system, so screw it. No point avoiding that part of the floor.

Her missing nail polish caught her eye as she picked mushrooms off the pizza. Courtney chomped on the slice, then laughed. *Monsters are real and I have to learn to fight them, but here I am, more worried about my nail polish and shitty pizza toppings.*

She burped, preoccupied with monster slaying, like the books she read back in her childhood, before....

I haven't read in months, not since that one beach day. Hopefully I still get a chance during training. A trip to Shannara could be a nice escape if fighting monsters isn't so glamorous.

She finished off the pizza and a second bottle of beer before heading back upstairs. The sword tucked neatly under her pillow, and she fell asleep shortly after crawling back in bed. Her dreams sent her on epic quests to ditch the retail job and focus on hunting monsters for money.

3

"Perhaps if you had not slept until one o'clock in the afternoon, we could have had time for a nice, long lesson," Ivan politely scolded Courtney from the doorway.

She squinted at the clock. "I'm sorry, but how are you so alert and ready to go after killing a gargoyle at 4:00 a.m.? And why are my glasses giving me a headache and blurry vision?"

"Gargoyle blood has several side effects, one of which is enhanced vision. If you remove your glasses, you will likely notice your vision is perfect. To answer your other question, I do not sleep. I have not needed to do so since the acquisition of my ring."

"Oh. I don't think I'd like that. Sleep is one of my favorite things. I enjoy dreams. They're a nice break from the reality of selling refrigerators." Courtney removed her glasses, blinked, and set them down on the nightstand with a shrug. "Well, I'm going to save a bunch of money not needing an optometrist anymore,"

"I do not miss the nightmares which haunted my youth of the atrocities perpetrated by the Soviet regime. Now, may I ask what you dreamed of last night?"

"I was selling an oven to a hefty smelly man with a speech impediment. Poor guy; I couldn't understand what he was saying and it was making him angry. Then he shed his skin and turned into a monster I got to use this on." Courtney patted the sword's handle poking out from under her pillow.

"That sounds... charming?"

"It's better than selling washers and dryers to teenage mothers who bring their crying babies into the store with them, then try to change dirty diapers on the merchandise. Nothing like retail to convince me I never want any little shitgoblins." Courtney enjoyed the sight of Ivan's face growing pale while she tied her hair back.

"Let us start our lesson for today. Draw your sword," Ivan instructed, ignoring the subjects of appliances and ill-tempered infants.

"We're really going to do this with a real, sharp sword and no instruction?"

Ivan nodded. "Mine is dull, so fear not. Cut me all you wish—if you can. I will heal instantly, even if by some miracle you manage to lop off a limb. Proceed."

Courtney lifted her pillow and grabbed her sword, but stopped with it partway out of the scabbard. Ivan's blade hovered an inch from her neck.

"I believe you may wish to be a little faster next time. The Sumerian would not be pleased to see his blade wielded so imprecisely. Return your sword beneath your pillow and we shall try this again."

Courtney tucked the sword back under her pillow, scowled, and waited.

"Proceed," Ivan ordered, charging her.

She drew her sword in time and blocked his swing, then ducked right as Ivan spun and swung from the other side.

"Fuck, you're fast!" She scrambled for a defense plan and shook her arm as it buzzed from the impact.

Relying on martial arts instinct, she tripped him. Ivan stumbled back a step. The brief respite provided allowed her to stand and mount a charge of her own. Ivan blocked her swing and nearly knocked her sword from her hands.

He paused to chuckle. "Very good. I am impressed you tried to take the offensive so soon. Now, move back to your bed and charge at me again. I will not be off balance this time, so think about how to surprise me."

Courtney stood by her bed for a few seconds, staring beyond her sword at Ivan.

"Do not look at me for answers. If I tell you what to do, you will not surprise me, will you? The element of surprise is one of the most important factors in battle, often deciding a fight in favor of someone with less size, strength, or skill—like yourself against a gargoyle, so I implore you to take this lesson in thinking outside the norm to heart. Right now this is more important than teaching proper sword techniques. Aside from a select few, gargoyles rely on claws and teeth."

She ran at him and feigned a swing. As he brought his sword up to block, she spun behind him.

He recognized her plan and ducked, but the weight of her sword kept the swing going cleanly over his head. Momentum threatened her balance.

Ivan flashed a grin as he tripped her; she pounded the floor a second later. Before she could think about blocking or getting up, the cold tip of his sword touched her forehead.

"That was a very good attempt, I must say. You have an instinct for this far beyond your years. Against a less experienced opponent, that could have been a brilliant tactic. Perhaps a bit less of a baseball swing may have fooled even me." Ivan gave her his hand to help her up.

"Yeah, it's not really all that fair trying to outwit a hundred-something-year-old dude with a thirty-year-old body that's still got great reflexes," Courtney said as she rubbed her tailbone. "Maybe I should've put the mats down first. Ow."

"The world in general is not a fair place, and there will be no mats when you meet your first gargoyle. I was only thirty when I fought an eleven-hundred-year-old warrior guarding the tomb of King Dugdamme. Admittedly, he may have been a little out of practice since he had not faced a challenge in over five hundred years." Ivan smiled at the gleaming blade of his practice saber.

"I don't think I'll ever get used to your concept of time," Courtney said as she picked up her sword, grimacing at the gouge it left in the hardwood.

"Do not try. I do not expect anyone to have an inkling of how different it is to live forever and be awake twenty-four hours a day. It is my life, and everyone else has their own life to live."

Courtney prepared to charge Ivan again, but he rushed to the offensive. She stepped forward and swung. With their two swords locked together, he pushed her back. His strength proved far greater than his handshake foretold. *Holy shit, is this guy part bear? I'm strong, but it feels like he could swat me aside like a damn fly. What the hell do I do?*

Overpowered, she ducked and stepped forward. The move took Ivan by surprise, and she threw him over her back with ease. He hit the floor as she spun around, and her sword poked his chin as he tried to get up.

"I never would have considered one could be the victim of a judo flip during a sword fight. You are learning in leaps and bounds and have accomplished something your uncle took six months to achieve. You either have warrior instincts in your blood, or I have become an exponentially better teacher since the 1970s."

"You're stronger than a damn ox, and four inches taller than me. Judo was the only shot I could think of to gain an advantage."

"Remember that when facing a gargoyle. While they do not use swords, they will get as close as possible and use their superior strength. I am nearly as strong as they, so your judo tactic shall be of great use to you—so long as you avoid their claws, beaks, or teeth. Not all gargoyles are alike, as you will find out. Now let us continue." Ivan pushed her sword aside and stood.

He brushed off his perfect white shirt and adjusted his collar before raising his sword to beckon Courtney forward. Her charge went by him as he spun and effortlessly dodged. She turned to swing but he was already behind her. Before she could do anything else, she felt the tip of his sword between her shoulder blades.

"You were toying with me before. You could beat me any time you wanted," she said as he pulled his sword away.

"I would not go so far as to say that I could defeat you at will. Ninety-nine percent would be a more accurate figure to use as a success rate."

"Are all Russians so self-satisfied?" Courtney grumbled.

Ivan laughed, then spun, halting his sword half an inch from her throat. He flashed his confident smirk. "Only those with good reason or who have had too much vodka."

A knock came from the doorway. Courtney glanced over to Hank peering in.

"Do you mind coming downstairs for a moment, Courtney?" Hank asked, then turned to Ivan. "Sorry to interrupt."

Courtney said to Ivan, "I'll be back," then to Hank, "I'll be there in a second."

Ivan nodded to acknowledge Courtney's promise as she left the room. Courtney followed Hank down the steps to the great room across from the kitchen, carpeted in the same green as the hall with walls of stained pinewood. Whenever she visited as a child, the patterns of the knots in the wood made her think of the faces of strange woodland fairies from an enchanted forest like in the books she used to read constantly, but now they struck her as an eyesore.

A signed Rod Woodson Oakland Raiders jersey hung in a display case on the far wall. No matter how poor the Raiders played, Hank religiously watched every game. A billiards table stood in the center of the far end of the room. Hank and Alec often used it whenever the curmudgeonly old British librarian would visit. Courtney avoided playing pool as a result.

Between the billiards table and television sat a leather couch with matching recliners to either side In the recliner closest to the door sat Luke Stillman, Courtney's boyfriend. Uncontrollable dark hair poked out from under his ragged San Jose Sharks hat and his scruffy beard had a few white hairs. He wore a hockey jersey, that of New York Rangers goaltender Henrik Lundqvist. Luke always joked how jerseys were great at hiding the true size of someone, which was why he had a large collection. Oddly, he didn't cheer for just one team, and only bought the jerseys of players from Sweden. Courtney assumed it was because he was born in Minnesota and his mother was of Swedish descent.

"What's with the big knife, and where are your glasses?" Luke asked, pointing out the sword she still carried.

"Oh, uh, um, heh heh," Courtney stammered, searching for a proper excuse. "One of Hank's friends is staying in the area for a little while, and he's rich and likes to play with swords. I thought it might be fun to learn. I didn't want to risk breaking my glasses so they're still on my nightstand."

Luke let out a sigh of relief. "I thought maybe you were going to snap and give me the haircut you've been bugging me to get. I'm guessing the rich friend owns the Bentley out front?"

Courtney laughed. Luke could lighten any mood with a well-timed wisecrack. "The haircut's a great idea. I'll have to do that sometimes when you're not expecting it," she teased as she set down the sword. "And yeah, the Bentley belongs to Ivan."

"Just make sure I'm not wearing any of my white road jerseys. I don't want hair on those," Luke said.

"Aside from cat hair, you mean? I didn't know the Rangers added orange to their blue jerseys. What are you doing here so early, anyway? I'm not even dressed yet," Courtney said, brushing away some of the cat hair.

Luke raised an eyebrow at her as he picked off more cat fuzz. "I'm on my way home from the DMV and figured I'd stop by to say hi. We're going to Mark's tonight. It'll just be him and his guitar on stage since they couldn't get a band."

"Perfect. Now I know what to wear. I've got some awesome new boots for tonight," Courtney said with a wider grin as Luke stood.

"I like the sound of that."

"Let me guess, you're going to wear that Lundqvist jersey," Courtney groaned.

"Why not? They do call him King Henrik, after all. He's damn good on guitar too." Luke winked.

"Just make sure you get the fuzz off, please."

"Of course. There's a reason I keep a lint roller in my car."

"Yeah. You have OCD when it comes to that Volvo. Don't try to make excuses for the little brush you use on the vents." Courtney rolled her eyes.

"It's the world's smallest hair brush. It does wonders maintaining the precise styling of my hair," Luke joked as the two walked past Hank and out of the room.

"You're so full of shit," Courtney said, giggling.

"It's why I have to wear so much aftershave. It covers up the smell."

Courtney giggled again as Luke reached for the door. They walked onto the small landing and she shook her head as she looked at the beige wagon in the circle. "Your car is older than Unc's hairstyle. Are you ever going to get something new?"

"Why? I can't afford a new car I actually want."

"Yet you can buy a new hockey jersey every other month and keep pouring money into the bland-wagon."

"It's Swedish," he said with a shrug.

"So is Abba, and you hate them," she said, giggling yet again.

"I'm a complicated person."

Courtney kissed him. "And yet so simple."

Luke smiled and sighed before walking down the steps. "I'll see you at six. Wear those awesome new boots you mentioned, and the usual green top. Please? Humor me on the last birthday before I become an old fart."

"Already knew that. Those couple silver hairs whispered it in my ear."

Luke waved, then unlocked the Volvo's door. Courtney leaned on the railing and watched him crank the engine repeatedly, but it wouldn't start. It finally stumbled to life after she stopped counting. A puff of black smoke popped out of the exhaust to commemorate the event, and the car wobbled before he pulled around hers to leave. She waved, watching until he drove around the bend beneath the arched tree branches and out of view.

Courtney passed Hank at the entrance on her way back.

"He said six, correct?" Hank asked.

"Yeah. Dinner at Mark's Bar & Grill. Hopefully I'll have time to run to the pharmacy to pick up some real nail polish and get my workout in after this sword lesson." She grabbed the weapon from the great room table.

As the two walked back up the stairs, Hank said, "Mark is part of our extended circle. He hasn't absorbed gargoyle blood, but we helped him with a gremlin infestation in the basement of his place. Occasionally we have our meetings there."

"So even Mark knew about this gargoyle shit before me? And wow, you seem to know everyone despite never leaving the house," Courtney said as they entered the second floor hall.

"That's not true. I don't know the people I've never met."

"No shit, Sherlock," she teased.

"Courtney, how many times do I have to mention your swearing?"

"Seems like a fuckton." She giggled as she passed Ivan, who winked at her and bit his lip, clearly trying not to laugh at the look on her uncle's face.

"Can I borrow that practice sword for a second?" Hank grumbled.

Courtney chuckled. "Okay, I'll try to be a good girl for a few minutes."

"I would prefer you not. Please, try to fight dirty as we resume the lesson," Ivan said, raising his sword.

Courtney nodded. Hank moved to the other side of the bed, out of the way. Ivan charged her. She dodged and took the offensive. He barely managed to block her swing and threw out his leg to trip her. She landed hard on her tailbone and let out a small pained squeak, but still blocked his swing.

"Are you all right, Courtney?" Ivan asked as he paused.

Courtney rose to her feet and nodded, gritting her teeth. She swung while his guard was still down. Ivan jumped out of the way to dodge her blow. He turned to attack, but Courtney lunged forward. She winced and let go of her sword as it sank deep into his chest, grinding against his sternum and ribs.

"Oh shit," Courtney said weakly, stepping back.

"No, come here," Ivan sputtered. "You need to withdraw your sword."

She froze for a moment, then moved back closer to him and tugged on the blade. It resisted. She yanked again. It took three tries to pull it out. No blood coated the blade. His chest wound trickled red before every drop sucked back into the gash, which mended itself immediately. The only evidence left behind was the hole in his shirt.

She stared. "Wow. Freaky shit."

"One grows used to it after eighty years. I have had much more grievous wounds than this before," Ivan stated calmly as he untucked his shirt to examine the damage.

Hank chimed in. "I accidentally chopped his arm clean off, just to see it float up and reattach itself."

Courtney shook her head. "I didn't really believe the whole immortality thing. That's one of the weirdest fucking things I've ever seen."

"It was only one of the weirdest sights? I am almost afraid to hear what ghastly occurrence could have surpassed it."

Courtney glanced back at Hank and smirked as he rubbed his forehead. *Heh, he knows what's coming. I can't wait to see Siberian Highlander pale again.* "Back in high school, I dated this guy named Brett. He was the quarterback of the football team, but was so shy on dates and couldn't keep a girlfriend. Luke and I ran into Brett a few months ago. The thing is, she's Brittany now. I'm glad she did what she needed to be happy and all, but it's weird to look back, thinking how my ex has a bigger chest than I do now. She went all out with her implants."

"I can see how that would be quite awkward. You are the winner in this debate," Ivan acknowledged, breathing heavily.

"Want to continue?" Courtney held up her sword.

"No, we are done for today. I will allow you to fit in the workout routine and pharmacy visit you mentioned before your date with Mr. Stillman."

Hank exited the room while Courtney put her sword away under the pillow. "You heard all that?"

Ivan nodded, but said nothing.

"Huh. So you've got freaky good hearing and super strength. Anything I can look forward to with the gargoyle blood?" she asked as she knelt beside her bed.

"Perhaps. It affects everyone a little differently."

Courtney nodded as Ivan leaned against her computer desk. *He must need a breather after healing.* "Are you going to hang out here all day?" she asked, digging her old black Converse out from under the bed.

"No. I will leave in a moment. I would like to make a quick suggestion."

"Fire away, Comrade."

"I should shadow you while you are on your date, just to be safe. Do not worry, I will keep my distance. I also know when to look away, as those pills beside your computer would suggest may be necessary," Ivan said quietly, not meeting her eyes.

"Um, okay. I guess I can deal with a distant guardian. You didn't say anything to Hank about those, did you?"

"No. He pointed them out. Your uncle explained he knew you were on birth control a while ago, but did not want to create an awkward conversation—that you would merely state you were an adult," Ivan answered as he slowly walked to the door.

"Thank goodness. It's weird enough talking about it to a Russian centenarian," she joked. "I'm going to need to come up with an excuse for not needing glasses. I told Luke I wasn't wearing them because I was afraid of breaking them while learning swordplay."

"Tell him we knocked your nightstand over while sparring and broke them anyway. We can get you new frames with fake lenses like the ones your uncle wears, though with thinner glass since he wants everyone to think his vision is terrible, as a disguise." Ivan nodded before leaving.

Courtney sighed as she looked at her glasses. She picked them up and snapped one of the hinges. "I hope I've got enough for new polish," she muttered as she slipped on the sneakers and grabbed her purse.

4

Luke locked the car as Courtney waited at the end of his apartment walkway.

"Why bother locking it? No one's going to steal it when the house across the street is empty until November—with a Mercedes sitting in the driveway. Hmm, big expensive thing or ancient brick that won't start.... Yeah, I'd totally take the Volvo," Courtney teased loudly.

She didn't mind yelling a little since no houses nearby were occupied. Luke rented a small single-story house at the end of a dead-end street, and the house across the way was a winter home for some rich New Yorker escaping the snow.

Luke caught up to Courtney. "You never know when someone is going to take an interest in your stereo and find an unlocked door to make their job easier. You're one to talk about paranoia, wrapping a sword in a hoodie. You really want me worried about the haircut?"

Courtney said nothing as she stepped forward cautiously. The combination of stiletto-heeled boots and high quantities of rum didn't mesh with loose gravel walkways. *At least all those free shots make it easier to pretend I can't see shit until I get those fake glasses. It took a lot more than normal to get buzzed, too. Maybe it's another one of those gargoyle blood things to get used to. Bullshit. Having to buy more booze to ignore any troubles when there's more of them? We ought to hunt down all the fucking monsters and be done with it.*

Courtney grinned at the thought of the hunt. Luke grinned back, clearly thinking her mind was on the date. The tumblers in the lock seemed a bit louder than she remembered, but Courtney brushed it off and kissed Luke's cheek as she slipped past him. "I'll meet you when you're done feeding the cat."

He kicked off his sneakers at the door while Courtney slunk down the hallway. Her ankle turned near the kitchen. She laughed awkwardly. "Take care of the little bugger. These boots need to go."

"Okay," Luke said with a chuckle. He passed her while she sat on the floor and set down the hoodie-wrapped sword.

Courtney grunted as she struggled with the high boot, listening to the cat meowing like a fiend in the kitchen. The boot pulled free—and the back of her head slammed into the wall. "Ow, fuck. I'm going to be dizzier."

"Are you okay?" Luke called from the kitchen.

"Never better," she slurred. "Just banged my head on the wall when the boot came off."

Luke laughed. "You probably had enough shots to match Bea's body weight. I'm surprised you're even walking straight. Poor girl jumped and smacked the bottom of the cabinet when you hit the wall."

"Sorry, cat," Courtney said as she set the stiletto boot by her sword. *Shit. I really should've said no to those last couple shots. Eh, fuck it. Ivan's watching the house. I need a little release after all the weirdness.*

The other boot came off easier, and she didn't hit her head this time. Courtney wobbled a little as she stood. No further balance issues happened as she dropped the boots by Luke's sneakers. Her head spun a little, but she wasn't sure if it was from the rum or the hit.

Courtney paused and looked out the front door's window. A man in a dingy hoodie walked by, but something about his gait seemed odd. She watched him stop and look at Luke's car for a few seconds, but she couldn't see his face. He turned and crossed the street towards the parked Merc. "Well damn, I guess you were right to lock the blahmobile," she said as she walked back towards the kitchen.

Courtney leaned on the doorframe and watched the cat dance on the counter as Luke chopped wet food with a spoon. Beatrix meowed repeatedly as he set the spoon in the sink. Courtney stood by the cat's tray. "Mind if I do the honors so she warms up to me some?"

Luke picked up the dish as the orange puffball tried to dig in while still on the counter, and handed it to Courtney. The cat sat back and blinked at her with big golden eyes, then meowed in agitation.

"Oh, come on. Just because I've never had a pet before doesn't mean I don't like you!" Courtney said in a squeaky voice. She waved the dish around a few times in front of the cat and watched the little pink tongue dart out before she bent over to place the dish. Bea jumped down and hit the edge of her water bowl with a paw. The water spilled over Courtney's socks.

She sighed. "At least it isn't"—*gargoyle blood again*. She almost blurted out gargoyle blood—"shit. Or a hairball."

Courtney petted the cat for a moment, then tugged off her wet socks while Luke rubbed the purring little fiend's hips. "I guess I know next time to leave shoes on until the cat is fed no matter how hard it is to stay upright." She glanced around the austere kitchen.

Luke laughed again as she draped her socks over the faucet.

Courtney shook her head. "I was going to ask where your dryer is, but I forgot you always talk about the laundromat."

"I do have one, but as soon as I turn it on the breaker trips. The landlord hasn't gotten around to replacing it. It's only been a couple months though, not like it's cost me a ton at the laundromat. Hopefully your socks dry before it's time to drop you off," Luke said.

"No big deal if they're not. This tile isn't half as cold as the iron stairs at home, and I don't think Unc will think anything too bad if I walk in the house barefoot. I'll just say the new boots weren't too comfy," Courtney said.

Luke nodded. "I guess. You know him way better than I do. How's the ankle?"

Courtney leaned her butt against the cabinet and looked down as the cat noisily munched away at smelly salmon. She leaned her head on Luke's shoulder and sighed. "My ankle was fine a few seconds later. Not worth even getting mildly agitated over, the ankle or the socks. I mean, it's not like they were staying on tonight anyway. It's my chance to do something a little special and private for your birthday. I even bought real nail polish instead of using a Sharpie." She wiggled her fingers to show off the usual black nails.

He wrapped an arm around her and said, "You know, I never noticed it was Sharpie before. That's kind of cool; another thing so different from all the fluff-heads who were desperate enough to date me before. I don't have to hold my breath and wonder what you're thinking. You just say it."

"Oh sheesh, don't get sappy on me now. I won't deal with that too well and you'll be calling your witch of an ex. I shudder, 'cause the couple Facebook posts you showed me told me all I needed to know about the bitch. I would've avoided the hell out of her in school, with different Berkeley shirts in a dozen pictures droning on and on about politics."

"Probably why she was single long enough to be desperate enough to say yeah when I asked her out," he said as he rubbed his stubbly chin.

She elbowed him playfully in the ribs. "Stop it. You look just fine, kind of like Brendan Fraser if he had a beard in *The Mummy*. Your gut's not half as big as you think. Just because you're going gray before twenty-nine isn't something to be ashamed of. Hell, if I had to deal with Kendra for any length of time I'd have white hair—if I didn't pull it all out trying not to kill her."

Luke kissed the top of her head. "See, I'm realizing the problem wasn't my looks, it was chemistry and lack of confidence. You're so damn hot, but I can talk about anything with you."

Courtney laughed. "Maybe we should let the rum do the talking."

Luke squeezed her closer. "There's a great thought."

Beatrix wandered away from her half-empty food dish as Luke led Courtney into the hall.

"Hang on a second," Courtney said as she picked up her hoodie and sword. "I've got to show this off better than I did at the house. Why do you think I dragged it along?"

"I don't think you've ever sounded more excited, even during that first striptease."

Courtney snickered. "Would it be a good striptease if it was wordy? Fuck no. I don't have all those fancy romantic poet words to spew when I want to get laid."

Luke opened his bedroom door and laughed. "It's so refreshing how blunt you can be."

She sat on the bed and pulled off her blouse. "I always forget about the itchy tag."

"I'll never complain," he said as he eyed her sports bra.

"Sword first." Courtney unwrapped the blade from her hoodie.

He reached for the zipper of his jeans, but she giggled. "I meant sword as in sword, not nicknames for anything else."

She handed him the hoodie and pulled the ancient Sumerian weapon from its worn leather scabbard. Her fingers ran along the red runes in the darkened steel blade as she smiled. "It's mine to keep. I love this thing. It's not super shiny. It's practical-looking. It's sharp, too. A real sword, not some dull practice dummy." Courtney beamed.

Luke stared at the emerald. "It's probably worth more than either of us make in a year. Hell, it's definitely worth more than my Volvo. This friend of your uncle just gave it to you to practice, even though it's sharpened?"

"You've heard of Volkodav Sekurities, right? He owns the company. The Bentley is a drop in the bucket to Ivan. It's so weird to think about when I had to switch to cheaper booze after my car insurance went up," Courtney said, still smiling at the sword.

"I sure hope someone else makes the decisions for the company. It's awesome you've got a real sword and you're so happy with it, it just seems weird when the guy hasn't known you for a full day yet—especially a sharp one when you've never used it before," Luke said.

"He had confidence I could do it after he watched my workout." Courtney paused and added, "I didn't know he was there until he clapped."

Luke laughed. "Yeah, you get so focused that someone could offer you a million bucks and you'd never notice."

Courtney breathed easier. "What a relief. I thought you'd be wondering why someone I don't know watched me work out."

Luke took off the jersey. "Who the hell wouldn't? Now that you've got a sword you ought to get cast in the *Red Sonja* remake, if they ever get one into production."

"Eh, I don't need to be seen in a chainmail bikini. I'd like a little more protection."

Beatrix charged into the room and turned to hiss at the doorway. "She wasn't referring to that kind of protection, Bea," Luke said. "Don't kill the mood before we even start."

Courtney put her finger to her lips as she heard a couple of thumps against the front door. She set the scabbard aside and raised the sword.

Luke grabbed her hand. "Damn it, could a burglar pick a worse time?"

Courtney pulled away and put her finger to her lips again as she stood. *Fuck. The gargoyles did come tonight. Why didn't Ivan get them first? How the hell am I going to explain this to Luke? Oh well, at least the room isn't spinning.*

"I don't think it's a burglar. It's worse, so hide," she said.

"Hide? Really?" Luke questioned.

Courtney took on the stance she'd seen Ivan use and hissed, "I mean it. Hide. Now."

Luke reluctantly obeyed. The sound of the front door splintering sent Beatrix under the bed with him. Courtney pushed the bedroom door so it was nearly closed and hit the switch on the wall. The faint light slipping through the doorway allowed her to see while still leaving enough shadows to conceal her. When the gargoyle entered the room, she would flip on the light and kick the door in hopes of knocking her adversary off balance before it knew where she was.

The next thump accompanied the sound of the broken front door as it tore free from its hinges and hit the floor. Her mind raced through Ivan's lessons from earlier in the day, then to the face of the dying gargoyle. She remembered the feeling when her sword plunged through Ivan's chest. The gargoyle replaced Ivan in her memory.

I can do this. Well, I better be able to if Ivan doesn't show up. Where the fuck is he? Courtney shook her head and focused on the noises beyond the door. Something growled. It was the same sound she'd heard up in the tower.

Luke whispered to her from under the bed. "What the hell was that?"

"You'll see soon enough."

Claws scraped against the wall. Raspy breaths accompanied heavy footsteps as the thing closed in. The creature stopped outside the door and breathed deeply before unleashing a ferocious roar.

That's a little terrifying. Please just shut up and come in so I can stick my sword through your face before the rum's courage wears off.

The door pushed slowly inward, allowing more light from the hall to enter the room. Claws reached around the edge of the door. Courtney flipped the light switch and kicked the door. It didn't budge. The creature flung the door instead, and it sniffed the air as it faced her.

Oh fuck, this is bad.

This gargoyle appeared different from the one Ivan slew, at least as far as facial features. Its mouth was more human than a beak, and filled with sharp, yellowed teeth. However, it didn't have a human nose, just two craters above the mouth for nostrils. Beady black eyes stared at her, set far apart and deep below a thick brow. Bat-like ears perched on the sides of the domed head, with two small horns protruding from the top.

The thing spoke in a gravelly voice. "I smell in you the blood of my brethren, and for this Edthgar demands vengeance." It lunged at her. She swung her sword. The blade glanced off its shoulder, but the gargoyle dodged and its claws missed her as she scooted out of the corner.

Shit, shit, shit, shit, shit. At least I'm faster than it is so I can get around it. Courtney spun and swung her sword to nail the gargoyle in the back of the head. The sword again failed to produce a scratch. The gargoyle turned to face her. It roared again, unfazed, and took a swipe at her, but she dodged again. As she dodged, she hacked at its hand. One of its fingers sliced partially off at the joint, so she tried for the elbow.

Her foe snarled, dodging the blow. It tackled her and pinned her down. The gargoyle's face twisted into something like a smile, and it sunk its claws into her right hip. She screamed. Rough laughter was its response.

The ugly beast leaned in close to her face, rotten breath assaulting her nose, and it said, "Only the beginning."

The gargoyle pulled its claws out of her hip and placed one clawed finger just above her belly button, running it gently up her stomach to the bottom edge of her bra, leaving a thin streak of blood behind. Courtney glared into its eyes and brought her knee up into its abdomen. All it did was give Courtney a sore knee.

The gargoyle chuckled. It abandoned her bra clasp, and instead ran its finger back down. Something green covered the gargoyle's face and pulled it away. Luke had wrapped Courtney's hoodie around the creature's head. Its teeth tore through the hoodie, which it tossed aside as it turned to Luke.

Courtney ignored the stinging pain in her hip, pushing herself to her feet and grabbing her sword again. While the gargoyle analyzed its new opponent, she lopped off one of its arms. The gargoyle let out a high-pitched whimper as she hacked at its knee. The weakened joint bent and dropped the monster to its knees. Its tiny eyes widened as Courtney spoke.

"This isn't a beginning. It's the end for you. Say hello to your brother, ugly fucker."

Her blade slammed into the gargoyle's neck, blood squirting from the wound onto the bed sheets. It grabbed at its throat with its remaining hand until she swung again. The arm fell limp, and the gargoyle dropped forward onto the floor. A final gurgle accompanied the puddle forming on the threadbare carpet.

"Don't touch the blood, but come on. We need to get back to the mansion. More might be coming," Courtney said to Luke.

He nodded without complaint and pulled the cat out from under the bed. Beatrix hissed at the dead body as Luke wrapped her in his jersey. Courtney reached for her shirt, but pounding on the window drew her attention. It was another gargoyle.

She yelled to Luke, "Get to the car. There's no more time."

He ran out of the room, carrying the cat in one arm. Courtney grabbed her hoodie and the sword's scabbard and followed him out. As Luke passed the kitchen, a third gargoyle jumped out between him and Courtney. She slashed at the gargoyle before it set eyes on her and dropped it to the floor. Her sword kept swinging at its neck until the head flopped away.

Courtney stepped over the head as Luke yanked on his sneakers and looked back for her. She waved him on, yelling, "Go! Start the car." She leaped over the splintered door, ignoring the boots. They'd take forever to put back on.

A large shadow blotted out her own on the gravel walkway. She looked up at the moon. Something was silhouetted against it. The winged shadow grew larger as it dove to the ground. It was a massive gargoyle, and Courtney froze as it landed between her and where Luke shoved his key into the Volvo's passenger door.

Courtney gaped at the horror in front of her. It had long arms that it used like a set of front legs upon landing. A long tail waved behind the thing with a spiked club on the end resembling long-extinct ankylosaurs. Demonic wings spanned thirty feet until they folded against the gargoyle's back. At the end of its thick, slightly elongated neck, its head had a snout like a dinosaur, filled to the brim with long, wickedly sharp curved teeth. The eyes glowed a dark shade of red and faced forward over the nose. Two horns projected above its brow, long and curved rearward with sharp points. It stood over seven feet tall on all fours.

Courtney stood petrified until the Volvo's engine sputtered. She took a step to her right, but the winged gargoyle inched forward. Her hoodie dropped as she wrapped both hands around her sword. *Nobody ever said anything about something this fucking big. I don't think any of the guns I turned down would've even touched this thing.*

Another engine besides the struggling Volvo drew her attention, but the gargoyle's eyes fixed on her. Courtney couldn't help a smile as Ivan's car blasted over the curb. She backed up a few steps. The gargoyle finally noticed the Mulsanne—too late. The Bentley slammed into it and plowed into the side of the house.

Ivan opened the door and stepped from the car. "Run to Luke. I will handle this." He held a large machine gun with a drum magazine on top, which Courtney didn't recognize. She picked up her hoodie and ran to the wagon.

Damn, maybe if they'd offered me that gun I would've had a harder time saying no.

Luke left the passenger door open so she could slide in. The engine started as she closed the door. Luke hammered the gas and shifted through the gears once on the street.

Courtney looked back to the house as the winged gargoyle rose upright, pounding its chest. Ivan removed the ammo drum from the gun and headed for his car. He emptied an entire magazine into the thing, but all it provided was a diversion. She looked away. Ivan would be fine no matter what. That's what she told herself, though concern for the Russian gnawed at her.

Well, that's new. Last night I wanted to kick his perfect teeth in.

Courtney put her hoodie on and discovered the large hole the first gargoyle bit from it, along with part of the zipper. *Guess the sleeves and back are all the coverage I'm getting.*

She checked the mirror again, then looked at Luke's red-faced scowl. His attention was already focused on her as he asked, "What the hell is going on? Monsters are trashing my apartment and you're hacking them apart with a sword. This is not even close to normal."

"They're gargoyles. Ivan hunts them down, and one got in the house last night. Ivan killed it, but I—"

A thud on the roof interrupted.

The Volvo's roof buckled an inch or two, and the winged gargoyle's claws poked through the fabric headliner. Courtney shrank down in her seat and thrust the sword up. Claws slid back out of the torn metal as the creature growled.

What's it take to get rid of this spooky shithead?

The gargoyle's hand burst through the passenger window, showering her with glass. Wicked claws swiped at her but only tore the unused seat belt.

Luke swerved back and forth, trying to throw the gargoyle from the roof. Courtney screamed as the right front wheel lifted from the pavement and slammed down hard. The winged gargoyle withdrew and clung to the roof, grip slipping.

Finally the gargoyle flung from the roof and landed on the road. Part of the roof peeled back like a sardine can, but Courtney let out a sigh of relief as the crumpled gargoyle lay motionless on the pavement.

Luke tried to regain control, but the Volvo's rear corner slammed into a telephone pole. It sent the battered wagon spinning back into the street and threw Courtney into Luke. She slid across the seat to get out. A piece of broken glass stuck in her lower thigh, but the winged gargoyle concerned her more as it rose again.

Luke shut the car's engine off before getting out. He struggled to open the dented back door, but it didn't stand up to his efforts for long, giving way so he could scoop up Beatrix. Courtney grimaced, yanking glass from her leg as she watched Luke hug the cat.

Approaching sirens caught Courtney's attention. Luke shook his head and muttered, "Great, now we have to figure out how to explain running from gargoyles and playing with swords to the police."

"Um, yeah. At least the gargoyle should be pretty easy to explain? It's hard to miss that big-ass thing," she said.

It stood again and looked around, disoriented by its head-first plunge into the newly cracked asphalt. When it spotted Courtney, the red eyes brightened, their luminescence making the air around it glow. It roared, yet the lights in the lone house didn't turn on.

Fuck. Nobody home. Who called the cop? A police cruiser whipped around the corner, its blue and red lights overpowering the glow from the gargoyle's eyes. The creature turned to face the car as it stopped. The way the thing's chest rose and fell looked to Courtney like it was laughing.

The officer, a lean black woman in her mid-to-late thirties, exited the car, pistol grip shotgun in hand. She fired into the gargoyle's face and it shrank away from her. Sparks flew as the shot hit its horns. A second blast hit the fiend in the face and it spread its wings. The third shot hit the nightmare in the chest as it took off into the starry night sky.

The cop motioned Luke and Courtney to her as she got into the cruiser. They climbed into the back; the shotgun and a rifle sat in the passenger seat. Courtney recognized the officer as Renee Nelson, who'd given her a warning for speeding a couple weeks ago.

"Thank you so much, Officer Nelson. We'd be toast if you hadn't gotten here," Courtney said, rubbing her thigh with a wince. "But, um, what are you doing here? Who called?"

"Your uncle called as soon as he saw the green dots closing in on the radar, and directed me over the radio. When we're up against the gargoyles, just call me Renee. I've been off duty for about half an hour." Renee pulled the car around in the direction of Hank's mansion.

"Oh. So the cops know about the gargoyles, too? How the fuck is this shit so secret? I feel like everyone knows about this stuff but Luke and I," Courtney said.

"You know more than I do, except that these things just wrecked my home and car. I'd like some answers here," Luke said, his voice low and his arms crossed as he glared at the sword across Courtney's lap.

First time I've seen him pissed. I'm kind of relieved he can be. If this shit didn't do it I'd think he was some sort of robot programmed to always be silly.

"We'll answer all the questions we know answers to once the threat of dying is a little lower, I promise," Renee said. "Did you touch gargoyle blood?"

Luke looked himself over and saw only a couple red spots on the shoulder of his white t-shirt where Courtney hit him during the crash. "No, just hers. Why? She asked the same thing with the one she killed."

Renee explained. "If you get gargoyle blood on your skin, the gargoyles will be after you just like her, thanks to last night."

Luke's jaw unclenched, and Courtney figured his anger faded a little as he remembered what she was trying to explain before the car crash. He patted her leg and shook his head. "Got a hazmat suit I could borrow?"

Courtney poked her boyfriend in the shoulder. "I stepped in a blood puddle last night. That's why they're after me, and why Ivan was showing me how to use a sword. It's why they trashed your apartment. I'm so sorry; I didn't mean to get you wrapped up in this shit. I, uh, almost blurted out the thing about gargoyle blood when the cat spilled her water."

"Well, it sucks, but I guess it's easier to take with a kung-fu gladiatrix around. You know, that *Red Sonja* chainmail bikini might be a nice way to ease the sting of it all," Luke joked.

"I'm not sure a bikini suits you," Courtney said with a straight face.

Luke blinked a second, then laughed. "It'd be painful, ripping out my chest hairs in all the little links. I think I'll take losing a shit apartment over that."

She kissed him and sighed. "I'm just glad we got out of there."

Renee cleared her throat. "Please keep on what clothes you have left. This Charger is pretty new and I don't need that going on in the backseat. Besides, who knows if Edthgar will come again. Be ready to fight some more," she said with a chuckle.

"Sorry, we kind of got interrupted at Luke's place. I might already be bleeding on the seat, though," Courtney said as she looked over her shoulder for any sign of the winged bastard. *Edthgar? The thing has a name and they know it? Wow, I'm stuck in the dark.*

"I figured. I'm a cop. Being observant is part of what we do. Why else would you be swinging a sword around half-dressed?" Renee said.

Courtney shrugged. "You've got a point, but if these things keep coming at night it's going to be rare for me to fight fully dressed. I'm not sleeping with everything on."

"If they're so into underwear maybe we could end this by finding their lair and stuffing it with Victoria's Secret catalogs," Luke teased.

Renee laughed. "If only it were so simple. We haven't found their lair, anyway."

"I really hope my green top is in one piece whenever we get back to your place, except maybe that annoying tag. Those boots were expensive, too," Courtney said.

An emergency call came over the radio for a fire at Luke's address as she finished.

"I guess that takes care of that," Luke said. "Fuck."

Courtney sighed. "And your jerseys."

Luke closed his eyes. "I haven't been to the laundromat in a week. My favorite ones are all in the basket in the back of... my car."

Courtney put her hand on his knee.

"You'll be able to get all of your stuff out of it from the impound lot, as long as gargoyles don't torch it," Renee said.

"Thanks."

Renee nodded and grabbed the radio handset. "Yo Hank, can you direct Ivan to 124 Seagrass Road? I'm not hearing anything from his headset."

"Will do. Are Courtney and Luke safe?" Hank replied.

"A couple cuts and scrapes, but nothing major." Renee wheeled the police interceptor up Overlook Road.

"Thank goodness, and thanks for getting there so fast," Hank said.

"No problem. What's the radar show?"

"More green than your lawn. We haven't seen this many in ten years. I need to do some preparations; be ready for anything when you get here."

"Okay. Good luck."

A gargoyle ran in front of the car, but it didn't faze Renee. She pushed the gas to the floor and ran down the gargoyle. It crumpled over the brush guard and rag-dolled off the road. One headlight went out.

This is going to be car insurance adjuster heaven tomorrow, if we live that long. Courtney shivered and looked out the rear glass again, but there was no sign of the winged asshole with the stupid name.

"That'll make some interesting road kill in the morning," Luke said.

"They carry away their dead when they retreat before dawn in any attacks. They don't want to be discovered by the general population. They like secrets, too," Renee said. She pushed the button on the handset. "Hope your preparations were quick. We're almost there."

As they slowed for the driveway, Hank said over the radio, "We've got three green dots outside the house right now. I'll meet you out there."

"Sounds good," Renee said. She turned back to Courtney and Luke. "Hope y'all want more. I always wonder why the hell I left New Orleans."

Renee pulled up behind Courtney's car and stopped. All three piled out, and Renee walked over to the passenger side. She grabbed the rifle from the seat, then handed it to Luke. "Ever fire one of these?"

"Not an AR like this, but my uncle in Minnesota has a couple AKs he made me and my sister try out as kids. I had a lot of fun. Always wondered why my parents never went back," Luke answered.

"Okay, you should be able to handle this. It's lighter and more accurate. It has a bit less kick to it than an AK, too. Only shoot when you've got a clear shot because I don't have any extra clips here, and once you run out all you'll have is a fancy club. I'll be back in a little bit; I'm going to give Ivan a hand. At least if I leave you this you'll be able to fight until I get back." Renee put more shells into the shotgun.

"Safety?" Luke asked.

"On the left side behind the trigger."

"Thank you," Luke said to Renee, who walked around the front of the car.

Hank descended the front steps quicker than Courtney thought he could, and gave Luke and Courtney headsets. Luke put his around his neck while retrieving the cat and jersey from the interceptor. Courtney put hers on. When Luke shut the car door, Renee drove away.

"With these, you two will be able to hear what I tell you is on the radar after I get back up there," Hank instructed. He scowled at Courtney. "Where are your clothes?"

"I'm covered. Mostly. Other things kind of happened that were a little more important than getting fully dressed again. Those boots take way too long to put on when there's monsters trying to kill you," she explained, looking down at her toes.

"Which explains your shirt how?"

Courtney shrugged.

Hank shook his head and said to Luke, "Just don't shoot her, okay? I know she must tempt you sometimes. God knows I'm tempted right now."

"Yeah, wouldn't dream of it when I apparently have to fight monsters I know nothing about. She's good practice for helping me deal with difficult customers," Luke said, a bit of anger returning to his voice.

Luke followed Hank up to the front of the house with the cat and jersey in his arms and the AR-15 slung over his shoulder.

Courtney called to him, "I'm going to make sure the cat shits on your precious jersey for that one."

Luke walked into the foyer, plopping the cat in the closet. It looked up at him, then at Courtney behind him as he hung up the jersey. "Stay. I'll be back—I hope," he told the cat. Luke sighed at Courtney. "Not that I've got a clue what I'm doing. You'd think maybe the cop could stick around and help."

"I barely know more than you do. Honestly, I don't think anyone really has a plan. We've just got to wade through the shit if we want to live," Courtney said, her eyes darting from tree to tree, searching for signs of the next monster.

Luke raised the headphones and grunted something she couldn't hear.

"I wish I'd thought of my sneakers while you were in there," Courtney said.

"We should've just stayed there, really. I wouldn't have to play soldier and you wouldn't have to play modern Xena."

"I think I'm better looking than Xena, though I kind of wish I had her armor. And a pair of fucking shoes."

"I'll go back for the damn shoes, and maybe hide until someone who knows what they're doing arrives to take care of this."

Hank chimed in over the radio, "Those three gargoyles are moving. Two around the tower, one by the garage."

"I guess we're stuck," Luke said as he faced the tower.

Courtney sighed, walking to him through the grass. Her back pressed against his and she faced the garage. Rustling in the bushes on Luke's side took his attention off Courtney. He fired a quick burst while she raised her sword and tried not to look behind her.

As Luke's gun fired, the garage gargoyle charged around the corner. It seemed startled to see Courtney waiting for it, and she ran at it swinging the sword. She clotheslined it. The blade sliced through its throat. The gargoyle flopped onto its back and clutched at the gushing wound, rolling around on the ground while Courtney hacked at the throat a few more times to finish it off.

One ran around the tower and Luke mowed it down. Courtney heard him ask over the radio, "So, uh, how many rounds does an AR-15 magazine hold?"

"Usually thirty," Hank answered, "Why?"

"Just wondering. I've fired about fifteen. I think."

"Let Courtney get the third. I'll bring another gun down; I don't have spare clips or ammo for yours. You two be careful since I'm not going to be by the radar," Hank advised.

Courtney looked to Luke and said, "I'll be fine. Stay here until you've got another gun."

"I'll be there as soon as he gets it to me, though. I'm not leaving you alone long, as terrifying as these things are," Luke said. "I'm glad I pissed before we left the grill, or my pants would be soaked."

Courtney snickered, then slunk along the side of the house with her sword raised. Her hip throbbed, but it was a peripheral thing she barely noticed. She found herself relishing the thrill of pursuit.

Okay, this is weird. It's like suddenly I'm hunting for sport. Man, I want to kill this thing. It's not just survival mode. Am I fucking smiling?

Leaves wiggled in the bushes. Courtney took a few steps towards the movement. Once she was a few feet away, a small rock flew past her and hit the leaves.

"Fuck," she said as she realized her mistake.

Courtney spun just in time to be tackled. The sword dropped from her hand and stuck in the dirt out of reach. Gargoyle teeth sank into her left shoulder as she reached towards her sword. She grunted as her knuckles hit a rock.

This fucking hurts, but you'll hurt worse soon. I'll kill your ugly ass. Courtney clenched her jaw, grabbed the rock, and slammed it into the side of the gargoyle's head. The gargoyle recoiled, ripping its teeth from her skin as it retreated. She dropped the rock, a burning sensation spreading through her shoulder. The creature grabbed her calf as she struggled to get up. Claws dug into her leg and her hands scrambled for grip in the dirt as the gargoyle dragged her to the tree line.

Gunfire caused the gargoyle to release her. Luke fired a warning shot and stopped a few yards away with his rifle aimed at the fiend. Courtney crawled over to her sword, aware again of the pain in her shoulder, hip, and calf as the battle rage melted away. The gargoyle snarled at Luke, then took a step towards Courtney. Luke emptied the AR-15 into the creature's abdomen. It dropped to the ground, but tried to push itself back up.

Luke walked up to it, ready to bash its head in with the butt of the rifle.

"No!" Courtney yelled. "You'll get splattered with its blood. I don't want you to be a target if I can help it. Let me do this."

She limped over with the sword and Luke backed off. Courtney weakly swung the sword with her uninjured arm while Luke looked away. The sound of racing engines approached. Courtney's blade barely hit the fallen gargoyle. It growled, unable to fight back. Another swing smacked it in the back of the neck. This did nothing to the gargoyle. She dropped the sword. Courtney fell to her knees and swore under her breath as weakness crept through her limbs.

Renee's cruiser and Ivan's somehow-undamaged Bentley stopped a few yards from Courtney. Luke helped her up as Hank ran over. They supported her and ran to the stairs, where Renee brought medical supplies. Courtney watched Ivan finish off the wounded gargoyle while Hank and Luke helped her sit on the steps.

Shit, I hate hospitals. I fucking hate hospitals, but oh man this is bad.

Another vehicle drove into the circle, but her vision blurred too much to tell what it was. The blood dripping from her fingers was pretty damn clear, though.

Secrets. Too many secrets. How am I going to explain this bite scar to Andrea? I'll never be able to wear a swimsuit or tank top again. Shit, shit, shit. I have to live first. This is bad.

Fabric tore, but it sounded distant. If it weren't for stabbing pain in her shoulder, she wouldn't have known it was her hoodie being torn away from the bite.

"Scott, got your whiskey handy? She's been bitten." It sounded like Hank's voice, but it could've been the tooth fairy. Everything was so hazy except the pain.

"Sure thing, old man," said the shadowy shapes behind her blurry uncle.

Something splashed on her wound, and her consciousness finally succumbed.

5

ourtney's fist drilled Luke's jaw. He dropped back into her computer chair, which rolled back from the side of her bed and almost tipped over.

Her eyes fluttered open as she sat up in bed. She rubbed her eyes and glanced around at her surroundings. No gargoyles, just her bedroom.

Luke flexed his jaw. "It's okay, you're safe."

She rubbed her eyes again. "How long have I been out and why the hell does my head hurt so bad? It's like the only thing I didn't hurt."

"Almost a day. How are your knuckles?"

"Shit. Guess I'm not working today. And they feel fine, why?" *Okay, I didn't hurt my knuckles, either. What the fuck?*

"You decked me a few seconds ago when I put my hand on your forehead to check your temperature. Don't worry about work; Hank called in for you already. I called my store and said I'd be out for a few days. They saw the news and figured that, anyway."

"I was having a pretty nasty nightmare about the winged fucker. Sorry, but I can't be held responsible for my actions while I'm sleeping." Courtney yawned.

"Kind of like your snoring?"

"I don't fucking snore."

"Ivan's got a video on his phone proving otherwise. It might be a side effect of the gargoyle blood though, among other things like your perfect vision so you don't need those sexy glasses anymore." Luke sighed.

"Oh fuck, why? I'm more disturbed about snoring than getting turned into ground beef by monsters. We made the news? And wait, seriously? You thought my glasses were sexy?"

"I loved your glasses. Not that you're not gorgeous without them; it'll just take some getting used to. As for the news, the cops fudged the report a bit. No gargoyles. There was a home invasion, but we got away. They chased us until we crashed, but you kicked their asses with kung fu. Their gang buddies burned my apartment as payback. As for your head, gargoyles have venom in their bites. We had to induce vomiting. Lots of whiskey."

"Oh. That explains the headache. How's my breath?"

"Like dog farts," Luke said, holding his nose.

"Well, just hold your breath. I'm not ready to move yet," she said as she lay back.

"Don't expect you to be. Want to see something cool?"

"Sure, I guess, as long as I don't have to get up."

Luke lifted the sheets at the foot of her bed and pointed to her calf. Courtney sat up. The claw marks were gone. *How?* She threw the sheets aside, but deflated as her hip remained bandaged.

"Don't look so sad; I'm taking it off now," Luke said.

He ripped off the tape and grinned at her screech.

"Ow, damn it!"

"It didn't bother you when I took the one off your calf. Didn't even stop snoring. Besides, payback's a bitch and my jaw wanted some."

"You're not going to leave this snoring thing alone, are you?" Courtney peeked at her exposed hip. Only a few faint scabs remained where the first gargoyle's claws sunk in.

Huh. Good thing I didn't get wounded anywhere that'd be visible all the time. This healing might be harder to explain than ditching my glasses.

"Hank figures snoring's a side effect of the gargoyle blood, just like this fast healing," Luke said.

"I guess I'll take snoring if it comes with healing. Glad I didn't get clawed two inches lower. These panties were expensive, and Unc would've had to take 'em off to do the bandages. Shit, that would've sucked."

"That's why I did the bandages. Did you forget about the glass in your thigh? Your jeans are shot. The bra too. That bite tore off a strap."

"Shit. How's the shoulder look?"

"Very red. A few little scabs. Hank figures you'll be one hundred percent by six." Luke tapped her wound and watched her scowl.

"I hear my name. What'd I do now?" Hank asked, walking into the room. He immediately looked away. "Luke, give her the blanket back so I'm not looking at my niece in shredded lingerie. Please."

"Yes sir," Luke answered. He wrapped the sheet around Courtney's shoulders. When she stretched her legs, her feet nearly came down on Beatrix, who lay on the floor by the bed. Pain lanced through her hip as she crossed her legs to avoid the cat, so she left her right leg hanging off the bed. "You can look now, Unc."

Hank turned to her while Luke sat in the computer chair and rubbed his chin. Hank spoke. "About last night. Obviously, quite a bit has changed. Luke no longer has his own place or vehicle. Ivan and I explained everything to him, and rather than accepting protection, he wants in on the fight. I don't think I've seen Ivan's eyes so wide as they were when Luke went off on him. Really entertaining. I've asked him to stay here for a while so he can learn. He wouldn't accept until he heard your opinion, but insisted he's learning anyway."

"Of course. I'll even share my room if you don't object," she answered.

"No objections. I saw the way you stayed up all night watching her, so that's settled," Hank said to Luke.

"What's the rent? That's kind of important too," Luke asked.

"For now, nothing. I know you lost almost everything, so I'll let you worry about getting all that set first. I know Ivan's given you some money, but you've got enough to replace without thinking about rent," Hank answered.

"Sweet. No complaints here. Hopefully the renter's insurance does its job and I'll be on my feet with a new apartment soon."

Hank nodded and said to Courtney, "Now Cricket, I know you don't care for the Pontiac. Since we were already discussing a new vehicle for you, I think we should give Luke your car. That'll allow him to get back and forth until he gets a vehicle of his choice."

"So the Jeep is still a go?"

"Nope. I checked and it's already sold. I had a different idea. Close your eyes and hold out your hands."

Courtney obeyed, half expecting to find sales ads to peruse. Instead, a small piece of cold metal dropped into her palm. A set of keys. "What are these for?"

"They're for your new car."

"I don't get to pick it out for myself?"

"No. I know you'll love it."

"What is it?" Her brow furrowed as she stared at the unmarked keys.

"It's in the garage already. Has been for years."

"Hold up," Courtney said quietly. "These are the keys for the Willys?"

Hank nodded and smiled.

Courtney yelled, "These are the keys for the Willys. Holy shit." She jumped up and hugged her uncle, barely missing the cat as her feet hit the floor. The sheet fell. Beatrix took up residence under the computer desk.

"I can't thank you enough." Courtney struggled to hold back tears.

"You could always put the blanket back on, and maybe work on your swearing. I'd be thankful for both," Hank suggested.

Luke picked up the sheet again. He wrapped it around Courtney as she let go of Hank. She looked at the keys again as the tears flowed, and she let Luke walk her back to the bed.

"You need more rest before jumping around like a teenager, and we have stuff to do a little later," Luke told her.

She wiped her eyes and nodded as she sat back on the bed. "I never get this emotional, except angry. Another gargoyle blood side effect?" she asked Hank between sniffles.

"Ivan said Anatalia experienced significant mood swings, so perhaps it is in women. She and Renee are the only women he's known to absorb their blood. It wasn't permanent. Only lasted a few months. Renee didn't get extra emotional, but had the munchies."

"Good. I hate crying."

"I know. I mean, this is the first time I've seen you cry. Even that Will Smith zombie movie didn't do it," Luke said.

"*Star Trek II*, when Spock dies," Hank fake-coughed.

Courtney gaped at Hank. "Unc!" She elbowed Luke and asked, "Do we have a new litterbox for your furball so I can wipe cat shit inside his welding mask?"

"Yeah, Ivan picked up cat stuff as soon as stores opened so we could keep watch over you. We still need to go shopping for me later, though," Luke said.

"We? We're shopping together? This is a huge step in our relationship, you know, especially if there's clothes shopping involved."

"It's not like we don't live together now," Luke pointed out. "We're only going to Bullseye Bargain Barn. I want some cheap clothes. And a toothbrush. And my kind of toothpaste, deodorant, all that happy stuff. You're not the only one who desperately needs their teeth brushed and a shower right now."

Courtney laughed. "I noticed. What are you going to do about that bloody T-shirt? You can't exactly waltz through Bullseye looking like *The Walking Dead*."

"Ivan's letting me borrow a leather jacket. I think it cost more than I make in a year, so I'm worried as hell," Luke answered, laughing. "But I think Hank has some important stuff to say before we plan a big shopping trip."

Hank nodded. "Yes, plenty. Last night you encountered one of the winged gargoyles. You can't kill them as easily as their minions."

"So I saw. I mean, it got right back up after getting hit by a car, filled with bullets, plowing headfirst into the road, and being shot in the head with a shotgun." Courtney shivered at the mental image of the beast pounding its chest.

"You have to cut off the horns before you can kill it," Hank said.

"So that's why Renee shot at the horns."

"Yes. Now if you'll let me finish, there's only three winged ones left. Last we knew, Grigori went into hibernation and Halgaard has actually aided monster hunters in Europe. The one you saw last night was Edthgar. We haven't seen him out of his den in close to ten years, so last night was an exceptional event. He must be quite interested in you. I'm sure his fascination will pass in a few weeks like it always does when someone new absorbs blood. We'll be back to occasional gargoyle sightings after that, but until then we have to take measures to keep you safe."

Hank paused to wipe his glasses on his flannel shirt, then continued. "So, Ivan and I insist you need a cell phone. We can't watch the radar twenty-four seven and you can't hide all the time. Your friends might figure out something is going on otherwise, and knowing how nosy Andrea is, we don't need her sneaking around and running into a gargoyle because she's curious where you went. As I said before, the gargoyles must remain a secret."

Courtney scowled, staring at her fingers gripping the sheets, and asked, "What kind of phone? What kind of bill do I have to budget in now? What kind of stupid name is Edthgar? If he weren't so huge and spooky I'd deck him for having a name I can barely pronounce."

"Ivan is out right now picking up a couple of smartphones to add to his plan and getting them set up by some of his tech people with apps to track you better. After the minion Havardr lured him away, I had to direct him on radar back to Luke's place and he barely made it in time," Hank answered.

"I'll try not to complain. What you and Ivan think is best works, as long as I'm still free to do normal life stuff. Avoiding Ed-Derp is worth a damn phone I guess." Courtney said her nickname for the winged gargoyle in a silly voice.

Hank chuckled.

"No complaints here. I won't miss my phone. Kind of always wanted to burn the thing, so I guess I got my wish," Luke joked.

Courtney changed the subject. "Have you ever killed a winged one? You had to learn the horn thing somewhere, right?"

"Yes, back in '89," Hank said. "Alec pored over a medieval-era tome detailing the killing of the winged one Chivamir during the Crusades. We didn't figure out the horns thing ourselves."

"Huh, the old perv is good for something. How'd you do it?"

"There's a series of tunnels carved under the town. The earliest ones were the lair of the winged one Mephallo, though we've added new tunnels over the years as an emergency shelter. Ivan wanted subterranean passages between his different businesses around here, and the discovery of Mephallo's tunnels was a pure accident."

Hank looked out the window with narrowed eyes as he continued in a quiet voice. "He killed a few good friends who went to investigate the mystery tunnels, and for the next few weeks he kept popping up and killing monster hunters. We finally lured him to a crossroads in the tunnels—packed with explosives. He lived through the blast, but the horns were gone and he was easy picking. I struck the killing blow with your sword."

His gaze moved to Courtney's pillow, and he gave her a sad smile. "It's actually the last time I used it. I switched to a claymore after that. The longsword took too many swings, and another man died before Mephallo fell. The claymore's extra heft would've carried it deeper earlier. Since then, Mephallo's blood pooled in moats there, and minion gargoyles won't pass his blood. So it's like a shelter now that the tunnels are rebuilt—a few small earthquakes happened after the explosion."

Courtney's stomach let out a thunderous growl. Luke slapped her stomach playfully and asked, "Does this shelter have Twinkies?"

"No. The gargoyles always retreat before sunrise, so it doesn't need many supplies aside from ammo and bandages."

Courtney put her hand over Luke's mouth before he could come up with a witty response to the unimaginable lack of Twinkies, and asked, "What's for lunch?"

"I already had mine." Hank headed towards the door.

"I'll cook up a couple of burgers while you take a shower," Luke answered.

"Just don't use up all of the beef," Hank said. "Ivan is going to fix some sort of Russian dish for dinner tonight and needs about a third of a pound."

"I want it cooked all the way through without being burnt. Think you can do that?" Courtney said as she leaned against Luke.

"I know how you always order them at Mark's, and mine are better. Your mouth is in for a spiritual experience," Luke gloated before kissing Courtney.

"It's got to be better than that kiss," Courtney joked. "We've both got awful breath right now."

"Burger breath will be better. You'll bow to the greatness of my burgers and pronounce me *King of the Spatula*."

Courtney snickered. "You're such a bullshitter. I bet these burgers taste like cardboard."

"Ah, a doubter I see. You'll be seeing the light when you take the first bite."

"How long have you been waiting to use that line?"

"It hit me three years ago," he admitted. "But it's a fact."

"Okay, well quit yapping and get cooking? Sorry, I'm no poet."

"Good thing, too. I don't think poets do too well against monsters," Luke said, deflating as he headed out the door.

Courtney tossed the sheet aside and looked over her hip again. *This healing is pretty great. I hope Luke doesn't decide he wants it, too. I don't want him to be targeted. He doesn't have the fighting skills I do. I'll have to check with Unc later and make sure that little ground rule gets set.*

She headed out to the laundry room to grab her towel and robe. As she entered the room, her little toe found the corner of the litter box. "Ow, fuck! This is going to take some getting used to," she grumbled as she limped to the bathroom.

6

The Pontiac's brakes squealed faintly as Luke stopped it behind Hank's Blazer. He shut off the engine and tried to remove the keys from the ignition, but they wouldn't budge. "What the hell? The keys are stuck."

"You have to put it in park." Courtney suppressed the urge to laugh.

He threw the shifter into park. "Damn automatics. I miss my Volvo."

Both exited the car. Luke gently closed the door out of habit, as his old car's door had a fussy homemade latch after the original broke.

"This is torturous, isn't it?" Courtney asked.

"Torturous isn't a strong enough word. These seats aren't comfortable like my worn-out vinyl ones. I loved the vent windows I could crack open for a little air. Everything about the seat and gauge locations is wrong. Hell, the steering wheel feels weird," Luke ranted.

"I felt the same way about my Mazda, but that wasn't anywhere near as different as your brick. I can't wait to see how the Willys is."

They walked over as Ivan polished the Bentley's wheels in front of the garage. Blinding sun reflected off the upright grill and forced Courtney to shield her eyes. Luke stuck out his tongue at Courtney as he pointed to his new sunglasses from their shopping excursion. "Once you start driving a standard every day, you don't want to go back. I kind of wish I was tagging along to watch Hank teach you, but Ivan wants to give me some lessons in performance driving," he said as she stuck her tongue out at him in return.

"What's he teaching you with? Not the Pontiac, I hope."

Luke pointed to the Bentley.

"Lucky bastard."

"Come on, you've got a classic now and you're jealous of a Bentley? Hank said the Willys is pushing 650 horses. Mulsannes have about five hundred," Luke countered.

Ivan laughed and put his hand on Luke's shoulder. "A stock Mulsanne has 500 horsepower and does not survive collisions with winged gargoyles, let alone escape without a scratch. Custom Mulsannes surpassing thirty million dollars—once all the modifications were finished—are a different story altogether."

"So what's *this* car putting out?" Luke asked.

"I have never had it dyno tested. The engineers who designed this engine surmised the output is over 1200 horsepower. However, this car is not the fastest since I do not need it to be. It simply needs to be able to move 7.5 tons at a brisk pace. The armor is quite heavy."

"Wow," Luke said. "It looks completely stock."

"That is the point. Only the interior is different, due to all the extra switches on the center console. Do not touch them during your lesson."

"Missiles behind the headlights?" Courtney asked.

"No. I admit the gadgets are tempting, but it would take eons to describe them and why they would be unwise to use on the daily commute." Ivan paused a moment. "Are you expecting company? Perhaps someone in a small roadster? I believe I hear a Miata."

"Yeah, Andrea. Wait, how the hell can you tell what kind of car it is?" Courtney asked.

"I listen," Ivan answered with eyes closed.

Andrea's blue Miata drove into view beneath the tree arch.

"I'll be damned," Courtney muttered.

Andrea parked next to the Bentley. She stepped out of the car and ran to Courtney, her long blonde ponytail whipping her back as her flip-flops slapped the pavement. Andrea wrapped her arms around Courtney and squeezed. "Gawd, I'm so glad you're okay! I saw the news. I can't imagine how scary that was," she babbled.

"Scary? I got to beat the living shit out of some thugs. I'd almost call it fun, but the car crash sucked. Luke has more to worry about than I do." Courtney extricated herself from Andrea's arms and forced a smile, despite the tears at the corner of her friend's green eyes.

Damn, that lie came easy.

Andrea hopped over to hug Luke. "I'm glad you're okay, too. Sorry about your stuff."

"Don't be. You had nothing to do with it. Besides, I'm moving in here now, at least temporarily. Big step up from my apartment. I'm more heartbroken about my Volvo than anything else. I mean, I've still got my cat and Courtney, so nothing important's changed."

"How adorable," Andrea teased. She turned to Ivan and asked, "And who's the hunk?"

Ivan raised an eyebrow as he held out his hand to shake hers. "My name is Ivan Trebeschkov. I am a friend of Hank Mays, and am visiting for perhaps a few weeks. It is my pleasure to make your acquaintance."

"Andrea Browning. Courtney's best friend since we were in diapers. Pleased to meet you too," she said, shaking Ivan's hand.

Andrea turned back to Courtney. "Don't make a habit of fighting with Brazo de Dios. That gang's bad news. You remember my ex, Javier, right?"

"How could anyone forget the douche?"

"One of them beat him to a pulp in San Quentin, and he was a tough dude," Andrea said.

"Come on, AB. I don't go looking for fights. Usually. This one found me, and if they try shit again, I'll keep going Bruce Lee on their asses. Javier wasn't a real fighter, just a run-of-the-mill thug," Courtney answered.

"You're impossible. Just be careful, please. Some of those guys are huge. And where are your glasses?"

"I broke 'em. Don't worry, if I wind up in a pinch against a bigger dude I'll use the five-point-palm exploding-heart technique," Courtney teased, referencing the *Kill Bill* films Luke loved.

"Dammit Courtney, you weren't trained by Pai Mei. You do flips and kicks in your room. There's a huge difference," Andrea countered.

Luke chimed in. "Courtney was up against a guy that was 6'6" and had a machete. By the time she was done, he was crying. She broke his leg so bad the bone was sticking out. She could've snapped his neck. They were scared shitless because she dropped him in about fifteen seconds, and they ran to their car with their tails tucked between their legs. That's when the chase happened. And after we crashed, those three came at her all at once and were on the ground in less than a minute. My warrior princess is incredible."

"Princess?" Courtney said, scowling.

"Well, I'm not standing around arguing when I've got groceries to buy," chirped Andrea. "I'll catch you later. Oh, and hurry back to work please. Filling in for you in appliances would royally suck. I'm glad they didn't try calling me in today."

"I'll be there tomorrow as long as I get a driving lesson with my new car."

"New car? Why do you need a new car? Luke does, but you don't. I mean, yours is right there," Andrea said, pointing to the Grand Am.

"I'm giving it to Luke. You'll see my new car tomorrow. It's one of Unc's projects."

"Oh gawd. Like you need a speedy gas hog." Andrea rolled her eyes.

"You never know with Unc. He might've built a Yugo that runs on hostile thoughts."

"You're smiling, so there's a big engine that guzzles gas and kills the environment."

"Come on, if Unc made a car that ran on hostile thoughts I'd never have to buy gas again."

"You're cheap, so that'd make you happy, and then there wouldn't be angry thoughts and the car wouldn't run."

"Touché," Courtney admitted.

"You said something about groceries, right?" Luke hinted.

"Gotta go! Later!" Andrea squeaked. She darted back to her car and hopped in. As the small roadster started, her hand waved in a blur. The car crept around the Bentley as Andrea winked at Ivan, then crawled around the circle to exit the driveway.

Once the car disappeared from view, Ivan turned to Courtney. "Your friend seems strange and quite annoying. Do I want to know what this 'hunk' term means in whatever modern slang she uses?"

Luke burst out laughing as Courtney flipped off Ivan.

"How did you come to associate with someone so odd?" Ivan asked.

"Like she said, we've known each other since daycare. We went through most of school together, except when I was in that awful private school. Her family moved to San Rafael after high school but we kept in touch those couple months and she helped me get the job at Motherlode when I came to live with Unc. I helped her look at apartments here when she decided to move out. We're like sisters. It's going to hurt keeping secrets from her. That lie came too easy about the gang."

"That is one of the most difficult aspects of this business. I fear Miss Browning may have too fragile of a psyche to cope with a revelation such as this, so it is best you get used to lying for her benefit."

"She's stronger than you give her credit for, but I won't mention anything. Unc went over the 'gargoyles have to stay secret' thing." Courtney crossed her arms and turned to Luke instead, but his attention was on the Bentley's blinding grill.

"Not even a scratch. What kind of super polish are you using and where can I get some for my next Volvo?" Luke asked.

"I cannot tell you any details as I am no chemist, but it is quite special. It is a two-part compound which one of my scientists developed. Separately, the two chemicals are unremarkable. Once combined, the resultant hardness is comparable to the surface of a diamond. This polish dries to be approximately 0.01 mm in thickness, yet will be unaffected by small arms fire. Four coats of this chemical render the paint beneath impervious even to fire from a modern minigun. I have been unable to think of a proper name for it, unfortunately. My mind is less imaginative than logical."

"I'd name it *The Shit* because it's awesome but reeks like rotten eggs." Courtney pinched her nose. "A little cucumber too? Weird."

"I don't smell anything," Luke said.

Ivan smirked. "That odor is not the polish. You smell the gargoyle hiding in the bushes, likely waiting until sunset to attack. Because of the blood you absorbed, all your senses are enhanced, not just your eyesight. I wondered how long you would take to notice."

"This whole time we've been talking there's been a gargoyle here?" Her eyes darted to the mansion's front door. "My sword is inside."

"Yes. It has been here since last night. It failed to retreat before sunrise, and has been hiding since then."

"Does the sun kill them or something?" Luke asked.

"No. They just prefer not to be seen, and daylight is detrimental to stealth. It could attack at any moment if it knows we are aware of its presence," Ivan said, opening the Bentley's door and pointing out his sword on the seat.

As he reached for the handle, the gargoyle bounded from the bushes. Ivan ripped his blade from the scabbard and thrust at the charging gargoyle, impaling it through the chest. He jerked the sword free from his dying opponent and swung, severing the head with enough force to send it bouncing into the bushes. The headless body toppled backwards.

Ivan wiped his bloodied blade on the corpse's arm, then grabbed one of the used polishing rags to completely clean the blade. He slid his sword back into its sheath. "The polish contains no sulfur. That is the scent of the gargoyles in this area. I suspect their underground lair has a high sulfur content, as natural gargoyle scent is faint, reminiscent of the cucumbers you detected. Well, minions of Edthgar, anyway," Ivan said, oblivious to Luke and Courtney gawking at the dead gargoyle.

"How did you do that so calmly?" Luke asked.

"A century of life has taught me a solitary, reckless gargoyle is little concern. The fact it failed to retreat last night suggested this one would be particularly imbecilic. Now, might I suggest you retrieve the spoils of your shopping trip and bring them inside so you have time before sunset for your lessons? I would prefer to be done then in order to have the proper amount of time to prepare my chebureki for dinner. It is a Russian dish I am certain you will enjoy. I also have a gift for each of you which could prove quite useful if you find yourselves unarmed against a gargoyle. I will share no further details to spoil the surprise."

Courtney took Luke's hand. "Food's a good reason to hurry. Come on, I want to get my lesson done so we can try this stuff sooner."

"Food motivates you more than a hot rod?" Luke asked.

"Well no, but it adds a little more. I barely feel my wounds now. I'm ready to move. Let's do this."

They walked back up to the Pontiac and retrieved the shopping bags. As they reached the steps, Courtney glanced back. Ivan stood over the gargoyle corpse with his hands on his hips, but stared toward the garage. "What's up? Thinking about polishing the Bugatti too?" she yelled.

Ivan shook his head. "No, simply reminiscing." His voice cracked as he looked away.

Luke squeezed Courtney's hand. "He looks like he could use alone time. Come on, let's reorganize your closet to fit my stuff. Give him some extra time before the drive."

Courtney watched Ivan as Luke held the door. The Russian kicked the gargoyle and muttered something, then sighed and stood with his eyes closed, hand on his forehead. "I wonder if gargoyles got his Anatalia and that's why he's so dedicated to this," she wondered aloud to Luke.

He shrugged. "That's up to him to tell."

Courtney nodded and followed Luke into the hall as the door closed behind her.

7

A metallic screech somewhere in the house awakened Courtney. She groaned. *Great. This shit again.*

She sat up and noticed she didn't have to wait for her eyes to adjust to the darkness. It wasn't a bright night, since fog rolled in off the Pacific, suffocating the moon and stars. *Cool. I guess this must be the gargoyle blood. Not quite like daylight, but damn.*

"What's up?" Luke mumbled as Courtney pushed the sheets aside.

"I heard a noise. Could be another gargoyle. I'm going to investigate." She slid the sword from under her pillow and headed for the door.

Luke half-fell, half-climbed out of bed. "Need a flashlight or the mini keychain light thing Ivan gave us at dinner?"

"No. I see fine. Stay here; I don't want you stumbling into blood like I did. Besides, I'm not trying to scare the gargoyle away with UV light. If there's one, it dies."

"I'm smart enough to wear slippers. It's a good habit to get in when there's a cat in the house. You never know when you're going to find a hairball," Luke advised.

ROGER SANDRI

"Well, stay here and protect the cat, unless cat barf is somehow toxic to gargoyles."

Beatrix sat up, ears pricked and pupils wide. *Something's definitely going on for her to be so alert.*

"Fine, but be careful," Luke said, stroking the cat's ears. "I don't want to have to sit up all night and play nurse again."

"Don't worry. I know what to expect now." Courtney grabbed her flannel and stepped into the hall. A brief glimpse of moonlight broke through the clouds and reflected off the emerald in her sword's handle. *At least it's a warm night so those stairs won't be fucking freezing.*

Gargoyle blood would warm them up.

The sword slid silently from its scabbard as she descended with a grin on her face. Images flashed through her mind of the gargoyles dispatched last night. Her eyes traced the length of the blade and noticed it was clean. *Well damn. Guess I need to thank someone for that. I sure didn't do it while I was hurt. Don't need blood in the sheath; that might stink.*

Light poured from the kitchen, and a shadow crossed the wall as something moved past the doorway. She dropped the scabbard and raised her sword overhead in a two-handed grip, approaching the kitchen with a smirk on her face and her eyes locked on the shadow.

Courtney strode down the center of the hall, carpet silencing her steps, then spun through the doorway ready to swing at whatever creature awaited her.

Instead of a gargoyle, Ivan was making himself a sandwich.

Ivan shook his head at her expression. "I was not aware midnight snacks were so frowned upon in this household as to draw the ire of a sword-wielding warrior woman."

Courtney blushed as she set the sword down on the island. "Midnight snacks are fine, but the 2:00 a.m. ones are a bit shaky. You're still in a suit and tie too, so that's really questionable."

"I do not sleep. Do you not remember that discussion?"

"Right. Sorry, there's just been a lot to think about the past couple days and not everything stuck, I guess."

"I thought myself to be quiet enough tonight, but apparently I was mistaken," Ivan replied, pouring himself a tall glass of cabernet sauvignon.

"Fancy red wine with a roast beef and cheese sandwich. Different."

"Red meat and red wine are a delectable combination." Ivan walked out of the kitchen straight through the doorway to the great room. He set the wine glass on the coffee table beside his sword. No lights were on, confirming Courtney's theory that perfect night vision was a gargoyle blood side effect.

She pointed to the table. "At least I'm not the only one paranoid enough to wander around with a sword in the middle of the night."

"When one stops being careful is when one most needs to be."

Courtney nodded as Ivan sat down. He raised the sandwich to his mouth, but before he could take the first bite he paused. A small squeal echoed through the metal staircase. "Perhaps it was not I who roused you from your slumber." Ivan sighed, putting down the sandwich and plate. He picked up his unsheathed sword and moved into the hallway. "I will go upstairs to lure our opponent down. I want you to stand halfway between here and the end of the hall until I return. Do this and we shall have our opponent in a two-on-one situation," Ivan instructed.

Courtney nodded.

Ivan crept down the hall while Courtney stood outside the door. *He's holding his sword awfully low. Weird. What are we up against?*

The squeal sounded different from anything she'd heard gargoyles make. Ivan's stance added to her doubt. He knew what it was but neglected to tell her. Courtney's mind raced, picturing everything from bloodthirsty leprechauns to a demonic Teddy Ruxpin. The thought of sharp teeth lining the drooling mouth of her beloved children's toy made her shudder.

Courtney's heartbeat accelerated as Ivan disappeared. She took a few shaky steps down the hall, then stopped and shook her head. *Ridiculous. What threat could something smaller than a gargoyle pose?*

The spider descending from the ceiling into the shower last week crossed her mind, along with how she'd let loose a scream worthy of a horror movie. Inevitably, she thought of a giant tarantula screeching as it crawled down the stairs.

A high-pitched giggle pierced her eardrums and Courtney nearly dropped her sword. The baleful sound set her ears ringing, chilling her to the bone. Another evil squeal of glee preceded a cacophony. Courtney wanted to run to her car and get the hell out of there, but instead she took a step forward.

Ivan stumbled around the corner, dragging his sword. A tremendous gash bled out across his stomach. Several small slices covered his face, and one eye hung from its socket. He stood straighter as the wounds closed and his eye sucked back into place. Courtney gagged at the grinding sound his shoulder made as bones shifted.

"You should see your face. It is quite amusing," Ivan said between labored breaths.

"What the fuck are we up against? It tore out your damn eye." She ignored his snicker at her expression.

Ivan faced the corner where the two halls met. He adjusted his stance lower and held the blade of his sword mid-calf level. "Two gremlins. They are exceptionally fast."

The gremlins' footsteps were silent as they descended apart from a barely audible ticking sound, like a dog's claws on a hard surface. When the noises ceased she knew the gremlins were on the carpet.

Two small creatures rounded the corner and peered down the hall. The gremlins looked fragile, with spindly limbs and thin bodies covered in dark gray fur. The larger one had black stripes on the forehead of its cat-like head. Their eyes flashed yellow-green in the light from the kitchen. Long, thin bat ears accounted for six inches of their height.

Courtney looked into the eyes of the smaller one. It stared back at her, twitching its ears like a curious cat. She thought it could almost be considered cute—until it opened its mouth and let out a shrill cry. Tiny, sharp teeth lined its narrow jaws and made the ones she imagined in Teddy Ruxpin's mouth seem harmless. Three-inch claws akin to needles burst from its fingertips before it ran at her. The larger one bounded towards Ivan.

Four pinpricks pierced her ankle before she could react. Courtney spun in time to see the gremlin leap at her. It missed as she dodged. The raging gremlin issued a zealous screech and leapt at her again. Her sword cleaved the gremlin through the waist. Both halves fell into the kitchen, spasming as the creature died. A small tape recorder was strapped to its back. An electrical pop sounded as blood soaked into the device.

Ivan fought the larger gremlin. Its claws jabbed into his shoulders to hang on as it tried to bite his throat. He held an ear in each hand, keeping the gremlin's mouth less than an inch away. Courtney kicked it, and the gremlin bounced off of the wall with a crack. It landed head-first on the carpeted floor with a pained *oof.*

The creature struggled to get up. Ivan planted his foot on the gremlin's back and pinned it before it could rise. "Would you kindly fetch a pair of pliers from the kitchen?" he asked Courtney as he examined the holes in his shirt.

She stepped over the twitching gremlin halves leaking blood in the doorway, then darted around the island. The cabinet doors squeaked as she grabbed pliers.

Ivan positioned the greasy metal jaws by one of the gremlin's fingers. "Now, press on the back of its hand."

She obliged, and the needle claws popped out for Ivan to clamp onto. Ivan spoke to the gremlin in what Courtney presumed was Russian. It hissed back.

He ripped out the gremlin's claw.

Huh. Maybe I should've cut off the other one's limbs if torture is the goal?

The creature shrieked as Ivan clamped down on the next claw. He repeated his question. Tears flowed from the gremlin's feline eyes as it spoke in a childlike voice. Courtney's ears rang from its scream, and her sword twitched in her hands despite the humanity its voice lent to the thing. Killing it would be so easy.

Hank stood at the end of the hall to watch the interrogation. Luke followed, despite Courtney's instructions to stay put, and he held the cat. Beatrix tried to conceal her head under Luke's arm. The gremlin's wailing must have been even more painful to her sensitive feline ears than the ache it sent through Courtney's skull.

Ivan finished questioning the gremlin and released it. Courtney swung her sword, but Ivan grabbed her arm.

"You're letting the creepy little shit go?"

He stared into her eyes as the gremlin stumbled away, wounded hand held in the other, tears in its eyes as it glanced back. "We now have a double agent. He has given us some very useful information for little more than a promise," Ivan said.

"How can you be so sure it's not going to double cross us?"

"Despite what you saw, gremlins are naturally peaceful beings. They stay hidden in forests and subsist on insects and small rodents. Tribal life is important to them. They form small communities around their chieftains. Edthgar knows this; he captured the leader of this tribe to force them into servitude. Gremlins are nothing more than pawns used for their stealth.

I promised this one his tribe will be free once Edthgar is killed. Freedom is a powerful motivator," Ivan explained.

The gremlin stopped to stare back at Courtney. Its ears drooped, and more tears streamed down its face. It said something in Russian to her before walking between Hank and Luke on its way to the stairs.

"What the fuck did it say?" she asked.

"He said, 'I am not an animal. I am a sentient being, with feelings.' He does not speak English, but he understands emotions and clearly recognized your intent to kill him as if he were a simple mouse."

"Mice don't try to tear out peoples' throats." Courtney stared at the blood on her sword.

"Correct. People, however, try to kill each other quite often. Brutality is a choice we make, and the gremlins are no different than you or I in that respect. Would you strike down a man who surrendered?" Ivan asked.

"It depends. I can think of a few I'd be happy to finish off."

Ivan sighed. "If a man were merely following orders because his family was being held hostage, what course of action would you take?"

"I'd ask who sent him and try to kill his boss. Otherwise, so long, creepy little shitstick."

"That is precisely what I have done. There are many strange creatures in this world. Some are savage beasts who desire nothing more than to do evil. Others, such as gremlins, merely want to live their lives in peace. Sometimes lines are blurred. This is one such case. Edthgar has evil in spades, and feels he must violate everything which is truly good in this world. In time you will learn which creatures deserve respect, and which creatures must be dealt with mercilessly."

Hank stepped forward and asked Ivan, "What did he have to say?"

"He said Edthgar sent him and his brother to spy on us, and to deliver a hit and run if they were noticed. Edthgar especially wants to know if we have his rune."

"Of course not. It's still tucked away in Romania, right?"

"Yes, but our new friend is going to tell him he couldn't find it before being discovered. Let Edthgar fear the possibility."

Courtney asked, "Um, what's this rune?"

Ivan sighed again.

Oh, great. Another long story. Hopefully he gets to the point before my hair goes gray.

"At one time there were thirteen winged gargoyles," he began.

"Hank told that bit already."

Ivan frowned and motioned a zipper over Courtney's lips, then continued. "The thirteen were summoned to our realm by a man who traveled dimensions and found himself unable to return. He brought his servants here to help him. To do so, he crafted thirteen runes, which turned out to be imperfect and transformed his servants into winged gargoyles upon their arrival. As long as he possessed the runes he could control them, but unfortunately, an untrustworthy mistress stole the runes. She lacked the knowledge that those runes could only be used by someone from the other dimension, and her actions freed the gargoyles. Before the gargoyles killed her, she hid the runes, and they remained hidden until Anatalia and I found them, which is when we were first attacked. I dispersed most of the runes around the globe to keep them hidden until I have rid the world of the last gargoyle."

"Does this sorcerer have a name? Must've been one shitty dude to let gargoyles rampage," Luke said.

"He has had many names, and still lives," Ivan answered. "The one he went by when we met was Baron Wolfgar von Teuffelmann. That name was bestowed upon him by a mistress in the 1880s. He searched for the runes in vain and was unable to bring himself to kill the gargoyles, for he remembers who they were before. They cannot kill him, either. Only someone of his own blood or one who wields a weapon with a particular enchantment can kill him."

"You know this guy?" Courtney growled.

"Yes. He spent part of the early 1900s in the Russian city of Petrograd, which you know as St. Petersburg. He sought the runes, but found only Lyuba Yemelina. They had a brief but fiery relationship from October to Christmas in 1907. She broke off their romance when she met her soon-to-be husband, Anatoli Trebeschkov. On July 17 of 1908, I was born. You see, I am not merely acquainted with the man—he is my biological father," Ivan explained.

Courtney gaped at Ivan, then shook her head. "The dark secrets keep coming like slow drivers when all you want to do is get home after work."

He smiled at her. "Now if you will excuse me, I have a sandwich to eat. Courtney, please mop up the mess from the dead gremlin before it stains the hardwood. We lack special cleaners for that, so it may take a bit of effort. Oh, and smash that recorder. It will be difficult for Edthgar to obtain another."

"Don't worry, Cricket, I'll handle this. I know you need to get some sleep so you can work tomorrow; well, today," Hank said.

"Just pass me some paper towels to wipe the sword off." Courtney glanced back to Luke waiting at the end of the hall.

"Of course," Hank replied. "One less thing I have to clean tonight, unlike last night."

"Thanks, by the way."

"Sometimes cleaning is therapeutic when all you could do otherwise is worry."

"I'm sorry I got hurt. It must've been scary for you, too," she whispered.

"It happens to us all sometime. Don't dwell on it." Hank handed her the towels.

"Thanks. I'll try," she said as she mopped the blade clean.

He took the dirty towels back. "Have a good night, er, sleep?"

"You too, Unc." Courtney headed back to the stairs, picking up her scabbard along the way to Luke.

8

"Wait up, Courtney. You wanted me to look at your new car, right?" Andrea yelled.

Courtney paused at the Motherlode exit sign. "I parked next to you, like always. Think I'd change that?"

"Well, it's some kinda fancy thing, isn't it? I'm happy you trust me parked near it," Andrea replied. They walked side by side down the parking lot. "Wow, I'm surprised how empty this place is. Like, come on, it's Friday night." Andrea gestured at the mostly empty parking lot.

"You haven't seen the movie ads lately, have you? Everybody's probably in the theater."

"Oh gawd, not that Batman thing. I hate action movies." Andrea rolled her eyes.

The two stopped between the Miata and Willys. "I'm no superhero fan either, but we're in the minority. If the ads weren't on literally every YouTube video I'd never know about it. More importantly, like the car? It's a '41 Willys."

"It's huge but I like the color." Andrea unlocked her Miata's passenger door.

"It's nowhere near the size of Hank's Blazer or Ivan's Bentley. Besides, everything looks massive compared to a Miata except Fiats and those shitty Smart things." Courtney opened the Willys' driver's door and popped the hood release, then headed to the nose to reveal the chromed engine compartment.

Andrea grabbed a pack of cigarettes out of her Hello Kitty purse. She tossed the bag onto the seat and removed a cigarette.

"If you want a ride you might want to think twice about lighting that," Courtney said, glaring at the cigarette between Andrea's fingers.

Andrea tossed the pack onto the passenger seat next to her purse and tucked the cigarette into her cleavage. "The hood kinda looks like a bird beak. Really shiny engine, too, wow. I could do my makeup in my reflection. How's it on gas?"

"Don't know yet. I haven't driven it enough to know exactly what kind of mileage it gets. I'll probably be broke, but it'll be totally worth it."

"I can barely afford gas for my car with how rent keeps going up. Your uncle must not charge much."

"You smoke Marlboros. Switching to a cheaper brand or quitting would save some."

"Giving up weed was hard enough once I realized my green thumb only extends to flowers. I'm not zen like you; I gotta have something to unwind and relieve the stress since I still gotta buy veggies. Can't get those to grow yet either."

"I'm not all zen. I like my booze and red meat too much. You can keep your vegetarian shit." Courtney slammed the hood shut.

"Well, don't bug me about my smoking and I won't bug you about eating Bambi."

"Venison isn't really my thing. Beef, though, fuck yes. The passenger door is on that side," Courtney said with a smile as she pointed to the other side of the car.

Andrea hesitated as she looked over the car's interior. "The seats are nice, but why does it need those ugly bars?"

"That's a roll cage. Unc thought about turning this into a drag car but decided to leave it street. Come on, get in. Don't be chickenshit."

Andrea pursed her lips as she climbed in. She fiddled with the seat belts for a moment until they clicked. Her face paled as she saw Courtney's smirk. "What's with these funky belts?" Andrea squeaked.

"Five-point harnesses. They're safer than normal seat belts."

Andrea bit her lip as she looked at Courtney, then asked in a squeakier voice, "Why does it need safer belts?"

"They're safer. Safety first," Courtney said with a wide grin.

Andrea's eyes darted over the dash, and her breathing hastened. "There's no vents for A/C or heat. There's no CD player, but I see speakers. Are you sure your uncle finished this thing?"

Courtney pushed a button on the steering wheel. A brushed aluminum panel on the dash slid aside to reveal the CD player. Andrea blinked at the stereo. "That's straight outta like 2004," she giggled.

Courtney put the keys in the ignition. "Another button opens the vents and turns on the radio. I can control it all from the wheel, except for adjustments to the heat and A/C. That's what the little dial by the shifter is for. Unc wanted the car to have a clean-looking interior." She pushed in the clutch and turned the key to bring the V8 to life.

Andrea covered her ears and yelled, "Is it loud enough? You won't hear the music—not that you listen to anything good."

Courtney winked as she turned on the CD player. "Unc almost put an 8-track in here. I tried talking him into an MP3 player, but a CD player was as modern as he'd go."

"MP3 isn't exactly modern, either, you know. Bluetooth is the new 'it thing' I so wish I had so I could play everything on my phone in the car. Of course, you don't have a phone so I guess you're outdated, too."

"Outdated? I just don't give a shit. Are you ready?"

Metallica blasted through the stereo and Courtney belted out something resembling lyrics mingled with discordant noise. As she stopped "singing" along, Courtney dumped the clutch and hammered the gas.

The Willys lurched forward and stalled. Her face burned. "Yeah, I'm still new to driving a standard."

Andrea rolled her eyes. "Ugly roll cage, weird seat belts, won't stay running. At least it's pretty on the outside. Not impressed so far. It's almost as bad as your singing."

Courtney restarted the car. "You will be. Let's try this again."

This time the car stayed on. Smoke billowed from the rear tires as the Willys rapidly accelerated. Courtney steered around one of the light posts, sliding the rear end and taking aim at Andrea's Miata. Andrea screamed at the top of her lungs when the headlights illuminated the smoke around her car. Courtney turned slightly and jammed on the brakes, stopping so the passenger side of the Willys faced the passenger side of the Miata.

Andrea fumbled with the belts for a moment and jumped out of the car. She knelt down and kissed the pavement.

Courtney cackled as Andrea got up. "Maybe you should quit smoking."

Andrea stood with her hands on her hips and glared at Courtney until the laughter ended. "Am I still welcome to swing by tonight or was that a hint you don't want company?"

"Of course. You're always welcome." Courtney dabbed her eyes with the back of her hand to mop away the tears of laughter.

"Will Ivan be there?"

"Probably."

"He's kind of cute. Is he single?"

"You'll have to ask."

"I will."

"I can't wait to see this," Courtney said with a mischievous giggle.

"I'll meet you there." Andrea closed the door on the Willys.

Courtney floored the gas and pulled away, leaving Andrea in a fresh cloud of smoke.

9

Andrea coughed and shook her head as she got in the Miata. She pulled off her sneakers and chucked them in the passenger footwell, then peeled off her socks. Her head leaned back as she sighed and unbuttoned the polo shirt. "Best part of getting out of work."

She coughed again as she reached for her pocket book. Her fingers hunted for her lighter, then tossed the bag onto her sneakers and removed the cigarette from her cleavage. "Bleh, this cig is wet. Dammit Courtney, you made me sweat wondering if you were gonna hit my car."

Andrea dug her keys out of her pocket and started the car. Her hand shook as she tried to light the cigarette. Once it finally lit, she dropped the lighter in her lap. "Easy girl, you're just spooked from that hell ride."

She turned on the radio to play her *Bob Marley Greatest Hits* CD as she enjoyed the first puff of smoke. Andrea's head rocked gently to the tune of the music, and she closed her eyes. Every work day she followed this little ritual before driving home. As "Stir It Up" came to a close, she opened her eyes again. For five and one-half minutes she'd separated herself from the world around her, and it shocked her to see a man in a hoodie slinking around the few cars in the parking lot, watching her. Something felt off about the guy without a glimpse of his face. Andrea got a bad case of the creeps, so she tossed the cigarette, then threw the car into drive.

Andrea checked the mirror while stopped at the lot exit sign. The hooded man was still back there, staring at the area she'd been parked. A police interceptor rushed down the road with its lights flashing, so she sat and waited despite her desire to get away from the man. To her surprise, the interceptor turned into the parking lot. Andrea watched the mirror and saw the creepy stranger run away.

"You'd better run, freak show. The fuzz'll getcha," Andrea said, pulling out of the lot.

She gradually accelerated up to the speed limit. It pleased her to see the road almost empty so she could drive her own speed without fear of being tailgated. Whenever someone rode her bumper, it made her paranoid, thanks to the memory of getting rear-ended while riding with Courtney in her little Mazda MX-3. Courtney came out unscathed apart from minor cuts and the heartbreak of seeing her beloved first car hauled to a junkyard. Andrea, however, had broken her wrist and received a concussion. Her wrist recovered, but her previously perfect vision didn't. Sometimes it embarrassed her, having glasses matching Courtney's, thanks to all the "twins" comments they heard over it and their eyes.

Andrea adjusted her glasses, unable to believe what approached in the opposite lane. An old Volkswagen Bus sped towards her, hazard lights flashing. As it blasted past, she blinked at the pink paint job with a white roof.

"Someone's in a hurry. Weird for an old hippie."

A red light forced her to stop. Red lights always made her antsy, but this was the light where the accident happened.

Courtney had given her a lift while Andrea's Volkswagen Cabrio sat in the shop for what seemed like the thousandth time. As soon as she'd recovered, Andrea had looked for a new car. She loved convertibles and marveled over the reliability of Courtney's Mazda before the big Lexus SUV squished it, so a Miata seemed cool. It was sporty, too, giving her the maneuverability to avoid bad drivers.

The light turned green, so she eased forward. A silver Toyota pickup blasted through the intersection in front of her. Andrea caught her breath as she started moving again and looked in the mirror. The license plate wasn't visible enough in the dark, but she made a mental note of the black cap on the bed and flashing hazard lights. "What's with these crazy people tonight?"

The full moon peeked through gaps in the thick cloud cover as she crested a small hill. "That's why everybody is so loony." Her mind kept drifting to the guy in the parking lot. Something was strange about him, but she couldn't imagine what aside from his behavior. She never saw his face, so it couldn't be that. It could've been a creepy woman, but the bulky body was more masculine to her. Whatever bothered her would go unknown since the creep was probably in police custody, and frankly she didn't want to know.

Andrea closed in on Overlook Road, but thought more about the eventful forty-five-minute drive than the teasing Courtney had in store for getting to the mansion late. Racing Courtney was pointless. Andrea took her time and enjoyed her smoke.

She turned up the driveway, forcing herself to ignore the stone gargoyles. Her palms grew sweatier than usual thinking about the creepy statues. Hank seemed fairly normal to her, but his taste in décor hinted at some secret below the surface. Five years of visiting the mansion gave no answers.

Andrea parked behind Luke's car, then slid on the flip-flops she kept in her purse. A quick breeze made her shiver, and as she thought of the man in the hoodie, Andrea put up the Miata's top and locked the doors. Ivan's Bentley caught her eye on her way to the front door, banishing the stranger from her mind. "Cute and rich. I hope you're single."

Courtney opened the front door and stepped onto the landing. "About time you got here. Come in."

"I'll be there in a moment," Andrea said.

"What took so long?"

"You probably drove faster, that's all. I had to enjoy my smoke first to relax after you tried to kill me."

"My car is so fun and fast. See why I love my Willys?"

"You have no idea how bad that sounded."

"Eh, whatever. We all say stupid shit now and then."

They both stepped into the foyer. Andrea kicked off her sandals next to Courtney's sneakers. "Come to the kitchen," Courtney said with a wink.

Andrea followed Courtney in and said, "Hi, Hank. Hi, Ivan."

"Hello, Andrea; what's new?" Hank asked.

"Nothing but higher bills."

Ivan poured drinks for himself and Hank, nodding to Andrea. "Would you like something to drink as well?"

"No, thanks," she answered as Ivan took the first sip of his drink. "You're kinda cute; are you single?"

Ivan spit his drink out on the island.

He coughed, then spoke in a shaky voice. "I am single, but unavailable. My heart was taken long ago and I do not foresee that changing any time soon."

"I'm sorry. Why do all the cute ones turn out to be gay?"

Ivan coughed again before answering. "I simply have no interest in dating. My darling Anatalia departed this world long ago and I cannot envision myself with anyone else."

"You're dating an astronaut?"

Hank tried not to laugh but failed miserably as Ivan bowed his head and muttered something in Russian.

Courtney put her hand on Andrea's shoulder, whispering in her ear. "That means she died, dumbass."

Andrea blurted out, "Oh gawd, I'm so sorry! I didn't mean to be so insensitive."

Ivan looked at his mess on the table. "It is quite all right. I am much too old for you, anyway."

"Come on, you can't be much older than thirty."

"He's so old his birth certificate is etched in stone and tucked away in a museum," Courtney muttered, winking at Ivan.

Hank took off his glasses and wiped his eyes.

"You were much too kind with your assessment of my age. That is all I will say on the subject. Allow me to mourn a good beverage gone to waste," Ivan said. He grabbed some paper towels and frowned at Andrea as he mopped up the wine.

Courtney pulled Andrea out of the kitchen. "Come on, I've got something to show you. Besides, I think Ivan needs some peace and quiet."

Andrea followed Courtney to the stairs.

"You really can get under anyone's skin. That's the first time I've seen him be anything other than the calm and perfect gentleman," Courtney said.

"My little talent. You're athletic and I know how to annoy people."

"Annoy. What an understatement." Courtney led Andrea up the stairs.

"These stairs are always cold. Isn't your uncle ever going to carpet them?"

"Don't be such a wimp. Imagine me trying to sneak down for a snack in January. Besides, Unc says if there was carpet, how would we hear bumps in the night?"

"Are you sure your uncle's as normal as he seems?"

"Is anyone truly normal?" Courtney asked as they stepped out on the second floor.

"I am," Andrea chirped.

Courtney snickered to disagree and stopped at the door to her room.

"Luke, I'm coming in!" Courtney yelled through the door. She turned to Andrea and said, "Stay here for a moment."

Andrea waited outside while Courtney went in for whatever she wanted to show off, staring out the window at the moon. It loomed large in the night sky as a beacon for the coyotes howling in the distance. A sudden swishing sound broke her trance. Courtney swung something large at her. Andrea shrieked and ducked.

Courtney laughed as she held a sword out for Andrea to see without the motion blur.

"Are you fucking insane? I nearly pissed myself! Crazy bitch!"

"I wasn't going to hit you, not even close. You should've seen your face. Priceless."

"Why the hell do you need a sword?" Andrea squeaked.

"Ivan likes to play with swords and needed a sparring partner because my uncle is getting too old, so he's teaching me. It even has emeralds in it." Courtney stuck the handle into Andrea's hand.

Andrea nearly dropped the sword. "Heavy fucking thing," she said as she handed it back.

"Come on, it's like three pounds. If Brazo de Dios ever come by here, they're toast. You don't have to worry about them hurting me."

"Do you mind if I go back downstairs and take Ivan up on his offer for a drink?" Andrea said with a shaky voice. She hustled down the stairs, silently praising her bladder control after an evening of so many scares.

10

Static filled Courtney's ears as she rode in the Bentley. She tapped her earpiece and the static subsided. "These sure are cheap earbuds," she said to Ivan.

"They are the same as those used by Special Forces in the United States military."

"No wonder. The government always buys from the lowest bidder. Maybe your company should design and make better ones," Courtney suggested as she looked out at rolling green fields lit by moonlight between clouds.

"I am well aware of this. The process is ongoing, but alas, a quality product is not designed overnight."

"Good never is, but evil always finds a way to be."

Ivan looked over and said, "I have not heard you say anything quite so profound before."

"I was quoting Unc. He was bugging me about how long I took to do my makeup before a date, so I told him you can't rush perfection. That was his response."

"I see," Ivan said, feigning surprise and failing.

"You're a terrible actor."

"What leads you to believe my expression was not exactly what I intended?"

"Uh...."

Ivan smirked. "Occasionally, due to my position of influence within a globally renowned company, I am required to attend social gatherings held by other affluent individuals. These are contrary to my reclusive nature, but alas, I must masquerade as a typical aristocrat despite the tedium which I disdain so much."

"You certainly have the vocabulary to pull it off," Courtney said, shaking her head.

Luke's voice issued from Courtney's earpiece. "Personally I would've used *ennui* instead of *tedium*."

"Hi Unc! You told Luke that word, whatever the hell it was, right?"

Hank and Luke had both stayed behind in the office. Tonight, Luke began training on the monster radar. Hank didn't have to work hard to convince Ivan of the need for a younger backup to operate the radar, since the only other person trained for it was the old librarian, Alec.

Luke opted to change the subject. "So, that was hilarious with Andrea tonight."

Courtney replied, "If you thought that was funny you should've seen what she did to Ivan. I didn't think he was capable of being so—"

"Irritated? Precisely why the prospect of a hunt tonight is so enticing. It will be delightful to release the aggression she incited," Ivan stated, barely containing his excitement.

"I still find it funny how you can hack gargoyles apart with your eyes closed and some little blonde intimidates you," Courtney teased.

Ivan said nothing. He stared ahead at the bright orange Lamborghini in front of them, which crawled along at five under the limit.

"Why the hell would someone drive so slow in a Murcielago?" Courtney asked, tapping her fingers on the Bentley's armrest.

"I suspect we are behind a drug dealer trying to be inconspicuous."

"Inconspicuous in a bright orange Lamborghini? Fucking brilliant."

"Would you consider drug dealers to be sensible individuals?"

"Good point," Courtney said as she looked back out at the rolling hills.

Renee's voice emanated from their earpieces. "What's the plate? I'm at our rendezvous point now."

"We should arrive shortly. As for the plate, it reads X-ray, Sierra, India, Victor, Four, Uniform," Ivan answered.

"That's one of the SFPD's informants. He's in on a big deal going down tonight. They're hoping to nail a guy with connections to Brazo de Dios so all the area PDs can finish picking them apart," Renee explained.

Courtney rolled her eyes at Ivan's self-satisfied smile. "Sometimes it's scary how much you know."

"It is merely the fact that I have eighty more years of experience in the world than you do. This has allowed me to gain tremendous knowledge of human nature and various other subjects."

"Sure, play the age card again."

"Remember, I also do not sleep. Because of this, I spend that time learning while you dream of dastardly customers at your workplace. It is nothing to be ashamed of." Ivan slowed for a sharp turn onto a gravel road. He pulled the big sedan into a clearing after a quarter mile, parking beside Renee's police cruiser.

Courtney's face wrinkled in disgust as her old boots sank into sloppy mud. She took a step forward so she could close the door, fighting the muck's suction. Ivan wandered back to the car's open trunk, unaffected by the surrounding quagmire. She slogged her way to the back of the car and stood beside Ivan.

An open case lay in the trunk. He screwed a silencer onto a pistol before sliding in a magazine. Ivan handed the pistol to Courtney. "Aim slightly lower than the location on your target you wish to hit. This Glock 21 fires silver-tipped .45 ACP rounds. I regret we have not managed to give you proper firearms training before throwing you into the field, but I am certain you will weather the storm if your instant sword prowess is any indication."

"Silver-tipped? We're hunting werewolves?"

A howl sounded from across the field before Ivan could answer. He pointed to the full moon as increasing cloud cover drifted across its light. Sprinkling rain fell, adding to the fifteen minutes of drizzle before Andrea left the mansion.

Renee noticed her glowering at the mud and headed to the Bentley. "Some nature nuts are converting a few acres here into wetlands for some sort of swamp bird sanctuary since we're just outside the boundaries of what the state considers to be the Point Reyes National Seashore," Renee explained. "They figure it might be a good tourist attraction with all the bird watchers coming here already. Anyway, they introduced some farm-raised cranes a few days ago, but they all disappeared last night. Of course, they called the cops to file a report for the missing birds—like we don't have a speeding ticket quota to spend our time on. Hank called me as soon as he saw orange dots on the radar, and I figured out where the birds went."

Courtney noticed the fisherman's waders Renee wore. She dreaded slogging through the slop but the thought of seeing Ivan's expensive suit and tie dirtied amused her. Renee snickered as Courtney bent down, checked the zippers, and tightened the buckles on her favorite old boots to ensure the muck couldn't rob them from her.

"Anything I should know about their tendencies so I don't wind up as Pupperoni?" Courtney grumbled at Ivan, still looking down at the muck. "You're great at sharing this kind of stuff ahead of time, like with the damn gremlins last night."

"They are fast and strong. Speed is their greatest asset, and they thrive on the thrill of the chase. Do not hesitate to fire if one is charging at you. These two will gleefully tear you apart. Do not think, just shoot. Renee will not be running at you, so do not be concerned about shooting her by mistake," Ivan instructed. He pointed to the blinder keychain hooked onto her belt and added, "If you get in trouble, that light will not help. Only gargoyles see that spectrum of light."

"Okay." Courtney switched off the gun safety and looked to Ivan as he closed the trunk. The gun didn't feel right in her hand. It wasn't the old Sumerian blade.

"I would say we are all ready. Luke, direct us to our target," Ivan said.

Luke's voice accompanied the constant static in their ears. "They're almost straight ahead of you, maybe a bit to your left at about a hundred and fifty yards."

Ivan said to Renee and Courtney, "I will stay to the left. Courtney, stay in the middle with Renee to your right. With you in the central position it will allow both Renee and I to come to your aid if necessary."

"Sounds good to me," Renee said as Courtney nodded.

The three walked to the edge of the tall grass. Courtney struggled with the mud. Her nose wrinkled with every step at the squelching sound from the mud's suction, especially as she watched Ivan move unhindered by the difficult conditions. She looked to Renee and took some solace in the fact she struggled with the muck, too.

A faint breeze accompanied occasional tiny raindrops. The grass moved as the hunting trio separated. Courtney took

THE DEN OF STONE

a deep breath and exhaled sharply. *Fuck, they'll see exactly where we are.*

She stressed about the lack of stealth until she noticed movement in the grass about seventy-five yards ahead. *Oh hey, they'll shake the grass, too. That makes things easier. Damn, so fast though. Ivan wasn't kidding.*

Courtney tripped as she caught her first glimpse of the dark hominid shape. The hunchbacked silhouette stopped and turned its lupine head to her, alerted by the loud expletive Courtney screamed as she fell. Mud splattered over her clothing and she swore again, but held onto the pistol. A hungry whine sounded fifteen yards away as she got back up to her knees and brushed off some of the mud.

Well, shit. I hope the barrel isn't clogged. Her hands shook as she aimed and pulled the trigger. The werewolf kept charging. Its eyes' amber shine focused on her as it closed in. Courtney fired multiple times, screaming a battle cry.

The werewolf jolted and lost its balance. Courtney fired again. The monster yelped. Momentum carried it the few feet to reach Courtney and knock her backwards into the mud.

It didn't rise.

Give me my sword and some gargoyles any day. This aiming and shooting shit is hard. One werewolf was down and breathing its final few shallow breaths as she stood, but one remained.

A howl pierced the night close behind, sending a deep chill down her spine. She spun and spotted the second dark shape, looming large and ready to pounce. Her finger twitched the trigger twice. One shot whizzed past the werewolf, but the second pull only resulted in a click.

Oh fuck, I'm dog food.

The beast's lips peeled back, revealing yellowed fangs, glistening with saliva in the moonlight. Foam dripped down its bony chin.

Courtney took two steps backward. It took four steps forward. She tripped again, but maintained her balance. The werewolf saw a moment's weakness and leapt. Courtney ducked to evade it. She heard three dull thumps, followed by a splat. The werewolf fell and slid to a halt inches from her feet. It convulsed for a few seconds and stilled.

Courtney jumped as something grabbed her shoulder from behind. She slipped its grip and spun around with the empty pistol held high to smash whatever was behind her, but it was only Ivan. Courtney hissed. "You scared the shit out of me!"

"You are quite welcome. Consider it vengeance for what your friend did earlier. I also see I was mistaken when I thought you would be a natural with firearms. You emptied the magazine and scored only three hits, which is quite poor accuracy. I will ensure you receive thorough firearms training. You may also want to look around for your earpiece; Luke is rather frantic you have not answered his queries on your condition."

Courtney yelled, "I'm okay, Luke!" then said to Ivan, "Well, considering I've never had to shoot anything before in my life I would've thought common sense might suggest a little training. If we're facing more of these nasty fuckers, I need a silver sword like the Witcher books."

"You are correct about the training. However, you never used a sword before and you took to the blade with aplomb. I was apparently mistaken in expecting you to be a natural all-around warrior based upon your sword training progression and the prowess you show in martial arts." Ivan added, "Luke is relieved to know you are safe."

Courtney grunted as she looked down for the earpiece, but her attention was drawn to the werewolf corpses dissolving. She covered her nose and mouth with her sleeve to prevent her gag reflex from kicking in. Her hoodie smelled like wet dog and made her cough. She looked away from the disintegrating corpses to see what she tripped over. A half-chewed crane lay in the mud. Courtney struggled against the tide rising up from her stomach.

Ivan saw her facial expression and guided her towards the cars with Renee close behind.

Once between the two cars, Ivan tried to comfort her. "Do not be concerned over the loss of your earpiece. I have many more in storage. The silver sword is an intriguing idea, though impossible nowadays. Advanced magic was required in the past to make the silver strong enough to be an adequate blade. That skill was unfortunately lost long ago when the last druids passed without recording the old elven knowledge."

Fuck the earpiece. Magic? Elves? Dissolving corpses? I'm supposed to worry about a cheap-ass earpiece with those bombshells?

Courtney swallowed hard. "Why do they dissolve like that? How the hell do you move through mud so easily? It's like you're a fucking ghost. And really? Elves?"

"The virus causing lycanthropy reacts severely with silver, creating acid in the bloodstream that burns away all bodily tissue. It is quite convenient since there is no corpse to dispose of. As for the mud, let me ask this: have you seen images of Russia in the spring?" Ivan ignored the mention of elves.

Courtney shook her head while Renee said to Ivan, "I'll make sure the police report says a coyote got the cranes." She added to Courtney, "There's a blanket in the back seat of the cruiser. I'll give you a ride home so you don't get Ivan's precious upholstery all dirty. It might be funny to see him swearing in Russian, but I don't know if you want to find out."

"Yeah, I'm good. For all I know he might make me scrub the seats with a toothbrush as a twisted lesson about destroying evidence, or just payback for the glass of wine Andrea made him spit out." Courtney opened the interceptor's door and slid in.

"I had not thought of that, but I will take note of it for future reference in case such a situation arises again," Ivan said with his trademark smirk.

"Please don't." Courtney pulled the door shut before he could add some further smug remark full of fancy verbiage.

Renee sat in the driver's seat. "Don't worry about a seat belt; I won't give you a ticket."

"Maybe I'll take a nap if I can ignore this awful smell. Fuck, those things stink," Courtney grumbled as she picked coarse hairs off her muddy hoodie and jeans.

"Sounds like a damn good plan to me. I'll turn down the radio and go smooth for you." Renee laughed.

Courtney lay on her side, wishing she was in Luke's old Volvo with his lint roller handy for the werewolf hairs. She sighed and closed her eyes as the Charger backed up. The car jolted as it ran over a rock, and Courtney groaned. "Nap or not, I just want a damn shower."

"Patience, Cricket," Renee teased in her best attempt at mimicking Hank.

He's going to love seeing all this mud in the laundry bin, if he doesn't make me get up earlier to wash it. I'll have to ask about this whole elf business. Maybe he'll be less evasive than Mr. Immune-to-mud.

11

uke leaned against the railing of the back porch with a root beer in hand. He put the glass bottle down to adjust one of his earplugs as Courtney reloaded her pistol.

Courtney wore noise-canceling headphones and safety sunglasses to combat the noise of the pistol and the glare of the setting sun. A paper target pinned to a hay bale across the backyard pond bore only three holes, all far from the center.

She lowered the gun and walked to the porch stairs, throwing aside the headphones. "I've gone through five clips and only scored three hits. I hate guns. I wish I could carry my sword all the time and not have to worry about this gun bullshit."

"If it makes you feel any better, I only got four hits on my target."

"Ivan gave you a revolver and you only fired six shots. That doesn't make me feel better at all. I suck at this shooting shit. I got like two minutes of instruction, and neither of them answered my question about the elves. It's like I'm supposed to figure it all out myself."

Luke shrugged and took another sip of root beer as Courtney swore again and picked up the headphones. "Ivan sure split quickly after my shots and the couple tips he gave you. Wonder what's up? I thought he'd stick around to watch you shoot and maybe help out some, like you said."

"I guess I shouldn't have told him Andrea would pop over. If I could figure out how to use the damn phone to translate I think I could've learned a few Russian swears."

"He's really intimidated by her? That's funny."

"I think deep down he likes her and doesn't want to admit it." Courtney winked as she put the headphones back on.

Luke raised an eyebrow.

Hank stepped out onto the porch and laughed. "He doesn't like her at all and prefers to minimize his interactions with non-monster hunters. It's also almost seven, so she'll be here soon," Hank said.

"Yeah, I figured. One last attempt at this shooting shit, then," Courtney grumbled. She squeezed off another four shots until the gun clicked empty.

"Maybe you should shoot while pissed more often," Luke said, looking through binoculars at the target as she tossed the headphones aside.

"Why?"

"Three hits, one near dead center."

"I still prefer the sword." Courtney handed the gun to Hank.

"A sword is great for one-on-one fights, but in a large attack you're going to get overwhelmed. Guns are necessary in many situations. Besides, I'd love to see you try to get a concealed carry permit for a sword. If necessary, you can tuck a pistol into your waistband and wear a baggy shirt. No one will ever know," Hank said.

"I know, I know. I'm just stating my opinion. But how the hell is Luke supposed to conceal that Dirty Harry revolver he got?"

"Fat man in a hockey jersey. If a jersey can hide my gut, it should hide a gun, even a big shiny revolver," Luke answered.

Courtney walked inside to find a mirror and fix her hair after the headphones messed it up. A car horn at the end of the driveway made her breathe deep as she pulled off the sunglasses. She left them on the pool table and gestured to her uncle to grab them while she went to get her new fake glasses.

A car door closed, followed by the slapping sound of Andrea running up the stairs in flip-flops. A series of rapid knocks on the door came next while Courtney ran her fingers through her hair.

Courtney yanked open the door, interrupting another series of knocks. Andrea's knuckles missed Courtney's shoulder as she almost fell through the open doorway. Courtney grabbed her friend's wrist to stabilize her and raised an eyebrow.

"Hi," Andrea said. "You're later than usual. I never get to knock twice. What's up?"

"I was meditating on the back porch," Courtney fibbed.

"I've never known anyone to meditate in tight jeans and stiletto boots. Oh, and those new glasses are great. You got the same frames again."

"Thanks. When the meditation mood strikes, I follow if I have the chance. You can't set aside special time when you work on a flexible schedule. The mood hit while I got ready, and these things were too much of a pain to get on to take them right back off again," Courtney answered, looking down at the boots.

"That makes sense. You and your damn boot obsession. I keep telling you how much some fancy sandals would suit you but nope, I'm just a little idiot without a clue about zen, right? So, are we doing anything tonight besides standing in the foyer? Aren't we supposed to be doing Luke's birthday dinner somewhere?"

"No. I was planning something, not meditating. I'm going to tie you up and shove you in the closet until Ivan gets here so he can torture you and get his revenge," Courtney joked.

"I'll tie myself up!" Andrea winked at Courtney. "Oh wait, that might be kinda hard."

Courtney stared at her for a moment, then shook her head. "He's out of town. As soon as I said you were stopping by he suddenly remembered a business obligation. I don't think you have to worry about getting hog-tied."

"Damn." Andrea looked at Courtney's hair and giggled. "Wow, you really were in the middle of getting ready. There's this one frizzy strand sticking out like six inches."

Luke jangled the keys to the Pontiac in the foyer while Courtney grumbled, running her fingers through her hair again.

"If we're going anywhere tonight I need to get to the car," Luke chimed in.

"Come on, we've got makeup to talk about!" Andrea squealed.

"Would tossing a mouse past you get you to pounce out of the doorway so we can get to the car, Miss Hello Kitty?" Luke pointed at Andrea's tank top.

"Gawd, I'll move. Leave the poor mousie out of this," Andrea said as she backed out onto the landing. She nearly fell as her heel moved past the edge, but she caught herself and giggled, looking back at the steps.

"Careful." Courtney grabbed her purse and followed Luke out the door.

The trio headed for the Pontiac, and Courtney pointed to the rear, smirking at Andrea.

"I've got to get in that tiny back seat? Well, damn, maybe I'll follow in my car wherever the hell we're going, if you let me stop for gas on the way." Andrea crossed her arms.

"You're the smallest." Luke shrugged as he got in the driver's seat.

"I'm hungry," Courtney said, fishing through her purse for a mirror to fix her hair. "Either get back there or get in your car if it's got enough gas to get to Inverness."

Andrea huffed and pushed the seat forward to get in the coupe, and once she was in, Courtney followed. Hank wandered out to the car and knocked on Courtney's window. She set the purse aside and rolled the window down as she lowered her glasses to look at her uncle.

"Do you have your phone with you in case anything happens while you're out?" he asked, leaning in.

Courtney pulled the phone from one of her hoodie pockets and showed it to Hank.

"Is it on?"

She frowned and pushed the button on the side of the phone.

"That's better. Don't turn it off. I'll be texting tonight and expect you to respond so I know it's still on," he said as he backed away from the window.

Courtney sighed and nodded.

Hank waved. "Have a great time and don't drink too much."

She waved back and rolled up the window as Luke drove around Andrea's Miata to head down the driveway.

"You got a cell phone? Little Miss I-don't-need-a-phone got a cell phone?" Andrea grabbed her shoulder.

"Yeah, I gave in. Unc talked me into it after the gang shit."

"When were you planning on telling me your number?"

"Um, it's just for emergencies so I wasn't."

"I'm hurt," Andrea whined as she swatted Courtney's shoulder with a flip-flop.

Courtney handed the phone to Andrea with a sigh. "I don't remember my number, so call or text yourself and you'll have it."

Andrea reached for the phone as Luke stopped at the end of the driveway. "Holy shit, you got an iPhone just for emergencies? What's that cost per month?"

"Not a clue. Unc is paying for it. He got one for Luke, too, since his phone burned in the fire. It's not like Unc worries about money."

"Can you ask him if I can have one?"

"Ask Ivan. I'm sure he'd love to have you calling him all the time," Courtney teased.

"I wouldn't call constantly. I'd send him pictures."

"Easy there. I don't think you're brooding and mysterious enough for his taste," Courtney said.

Andrea blinked at Courtney but said nothing. She handed the phone back with the wallpaper set to a picture of herself frowning as Luke braked at the end of Overlook Road. An electric blue compact sedan with a wing on the trunk blasted past. Andrea's eyes widened at the loud exhaust on the tuned car.

Let's hope this gets her mind off Immortal McFuckface.

Luke pulled out onto the main road. "Looks like Chris is already on his way. I'll bet Tad loved putting that new wing on for him."

"Who's Chris?" Andrea asked. "You haven't told me where we're going yet except that it's in Inverness."

"Chris is my best friend. He plays with computers for some programming firm in San Rafael. I've never heard of the place but I guess it's a good job," Luke answered.

"Does he make a lot of money?"

"You're a gold-digging bitch, you know?" Courtney teased.

Andrea ignored Courtney, focusing on the blue car at the red light ahead. As Luke stopped next to Chris, Andrea tapped Courtney's shoulder. "The big green thing Ivan has doesn't look half as good as that."

"Seriously? It's just a tuned Lancer. My Willys would smoke it."

"You and your gas guzzler. What's Chris look like? I can't see through the tinting," Andrea asked.

"Kind of like Sloth from the Goonies," Luke joked.

"Oh gawd, no wonder he wanted tint," Andrea said with a look of disgust.

"I'm kidding. He looks like Jack Sparrow without all the pirate stuff," Luke said.

"Huh?"

"He makes you think of a pirate with the hair and goatee. When he started growing it out back in senior year, we started calling him 'Captain McClennan' or 'McCap'n.'" Luke laughed.

The light turned green and the Mitsubishi rocketed away, giving Andrea a chance to notice the license plate. "MCCAPN. I love it."

Luke accelerated slower, watching a police cruiser parked in front of the bakery ahead, but it was unattended. "Must be getting donuts," he joked.

"Are we going somewhere that sells donuts?" Andrea asked pointedly.

Courtney's phone buzzed, and she ignored whatever Luke answered. *Damn Unc, didn't even give me five minutes.* She answered his text with a poop emoji, something she'd discovered by accident when he'd first shown her how to use the phone.

The trio stayed quiet for a while, enjoying the scenery. No matter how often Courtney passed through this area, the view never got old. She often fantasized about a little cottage on a secluded beach, spending her days relaxing to the sounds of the surf and doing her workouts on the fine beach sand. In recent months, however, these fantasies included Luke tinkering with his old Volvo beside the cottage. As she thought about what would replace the old wagon since he wouldn't keep the Pontiac, her mind turned a few nights earlier to the demise of his beloved beige block of steel. Edthgar loomed over her and reality snapped back as they entered the parking lot at Mark's Bar & Grill.

"Wow, we're here already?"

"You really zoned out for a moment there, zen master," Andrea remarked.

"I guess so."

Luke backed into a parking space beside Chris. As the trio exited the Pontiac, Andrea noticed a silver Tacoma with a cap across the small, unpaved lot. "Who drives that? The asshole cut me off last night after leaving work," she barked.

Luke answered. "That's Scott Zolansky's truck. He's a regular here."

"Yeah, a regular drunk. Now I know why he cut me off. Too shitfaced to pay attention to the road," Andrea snarled as she started off towards the truck.

Luke stopped her. "No, the guy doesn't drink. He's a private investigator. He gets quite a few leads here and probably had to act on one right away."

Andrea blushed and looked at the ground. "I'm sorry I was going to make a scene like that. Where's Chris, anyways?"

"On his phone in his car. Some of his coworkers are more clueless about computers than Courtney, and they're always calling him. That's my guess anyway," Luke answered.

"I know enough about the things to piss me off. For something that's supposed to make life easier, they complicate the living shit out of it," Courtney said.

Andrea ignored the computer talk. "It was so weird last night before you tried to kill me with that sword. First a cop swerved into the parking lot and then after I left there was some old pink VW bus speeding that way and then after that this Scott guy zoomed through a red light in front of me and they all had their hazard lights going except the cop because of course cop cars have light bars on the roof but it was still weird."

"Holy run-on sentence, girl." Courtney tried to think of an explanation other than the one creeping into her mind: Andrea saw some monster hunters in action. She needed a moment to form a suitable response.

Luckily for Courtney, Chris got out of his car. She pointed him out to Andrea. "Hey AB, meet Chris."

Andrea turned to see Chris stuffing his phone into his khaki cargo pants. She stared at the tall man in his loose-fitting denim button-down shirt with rolled-up sleeves. He wore dark brown boots, which were mostly covered by baggy cargo pants. Shaggy black hair fell past his shoulders, and a thick goatee covered his chin. Courtney grinned at the look on Andrea's face.

"Wow, yeah, I totes see the modern pirate thing. He's way too hot for a programmer," Andrea whispered to Courtney.

Chris stopped to talk to Luke. "Dude, it's going to take some getting used to, seeing that thing instead of your Volvo. Oh, and happy birthday. The last year of your twenties, old fart."

"Thanks. Don't get too used to this. I hate the thing. I just need to get back on my feet financially and I'm ditching this," Luke said.

"So no new jerseys then, eh?" Chris pointed to Luke's old Whalers shirt.

"Not for a little while. By the way, meet Courtney's friend, Andrea." Luke directed Chris's attention to the blonde.

Chris held out his hand, smiling. "Chris McClennan. Pleased to meet you, m'lady."

Courtney tried and failed to contain a snicker.

Andrea didn't notice the derisive laugh. "Andrea Browning. Nice to meet you. You really do look like a pirate, like Luke said. He tells me you do computer programming—sounds like a good job."

"I hear the pirate thing all the time. The job sucks but it pays well." Chris' hand still rested in Andrea's tiny one. "What does a perky blonde like you do for a living?"

"I work at Motherlode."

"I'm sorry to hear that." Chris added, "Retail sucks *and* has shit pay."

"I love retail and all the different people I meet."

"You're a better man than me. Well, not literally."

Andrea laughed. "So why don't you like your job?"

"Having to program shit for people who are clueless about what they actually need is horrible. I had to explain to someone last week what the cursor is," Chris explained.

"Isn't a curser someone who swears constantly at computers because they fucking hate the things?" Courtney joked.

"Different kind of cursor, but yeah, that describes you to a T."

"So what do you want to do for a living?" Andrea asked as Courtney bowed.

Chris slid his round-framed aviator sunglasses down his nose, revealing deep brown eyes. He looked directly into Andrea's as he answered. "You'll be the second to know when I figure that out. Oh, and, uh, you can let go of my hand any time you want."

Andrea looked down. She blushed and giggled as she released him. Courtney winked at Luke, who winked back. "Why would I be the second?" Andrea asked.

"Well, obviously when I figure things out I'll be the first to know, which would make you the second. Right? Simple math."

"Right," Andrea replied, nodding slowly.

Luke interrupted. "Now we just have to wait for Tad and Heidi to get here."

"Hope his Olds didn't break down. That thing is a bigger shitbox than the Volvo." Chris slapped himself in the forehead. "Sorry man, didn't mean to pour salt in the wound."

"It's okay. Like you said, it'll take a lot of getting used to," Luke said.

A sour exhaust note drew the foursome's attention to the white and gold Oldsmobile 4-4-2 turning into the parking lot. "It didn't sound that bad the other night, did it?" Chris asked.

"No. Something must've gone in the exhaust since then. Poor Tad," Luke answered.

The Olds seemed to emit a sigh of relief from under the hood as the engine shut off. Tadeo Camino got out, and Heidi Yamada followed him out the driver's side. "I'm getting really tired of climbing over the shifter," Heidi said, adjusting her white knit jacket and artificially curly dark hair.

Courtney ignored their usual light-hearted insults as Tadeo rubbed his tanned, bald scalp.

Andrea whispered to Courtney as Tad and Heidi continued bickering. "How the hell do these two put up with each other?"

"Tad likes a challenge," Courtney whispered back. "They do like each other, I think." Andrea nodded as Tad and Heidi quit arguing and walked over. They both said happy birthday to Luke, then introduced themselves to Andrea.

"Tadeo Camino." Tad held out his greasy hand. "I'm a mechanic, but the dirty shirt and name tag probably gave that away."

Andrea shook it. "Could've been a plumber too, which would've worried me with the dirt. I'm Andrea Browning. I work at Motherlode."

Tad chuckled as Andrea turned to Heidi and repeated her introduction.

"Heidi Yamada. I'm a part-time chef here. My sister Kimiko tends the bar and does the bookkeeping."

Andrea asked Heidi, "Since you cook here, do they serve anything for vegetarians?"

"Yeah, come in and check out the menu."

The group walked up to the naturally aged wooden building. Chris led the way to the red-painted porthole door, borrowed from a decommissioned fishing boat when Mark built the place. Chris held the door open for everyone and followed them down the short hallway lined with pictures of cars, stars, and guitars.

At the end of the hall, a petite, pale brunette in a blue dress stood behind the tall reception desk. Her blue eyes brightened at Chris and she flashed a wide smile her thin, freckled face barely contained.

He walked up to the desk. "Hey Lacy, is my usual table open?"

"Of course. Daddy saved it for you. Party of six tonight, I see. Two bills for three each?" Lacy asked in a squeaky voice.

"No, I'll have a bill for four. Heidi'll have her usual for her and Tad."

Lacy jotted the information on a notepad. "Got it. Follow me." She flashed another wide smile as she sidestepped from behind the desk. Her garish turquoise cowboy boots thumped against the dark stained wood floor as she led them past the stage. On the stage, on a tall wooden stool, sat Mark DiSandis, a heavily tattooed man with spiky short gray hair and a bushy goatee. He picked slow blues notes on an old black Les Paul with gold inlays and a matching gold tremolo.

"I'll be there in a second, just let me grab a quick drink to hold myself over until food," Courtney said, peeling away from the group. She stopped at the bar next to a short thin man with thick dark curls.

"Hey, Courtney. Want your usual?" Lacy's twin sister, Stacy, asked from behind the bar.

"Yep, always rum and coke."

As Stacy nodded and turned around, the man next to her leaned over. With a Brooklyn accent, he said, "Ah, not the whiskey type? Sorry that's what we had to pump in you the other night for the bites."

"You must be Scott. Thanks for the help. I'll buy you a new bottle sometime to replace it. Jack, Jim, Seagrams?" Her voice trailed off as Scott shook his head.

"Brand doesn't matter. I only keep it around in case of bites. I saw enough of what drinking did to my pop back in Flatbush. If you want rum, buy that for 'emergency use,'" he said with a wink, then sipped his coffee.

"Sounds good. Thanks again. Oh, who drives the VW? My friend Andrea saw some of you guys last night, I think."

"Aramis Mendoza."

"Really? The vet fights mon—," Courtney said until Scott zippered his fingers across his lips.

"Nice to meet you in a peaceful moment," he said as Stacy handed Courtney her shot glass.

"Thank you," Courtney said to Stacy, then smiled at Scott as she headed toward the corner table Chris always reserved.

"Lacy sure seems to like you," Andrea said to Chris as Courtney approached.

"Her and Stacy are my cousins and also Mark's daughters. He's my mother's brother. She fell for a Jamaican guy after her first divorce, and along came me, the half-black sheep of the family with no musical talent."

"So that guy on stage is your uncle?"

"Yeah, that's what they tend to call your parent's siblings," Chris teased before continuing. "That's why I get a family discount. Heidi gets an employee discount that's somehow higher than the family discount—that's why her and Tad pay separately. So, what do you think of my uncle's playing?"

Courtney tuned them out as her phone dingled again. She whipped it out to see a text about her car's extended warranty, muttered under her breath, and dumped the phone on the table to return to the real conversation.

"I can't help noticing those three birds on your shoulder. Nice tattoo. I'm guessing that's for Bob Marley?" Chris asked.

Andrea nodded. "You got it." She shoved her chair back and raised her leg to the edge of the table, shoving up her corduroy pants to expose her ankle. Chris put a hand to his chin, arching an eyebrow at Andrea's foot on the wooden table.

"Bee Happy!" she chirped as she pointed to the tattoo of a buzzing bee with script beneath it.

Chris chuckled. "That's, uh, creative."

Luke winked at Courtney as a new waitress wandered up to the table to hand out menus. "I'll be back to take your orders in a few," she piped.

"Has anyone ever had the beer-battered fish? How is it?" Andrea asked.

"It's fantastic. A seafood lover's delight. I'm having that myself," Heidi answered.

"I think I'll get that with the Mediterranean Greek salad and an iced tea," Andrea said.

"I thought you were a vegetarian?" Chris asked, confused.

"I am."

"How can you eat fish then? Fish are animals, last time I checked."

"Because I'm a bit different," Andrea answered, squeezing her eyes shut and sticking out her tongue.

"No kidding. I couldn't tell."

Courtney bit her lip and tried not to laugh.

Andrea asked Chris, "How come you're the only guy at this table without a date?"

"Probably because I'm single. How come you didn't waltz in here on the arm of some burly dude?" Chris replied.

"Because I'm a lesbian," Andrea said with a straight face.

"Oh." Chris deflated a bit.

"I'm actually bi, but really it's 'cause I'm single at the moment, too."

Chris grinned. His smile grew wider as her eyebrow raised. Courtney guessed Andrea's tattooed foot was rubbing his leg under the table while her hands held the menu primly. "Really? I'm shocked no one is with a shy and lady-like pescatarian like you seem to be. That's the proper term for a proper lady who's a vegetarian except for fish."

133

Courtney couldn't contain her laughter this time, but he and Andrea were too preoccupied with each other to notice. They also failed to notice as Courtney told Luke, "You owe me ten bucks. I told you I'd make her forget about Ivan within a week. Cough it up, you cheap bastard."

Luke fished his wallet out of his back pocket as the waitress returned.

12

Heidi stumbled out the doorway first as Tad held the door for everyone. Andrea followed Chris over to his car, and Courtney checked the latest message on her phone from her uncle. *"Make sure Andrea leaves quickly. We might have some unwelcome guests."*

"Shit," she grumbled as she typed, *"OK."*

Scott rushed past her to his truck, and nodded as he flung the Tacoma's door open. She shot back a fake smile as she shoved her phone back in her pocket.

"Unc is expecting company, so get your car fast and leave, please," Courtney yelled to Andrea.

"Oh, don't worry, I've got some stuff I wanna do. I'll be gone in a hurry!" Andrea waved at Luke and Courtney from Chris' door. "See you guys back at your place."

Tad saluted Chris and Luke. "Have a good night, broskis." The three got into their cars. Tadeo left the parking lot first, followed by Luke, and Chris last.

Luke looked in the rear view mirror at the reflection of the Mitsubishi's headlights behind them and asked Courtney, "Was it really worth ten bucks to see her almost slobbering over Chris?"

"Priceless. I wish we were having as much fun as them tonight. We might have some visitors of the scaly persuasion. At least you won't ruin the new hat I got you, since you still insist on wearing that ratty old one."

"I really do appreciate the new hat. An original from the Sharks' first year, in new condition, was some find. I'm honestly kind of afraid to ruin it. I'll wear it on special occasions instead of this one, okay?" He fiddled with the different stalks until the wipers turned on.

They passed a boarded-up gas station with graffiti painted over one of the windows. Luke swore under his breath as a pickup pulled out in front of them and turned left immediately without a turn signal. He and Courtney raised their middle fingers at the back of the truck, though the driver would never see it in the dark.

"Well, at least I'll get to take out some frustrations on monsters tonight if I can't do it to idiot drivers," Courtney muttered.

"Guess I won't be catching the end of the Sharks game."

"Thank you, gargoyles," Courtney said with a grin.

Both fell silent. Thickening fog obscured most of the scenery Courtney had enjoyed under the setting sun. Darkness enveloped everything but what the car's headlights revealed. The fog distorted shadows of familiar sights, shrouding them in an enticing air of mystery.

The red traffic light ahead lent an eerie glow to the hazy night. Courtney sat up, squinting at a dark shape creeping towards the road from behind the wooden sign for the pizza place she always avoided because it resulted in frequent noisy bathroom visits.

"Luke, look out my window," she squeaked, grabbing his arm. He turned to the shape in the mist as Chris' car rumbled to a halt behind them.

Courtney's superior night vision caught light glinting off claws that poked from its hoodie. "It's a gargoyle dressed as a human. When the light turns green, I want you to pretend you're me and hopefully as we speed away Chris and Andrea won't notice it there, okay?"

"Got it."

"Good. Now we just need the fucking light to cooperate," she said, grabbing the UV light off her belt in case the gargoyle got there first.

The disguised gargoyle took a step towards the car, reaching for the passenger door. Courtney pushed down the lock with the gargoyle a few feet away. It took another slow step closer. The light turned green. Luke accelerated away, and the squealing tires drowned out the sound of claws scraping the car as the gargoyle lurched for the handle.

Courtney looked in the side mirror to see Chris steer around the gargoyle as it stumbled into the road. She hoped Chris and Andrea didn't see the monster hidden by the hooded sweatshirt. Ways to explain the existence of live gargoyles bombarded her mind.

"That was close," Luke commented.

"We're not out of the woods yet. What if Chris and Andrea saw what it was?"

Luke's eyes widened as he muttered, "Shit."

Courtney's phone vibrated in her hoodie pocket. She raised her fake glasses and checked the screen as she pulled it out. It was a text from Andrea.

She swiped the screen to read the text aloud to Luke. "'Why'd you do that to the homeless guy? He,'—uh—'prolly?' The fuck?"

"Text speak. Go on."

"'He prolly just wanted money for food.' Damn, numbers instead of words. Learning this shit is going to be like another language, and I barely passed Spanish."

Luke snickered. "I guess they didn't see it. That's good."

Courtney breathed a little easier knowing the secret of the monster hunters was safe. "I'm texting her back, 'The guy had a knife.'"

"Sounds good to me."

Courtney tapped away at the screen slowly and swore under her breath at the typos before sending her response. "This tiny touch keypad sucks," she complained.

"Turn it sideways. The keys will get bigger."

"Oh." Courtney blushed.

The phone vibrated in her hand again before she could stick it back in her pocket. This time it was Hank calling. "What's up, Unc?" she asked.

"I see on the radar you just had a close encounter. Is everything all right?"

"Yeah, we're fine," she answered.

"Did Andrea see anything?"

"No. She's riding with Luke's friend Chris. The gargoyle wore a hoodie and jeans, trying to look human. The thing was hanging around Luke's place the other night, but I thought it was just a homeless guy then. If I'd known then, maybe I...."

Hank interrupted. "That's Havardr, one of Edthgar's top minions. It's better you didn't know. He's a formidable opponent. He's a former follower to another winged one, Halgaard, but grew bloodthirsty and joined Edthgar. They must be planning something more than one of their usual small attacks tonight," Hank said.

"Like what?" Courtney asked.

"A pack of six showed up behind the mansion after I texted Scott and Renee to intercept a couple down the road, so I'd say they're still quite interested in you. We've not seen this much activity in years."

"Good thing Andrea is in a hurry to leave after she gets her car."

"Yes indeed. Mendoza, another of our group, should be here shortly to lend a hand. Ivan is also on his way, so hopefully their presence keeps the gargoyles away for Andrea. I'll meet you in the doorway once she's gone, with your sword and a gun for Luke. See you soon."

"Okay. We'll see you in a few." Courtney hung up and turned to Luke. "Definitely a fight tonight. There's six gargoyles behind the house."

"Not the romantic after-dinner I was hoping for," Luke joked.

Courtney laughed. "Killing monsters isn't fun?"

"There's a bit more danger involved. Frolicking under the sheets has—"

Courtney interrupted him. "That danger could make the after-party even more satisfying."

Luke cocked an eyebrow at her sideways grin. "I like the way you're thinking," he said as he steered the car up Overlook Road.

Courtney's heart quickened over speculations about the upcoming battle. As her mind played through different scenarios, she felt her smile widen. She found herself looking forward to it, understanding the phrase, "the thrill of battle." Her senses tingled as she recalled the feeling of her blade slicing through a gargoyle, the sounds of a fearful gargoyle aware of its imminent demise, but most of all, the sight of their blood glistening on her sword.

The fantasy broke as Luke stopped in the circle behind her uncle's truck and the VW Bus Andrea mentioned the other night. Hank stood in the doorway, though he held no weapons.

Luke shut off the engine and pulled the key from the ignition as Courtney stepped out of the car. Chris stopped behind Andrea's car, and she jogged to it. "Have a great time!" Andrea yelled to Courtney.

"You too," Courtney said, hoping her friend's shouting didn't draw out the gargoyles.

Andrea waved and tucked herself into the small roadster. Courtney breathed a sigh of relief as both Andrea and Chris departed the circle and drove down the driveway.

Good. Both got away without the gargoyles coming out.

Hank beckoned Luke and Courtney towards the house and pointed up. Edthgar perched upon the mansard roof with his long arms resting on the railing. He looked statuesque. The only signs he wasn't carved from stone were the scarlet glow in his eyes and the slowly turning head. The beast's gaze focused on something distant. Courtney suspected Edthgar recognized Ivan's Bentley and watched his immortal adversary approach.

She didn't care to find out, so she grabbed Luke by the wrist and pulled him to the door. Once inside, Hank led them to the great room. Courtney found her sword waiting for her on the pool table, where she left her purse, phone, glasses, and the scabbard once she pulled her sword free. Hank handed Luke an AK-47, keeping the Thompson for himself.

"Ivan should be here in a few minutes," Hank said. "We'll let the gargoyles in. Mendoza's still outside, and he'll have his gun ready in case they try to escape."

"Shouldn't we be whispering? How long's the big ugly been up there?" Luke whispered.

"Edthgar arrived just before you did, and there's no need to be quiet. This entire building is soundproofed as long as all of the outside doors and windows are closed," Hank answered.

"Big ugly sounds a lot better than Edthgar," Courtney grumbled. "Stupid name. Makes me feel like I'm going to drool every time I say it." She held the sword close to her face and closed her eyes. The gargoyles she killed days ago passed through her mind and allowed her to focus. Externally, she appeared calm. Only she was aware of her building excitement.

Hank instructed, "Luke, we'll stand by the speaker on the wall behind the right recliner and aim at the doorway. Ivan and

Courtney will be behind the other recliner with their swords to fight off whatever we don't hit. As soon as they engage the gargoyles, I'll pull this speaker down to open the trap door to the tunnels. When I do, go to the pool table. The throw rug closest to the hallway door will pop up and reveal a staircase. Go down it, but be careful. It's pitch black at the bottom. I'll guide you in the dark. Understood?"

"Understood," Luke confirmed.

Courtney breathed slow and deep, tightening her focus. She stepped from the pool table towards the chair. Her eyes stayed shut because she knew where everything was in the room, but also because the fight playing through her fervent imagination was more interesting than anything her eyes could reveal at the moment.

Hank gave more instructions. "When the trap door opens, the front door will automatically close. If any more try to come, Mendoza will pick them off at the door."

A gunshot rang out in the night, and Courtney's eyes flew open. The real battle was about to begin.

"I thought you said this place was soundproofed?" Luke questioned Hank.

"They can't hear us, but we can hear them. Think of it like a reverse interrogation room."

Courtney ignored the conversation and listened to the front door opening as Ivan entered the house—without shutting it fully. He wandered in the great room doorway, holstering his pistol with one hand and carrying his sword in the other. She watched him pause to remove his red tie and toss it on the hallway floor.

"Damn, you must really hate that tie," she said.

He whispered to her, "That expression of befuddlement nearly lends you an air of innocence, Miss Mays," before saying aloud to Hank, "Edthgar evaded the GPS bullet. I suppose I shall call my scientists come morning and request they produce more prototypes."

Hank nodded while Courtney whispered back to Ivan, "Nearly?"

"You are, after all, holding a sword, and your stance would suggest even to the uneducated that you are quite eager to put it to use," he replied.

Courtney grinned and looked back to the doorway. Shuffling sounds outside the front door indicated the time for battle neared. She relished the chance to bloody her blade again.

A shadow, which wasn't visible on the dark carpeting, fell over the bright red tie in the hall, and Courtney understood Ivan's tie disposal. He knew exactly where the gargoyle was before it came into view because of the shadow over the tie. Ivan winked at Courtney.

The first gargoyle stopped near the doorway and crouched down, examining the tie. A second stood behind and stared down at the red silk, its monstrous face showing childlike fascination. Gargoyle number three turned its head and peeked into the great room. It growled and pointed to alert its compatriots they were not alone.

Hank fired a quick burst from the Thompson through the third gargoyle's face and disintegrated the top of its head. Luke dropped the first gargoyle with a few rounds to the chest. The second gargoyle used the first's body as a shield as it entered the room.

While Courtney spun behind the gargoyle, Hank pulled down on the speaker and Luke moved to the tunnel entrance. She swung the sword into the back of its neck, slicing lightly. The gargoyle turned to face her, ignoring Hank as he followed Luke down the tunnel stairs. The last three gargoyles charged into the room at once. Courtney ducked; one of the leaping gargoyles tackled her bleeding attacker over the couch and down the tunnel stairs.

She grinned at the two gargoyles remaining in the room and motioned them forward. Ivan moved to her side. He flinched at the sounds of gunfire in the tunnels and outside the house, but Courtney ignored it, charging at the gargoyles. One tried to tackle her but failed as she thrust the sword up under its chin and through the top of its head. The blade stuck for a moment.

Ivan engaged the other gargoyle. It slashed at his face, but missed. He kicked its knee, dropping the beast to the floor. Ivan placed his sword's blade at the base of its skull as it clambered to its hands and knees. Another burst of gunfire erupted in the tunnels below. Ivan moved to the tunnel entrance. "I will leave this one to you."

Courtney nodded and yanked her sword from the dying gargoyle. Ivan's vanquished foe crawled towards the hallway. Courtney walked over and slammed the sword into its armored back, pounding the gargoyle flat against the floor. Its beady reptilian eyes locked on the bloodied blade of her sword before she jammed the tip into its left elbow.

"Any last words?" she said as she cut into its right bicep.

The gargoyle grunted, but said nothing.

"Sweet dreams, shithead." Courtney hacked through its throat.

Since the only remaining gargoyles she could do anything about were down in the tunnels, she headed into the inky depths. Her boots clicked against the concrete steps, and the echoes seemed amplified, as did the sound of her breathing. They drowned out the rapid gunfire outside the mansion.

Good. Let them hear me. Let them come to me.

Despite her night vision, her eyes took a moment to adjust to the inky darkness. Once acclimated to the encompassing murk, she spotted a gargoyle corpse on the floor about fifteen feet ahead, Ivan's sword firmly entrenched in its abdomen. She walked closer to the dead creature. Each step grew louder.

"Maybe I should've worn my old ass-kickers instead of the new stilettos," she muttered as she looked over the dead gargoyle.

Once past the body, she spotted Hank's gun on the floor. Blood speckled the wall and formed a line leading deeper into the tunnels. She knew without looking closer it was human blood, and fear crept into the back of her mind. It wasn't Ivan's blood, because it would have already receded back into his wound. The blood was either Hank's or Luke's, and neither were immortal. Ivan abandoning his sword hinted whoever was hurt must be bad off and desperate for medical attention. They must have run for the safe space, wherever it was.

She swallowed hard, but pressed onwards following the blood trail. The corridor ended. She needed to choose the tunnel to the left or to the right. The drops of blood grew further apart, but a couple spots dotted the left passage floor.

A few steps into the next tunnel, a growl echoed from the depths behind her. She turned to await the final gargoyle's charge, hearing its running steps pounding against the concrete. Instinct took over and she ran towards her foe. Its silhouette became visible thirty feet away.

Courtney belted out a war cry as she swung the sword. The gargoyle stumbled, clutching at its hip while she attacked again. The edge of her blade sunk into the side of the gargoyle's neck, blood spraying from the wound as she slid the sword free. The gargoyle crumpled to its knees. She finished beheading it before it could reach for the neck wound.

Courtney paused to relish her adrenaline rush for a moment with the last gargoyle vanquished, then resumed her search for the end of the blood trail. As the adrenaline faded, her heart pounded in her chest. Once she found red drops on the floor again, she thought of her uncle or Luke severely wounded. Courtney sprinted as well as the stiletto-heeled boots allowed. Despite the thunderous echoes of her steps, she heard nothing over her hammering heart and frantic breathing. She dreaded what waited at the end of the trail, yet needed to know the answer.

The blood trail stopped abruptly. She dropped the sword and hunched over with her hands on her knees to catch her breath. Her lungs burned, and it felt like she'd been running for hours. "Fuck," she wheezed.

She had no more blood to follow, and no sign of the others. The trail could lead her back to the stairs, but what good would it do if someone was dying? Her mind filled with muddled images of her uncle bleeding to death, or Luke's prized Whalers jersey stained red.

"Luke! Unc!"

A voice responded not too far away but she couldn't discern who. It could only be who she sought, no matter which of the three responded. She stood and took a shaky step forward, repeating her cry.

Another shout followed, and this time she recognized Luke's voice calling her name. She left her sword where it lay and shouted again as her legs pumped faster. Faint light emanated from a corner ahead of her. Around the corner, the source of the light came into view along with three people standing. Luke yelled her name again and her uncle held Luke's shoulder.

"Unc, what happened?" Courtney called.

Before he answered, she fell. The splash surprised her, and she breathed in sharply. A metallic taste filled her mouth and lungs as the light disappeared over her head. Courtney flailed for a moment before her feet hit the bottom of the pit. Whatever liquid she fell in suppressed the sound from above enough so she only heard a dull hint of shouting.

The outline of a man appeared above, showing the surface wasn't too far overhead, so she thrust upwards with her legs and grabbed the edge with her fingertips while struggling to breathe.

She coughed and hacked as Ivan pulled her the rest of the way out. The fluid from her lungs forced its way up and barely missed Ivan as it splattered the concrete. Blood flowed across the floor. Her limbs were coated in red while she sputtered.

"I see you forgot about the moat of winged gargoyle blood around the safe space, or perhaps you wished to try a different shade of red for your hair?" Ivan teased, slapping her back to make her cough up more blood.

"There's a board across the moat literally three feet from where you fell in," Luke said, as Hank held him back.

Courtney looked to her uncle as she gasped for air.

"Don't worry," he said. "I'll be fine in the morning. I took a glancing ricochet. Same shoulder wounded in 'Nam. Ivan already got out the bullet."

Courtney nodded as she sat, still struggling to breathe but improving. Ivan crouched down and looked her in the eyes. "Whenever you are ready, we will proceed back up to the house. I believe you are in desperate need of a shower while I clean up the bodies and blood."

"Just get me the fuck out of here," she croaked.

Ivan stood, pulling her up with him. "Let us go then." He pointed out the narrow board positioned over the blood pit as he led everyone away from the light. Ivan pulled out his phone and read something on the screen, then added, "Mendoza is on his way while Scott and Renee watch the entrance. Should I tell him to hold off so you can meet him in a less messy outfit?"

"Fuck it, who cares? Let's get the intro over with so I can take a shower."

Every step squished from the blood pooled inside her boots, and every inch of her skin tingled. Courtney grimaced until she caught her breath, then tugged on Ivan's arm to signal a stop. "Will the cleaner get all the blood out of my clothes?" she asked.

Ivan nodded and made to continue, but she didn't budge. "Help me get my boots off first and dump out the damn ponds."

Ivan chuckled and said, "Very well. That would be uncomfortable."

She sat and stretched out her legs, catching her breath as Ivan knelt beside her.

Hank continued to hold Luke back. "Remember, that's gargoyle blood. You don't need to touch that. Let Ivan handle her until she's cleaned up."

Luke nodded as he watched Courtney breathe easier.

"I want a hug as much as you do, but Unc is right. You don't want this curse, and it'd be terrible if that expensive jersey got dirty," she wheezed.

"I'm more worried about you than a damn jersey," Luke said.

Ivan dumped the blood from one boot and set it beside Courtney. She smiled up at Luke as she leaned her head back against the wall, ignoring Ivan's hands slipping against the other blood-slicked boot. "I promise I'll make it up to you later," she said.

Her uncle muttered under his breath and looked away as Luke grinned.

The other boot's blood splashed against the floor. Courtney pushed herself to her feet.

Footsteps approached down the tunnel, and a tall, muscular man with long dark hair and a thick handlebar mustache came into view. A machine gun and large ax were strapped to his back, and Courtney's sword was in his hands. The smile on his weathered tan face faded as he saw the blood dripping from all over Courtney. He said something in Spanish, using his free hand to motion a cross over his chest.

"She is all right, but fell in the blood of Mephallo," Ivan said.

Mendoza nodded. "Pleased to meet you. *Los diablos* sure seem interested in you. I had to shoot another four after these six *pendejos* followed you inside."

Courtney smiled. "Nice to meet you, too. I think you can forgive me for not shaking hands right now."

He nodded as Ivan said, "So ten total, then. We have not seen so many in over twenty years so soon after another assault."

"Thirteen, actually. Scott and Renee got two before another jumped them," Mendoza said.

"Fifteen. Havardr almost intercepted Courtney and Luke on their way home from Inverness, and Edthgar was on the roof," Hank added.

Courtney shoved her boots in Ivan's hands. "Whatever number, I'm taking a damn shower. Fill me in after."

Ivan gaped at her as she wandered off past Mendoza, who laughed at the expression on Ivan's face.

"If you want to do something useful in the meantime, why not look at the radar map where they popped up so you can find their lair?" Courtney yelled. "Try being proactive instead of waiting for the fuckers to come after me."

She kept going and paid no mind to anything anyone said behind her.

13

Two weeks passed without a gargoyle encounter, or any luck finding lairs. Ivan said he figured the heavy losses suffered in one assault meant the gargoyles were busy regrouping, so it was essential to carry on with normal life in order to avoid arousing suspicion from their friends. Something resembling routine settled in, for Luke at least. He watched sword training between Courtney and Ivan whenever he was home. She stayed edgy due to Ivan's constant questions about side effects of the winged gargoyle blood she hadn't felt yet and his criticism of her sword technique. Luke suspected Ivan's criticism was more about drawing out her anger. Every time he did, the Russian wound up on the floor healing himself. Once, she kept pressing while he was down, hacking away and screaming.

The most recent lesson lasted five minutes before Ivan's lower jaw hit the ceiling. As the rest of his body hit the floor, she jabbed her sword's tip into his butt. "You keep yapping about my lack of a set technique being a disadvantage, but I can predict most of your moves. Didn't you say surprise was huge in a fight? If I don't stick to one style, no one can predict my moves." She withdrew her sword and watched his blood slough away as it seeped back into his wounds.

Ivan rubbed his jaw once it reattached, then groaned. "I am not the only swordsman in this world. Do not judge your progress solely on your berserker rage matching well against me."

Courtney sheathed her sword and huffed. "Well it's not doing me much good kicking your ass so easy. Maybe you should try something different next time. Try predicting what I'll do so I have to think harder on how to ruin your next dress shirt. I'm getting some water."

As she left the room, Ivan turned to Luke. "Her strength and speed have increased exponentially in the past two days, as has her temper. The blood of Mephallo is finally settling in. I will be at the library working on some research this evening, so please keep a close eye on her while your friends are visiting. I believe she could use a break from my questions and lessons."

"Anything in particular I should watch? You know, besides the hole in the wall where she flung the bedroom door open this morning?"

"Just anything unusual. You would recognize the signs better than I."

* * * * *

Courtney rushed past Luke to turn on the outside lights as Chris parked.

Luke leaned against the great room door frame while she waited at the front door to greet their company. Courtney hummed and tapped her foot, peering out the window. "Holy shit, she's in a flowery skirt."

"Wow," Luke replied.

"It's been two years since I've seen the hippie dress up for anything besides Halloween, and that was for court. I feel under-dressed now," Courtney joked, looking down at her loose jeans and old brown biker boots.

She opened the door for Chris and Andrea as they reached the stairs. As Andrea walked past, Courtney made a point to check her out and attempted a sad wolf whistle.

Andrea turned to her, curtsied, batted her eyelashes, and said in a mock aristocratic Southern accent, "Why thank you for the compliment, Miss Mays; you are much too sweet."

Luke stifled a snort.

"You're even wearing contacts instead of your hipster glasses, and high heels. This kind of effort from you can only mean one thing. Let me go grab my phone so I can get video when you propose to Chris. A proposal after two weeks, insane," Courtney teased.

Andrea watched every step she took as she hobbled to the leather couch. She held her arms out to maintain her balance as she flashed a quick middle finger to Courtney. "Did you forget you've got the same frames I do? Besides, if my glasses are hipster, what do you call your uncle? Those things are thicker than armored glass."

"I call him Unc and don't mention the glasses because he could raise my rent."

"Yeah, smart. And the heels?" Andrea plopped on the couch. "These things are pure evil. I feel like I'm gonna fall over with every step. How the hell do you walk in those fancy boots?"

Andrea kicked off the shoes and brought her legs up onto the couch while Courtney answered, "I have supreme balance, like a ninja. It's gotten better with my workouts than it was doing gymnastics."

Luke bumped fists with Chris and nodded in greeting. They watched Courtney and Andrea prattle on about wardrobe choices.

"How can they talk so much and say so little?" Chris whispered.

"It's a talent almost every woman I've met has, though I haven't seen Courtney do it much. I think Andrea brings it out of her."

"Oh for fuck's sake; they're comparing eyeshadow now."

"I've got some beers in the fridge," Luke suggested.

"Hold that thought," Chris said. "I need to do something first. Watch and learn."

Luke crossed his arms and tried to conceal a devilish grin.

Chris adjusted his collar before blurting in an effeminate tone, "Oh my god, Luke, those sneakers are like, totally fabulous. You must've gone to Hilltop."

Courtney and Andrea stopped and stared while Luke tried to keep a straight face. "Bullseye Bargain Barn."

"Wow, those are from Bullseye? That's, like, a total shocker. Were they on sale?"

"Yep."

"I love what you've done with your hair. That style, it's like, wow. How did you get one side to stay flat like that while the other is sticking up all jaggy and stuff?"

"I took a nap."

Chris tried to squeal but wound up coughing instead. Luke gave in and snickered.

"That was almost as painful as hearing about all those layers of makeup," Chris joked as he rubbed his throat.

Andrea did a quick search for something to throw. Her hand rested on the TV remote for a moment, but instead she picked up one of the high heels to toss playfully at Chris. She missed, and the shoe landed silently on the carpet. "Okay, you made your point. So what are we watching tonight?" Andrea asked.

"I was thinking Food Network. Maybe they've got some sort of special on steak. Makes my mouth water just thinking about a perfectly cooked steak. I might bite a cow or something if this craving gets too strong, or go get a burger," Luke teased.

Andrea threw her other shoe at Luke. It bounced off of his stomach, so he feigned pain.

"I'll go get a DVD," Courtney said as she wandered out into the hall.

"I'll follow you up," Luke said. He picked up the shoes and said to Andrea, "Since you don't need these anymore, I'll bring them up to your room."

"Oh, no you won't!" Andrea screeched.

"Try and stop me," Luke said as he ran to the stairs.

Andrea jumped up from the couch and ran after him, but stopped at the bottom of the stairs, scowling up at him with her hands on her hips. "Dammit Luke, you are such an asshole sometimes! It's supposed to get cold tonight and those steps are going to be miserable!"

He snickered, walking beside Courtney until she stepped off of the spiral on the second floor.

She raised an eyebrow when he didn't follow. "The guest room is next to ours, remember?"

"Yeah, but I'm putting them in the tower."

Courtney giggled before continuing down the hall.

Luke walked to the top of the staircase. The hair on his arms stood as he entered the circular room. He set the heels down on a bench and one of the windows flapped open.

"You always forget to close these, Court," he whispered.

Something shuffled behind him as he reached for the glass. He spun around and spotted eye shine under the bench. Too big to be a squirrel. Beatrix? No, the cat didn't like the tower. She ran back downstairs the one time he brought her up. Luke's fingers trembled as he pulled the window shut and latched it, but his eyes never left the shadows under the bench.

153

At least it's small, whatever it is. Hopefully I can get downstairs and grab Courtney before it attacks.

Luke swallowed hard and took a step towards the stairs. The green shine returned as his angle to the bench changed, and the eyes followed his movements. They approached the edge of the shadows. Luke took a deep breath.

A gremlin crawled out from under the bench, with black stripes on its forehead.

"You're the same one from a few weeks ago," Luke said as he crouched to meet the gremlin's gaze. It twitched an ear and exhaled as it came out into the open, babbling.

"I'm sorry, but I don't speak Russian."

It spoke again, a bit clearer but still in Russian.

"For Pete's sake, you're going to have to speak English if we're going to get anything out of this little chat."

The gremlin's ears perked up as it said to him, "Petr. Petr Timur." It held out its tiny fingers.

Luke shook the gremlin's outstretched hand. "Luke Stillman."

The gremlin's eyes shone like emeralds as it hopped and stared up at him. Luke couldn't help but think of a cat, until the gremlin said his name. He spoke again, but Luke only understood one word. "Yvonne? I only know one Yvonne, and you sure as hell don't want anything to do with her. I wouldn't wish her on anyone. She'd probably dress you up in little knit overalls like she does with her pug."

Luke jumped at Courtney's voice behind him. "What's taking so long? I thought you were dumping the shoes and coming back down."

Luke moved to his left to reveal Petr.

"Dammit Luke, you should've come down and told me to get the sword," Courtney hissed as she backed onto the stairs.

Petr's ears drooped. He backed toward the bench.

"Court, this is the same one from the other night."

"So? It's got a lot of nerve coming back here."

Petr glanced at the window and flinched. The gremlin shook as he watched Courtney. He reminded Luke of a scared chihuahua, especially as Courtney stepped forward and he shrank back, ears dropping even further.

"So? He's here in peace. He could've skewered my eyes with those little claws as soon as I found him. He even introduced himself," Luke said, holding Courtney back with one arm.

Petr tilted his head up at Courtney.

"So, what the fuck do we do?" Courtney said to Luke, avoiding looking at the gremlin.

Petr stepped towards Courtney with his hand outstretched and squeaked. She stared down at him as he said his name.

"Well, what are you waiting for?" Luke hinted.

Courtney sighed, knelt down, and took Petr's delicate hand. She shook it and introduced herself, then let go quickly. "We still need to do something about this. We can't let Andrea stumble into a fucking gremlin when she comes looking for her shoes," she said to Luke.

Petr spoke again.

"Yvonne? Who the hell is Yvonne?" Courtney said.

"No clue," Luke answered. "Hank is probably our best bet at finding out who Yvonne is and figuring out what to do since we have company."

"Yeah, you're right. If it stays in his office there's no chance Chris and Andrea will see it. I don't like it being around those guns, though."

"Petr. Not it. Petr. Besides, can you picture this little guy trying to pick up the Thompson? It weighs more than he does."

"Whatever. Let's just do this."

Luke beckoned Petr forward and motioned for him to follow down the stairs. The trio walked to Hank's office, with Luke making sure to shield Petr in case Chris or Andrea were looking for them.

As Luke raised his fist to the door, Courtney said, "I'll head down with the movie and tell them Bea barfed, so you're cleaning it up, I guess."

"Good cover."

Courtney departed, scowling at Petr while Luke knocked.

"Who is it?" Hank said from inside.

"It's Luke, and a visitor."

"What kind of visitor?"

"The furry two-foot-tall kind with a claw missing."

"I'll be there in a moment."

Luke heard a series of clicks as Hank slid open the deadbolts and unlocked the door. It cracked open. Hank peered out at Luke.

"Bring him in. He can hide out here until Courtney's guests leave, even if he doesn't have any useful information."

Luke led Petr into the office and watched the gremlin's pupils shrink into slits due to the bright computer screen. Luke wondered if the gremlins shared a common ancestor with cats when they evolved.

Petr insisted on introducing himself properly to Hank. Afterwards, his eyes darted from Hank to the screen, the cabinets, the sword rack, and finally the gun on the table. The gremlin screeched and backed towards the closed door. Hank glared at the gremlin, putting a finger to his lips.

Petr froze until Luke said to Hank, "Petr mentioned someone named Yvonne a couple times, but that and the introductions are all I can get out of him because he's speaking some other language. It sounds like Russian."

"Ah, he's here to give Ivan information. He's asking for Ivan, but with his accent you're thinking Yvonne," Hank explained.

"Makes sense. Ivan went to the library, right?"

"He didn't tell me. My assumption is he either went to San Rafael to speak with his scientists or to chat with Alec at our archives in the library, but he could've gone anywhere. For all I know he could've hopped on a plane for Romania."

"He mentioned the library to me, but what's in Romania?"

Petr whispered, "Teuffelmann."

Hank nodded to Petr. Luke's breath caught at the mention of Teuffelmann.

"What makes you think he'd do that?" Luke asked.

"He mentioned offhand it might be useful to have information on Edthgar's personality before he was summoned here and became a gargoyle. There's only one source for that. Like I said, though, he's probably off to San Rafael or the library."

"But there's a chance—"

"Yes, a slim one. I highly doubt he'd fly overseas without saying so first, considering his interest in Courtney's symptoms from Mephallo's blood. He wouldn't disappear for days without saying anything either, and it takes time to get to Romania. His damn plane is almost as old as Courtney's Willys. However, speaking of Courtney, we both know how impatient she can be. I'll keep Petr here until Ivan gets back."

Petr seemed to understand as he shuffled over to Hank.

"Sounds good," Luke said. Though he tried to block the thought from his mind, the thought of Ivan needing to ask Baron Wolfgar von Teuffelmann for advice left him shaking his head. He looked back at the gremlin's big bright eyes and managed to find a smile for the tiny creature. Petr waved to him as he exited.

Luke rushed downstairs to the great room. The sooner he flopped beside Courtney and focused on whatever movie she chose, the sooner his nerves would settle. Probably.

Courtney sat on the arm of one of the recliners, so he plopped into the chair beside her.

"Is Bea alright now?" she asked.

"Yeah," Luke fibbed. "Everything's cleaned up. I'm glad she ralphed on your hardwood floor and not the carpet. That would've been a bitch to clean up. What movie'd you grab?"

Courtney held up the empty case for John Carpenter's *The Fog*.

"Why did I bother asking?" Luke teased. "You're worse with that than I am with *Pulp Fiction* or *Kill Bill*."

"Common courtesy. Besides, Chris hasn't seen this," Courtney said as she picked the remote back up.

Courtney slid off the arm of the chair to lay across Luke's lap as the movie started. He tried to wrap his arms around her, but she smirked and shook her head. Courtney stretched her arms above her head and grabbed the bowl of popcorn on the table. "Snacks before snuggles." Courtney winked.

"Okay, fine," Luke said with a grin as she giggled, tossing a piece of popcorn towards her mouth. He laughed as the popcorn bounced off her nose. Thoughts of the baron flitted through his mind and dulled the moment. He pictured some crazed old wizard cackling as he summoned armies of gargoyles to commit unspeakable horrors upon the world, like raiding Wendy's and denying the pleasures of the Baconator to mankind or stealing Courtney's beloved aluminum popcorn bowl.

Courtney arched an eyebrow at him. He figured she sensed his unease but wouldn't ask while Chris and Andrea were around. Instead, she rubbed his thigh with her hand. His thoughts gradually shifted to the moment. The cackling wizard retreated away, though whispers of impending doom and burger cravings lingered.

14

Courtney removed the disc and pressed the power button. The retracting tray buzzed louder than usual, but she figured it was her imagination running wild. She couldn't wait to ask Luke what Hank said to leave him so troubled. She popped the DVD back in the case and studied Luke's eyes to see if she could glean some sort of clue about his mood. His cryptic gaze concerned her, but she tried to conceal it with small talk. "So, Chris, you're the only one here who hadn't seen it. What'd you think?"

"I liked it," Chris said as he nudged Andrea to wake her up.

"Anything stand out?"

"You're going to make me go into detail? I didn't know there'd be a quiz at the end. School was a long time ago."

"Well, she can't say much," Courtney said, pointing to Andrea stretching and yawning.

"You missed the movie," Chris teased Andrea.

"Just because I slept doesn't mean I missed it," Andrea countered.

"I really liked it. It's refreshing to see something with real special effects instead of a modern CG-fest reliant on graphics instead of an original plot."

"A computer programmer complaining about CG? Now I've heard everything. CG doesn't bother me one way or the other; I just don't like horror movies." Andrea turned to Courtney and added, "You couldn't pick a cheesy romance for date night?"

Courtney rolled her eyes while Chris answered. "I get that. CG doesn't require ingenuity. Don't get me wrong, computers are great, but you can generate anything you want for a movie. You don't have to play around and figure out how to do real world effects nowadays. That was an art form. Animatronic dinosaurs are what made *Jurassic Park* great and those took loads of creative thinking. That's always been interesting to me. When I was a kid I was always taking shit apart and putting it back together."

"Sometimes back together. Don't forget the VCR," Luke teased.

"I'd like to, but I don't think you or my mom will let me," Chris said. He muttered to Andrea, "No one ever mentions the dozens of laptops I've fixed."

"Aw, it's okay. You can tinker with my oven any time."

"Thank you." Chris glared at Luke while patting Andrea's shoulder. He explained further, "I love playing with hardware. It's what got me into computers in the first place. I always want to know what makes things tick. It extended into software and programming."

"Hardware," Andrea snickered, glancing down.

"Too bad your curiosity didn't extend to your Passat. Tad still has nightmares about breaking his knuckle working on that thing," Luke said.

"Germans over-engineer shit for the sake of over-engineering shit," Chris defended.

Andrea stood, stretched again, and said to Courtney, "Do you mind keeping me company while I go out for a quick smoke? If there's gonna be car talk I might fall asleep again."

"Sure. Let me put the movie away first, okay?"

"'Kay," Andrea chirped.

Courtney swayed as she entered the stairwell, leaning against the wall until the dizzy spell passed. When she ascended, the hairs on the back of her neck tingled and pressure around her right eye socket throbbed. The echoing metal steps rang in her ears. Courtney shoved her free hand into her pocket and shivered. "Fucking headaches," she muttered as she exited on the second floor.

She stuffed the movie into its place in the top slot of the DVD rack beside her computer. Luke's cat slept on her hoodie on the bed, so Courtney eyed the flannel shirt on the door knob.

Another dizzy spell hit. It lasted longer than the first, and additional pressure throbbed around her left eye socket and in her sinuses. Courtney closed her eyes and lowered her head, thinking about Andrea's frequent migraines, stemming from the concussion sustained in their car crash a few years ago. If the little hippie could power through migraines at work and still smile at customers, Courtney could grit her teeth and deal with her best friend needing a smoke. After meds.

The small keychain UV light Ivan gave her was the first thing she saw when she opened her eyes. She clipped it to a belt loop on her jeans, then popped on the flannel.

Courtney grabbed aspirin to beat the headache in its early stages. Crinkling from the plastic cup dispenser beside the medicine cabinet sent a bolt of pain through her forehead. As she filled the cup with water, the dripping faucet seemed amplified, as did the squeaking cabinet hinges.

She downed the pill, then frowned at her reflection. *Shit. What if this is the winged gargoyle blood?* Regular gargoyle blood improved her senses, so more powerful gargoyle blood boosting them further seemed logical. Ivan warned her some symptoms might take a month to manifest after the initial absorption, and since she'd fully immersed in the blood moat, side effects were likely.

Courtney dismissed the notion as she tossed the plastic cup into the trash and walked back out into the hallway. "Just a headache," she whispered.

The echoes in the metal stairwell reverberated in her ears. She squinted as the ringing pierced deeper into her head. "Halle-fucking-lujah," she muttered as she stepped onto the carpet and her steps silenced. Another brief dizzy spell replaced the ringing in her ears, but she ignored it.

Andrea waited by the foyer, holding her lighter and a pack of cigarettes. She cocked her head at Courtney's frown. "You look like something's bugging you."

"Just a little headache," Courtney answered as she did up a couple buttons on her shirt.

"You should take something for it," Andrea suggested.

"I did. Aspirin doesn't work instantly," Courtney snapped back.

"Okay, just trying to be helpful."

Courtney nodded as she slid open the foyer closet and grabbed Andrea's light denim jacket.

"Thanks," Andrea said as she put the jacket on without zipping it. "I wish I'd thought to ask you to grab my shoes while you were up there. I already feel chilled."

"Luke put 'em in the tower." Courtney tried not to laugh at Andrea's expression of disgust.

Andrea pointed to Courtney's work sneakers in the corner of the foyer. "What size are those?"

"Seven."

"Fuck. Too small. How do you have smaller shoes when you're taller?"

"I guess you're part hobbit without the hair? Just go up to the tower. That echoey staircase isn't good for my headache right now. Or just be your usual hippie self and skip them like a true hobbit," Courtney said, walking out the door.

Andrea followed her out. "Hippie hobbit it is. Slivers don't scare me that much. Those metal steps are going to be like ice tonight."

They walked down the steps to the blacktop. Andrea lit her cigarette and shivered. "It must be in the fifties now. I should've squeezed into your work sneakers."

Courtney shrugged, walking around to Andrea's other side. The wind shifted and blew smoke at her.

"Why'd Luke have to go and put my heels all the way up in the tower, anyway? I'm going to have to have Chris get 'em later 'cause I'm not going up any more of those cold-ass steps than I gotta."

"It's not like you need them until morning with how you complained, my dear hobbit. You probably shouldn't have chucked them if you wanted them handy."

"Well sorry, but Luke knows I'm vegetarian and made that burger joke anyway. I couldn't ignore it."

Courtney raised an eyebrow at her and snickered. "Maybe it was a fish burger since you're not really a vegetarian?"

Andrea puffed smoke in Courtney's face. "Pescatarian sounds more like some sub-sect of a religion."

"Ah, so you're Sister Andrea the hippie hobbit now? 'Thou shall not eatest beef, but fish are allowed. Now as penance I must go on a barefoot pilgrimage with my cigarette to apologize to dear Mother Earth for thinking how yummy her fuzzy creations can be,'" Courtney said in a melodramatic tone, miming a cross over her chest.

Andrea shook her head and changed the subject. "Think we'll get stuck working Black Friday again? I hate that; I wanna shop then, not wait on other people getting all the good deals."

"I don't really care. I'm doing all my shopping online. I hate people more than computers."

"Where's the fun in that? Your martial arts would make you a fantastic holiday shopper."

"For always preaching peace, love, happiness, and modified vegetarianism, you sure love your shopping with a side of unrestrained violence."

Andrea blushed.

Courtney added, "Besides, I have enochlophobia."

"Umwhataphobia?"

"Enochlophobia. Fear of crowds."

"So that's what you call that. I almost forgot. It really bugged you through school, almost as bad as those four girls when you were stuck in private school. I'm surprised you don't have panic attacks on Black Friday at work."

"I'm too busy to notice since I'm concentrating on one customer at a time and blocking out the rest. Don't worry, I'm not worried about your Halloween party. I know it's never big."

Andrea laughed. "You knew what I was going to ask next."

"Of course. You're easy to read."

"So are you coming?"

"You haven't set a date yet."

"But I can't until we get our work schedules. We're always off the same days so it can't be too hard to say yes or no," Andrea pressed.

"This year I have Luke to consider. It wouldn't be fair to go without him. He has to be to work at 7:00 a.m. so he can't be up too late for a party," Courtney said.

"He can just call in sick. It's what Chris is going to do."

"Luke used up all of his paid time off after his apartment burned down, remember? He can't really afford to take more."

"Being adults sucks sometimes," Andrea sighed, staring down.

"If you miss those kindergarten finger paintings so much you could always check into a mental hospital. I'm sure they'd be glad to have you."

Andrea smirked. "Bring Ivan if Luke can't come."

Courtney burst out laughing. "I don't think he knows what Halloween is."

"Well phooey to Mr. Fancy-pants and his blingy-mobile then. Is he out tonight 'cause I'm here again? I really made an impression on the poor guy."

The scent of cucumbers hit Courtney. She glanced to the side and caught a glimpse of claws retreating into the bushes. "Fuck," she muttered, shaking her head.

"What's wrong? Is it the headache?"

Courtney nodded, watching where the gargoyle disappeared. "Hurry and finish your cigarette. I'm starting to get chills now, too. And my head —"

The door clicked, interrupting her. Andrea dropped the cigarette and squeaked.

"Did Luke just lock us out? Dammit, now I really wish I'd grabbed your sneaks. I don't want my toes to freeze off out here." Andrea hopped up the stairs and grabbed the door handle. She jerked her hand back and yelped, "The door just zapped me!"

"It must be midnight. The alarm system automatically locks then," Courtney explained.

"You've got your keys, right?"

"They're sitting next to my computer. You've got your phone, right?" Courtney said, pointing to Andrea's cleavage.

Andrea pulled out her pack of cigarettes and lighter. "It's in my purse on the couch. What do we do now?" She shifted from one foot to the other for a few seconds, then pounded on the door, screaming. "Let us in!"

"Stop it, you're killing my head," Courtney grumbled as she tried to think of a plan. She swore and shoved her hands into her pockets. The UV light jingled as she did and cleared some of the worried haze from her thought process. "There's a spare key in one of the statues at the end of the driveway."

"We have to walk all the way down there? The house lights don't reach that far. How will we see?" Andrea complained, staring down at her feet.

Courtney tried the light on her belt. It barely produced a visible beam. Even though she'd be able to see because of the gargoyle blood, Andrea couldn't know. She also didn't want Andrea walking around blind, so she breathed deep and thought again. Her gaze fell upon the dropped cigarette smoldering on the asphalt.

"Your lighter," Courtney said as she stepped on the cigarette to snuff it out. "Light up another cigarette and hand me the lighter."

Andrea came back down the steps and joked, "You're like the female MacGyver. You just need a working flashlight."

Courtney took the lighter and fiddled with it until she got it to light. "Stay close. I want us both to be able to see where we're going."

"I'm not standing here alone, that's for sure. This place is creepy at night." Andrea puffed on the cigarette.

Courtney held the lighter in her left hand, closer to Andrea. Her right hand held the UV light, ready to use if the gargoyle approached. The increased sensitivity of her nose told her there was only one, but one was a threat while unarmed. Courtney hoped it would stay away since it was outnumbered.

She doubted it.

Damn headache made my thinking sloppy, but I'm not failing Andrea.

The duo set off for the end of the driveway. Andrea's breathing and heart rate accelerated. Her friend was cold, scared, and knew something wasn't right despite Courtney's best efforts to hide it. Her inability to tell Andrea what was going on tore at her conscience. Courtney wanted to spill the beans about everything, but Ivan was right, and especially in this instance, gargoyle knowledge would be a major detriment to Andrea's frame of mind. Courtney came up with a quick fib. "There was a bobcat lurking this afternoon."

"Must've been some kind of special bobcat to worry you. I think they're super cute." Andrea's demeanor settled. Courtney breathed easier, but still hated lying to her friend.

They pressed onwards without a word until the bushes rustled, breaking the silence. Courtney brought up the UV light and aimed it into the gargoyle's eyes. It tore off in the opposite direction. She stood still for a second, marveling that she'd managed to aim the light before seeing the gargoyle. With any luck, Andrea didn't notice either the aim or what lurked in the darkness.

"What the fuck was that?" Andrea whimpered.

"Deer," Courtney lied again.

"You've got better eyes than I do. It almost looked like one of those ugly statues came to life," Andrea said, shivering and dropping the cigarette.

"I guess your contacts aren't as good as my glasses. We're not far from the statues. Wait until we get there to light up another cig."

"What about this one? I can't put it out myself." Andrea pointed down at her feet.

Courtney stomped the cigarette and joked, "Your toes might warm up, Sister Hobbit."

"If I'd known we were gonna get locked out I definitely would've squeezed into your tiny sneakers. Chris'll have to give me a rub to get warm again."

"Poor Chris. Hindsight's 20/20, I guess," Courtney said as they walked the rest of the way to the statues with no sign of living gargoyles.

"Gawd, those things are so damn creepy." Andrea took back her lighter and lit the next cigarette.

Courtney snatched the cigarette from her. "Keeps the weirdos away. Well, except you."

"And the ones who live here." Andrea gave Courtney's shin a playful kick.

Courtney set the cigarette down under the statue so Andrea could see what went on. She searched for the recessed button on the tip of the statue's folded wing, fumbling around until the button pushed inwards. The key fell from the statue with a metallic clink. Pain shot through Courtney's head and dropped her to her knees while she screamed her favorite four-letter word.

"Are you all right?" Andrea asked, picking up the key.

Courtney nodded as she collected herself. "It's the headache. That high-pitched clank really hurt."

Andrea helped her up, then lit the lighter again. Courtney snuffed out the cigarette under the statue and rubbed her forehead.

"It's really funny how your uncle hid the key up the statue's ass," Andrea joked.

"He does have a different sense of humor."

"I'll bet you never expected to get bailed out by my smoking, either."

Courtney looked at her without a word as they walked up the driveway. They continued in silence until the breeze kicked up. The lighter flickered and Andrea zipped her jacket. "I really didn't need that extra chill," she complained.

"You did say it was supposed to drop below fifty tonight. I guess the weatherman was right for a change."

"Always when you don't want them to be," Andrea whined.

"At least they were wrong about the rain," Courtney said, trying to put a positive spin on the night's events.

"Don't jinx it now!"

Courtney winced at Andrea's sharp tone.

"Sorry," Andrea whispered, patting Courtney's arm.

As the lights from the house came into view, Courtney heard more distant rustling in the bushes. She swore and tried to formulate a plan to convince Andrea to hurry without sensing the danger approaching. "You know what'll warm things up before we get inside? A race to the door," Courtney said, then took off.

"That's not fair! You've got shoes!" Andrea yelled as she jogged after Courtney.

Courtney tripped on her way up the stairs and slammed her side into the top step. She struggled to breathe as Andrea stepped over her to slip the key into the door.

"What happened?" Andrea asked.

Courtney needed a moment to breathe again, and when she did, the pain in her side made the headache seem minor. She croaked out, "The headache is affecting my balance."

"Excuses, excuses. You just don't want to admit a smoker with no shoes and a little gut kicked Miss Athletic's ass in a race," Andrea gloated as she helped Courtney up.

"Think whatever you want," Courtney wheezed. "I might've busted a fucking rib."

"Do you think you'll need a doctor?" Andrea asked.

The door opened before Courtney could muster an answer.

"A doctor? What about doctors?" Luke asked, "And what the hell was that thump?"

"That was me crashing into the steps," Courtney groaned.

"The alarm system locked us out, so we had to get the spare key, so Courtney thought it'd be fun to race back up here but she tripped and *boom!*" Andrea twittered without breathing between words.

Andrea grabbed the key as the trio shuffled inside. Luke ushered Courtney to the couch and made her lie down. Chris moved to the doorway to stand and watch with Andrea.

Luke pulled up Courtney's shirt. "Why didn't you call me or Chris?"

"My phone is in my purse on the table. Court probably left hers upstairs with her keys. I screamed for you but I guess you didn't hear," Andrea answered. She looked at Courtney's side and her face contorted in horror. "Oh gawd, Court, there's a big bruise forming already."

Chris pulled her into the hall and said, "Let's head up to the guest room and give them a bit of privacy, okay? You need to get warmed up anyway."

Andrea nodded, sniffled, and wiped away a tear. Chris led her away from the doorway.

Courtney pulled her shirt down and sat up. "Get the door locked back up nice and tight."

Luke went to the door as instructed. Courtney listened as Andrea went up to the second floor with a little yelp at each step, and Chris clomped upstairs ahead of her. The individual tumblers clicked as Luke locked the door. The button presses to reset the alarm beeped as if she were beside the door.

Once Luke returned to the great room and she was satisfied Chris and Andrea wouldn't be able to hear her, Courtney explained. "So much for no gargoyle activity in two weeks. There's one stalking in the bushes. I chased it away with the UV light, but it was coming back so I had to rush Andrea up here. I've got a nasty headache. I lost my balance running up the steps. My senses are going crazy now, too, and not helping the headache."

"At least we know the light works." Luke unclipped it from her belt loop. "Come on, let's get you to bed. I'll grab some ice on the way up. You get undressed while you wait. Doctor's orders, *capiche?*"

Looking into his bright blue eyes sent a bolt of warmth through Courtney. She smiled and made an okay sign with her hand. Luke handed back the light as he helped her up.

"I'll be there in a few," he said as he followed her into the hall.

She gave him another okay sign and a smile as he went into the kitchen. Breathing hurt, but her ribs would heal by morning. The headache was a greater concern as she lumbered up the steps and metallic echoes assaulted her ears. Other sounds filled her head as well, like the freezer door closing down in the kitchen. The ice cubes rattled in the bag Luke put them in. She could even hear the heartbeats of everyone in the house and discern the rapid rhythm of Petr's little gremlin heart.

Courtney no longer doubted these were side effects of the winged gargoyle blood, as Ivan warned. She rubbed her forehead, fingers trembling. *Fuck. What's next?*

15

Courtney stared at her bloodshot eyes in the bathroom mirror. Her eyelids felt heavier than anything the world's strongest man could lift, yet sleep eluded her. The headache had passed, but her senses chugged along hyper-alert. Every noise in the house assaulted her ears, no matter how slight. The squeaking springs from the guest room bed annoyed her most. She heard Andrea's accelerated heartbeat, but Chris's heart beat at a relaxed rhythm.

Must be having nightmares about the thing in the bushes.

Courtney slapped the sink and grimaced as her ears rang. Andrea couldn't sleep because the damn gargoyles gave her nightmares, and she couldn't sleep because of sensory overload.

Petr's squeaky snores from on the third floor also annoyed her. She wished she could get away with silencing its snores with her sword, but it was probably best to let the creature disprove its loyalty before killing it. Who knew if the repulsive little fiend really did serve the gargoyles, but if she was right and it proved disloyal, she'd dispatch the vile beast with a smile.

One side of her lips quirked upward in her reflection, but she wiped away the grin and shuddered. Aggressive thoughts were nothing new, but the glee she felt at the thought of watching the life drain from the gremlin's spindly body disturbed her. If the winged gargoyle blood heightened her aggression further....

The Bentley's powerful exhaust note growled as if it were beside her, even though it entered the driveway a few hundred feet away. The brakes squeaked as the car stopped in the circle. When Ivan shut the engine off, she heard the rattle of an exhaust hanger loosening. Hitting Edthgar apparently did have some effect on the armored sedan.

Courtney closed her eyes and shook her head in an attempt to ignore her senses. The car door shut with a solid thunk, proving her efforts futile. "Fuck," she muttered as she leaned on the sink and buried her face in her arms.

Every step Ivan took toward the door hammered against her feeble sanctuary. The tumblers rattled as he unlocked the door. He reset the alarm, and every button push set her ears to ringing at a higher pitch. Even though he moved as quietly as she did, she still heard his carpet-cushioned steps. Thankfully he tread softly up the metal steps, so the echoes caused only a little more pain than the alarm system button beeps. The hallway carpet muffled his steps again until his shadow appeared in the doorway out of the corner of her eye.

"My senses are going crazy. Is it the winged gargoyle blood?" Courtney asked.

"Yes."

She smelled tea on his breath, and a faint scent of old books wafted into the bathroom. He'd been at the library. "How do I settle them? I haven't slept at all," she said with a groan.

Ivan stepped forward and placed his hand on her shoulder. "Should I ever discover a way to do so myself, I shall let you know."

"This shit is permanent?" Courtney blurted, regretting the volume of her voice and hoping she didn't awaken anyone.

Ivan rubbed her shoulder and answered, "It has not faded in seventy-five years, so that would be my assumption. It is one reason I no longer sleep."

"I don't have a fancy ring so that's not an option. How do I get used to it?"

"In time your body will adjust and this will seem normal. I am certain you will find your own way. I have never known another person, aside from perhaps Luke, who could sleep as much as you do."

Courtney turned around and smiled. "How can you tease me and make me feel better at the same time?"

"I learned the English language in the early 1930s. You were born in 1990. I merely have sixty more years of experience with English than you do."

"I bet you're one of those weirdos who reads a dictionary for fun," Courtney mumbled, rubbing her eyes.

"Why would that be considered strange?"

"I read stuff like Terry Brooks or Tolkien for fun, the kind of shit that tells a story, not tons of information most of us never need. It's been a while since I read, unfortunately, but screw the dictionary."

"I eagerly anticipate each new edition of the dictionary so I may learn new words. Knowledge is a wonderful thing. It is not strange. Strange is a word I would use to describe this text-message speak your generation has created."

"My generation? I don't understand the shit, either. I'll never get used to your age since you don't look much older than Luke. It must be so weird seeing your friends grow old while you stay the same. I mean, you've known my uncle for like forty years."

"You have no idea. It is immensely difficult. I have watched many friends grow old and die. I have wanted to give them the ring to avoid losing them, but that would merely prolong their suffering, end my life, and break a promise," Ivan said in a somber tone.

"Wow, no wonder you drink so much," Courtney teased in a desperate attempt to lighten the mood.

"Alcohol has no effect upon my brain due to the ring. I simply enjoy the flavor of fine wines, and harder spirits serve as a vessel to reminisce upon my younger years and adventures with Anatalia. I foresee you and Luke creating similar memories in the future. I do hope you two know how fortunate you are to have each other. The business of fighting monsters can divide even the most devoted couples, yet it seems to have drawn you closer together."

"He's cooked some fantastic bacon double cheeseburgers for me a couple times, so I think he knows. His humor keeps me going when shit gets me down. What do you think?"

"My opinion is he knows he is lucky, despite the gargoyle threat. I also suspect he fears more for your safety than his own, and feels he must make the most of every moment with you because it could be the last. After all, you are not exactly what I would call a careful fighter. You use your emotions to great advantage in battle, which makes you deadly and unpredictable, yet leaves you open, like the night you were bitten. You are not invincible. Always remember this fact and fight in a more controlled manner. By all means, continue your emotional style, but calculate your risks. Your enhanced senses will aid you in having greater awareness, and as such, greater survivability. Luke will thank you for it. He is devoted to you enough to risk his life in the fight against the gargoyles. Reward him by easing his concerns for you."

"Deep stuff," Courtney said, wishing she had a more suitable response.

"Before you were born, there was a woman your uncle cared for deeply. He tried to leave monster fighting behind for her.

I never met her, but I heard in his voice he felt she was his one and only. Luke speaks of you in the same manner. Unfortunately for your uncle, one cannot simply retire from fighting the gargoyles, and once she learned of the war with them it proved she did not reciprocate his devotion. She left him in the night, without a note. I know he never told you this story. You must not let him know I have done so. It is his secret, but I believe the comparison necessary to show the depth of Luke's support," Ivan said.

"Wow," Courtney said, still unable to process a fitting response. "Do you mind if I ask something personal?"

"No matter my answer, I know you will ask anyway. You have my permission."

Courtney swallowed. "What happened to your love?"

Ivan sighed before he answered. "We both lived for the thrill of treasure hunting in the most remote and dangerous regions of eastern Europe and western Asia. It was on one of these adventures we first encountered the gargoyles. Anatalia was severely wounded, and for the first time tasted her own vulnerability. Up to that point she viewed herself as unstoppable.

"After, she became so concerned about mortality that she lost focus and sustained further injuries. I left her in the care of a group of gypsies to search for a mythic ring which would grant immortality to its keeper. I wanted it for her so she would regain her confidence and I could bring back the old Anatalia I loved so deeply.

"I returned too late. She took her own life while I was away. The gypsy healer heard screams and found Anatalia with a knife in her hand and her throat sliced wide open. She could not stop the bleeding despite her advanced magical healing knowledge. The eldest mystic surmised the thought I could be just as vulnerable drove Anatalia to madness. At that moment, I promised her I would never falter in my newfound quest to rid the world of gargoyles. So the ring became bound to me, for Anatalia." His voice wavered as he said her name at the end of the story.

"I'm so sorry." Courtney held back tears and gave Ivan a brief hug. She recoiled due to the pain from her healing ribs.

Ivan raised an eyebrow. Courtney lifted her tank top and pointed to her ribcage as she tried to catch her breath.

"Perhaps I should have given you the speech sooner about lacking invincibility."

Courtney shook her head, wiping her eyes. The pain from her ribs had loosened her focus on preventing tears over Ivan's story. "I might've ignored the message a couple hours ago. This helps put it into perspective."

"I believe both of you have what it takes to succeed in this battle as long as you work on certain attributes. You know what you need to improve, and I am certain you are perceptive enough to know what shortcomings you need to advise Luke upon."

"Physical conditioning."

Ivan nodded. "He has stirred in your bedroom. Perhaps this would be the perfect opportunity to broach the subject to him. I need a sandwich.'

As Ivan turned around to exit into the hall, Courtney asked, "How do you know he's awake now?"

"I know because my senses have not relaxed. Yours have. Since you accomplished that, have a good night, Miss Mays."

Courtney smiled. "Enjoy your sandwich, since I can't really say 'good night' to someone who doesn't sleep."

Ivan chuckled as he wandered down the hall. Courtney looked into the mirror for a moment, pleased to see a normal smile instead of the devious one from the thoughts of slaughtering Petr. She peeked out the window and saw the bushes rustle, no doubt because of the gargoyle spy. If Ivan ignored its presence, she could, too.

Courtney slid in the half-open doorway and stepped over the cat on her way to bed. "Are you awake?" she asked Luke as she crawled under the sheets.

"Somewhat," he mumbled.

"I thought I was quiet," she said.

"You were. Bea wasn't when she jumped down. She's clumsy for a cat."

"Oh," Courtney said.

"So what's up? You and Ivan must have talked about something important, right?"

"My enhanced senses, his lost love, and our future," she answered.

"What about all that?"

"Well, the senses are permanent, so I have to get used to this shit."

"That's cool, honestly. You'll be able to warn me when your uncle rips one of his silent but violent bombs."

Courtney giggled. "Believe me, with how strong my sense of smell is now, I'm running when one of those fuckers slides out. Lay off the aftershave, too."

"Noted," Luke half-said, half-yawned.

"I asked Ivan what happened to Anatalia. She hunted treasure with him but got hurt. He went to find the ring for her, but she committed suicide because she was too scared he'd get hurt, too. That brought up our future." Courtney paused as her head hit the pillow.

"Continue," Luke mumbled.

"I'll be more careful so you're not as worried about me when we're killing monsters."

Luke rolled over and gently poked her ribs. "Be more careful all the time. You're the clumsiest damned ninja-warrior-gymnast princess I've ever met," he teased as she swatted his hand away.

"I'm the only damned ninja-warrior gymnast you've ever met," Courtney giggled. "That makes me the most graceful too. I'm no princess, though. Fuck that shit."

"Well, yeah, but graceful people don't usually lose fights with their front steps."

"You're the heaviest gargoyle-killing comedian I've ever met," Courtney teased back.

"Fat guys are always funnier, and this gut helps cushion blows."

"I'm serious. The shape you're in, you'd get torn apart if you had to get in close with a gargoyle. You need to get a workout routine going and get fit. I can't focus in a fight if I'm worried about you getting hurt," Courtney countered, squeezing his hand.

"If you put it that way, I suppose I could fit a little something in. There's one condition though. I had to miss my Sharks while Hank's beloved Raiders lost again, but there's a TV sitting in your closet unused."

"You want to defile my room with toothless grunting Canadians fighting over a rubber disk? I don't know."

"Don't worry, I won't interfere with your precious workouts. Besides, there's Swedish players too; they're not all Canadian."

"We may have a deal, but let me think on it some more, okay?"

"Awesome. Now how about a little exercise before going back to sleep?" Luke suggested as he pulled her closer.

"I think I can ignore my ribs for a bit."

16

Courtney set her comb on the bathroom counter and reached for her robe. A car engine accelerated up the driveway; she turned to look out the window as she tied the robe. After the initial shock passed, the enhanced senses became enjoyable. Just by sound she knew it was the Pontiac coming up the driveway. As soon as it came into view and confirmed her hearing was right, she smirked and shut the curtains.

Courtney hummed on her way to the laundry room. As she chucked the towel in the hamper, a wider grin crossed her face. Her fingers untied the robe on her way back to their bedroom. *Let's give Luke a nice surprise.*

She walked through the open doorway, giggled, dropped the robe—and shrieked at Ivan sitting on the bed. He averted his eyes as she scooped up the robe.

"I'm decent now," she said, blushing.

Ivan avoided looking at her, instead facing the wall and nodding to acknowledge her statement. Courtney looked to the doorway as Luke charged up the stairs.

"What the hell was that scream?" Luke asked.

"Courtney...." Ivan started, paused, and stammered, "She will tell you later. All I will say regarding the matter is how glad I am Hank had a prior engagement and could not be here."

Luke shrugged and gave Courtney a peck on the cheek, but pressed no further.

"So, um, what's up?" Courtney asked.

"I thought I should share some of the information Petr gave us. I discussed it with Hank and Alec this morning, so they are aware of the plan I feel we need to institute," Ivan said, stopping as Luke looked between him and Courtney.

"Alec?" Luke asked.

"The pervy old librarian Unc has over sometimes."

"Oh, the Brit."

Courtney nodded while Ivan continued. "Petr heard through other members of his tribe that Edthgar desires a human queen. Scrolls my father hid in medieval times now reside in our library, and Alec analyzed some. He found references to human women being taken by the gargoyles and subjected to torture and sorcery to break their will, at which point they became vessels for entities summoned from the realm my father and the gargoyles came from. Once this process was complete, the power of the gargoyles grew immensely because they could access innumerable arcane abilities. We would obviously prefer this situation not occur."

"So why hasn't Edthgar taken a queen? Does a woman have to meet some sort of special conditions to be taken?" Luke asked.

Courtney swallowed hard and leaned against Luke. *Shit. I think I know what's coming.*

"The texts do not say. They merely describe the perilous situation our ancestors faced due to the exponential growth in gargoyle power. I do believe, however, there are certain qualities a candidate for queen must have. Perhaps they must have absorbed gargoyle blood," Ivan said, looking into Courtney's eyes.

Courtney's heart stopped. The thought the gargoyles wanted her to be theirs disturbed her more than dying at their hands.

Still looking into Courtney's eyes, Ivan continued. "Judging by your expression and the color draining from your face, I assume you surmise our suspicions. Your uncle and I believe it would be best if you were kept under surveillance at all times you may otherwise be vulnerable."

"How are you going to do that discreetly? People might get suspicious," she said.

"Officer Nelson will shadow you, along with Scott. Should they prove too conspicuous, say you are being tailed because of evidence of a threat from Brazo de Dios. That would be plausible, considering the news story following the incident which brought Luke into our fold."

"Sounds good."

"I need to discuss another precaution with you. Since there is considerable threat to your safety, your uncle and I both feel it would be sensible to have your car retrofitted with armor in a manner similar to mine. Fear not, you will notice no difference in performance when the task is complete. In the meantime I will loan you the Bentley. I shall enjoy driving my Bugatti, as it is presently more important for you to have the enhanced protection."

"You've got to be shitting me!"

"You do not have to act so insulted. I am aware the Bentley is not as attractive as your car, but I am certain you will enjoy it once you have driven it."

Courtney shook her head and corrected Ivan. "No, no, I'm not insulted. I'm surprised you'd let me drive something so expensive."

"Luke drove it less than twenty-four hours after demolishing his Volvo. Did I not also offer you the opportunity to someday drive the Bugatti, which is a priceless vehicle that cannot be replaced? I can have a new car built to my specifications should something inconceivable happen to the Bentley. Remember, though, this car is armored. If it can ram Edthgar and emerge unscathed, I am certain it will survive anything you could throw at it."

"One of the exhaust hangers is rattling, so not totally unscathed."

Ivan sighed. "It rattled six months ago."

"Oh, okay. But there's also the fact a Bentley isn't exactly in my price range. How do I explain to coworkers when I show up in that thing?"

"A 1941 Willys Americar is inexpensive? Your coworkers are aware of the business your uncle runs, along with his wealthy connections. Tell them one of his customers is doing him a favor because you destroyed the transmission in the Willys. It sounds plausible to anyone familiar with your driving."

Luke smothered his laughter. Courtney elbowed him in the stomach. "Good point," she grumbled.

"With that discussion settled, I shall allow you two a moment of discussion amongst yourselves." Ivan stood and departed the room.

"He sure didn't waste any time leaving," Luke commented.

Courtney blushed. "I was going to surprise you, so I dropped the robe as I walked through the door. Well, Ivan was sitting there and—"

Luke burst out laughing. "He got a show, eh?"

Courtney threw the robe to the floor and walked to the dresser. With her hand on the top drawer, she grinned at Luke. "Any suggestions?"

"What's the number to call in to work?"

Courtney chuckled and said, "I wish I could."

"I definitely could've used that surprise after today's news at work," Luke lamented.

"What happened?" Courtney pulled out the drawer.

"The old man Goldman is retiring and his kids don't want the business or any part of tracking down rare car parts, so the store is closing."

Courtney walked over, still naked, and hugged him tight. "Now I definitely need to go to work to help pay off your debt to Unc and Ivan."

"It's not closing until spring, but you can keep hugging."

Courtney let go and darted over to the dresser. She pulled underwear from the drawer, much to Luke's dismay. "I've got to make money before the holidays so I can afford something Ivan might actually want," she said.

"I don't think there's too many material things he wants." Luke sighed while watching Courtney pull up a looser fitting pair of pants than usual.

She noticed Luke looking at the pants. "If the gargoyles are after me, I can't have tight clothes restricting my movement. Being sexy doesn't matter if I'm turned into the gargoyle queen."

"Can we find their lair and set off an underground nuke? I don't know if I can take a world without sexy Courtney."

"I'm not sexy all the time?" she joked, tucking a polo shirt into her waistband.

"Well, yeah, but there's an extra level of sexy when you're in tight clothes that show how fit you are," Luke quickly backtracked.

Courtney sat on the bed to put on her socks. "I guess it's true what they say about opposites attracting."

Luke glanced down at his baggy jersey as she walked over to her computer desk to grab her belt, keys, phone, UV light, glasses, and wallet. He laughed. "I hate Sundays. I get home and you have to leave."

She kissed him. "You could always join me. You love movies; I'm sure you'd be great at selling them."

"Fuck retail. I'd rather commit *seppuku* with your sword."

"And soil your Lidster jersey?"

"Lidstrom. I'd take it off first and leave a note requesting you create a shrine to the greatest Swedish defenseman in history."

She kissed him again. "I'll catch you later."

"Okay, have fun at work."

Ivan waited in the hall, holding up his keys. "Do not touch the center console buttons. Doing so could activate one of many systems we do not have time to discuss, such as the UV headlights and flamethrower exhaust. Stick to the radio and climate control systems. Do not push the bottom right corner of the horn. Resist smoky burnouts. Do not eat or drink in the car. Understood?"

She nodded. He dropped the keys into her hand. "Excellent. Enjoy your day purveying appliances to the plebeian masses."

"Thanks. I think."

"Perhaps I should use smaller words since you show particular disdain for the concept of reading the dictionary to expand your vocabulary?"

"Yeah, and maybe some contractions." Courtney jogged towards the stairs, jangling the keys in front of her as she went.

Ivan chuckled. "Either way, go careful. I will discuss further business with Luke until you return."

17

"Come on, Court, hurry up!" Andrea tapped her foot by the sliding doors at the Motherlode entrance.

"We're the only two left to close. There's no need to hurry," Courtney grumbled.

"I need my smoke. As honored as I am Lizzie trusted me with a key, I'm overdue for a cigarette."

"Sounds like a personal problem," Courtney teased while zipping up her hoodie. "Besides, Lizzie did this 'cause she's a lazy bitch. She knows you won't screw her over, but it's mainly because she wanted to skip out and see a movie."

"But she had a headache."

"And that's why Todd left at the same time. You're so naïve sometimes."

Andrea pulled a piece of scrap paper from her pocket and punched a code into the keypad. The two hurried out and waited for a beep, then Andrea stuck the key into the door to lock it. They wandered side by side to their cars, which were the only ones left in their section of the lot. A police interceptor sat in the far corner.

"I see they're ready for your shenanigans," Andrea said, pointing out the Charger.

Courtney looked. "Oh, that's Officer Nelson. She's a family friend. She's also running surveillance on me because of a threat from Brazo de Dios."

"What'd I say about that gang? They're bad news. And you call me naïve."

"You like the Bentley?" Courtney changed the subject.

"It's a big green blingy brick. Your Willy Wagon looks better. At least it's curvy."

The two stopped between their cars. Something moved by the corner of the building and Courtney knew the gargoyles were coming for her. It was the same one in a hoodie from the foggy night. "I think we should get going pretty quick," she suggested.

"You can go if you want. I need my smoke." Andrea turned to look towards the disguised gargoyle. "Why does that homeless guy creep you out so much, yet a gang doesn't scare you? I mean, yeah, he spooked me the first time I saw him here, but if he didn't get arrested he must be okay."

"I'm pretty sure he had a knife the other night. Brazo de Dios is organized; this guy is alone. He could be some lone wolf psycho type, or who knows, he could even be Brazo de Dios. I'll stay with you until you finish your smoke. Who's to say they wouldn't try to kidnap my best friend to get at me? I don't trust the weirdo slinking around."

"He could be a very nice homeless guy with some illness causing him to move funny. I appreciate your concern though," Andrea said, lighting her cigarette.

"I've got a lot on my mind lately, so I'm always thinking worst-case scenario. Sorry." Courtney leaned on the Miata's front fender to keep an eye on the incognito gargoyle.

"You're not pregnant, are you?"

Courtney raised an eyebrow. "What the fuck would make you say or think that? You know I don't want any little shitgoblins."

"There's not much that'd make you so melancholy or touchy. And you know, accidents happen, and Luke lives with you now."

"What's with the big words? Trying to impress Ivan?" Courtney snapped.

Andrea blinked rapidly at her. Courtney sighed and looked at the ground. "Sorry, the creepy guy worries me. So do my ribs and Luke losing his job. Then there's figuring out what to buy a billionaire for Christmas. Damn sales scam day."

"And you broke the Willy Wagon."

"Do you know how bad it sounds when you call it that?"

"Well yeah, that's why I do it. Why is Ivan still there, anyway? You'd think a billionaire would just buy a new place."

"He's having more issues dealing with the insurance than expected, and doesn't want to tie himself to a house he doesn't really like. His other home is in Romania, which makes it hard to battle with insurance in California," Courtney answered.

"Oh." Andrea blew smoke at Courtney.

Courtney walked to the rear of the car and leaned on the trunk. She only looked away a few seconds before pounding footsteps caught her attention. "Duck!" Courtney yelled, pulling Andrea down out of the path of the gargoyle leaping over the Miata.

The gargoyle spun upon landing and swung its fist at Courtney, who dodged. The punch connected with Andrea's cheek, dropping her to the pavement. Her head bounced off the ground and she lay still.

Courtney screamed as she delivered a roundhouse kick to the side of the gargoyle's head, sending it sprawling. She jumped on it and rained her fists down on its face, splitting her knuckles while knocking a couple of jagged teeth from its lipless maw.

The gargoyle thrust its knee up into her stomach, tossing her easily onto the hood of the Miata. It rose to its feet and pulled a dagger from its waistband. Courtney rolled off of the hood as it leapt at her. Claws plunged through the windshield, showering the interior with glass. Unfazed, it rolled off after Courtney, slashing at her with the knife.

Courtney moved around the car as smoke rose from the roof where the cigarette ignited the fabric. She almost bumped into Andrea, who pushed herself up to her hands and knees.

Courtney stood between her friend and the gargoyle. "Come on, you ugly fuckface. Come and get me."

It did, thrusting the dagger forward. Courtney kicked the dagger away and smiled as the gargoyle's arm bent backwards at the elbow. It grunted and barreled into her, throwing her over Andrea as her friend fumbled around for her glasses. The crunch Courtney felt under her shoulder upon landing pinpointed the glasses' remains.

The disarmed gargoyle stepped around Andrea and thrust its claws at Courtney. She squirmed out of the way and its claws drilled into the asphalt. It yelped in pain, allowing Courtney to wriggle free. She kicked it in the wounded arm and watched its elbow buckle under the gargoyle's weight. Its face hit the pavement as she stomped on the back of its head.

Andrea screamed. Courtney abandoned the fight and darted the few feet over to her. "I cut my hand on something. I can barely see," Andrea whimpered, tears rolling down her face to mingle with the blood from a scrape on her cheek.

Courtney looked down and saw the dagger. "This guy's still dangerous. Hang on and I'll get you to a doctor when the fucker's done for," she said, snatching up the knife.

Andrea nodded and winced as she leaned against the Bentley. She held her cut palm in a fold in her jacket and kept pressure on it with the other hand.

"Be careful," she told Courtney.

Courtney said nothing as she turned back to the stricken gargoyle. It dragged itself up using the burning Miata's door handle and glared at Courtney. One almost-human eye was closed as blood poured from the gargoyle's forehead. The open eye looked past Courtney at Andrea.

"We're not done yet. You're still breathing and I intend to change that." Courtney jumped and pounded it in the chest with a kick, knocking it back onto the Miata's roof and collapsing the weakened fabric.

The gargoyle stood and tore off the hoodie, material smoldering from the car's fire. The creature wobbled as it saw Officer Nelson blasting across the parking lot in the Charger. It stepped away from the flames.

Courtney took advantage of the brief distraction, running forward to jam the dagger up under its jaw, then slicing down its throat. The gargoyle grasped at the wound and gurgled as it fell to the ground, every major blood vessel in its neck severed by the knife.

Courtney wiped the knife off on her hoodie as Renee stepped out of the police cruiser. Renee tossed a moist towelette to Courtney and grinned at the dying gargoyle, then looked over to see Andrea fall as she passed out again.

"Get yourself cleaned up so you don't get any on your friend," Renee advised. "That's got the same cleaner in it that dissolves the blood." She held a first aid kit in her other hand and walked over to attend to Andrea. "Once you're clean and I've got her field dressings done, get her to Sir Francis Drake Memorial Hospital. Two driveways past the main entrance you'll find a dirt road leading up to a small hidden parking lot. Scott'll meet you there if I'm still tied up here. He'll bring the two of you in to see Dr. Nathan O'Rourke. He's our private doctor and he'll be able to keep any gargoyle details a secret. Hopefully your friend didn't see too much."

Courtney scrubbed her hands, wincing as the cleaner seeped into the cuts on her knuckles, while Renee wrapped Andrea's sliced fingers. After cleaning her hands, Courtney wiped off the dagger and examined it. The copper blade had natural green patina everywhere except the sharpened cutting surface that shimmered under the parking lot lights. The bone handle had what she assumed to be old Celtic designs carved into it. Warmth radiated from the knife as she studied it. Something was special about this dagger, but whatever it was eluded her.

"Courtney, did you hear me? We need you to unlock the car," Renee said, shaking her by the shoulder.

Courtney snapped back to reality and pulled the keys from her pocket. "Sorry."

Renee shoved Andrea into the passenger seat while Courtney took off her hoodie. She cut off part of a sleeve and wrapped the blade in it before tucking it into her waistband. The rest of the hoodie went in the fire.

Andrea woke up and asked Renee, "What's going on?"

"A gang member attacked you and Courtney. You're hurt, so Courtney is going to drive you to the hospital. We've got reports of more Brazo de Dios members incoming so we don't want to risk an ambulance crew until backup gets here," Renee said. Andrea tried to look past her, so she added, "Don't look; it's not a pretty sight. They set your car on fire."

Andrea started crying while Courtney walked to the driver's side of the Bentley. As she got in, Scott pulled into the lot next to her. She rolled the window down as he stepped out of the truck. He'd seemed taller seated at the bar.

"I'll meet you at the hospital in a little bit," he said. "There's more company coming so I'm gonna lend a hand here until Renee's backup arrives."

Courtney untucked the dagger and left it in her lap. Scott loaded his shotgun as the Bentley's window rose, and Courtney sighed watching the preparation for battle. She wanted to stay and fight, but Andrea needed help more. The throttle would have to bear the brunt of her anger instead of more gargoyles. She hammered the gas, stopping the window with it cracked open a hair.

"We'll get you patched up in no time, AB," she whispered to her friend.

"My head hurts so fucking bad."

"That thug had a pretty mean right hook. You went out like a light and hit your head on the ground, so you've probably got a concussion." Courtney stopped at the light by the parking lot exit.

"I just hit it on the window again with you playing Speed Racer. I've had one before. Remember the crash that left me needing glasses in the first place? This feels—" Andrea whined until a shotgun blast and several shots from a pistol interrupted.

Courtney fought the urge to return to the fight. The pained look on Andrea's battered face made her refocus on her mission. Courtney rolled the window completely shut to block the sounds of the parking lot battle. Despite the car's luxurious sound insulation, gunfire was still audible because of her heightened senses. "Maybe the radio'll block out the noise," Courtney muttered.

"You still hear stuff?" Andrea asked.

Courtney glanced over and shrugged as she fiddled with the volume. Though the classical music filling the cabin wasn't to her liking, it beat the cacophony of the battle she was running from. She'd not yet figured out how to change the station on the radio, and didn't want to risk setting off some secret weapon system hidden in the car while she had Andrea with her. Missiles might be hard to explain.

"I should've listened to you about the homeless guy. Did you kick his ass for me?" Andrea asked.

"Yeah, you could say that." Courtney accelerated away from the light when the green turn arrow appeared.

Andrea clutched the armrest. "What do you mean by that? You either whooped him or you didn't."

"I took his knife and kind of opened up his throat." Courtney hoped her excitement wasn't evident in her voice.

Andrea stayed silent for a few seconds. "I hope you don't get charged."

"Officer Nelson witnessed the whole thing before she made it over to us. She said she'd back me up if that happens, but she doubts it will. Brazo de Dios would be insane to try to do anything in court with their track record." Courtney knew nothing would come of the incident outside there being one less gargoyle in the world.

Andrea looked ahead. "I don't know why I'm trying to look at scenery late at night when I can't see and have a massive dizzy spell. I hope they find my glasses."

"I already found them."

"Well, hand them over, then. I hate feeling blind."

"I can't unless you want the piece of lens stuck in my shoulder."

"Can I have yours, or do you need them to drive?"

"Uh, yeah. You don't want me driving blind. Different prescriptions anyway." *Not that they'd do anything for you, since they're fake.*

Andrea slumped down further, sighing. "At least I've still got my old glasses at home as spares. It's gonna suck having to find a new best friend if Ivan kills you for bleeding on his seat."

"You're in the same boat as me with your fingers bleeding through the bandage. Maybe he'd buy a new car. Rich people are funny like that."

A large dark shape loomed in the road ahead.

Edthgar.

The extra UV headlights on this thing could come in handy right now if I knew how to fucking use them.

"Hold on," she yelled as she took evasive action. Courtney swerved the Bentley into the grass on the side of the opposite lane and missed the winged gargoyle by inches before sliding back into the proper lane, continuing toward the hospital.

"Fucking deer," Courtney lied. She checked the mirrors to see if they were being pursued. Nothing was there. Edthgar must have flown away since she escaped him.

"Now I know my head is fucked up. I could've sworn that looked like one of the ugly statues at the end of your driveway, just like the other night."

"At least your wild imagination is intact." *This lying hurts so much, especially since a gargoyle did this to her. Damn you, Ivan. How the fuck am I going to keep this up when it's so soul crushing?*

"I'm getting dizzier," Andrea complained.

"Hang on, we're almost there," Courtney said, pointing to the hospital sign ahead. "We're going to a private driveway to get you in quicker. Officer Nelson let a doctor friend of hers know we're coming."

Andrea moaned an incoherent response.

Courtney turned off the radio. Whatever Tchaikovsky tune played was beginning to annoy her. She needed to concentrate to find the proper driveway.

"I can't wait to have my car and music back," she grumbled as she passed the first driveway after the main entrance.

She spotted the hidden entrance and slammed on the brakes, barely making the turn. Andrea groaned in discomfort as the car bounced over a large bump. Courtney slid the car around an uphill turn. "Damn, no wonder rally racers use shitty little hatchbacks," she muttered as the driver's side mirror clipped a hanging branch.

At the top of the hill they pulled into a small paved lot riddled with cracks and bumps. The Bentley's headlights illuminated dirty streaked walls with faded white paint. The windowless building had one dim light over the wide, featureless gray door, and green backlighting on the buttons to a keypad beside it.

Courtney climbed on the brakes to stop the car. "I think we're here."

Andrea nodded for a moment but winced. She unbuckled the seat belt and spoke in a feeble voice. "This car might be uglier than yours, but at least it has real seat belts."

Courtney smirked and tucked the dagger back into her waistband as she exited the car. Andrea fainted again. Courtney darted around the front, then she realized she'd left the engine running. She started back to the door but stopped at the sound of wings beating overhead. A starlit shadow crossed the uneven parking space lines, and she swore as she inched towards the rear of the car.

Edthgar landed by the left front fender and stared through the glass at Andrea. He turned to look at Courtney, eyes glowing like brake lights. She reached for the UV light on her belt and grasped at a torn loop.

"Fuck me," she stammered. *Must've lost the light in the fight.*

Edthgar made a sound like a dry laugh and approached her. Her legs resembled Jell-O as she backed around the trunk. The winged gargoyle had her cornered with no UV light, no sword, and no way to fight back unless Scott arrived or the doctor came out with a gun. It wouldn't accomplish much, but she withdrew the dagger from her pocket.

At the sight of the dagger, Edthgar roared and charged. He knocked it from her hand and backhanded her, tossing her onto the trunk like a rag doll. The dagger bounced along the concrete and stopped a few yards behind the car while Courtney wiped blood from her lip.

She crawled onto the roof and stared at the enraged gargoyle, baring her teeth and raising her fists. Her aching jaw dropped when Edthgar went to retrieve the dagger.

Well, shit. Now I know there's something special about that knife.

Flames erupted from the car's exhaust and engulfed Edthgar. The winged gargoyle flailed in the inferno before taking off into the night sky, leaving a trail of fire in his wake. His horns glowed like molten glass.

Courtney blinked repeatedly, unable to believe her luck. She looked through the rear glass to see Andrea slumped over against the center console, which must have activated the flamethrower.

Courtney cackled and yelled at the sky, "What's the matter, shitstick? You don't want marshmallows and campfire stories?"

The flames died down and the engine sputtered, out of fuel from the flamethrower's thirst. Two dark streaks on the concrete extended back from the car's dual exhaust pipes, and small fires flickered as far as twenty feet behind the car where grass poked through the cracked pavement.

Courtney hopped down from the roof and walked over to the dagger. Somehow it was cool as she picked it up, despite how flames roared around it less than a minute ago. She didn't know what intrigued her so much about the dagger, but if Edthgar reacted this strongly to the sight of it, she had to have it. Her torn hoodie sleeve sat unburnt a few feet from the back of the car. She picked it up and wrapped it around the dagger before tucking it back into her waistband.

Courtney opened the front passenger door to fetch Andrea, listening as brakes screeched at the bottom of the driveway. "Come on, we need to get you in so the doctor can patch you up," she said, but Andrea was unconscious.

Scott pulled up next to the car as Courtney hauled Andrea out. "You need to lose a little weight," Courtney muttered since Andrea wouldn't hear.

"What's with the fires and that god-awful smell?" Scott asked as he hopped out of the truck.

"Barbecued gargoyle wings. The Bentley's flamethrower saved my ass when she fell on the buttons."

Scott helped Courtney lift Andrea. Courtney held her by the underarms while Scott held her legs as they headed towards the door. "Edthgar doesn't like playing with fire, eh? We'll have to remember that," Scott noted.

The trio arrived at the door. Scott set Andrea's feet down and pushed the intercom button at the top of the keypad. "Burrito," he said into the microphone under the speaker.

The door clicked and swung open.

"Renee must be hungry again. She always makes food passwords when she's hungry," said the doctor holding the door.

They dragged Andrea inside and lifted her onto a stretcher. Scott turned to the doctor. "Andrea doesn't know about the gargoyles. You'll have to transfer her out of our private section ASAP."

"Will do, after we've done a few tests and X-rays to see if she needs emergency surgery," the doctor said.

Two nurses took Andrea away and checked her vital signs en route to wherever their destination was. Courtney gave the doctor a concerned look.

"We'll take good care of her. Nurses Hooper and Meyers are the best I know, and we're privileged to have them as part of our group. Do you need anything? You look pretty rough yourself," the doctor said to her.

"I'll be fine, Doctor, uh, Mulder?" The doctor resembled the alien-seeking FBI agent of X-Files fame and wore no name tag.

The doctor chuckled and patted Courtney on the shoulder. "O'Rourke, actually, but I get the Mulder thing all the time. Please, call me Nathan. There's no need to be formal in our circle. Our waiting room is at the end of the hall to the left." He pointed.

"I'll let you know when she's transferred to a room in the main hospital. Don't contact her family until then, because if they arrive at the main entrance before she's transferred the receptionist won't know anything about her and things'll look suspicious." He walked off in the direction the nurses wheeled Andrea.

Scott put his hand on Courtney's shoulder. "Trust me, she'll be fine. He's the best doctor I've met, and I've wound up here several times. This private wing has all kinds of equipment other hospitals don't know exist yet. Ivan paid for this addition and everything in it. The few doctors and nurses in this section all used to work in his companies' labs or were vetted carefully by his security firm. Besides the small staff here, the rest of the hospital thinks this is storage for old equipment. Pretty cool having our own little private hospital, eh?"

"It would've been nice to get hospital care the night I was bitten," Courtney muttered, rubbing her injured shoulder and looking at the bleeding cut on her fingertip.

"Gargoyle venom acts fast, so there wasn't time to transport you. We had to get it out of your system right away. The quicker you puke, the better."

"Do you have pliers on you? Let's get this piece of glass out of my shoulder."

"Yeah, I've got a multitool," Scott said as the two wandered down the hall.

Art by Tony Paz (@tony.the.tainted on Instagram)

18

Something was after Andrea, but she didn't know what. She hadn't seen or heard it, but something was chasing her through the empty hospital halls. No one else was around, which disturbed her even more. Whatever was after her ensured she was alone—a plaything in its own personal playpen.

Andrea shuddered at the thought. It was chilly in the hospital too, and she only wore a paper gown. Thinking of her butt visible through the flapping gown led to worse thoughts about what kind of misdeeds her pursuer might have in mind if it caught her.

Lights flickered everywhere she looked, lending the hospital a post-apocalyptic feel beyond the lack of workers and stacks of supplies strewn haphazardly about the halls. The thing following her was a cunning foe, not some mindless zombie. Thinking of her pursuer as a creature scared her, but somehow she knew it was without seeing the thing. She had to be smart to avoid whatever was coming for her.

Andrea stopped running. Her feet slapping the dirty white linoleum and her labored breathing made it easier for the thing to track her. Stealth would be key if she hoped to escape. Besides, her hazy vision without glasses put her at risk of tripping over something she couldn't see and belly flopping in the hallway.

The hallway to her right was lit a bit brighter, so she headed there. Andrea tried doorknobs as she moved down the hall. All were locked. They had card slots to open them like a hotel. The hospital felt more unreal as she wandered further, glancing over her shoulder in case something emerged from the dark behind her.

At the end of the hall she turned right again. A couple of rooms lacked keypads, so she tried each door until she reached the last room on the left. The handle turned in her hand. Andrea exhaled as she pushed the door open. The door swung silently on its hinges and she stepped inside. It latched behind her without a sound.

"Gawd, what a relief," Andrea whispered as her fingers hunted for a light switch. The lights popped on to reveal an unoccupied recovery room. The bed was tightly made and something was written on the whiteboard under the high wall-mounted television.

She moved closer to the board to see what it said. *"Tem um faytham mo banrione."* It obviously wasn't English, but what language it might be escaped her. Spanish would make sense on a board, but it wasn't that either, leaving her with another mystery to ponder.

A small closet stood beside the whiteboard. She opened it and peered inside. A white lab coat hung on a hook. Andrea untied her gown and tossed it on the bed. Chills ran across her as she put on the coat. Something in the pocket bounced against her thigh. She pulled out a pack of cheap cigarettes, with a pink plastic lighter tucked into the plastic wrap.

Andrea buttoned up the lab coat. It wasn't much, but she felt better protected than in the silly gown. At least her butt was covered. "They're not Marlboros, but I guess they'll do," she said as she contemplated the cigarettes in her hand.

Andrea wandered into the bathroom and sat on the toilet. The fight in the parking lot denied her the chance to finish her after-work smoke, and if this creature was going to find her anyway because she couldn't find a way out, she might as well enjoy one last puff before whatever grisly fate awaited her. Three cigarettes remained in the pack after she removed one and stuck it between her lips.

As she brought the lighter up to her mouth, something roared in the hallway.

19

"Some of my nightmares were horrific. Whatever drugs they gave me were bad news. I'm glad they kept waking me every couple hours 'cause of the concussion," Andrea said to Courtney as they exited the hospital.

"I still can't believe your parents didn't come and visit. Petaluma isn't a long drive." Courtney held Andrea's arm to steady her.

Andrea shielded her eyes, so Courtney handed over her own sunglasses, pulling her fake glasses from her pocket and putting them on.

"Thanks. I understand them not coming. You said I'd be okay and was only being kept for observation. It's Monday morning. Dad's busy with his law firm and Mom doesn't drive. It's not like I was in danger of dying."

"Yeah, but your parents are the kind who care and you're their only child. I'd be there if I was them. Hell, even my shitty father would visit if I got mauled by a gang. Probably."

Andrea sighed. "Well, you're here for me. What are best friends for? That thug might've killed me if you hadn't been there. I'm glad the news changed the details for you."

"I didn't see the news. Sleep was way more important. I'm a bit sore but I was able to refuse treatment. All my shoulder needed was a band-aid."

Sleep hadn't happened because she'd spent the night crying in Luke's arms, concerned for Andrea despite Dr. O'Rourke's assurance. She'd waited until Andrea was transferred to a regular room to leave because it meant things really were fine. Her mind was too busy to pay attention to talking heads spouting news on TV.

Andrea filled her in as they stopped by the rear door of Hank's Blazer. "They said he fell on his own knife after one of your kicks. You were right about Officer Nelson having our backs. I'm just scared Brazo de Dios might come after me now, too."

Courtney opened the door for Andrea. "If they do, I'll kick the shit out of them. The Drake's Landing Police want them gone too, and this little feud's left the gang wide open. The doctor said the cops killed a few more gang members last night. Eventually Brazo de Dios will either give up, go to jail, or die."

Andrea scooted across the leather bench seat so Courtney could get in. "Easy, Killer. They might be horrible people, but they're still people," Andrea teased.

"You better not call me that all the time."

"Only when I want to annoy you."

"So yeah, all the time. Wonderful. You're going to make me regret saving you."

"Easy there, Killer," Hank said, looking in the rearview mirror at Courtney scowling in the back seat.

"Unc, you volunteered for 'Nam."

Hank got the Blazer moving as he said, "Yeah, but I've never tried to convince anyone I was right in the head."

Courtney had no response. Andrea giggled. "You really must have a lot on your mind. You've always got a comeback, even if they suck sometimes."

"So you were listening last night."

Andrea shrugged at Courtney's scowl until a yawn broke her expression.

Hank chimed in. "You know, despite her cold demeanor, she cried for you last night."

Courtney glared at the back of her uncle's head.

Andrea looked over at Courtney. "Really?"

Courtney nodded slowly, sighed, and said, "I told you I've been thinking worst-case scenario lately. The doc said there was a chance you could have a some-fancy-word hematoma and have to be placed in a coma. I couldn't take the thought of you as a vegetable because of those Brazo de Dios asshats."

She looked at Andrea's bruised face, scraped forehead and cheek, and her quivering lip. Courtney teared up again, but she fought them back.

"I'm touched," Andrea said, voice wavering. "I'm glad you're my best friend." Tears started to roll down her face.

"Fuck," Courtney muttered as she looked away. She glanced back to Andrea with her own cheeks growing wetter. "If you tell anyone I cried, I'll send you right back to the hospital."

"I'll bet you would've cried if you hit that deer in Ivan's car," Andrea said.

Courtney took off her glasses, wiped her eyes, and changed the subject. "I'm sure Unc doesn't want to watch a cryfest, so let's talk about something else. You're going to need care to make sure you don't slip into a coma while you sleep."

"Yeah, but my insurance won't cover a visiting nurse. I'm gonna have to risk it."

"What Courtney is getting at is we're offering you a place to stay so you won't be alone," Hank said. "She told me about the uneven steps in your apartment and how bad they'd be for someone in your condition. I watched your wobbly walking through the parking lot and I agree. You'll be prone to dizzy spells and poor balance for a few weeks, which is a bad combination for someone alone in a cheap, poorly maintained apartment."

Courtney added, "We'd be able to get you to doctor's appointments easier since we wouldn't have to go to your place to pick you up."

"And since I don't have a car anymore," Andrea complained as they drove past where crime scene tape flapped around the burned shell of her Miata. She shivered. "We're parking in a different spot when I'm cleared to go back to work."

Courtney nodded. "So you'll stay with us?"

"Let me think about it. I wanna talk to Chris first. He's probably still sleeping after his double shift and hasn't heard. Somebody's gotta take care of my plants if I stay with you."

"No problem. We want you to do whatever you feel most comfortable doing," Hank said.

"Even if that's weaseling your way into moving in with Chris, speedy," Courtney said.

Andrea giggled, grimaced, and rubbed her forehead. "You guys feel more like family than my family."

"Well, yeah, we care enough to see you when you're in the hospital."

"I just had a thought. If I wound up a vegetable, would that make me a cannibal?"

"Don't strain your poor scrambled little brain there, silly," Courtney said, tapping Andrea's shoulder.

Andrea put her hand over Courtney's, and as they looked at each other's faces, Andrea sighed, fresh tears glistening in the corners of her eyes.

"Oh fuck, not this shit again," Courtney said as she looked away.

Hank cleared his throat over Courtney's language.

"Stuff it, Unc. I got under two hours of sleep after killing someone. I don't have the mental energy to dance around swearing."

Hank laughed, but the rest of the drive passed in silence as Courtney avoided getting emotional again. When they approached the Mays mansion driveway, Andrea broke the silence.

"Those statues seem extra creepy today. I could've sworn one was in the road last night, but I know it couldn't be. It's just the concussion affecting my brain. Still, one of them was after me in my nightmares. It was chasing me through the hospital."

Courtney answered, "No, you're right. Gargoyles are real and they're trying to kill me."

Hank's hands tightened on the wheel as he slowed for the driveway.

Andrea giggled. "Luke is rubbing off on you. You said that with such a straight face I almost thought you were serious."

Hank held his breath until Courtney finished. "Yeah, great joke. Want to hear another? Ivan is immortal. He's over a hundred years old."

Andrea laughed and took off the sunglasses again to wipe her eyes. "You've got me crying again," she said, still giggling as she put the glasses back on.

Hank breathed easier as he stopped the Blazer by the entrance. "I'm going to discuss accommodations with you, should you decide to stay with us for your recovery. Courtney has to speak with Ivan for a moment," he said to Andrea.

"Okay. Did you know this would be the perfect setting for my Halloween party?" Andrea asked Hank as everyone got out of the vehicle.

"Absolutely not," Hank said.

"I'll be in shortly," Courtney said to Andrea. She wandered over to Ivan polishing the Bentley's grill.

"I can tell you wish to partake in some serious advice," Ivan said, draping the chamois around the hood ornament.

"I know you told me to keep Andrea out of the loop with gargoyles, but I think she needs to know. It'd do her more harm than good being kept in the dark at this point. I mean, one sent her to the hospital and she saw Edthgar. She's in denial, but I think she knows what she saw and it's going to drive her nuts if we keep telling her she's imagining things."

Ivan nodded. "You know her better than anyone else in our group. I clung to the hope we would not reach this crossroads, but that was folly. Your uncle and I discussed this before you awakened this morning. We agreed it would be best for you to make the call."

"Will you back me up?"

"Of course. We strongly believe you can make a better decision regarding Andrea than we can. We should do it straight away. Petr arrived early this morning and we have not had the opportunity to glean whatever information he has for us yet due to last night's attack."

Courtney swallowed hard. "Okay, let's do this."

They walked up to the house. On their way to the landing, Ivan paused and looked down at his trembling hand. "Would you believe this has me more nervous than anything prior to the fall of Mephallo?" he whispered.

"Considering your first meetings with her, hell yeah. I'd believe you if you said you've never been this nervous before." Courtney opened the front door.

"I do not think anything in this world could rival the nerves I had proposing to Anatalia."

"Good point."

Hank and Andrea sat in the great room. Ivan whispered in Hank's ear as Courtney dropped on the couch beside Andrea.

"I'll be up in my office when you're ready. Courtney has something important to talk about with you," Hank said as he exited.

"If she's going to talk about important stuff could we have some privacy maybe?" Andrea said to Ivan.

"It's okay. He's part of the important stuff," Courtney said.

"It is quite all right; you may have your privacy," Ivan said to Andrea. He turned to Courtney. "I will be in the kitchen when you need me."

Ivan departed and Andrea said, "Okay, I've got stuff I have to get off my mind first. I'm worried I'm losing my mind."

"You did that when we were in diapers. Remember, you wanted to be friends with me."

Andrea rolled her eyes. "I mean it. I've seen things I know I can't be seeing lately, really weird things."

"What kind of weird things?" Courtney asked, hoping Andrea would bring up the gargoyles so she didn't have to.

"I don't know. Would you still be friends with me if I was a crazy bitch?"

"Of course," Courtney said. "What did we talk about at the end of the driveway?"

"You're gonna make me think hard? I'm not supposed to with my concussion. Gawd, I have trouble thinking when I'm not a walking scrambled egg that didn't crack."

"The statues. What did we talk about after the statues?"

"Um, my nightmares from last night? Then there was the joke."

"It wasn't a joke."

"But you said it was."

"The gargoyles are real. The creepy homeless guy? Gargoyle in disguise. You saw a winged gargoyle in the road, not a deer. Brazo de Dios didn't send you to the hospital, a gargoyle did. You're hurt because they're after me. It's my fault," Courtney said, meeting Andrea's worried gaze.

"That—that just can't be. It can't."

"It is." Courtney pulled up her shirt to show her healed ribs. She took off her fake glasses and handed them to Andrea.

Andrea stared through the plain glass lenses and poked Courtney's side. She blinked repeatedly, her jaw hanging open.

"But, but, I saw the bruise a couple nights ago. I saw you break them on the stairs. These glasses are fake. Just—how?"

"The night before the fire at Luke's apartment, I absorbed gargoyle blood. Ivan killed one in the kitchen and I stumbled into the blood puddle. Their blood affects a lot of things. I've got enhanced senses, I'm stronger, I'm faster, and I heal faster. Enhanced senses means my vision is perfect now and those glasses are to keep up the illusion of the old normal me. Since I absorbed their blood, they're after me. Brazo de Dios isn't, but they're a good cover for the police to use to hide the gargoyles' existence."

"You're serious. You're really serious."

"That's why I need the sword, to kill monsters to protect myself and others, like you."

"And you didn't tell me?" Andrea said, sniffling again as she handed Courtney the fake glasses.

"You may place the blame on me. I instructed her to tell no one, as I now tell you," Ivan said from the doorway. "The existence of the gargoyles and other unsavory creatures that befoul our realm must remain a secret to the general public to avoid mass hysteria. The police are well aware of their presence and are involved in the cover-up, as are all governments of the world who have reason to be aware of the existence of the gargoyles. All agencies and governments feel it is in the best interest of public safety to keep the gargoyles secret and fight a small-scale shadow war against them."

Andrea looked to Courtney but pointed at Ivan. "You must've been joking about the immortality thing, right?"

Ivan unbuttoned his crisp white shirt and held up a kitchen knife. He ran the knife across his chest. Blood poured from the cut, then receded back into the wound. The cut sealed as the last drops sucked back in. "I was born in Saint Petersburg on July seventeenth of the year 1908. I have not aged since

I acquired this magical ring before the Great Patriotic War, known to you as World War II." Ivan pointed to the ruby ring on his finger.

Andrea stared in silence. Finally, she said, "You're the only hundred-something guy I wanna see without a shirt. You should skip it more often."

Ivan's fingers moved at light speed to button the shirt back up. He cleared his throat and said to Courtney, "Had I foreseen this awkwardness I would have had you run me through again."

"So, um, what am I going to have to do?" asked Andrea. "Am I going to have to kill monsters? I'm not sure I can. Peace and love are more my thing."

"No, you didn't absorb any blood. I kept you away from the puddles. Just be watchful and keep the secret," Courtney said.

"Thank goodness," Andrea sighed.

"There may still be a threat to your safety, one more reason we all believe you should stay here through your recovery," Ivan suggested.

"How well defended is this place? I mean, Courtney said you killed one in the kitchen. How'd it get in?" Andrea asked.

"I let it in so I could kill it," Ivan answered.

Andrea gaped at Ivan's calm explanation.

"Come up to Unc's office. I'll keep you steady up the stairs and we'll show you the secrets of the house," Courtney said, standing and holding out her hand for Andrea.

Andrea took her hand and they followed Ivan up to the third floor. She wobbled, but Courtney steadied her as promised.

Damn, listen to her heart race. Reminds me of how scared I was that first night. "Don't worry, nothing is going to jump out at you. I think." Courtney winked.

"You think?" Andrea squeaked.

Ivan opened the door and Courtney led Andrea inside. Andrea squeezed her hand tightly as she looked at the arsenal on display. "All these guns and you chose a sword? I thought I'd lost my shit," Andrea teased.

"Have you ever seen a samurai with a gun?"

"No, because they're all dead."

"Did Bruce Lee use guns?"

"He's dead, too."

"Fine, I'll admit it. I can't hit shit. I'm a lousy shot."

Andrea pointed to the central table. "When did you get a second cat?"

Petr was curled up on the table, taking a nap.

"That's no cat, it's a gremlin. His name is Petr. You won't get much out of a conversation with him though; he doesn't speak English."

Andrea moved closer for a better look. "I can't wait to go to my place and get my spare glasses so I can see. He's a cute little guy."

"You haven't seen his claws and teeth yet," Courtney said.

Ivan whispered to Petr and gently tapped his shoulder. Petr lifted his head, blinking rapidly and twitching his ears. He looked around until his gaze fixed on Andrea.

Hank walked over from the monster-tracking computer. "Go ahead and introduce yourself."

Andrea stepped up to the table and held out her trembling hand. "Hi, I'm Andrea."

Petr placed his hand in hers, looked her in the eyes, and said, "Petr Timur."

She gently shook the gremlin's hand. "You're an adorable little guy."

Ivan translated for him. Petr smiled, ensuring she saw his wicked teeth.

"Okay, so maybe adorable isn't the right word," she squeaked.

Hank laughed and led her over to the computer. "This system tracks monsters. It's daylight, so you won't see anything other than white dots. Those are people who have absorbed gargoyle blood. There's no new ones, so we know you're safe. The radar has a few blind spots, but anywhere you go is covered," he explained.

"What's the purple dot? Is that Petr?" Andrea asked.

"No, that's Ivan. Purple dots signify undead creatures, but for some reason the system reads him that way. Gremlins don't register because they're too small," Hank answered.

He picked up a couple UV lights from beside the computer and handed one to Courtney. "Ivan scrounged up a couple more lights from his lab's warehouse this morning since Renee found your old one burned up under Andrea's car. Try not to lose this one."

He turned to Andrea and handed her the other light. "This looks like an ordinary keychain light, but it's not. It gives off a special UV light humans can't see. It blinds gargoyles temporarily."

Andrea looked to Courtney. "So that's why your light looked like it didn't work when we got locked out."

"Yeah. I used it to drive away a gargoyle, not a deer. I didn't need light to see either, since my vision is enhanced by the gargoyle blood. I see just as well at night as in daylight," Courtney explained.

"So, what should we show your friend next to convince her she will be safe here?" Ivan asked Courtney.

"The tunnels?"

"I'm convinced. Just tell me about the tunnels; I don't need to see them," Andrea said.

"There is a network of tunnels beneath the town. The entrance from this mansion is hidden by the pool table, and there are other entrances in the library, my lab, and my warehouses. If a situation grows too dire we can hide out until daybreak. The gargoyles will always leave before sunrise. As fearsome as they may seem to you, they are afraid of the public knowing of their existence because they believe humanity will band together and exterminate them," Ivan told her.

"So why don't we just let the public know so that can happen?" Andrea questioned.

"Many innocent people would be unnecessarily slaughtered by the gargoyles. Keeping everything under wraps ensures only those waging the war are put at risk."

"Okay, this is unrelated, but I kinda want to see this fancy Bugazzi thing Court bragged about the other day," Andrea said.

"Ah, the Bugatti. That can be arranged. Follow me." Ivan led Andrea and Courtney back into the hall while Hank stayed at the computer. Courtney again steadied Andrea as the trio descended.

As they approached the door to the shop, Ivan said, "The garage is also heavily reinforced in the event we are unable to get to the tunnels or an earthquake renders them unusable. It is fireproof and can be sealed completely. As such, the cabinet with the welding tanks in it has a hidden compartment containing oxygen tanks so we may survive here overnight if necessary."

"How do you know so much about this house when you've only been here for about a month? Did her uncle tell you every detail about it when you arrived?" Andrea asked.

"I designed the house. All of the security features were handled by one of my companies, Volkodav Securities," Ivan said.

"Oh. I always thought her uncle was the one with weird taste."

"He had input on the styling. He is quite fond of Victorian architecture, yet also thought a stone fortress would be nice due to the nature of the building. We combined the two styles and I added the onion dome atop the tower. The dome hides the special antennae and sensors needed to work the detector," Ivan explained.

"So that's what interferes with electronics."

"Precisely," Ivan said as they entered the garage. "It is also why I gave Luke and Courtney special smartphones that resist most forms of interference." He pointed to his car. "This is the 1930 Bugatti Type 37 Courtney spoke of, and I have owned it since it was new."

"It's gorgeous. I love how you've kept it original." Andrea walked over to the car.

Courtney rolled her eyes, remembering her comment about it needing restoration. Ivan smiled and placed his hand on the dented fender. "Yes, the dents and scratches tell the history of this automobile, and it would be shameful to discard that history." He rubbed the fender. "We should all be proud of our scars, because they tell the story of how we became who we are and what we overcame."

Andrea looked down at her bandaged hand and felt the scrape on her forehead with the other. She nodded and turned to Courtney. "I understand now why you said it was priceless."

"I would offer you the opportunity to sit in it for a moment, but as you can see, it has no doors and the raised sides may be difficult for you to step over with your current balance woes. Perhaps another time."

"I'd like that," Andrea said.

"Now, let us return to the great room. We have much to discuss regarding your arrangements here during your recovery and about monsters in general so you can feel safe with the knowledge of how we fight them. I also need to speak with Petr to see what information he has for us today."

Ivan glanced back at the Bugatti, then to Andrea. Courtney saw the faintest trace of a smile form, but he quickly wiped it away. She muffled a snicker as she shut the door to the garage behind them.

20

Andrea found herself wandering through the halls in the lab coat at the empty hospital again. This time she knew she was dreaming and what she was up against. She scoured every room she could get into, seeking anything useful.

Hallways and empty rooms formed an endless labyrinth beyond the size of the real hospital. She eventually reached a hall ending in a door instead of yet another hallway. Debris was strewn throughout. She carefully stepped around hazards as she tried doors lining the hall. The gargoyle roars all sounded distant, so she didn't need to hurry yet.

Something drew her to one room. She stared at the door. Nothing seemed different from any of the other rooms, yet she felt it would be another story behind the door. A box of unopened syringes lay on its side in the hall, its contents spilled across the doorway.

I'm not risking stepping on needles. Nope nope nope.

As she knelt to push aside the needles, a shadow moved across the light visible beneath the door. She gasped and fell backwards, scooting away from the door.

"Hello?" came from inside the room. Andrea recognized the soft voice as her coworker, Lizzie, but something was a bit unreal about it.

Andrea stood and brushed off her rear end. She reached for the doorknob, but it rattled in her hand and wouldn't open.

"Who goes there?" said a nasal male voice. It must be Courtney's father. He was a doctor, but in San Francisco, not this hospital. The hairs on the back of her neck stood on end. Hollister Mays gave her a bad case of the creeps from the word go, with the odd looks he always gave her when he thought she wasn't looking.

"Tem um faytham mo banrione," said a gravelly inhuman voice, behind the door but also echoing in her head. Edthgar. It had to be the voice of the winged gargoyle.

The light under the door changed to glowing red and oozed farther out into the hall. Andrea felt a slight burning sensation as it spilled over her toes. She backed up and moved out of the light. As soon as she moved, the doorknob rattled, and smoke wafted out from under the gap. A large shadow blocked part of the light, and as something bumped the door, she swallowed hard and smacked into another door behind her.

Edthgar roared inside the room and pounded on the door, sending Andrea into a run. Her feet slapped against the dingy linoleum as she dodged or jumped over debris, but she didn't look back as she focused on avoiding the junk on the floor. She ignored all doors except the one at the end of the hall, hoping it wasn't locked.

Andrea's left foot caught on an overturned computer cart as she leapt, slamming her into the floor. She slid a few feet on the linoleum and something sliced into her right arm. Her foot throbbed, and she surmised a couple of toes broke, but there was no time to cry about it.

The copper-bladed dagger Courtney showed her earlier lay a few feet back with Andrea's blood on the blade. It wasn't much against a gargoyle, but better than nothing. She tucked it into the coat pocket and half-hobbled, half-ran the rest of the way to the door.

"Gawd yes!" she cried as the knob turned.

The door swung open, revealing a stairwell. Andrea descended the stairs as quickly as her injured foot allowed and cursed the fact none of the rooms she'd been able to check had anything of value in them, like shoes that fit.

The door at the bottom hung open on damaged hinges. Andrea stopped and listened, afraid the gargoyles might spring a trap for her. Silence waited beyond the doorway, so she moved through with the dagger in front of her, stepping over a smashed printer on the carpeted floor.

She limped past a row of cubicles to the reception desk. A vase with wilted roses sat on the counter, but the pistol next to it interested her more. Even though Andrea knew she was in another nightmare, firepower couldn't hurt anything.

Her fingers reached for the pistol as a chill ran across her bare legs. "What the hell?"

Past the flickering computer monitors a window was cracked open, and beyond the window, flurries drifted around pine trees to the snow-covered ground. Andrea had never seen real snow in her life, and stood watching it until a crash sounded a couple of floors above her.

She grabbed the pistol; since it had some heft to it she knew it was loaded. Her eyes drifted back to the falling snow, and goosebumps rose on her arms from the cold air. *Gawd, I hope I can find something warm before the gargoyles come down here.*

Andrea crawled over the counter and into the chair to check what might be left behind the desk. She stuffed three clips of pistol ammunition into the lab coat pockets as she searched around the computer. A bag hung on the back of the chair. Inside she found a dress, a pair of high heels, a key, and a note.

"Dearest Michelle, here is the key to room nine at the Bay Walk Motel. Meet me there at seven in this outfit, and we'll have a great time that's very against company policy for coworkers. Yours, Nathan," she read aloud. Andrea giggled, remembering her doctor introducing himself as Nathan O'Rourke.

She pulled the white dress out of the bag and checked the size. It'd be a tight fit, but she took off the lab coat and squeezed into it. If she had to go outside at least she'd have another layer of clothing.

The red heels had a wide enclosed toe, and she grinned until she saw the size tag. Andrea sighed and stuffed them back in the bag with the key and note. There were other cubicles to search, so hopefully someone who'd abandoned this horrible dream hospital left winter boots behind that might fit.

Another crash sounded above. She swore under her breath and put the lab coat back on, then limped to the next cubicle to continue her search.

Grunts from the stairwell put an end to that. She ran as best as she could out into the lobby with the pistol drawn and ready. Two doors stood to either side before the exit, but as she tried the handles she swore—both were locked. Her only escape was out the main entrance into the snow.

The gargoyles scoured the cubicles for signs of her presence, throwing computers and chairs around in their search. Andrea moved to the sliding doors. One of the gargoyles entered the lobby and pointed a black claw in her direction. Its toothy maw opened to roar.

"Leave me alone!" she howled as she fired the pistol.

One of her three shots careened into the open mouth and spread gargoyle brains across the off-white wall behind it. Andrea turned and ran for the door, ready to shoot the glass if these doors also turned out to be locked.

The doors silently slid open and she ran out into the snow. Her injured foot throbbed and she winced with every step crunching through calf-deep snow, but escape was more important than pain. What did the gargoyles want with her? She didn't want to find out. Andrea kept running towards the trees. It was a nightmare and the cold wouldn't hurt for real, but maybe the gargoyles could.

She stopped by a pine tree and turned to see if her pursuers were close. Her jaw dropped. The hospital was gone, and no gargoyles approached behind her. An ice-covered lake and mountains loomed in the distance. A castle stood nestled between a couple of mountains.

"Whoa. I'm definitely not in California anymore."

Despite the cold, she couldn't help but look around and marvel at the gently falling flakes and undisturbed snow around her. The only prints were hers; they appeared out of nowhere in the middle of the clearing. She wished for boots again, or anything more than the light dress and lab coat, but it didn't really matter. It was a dream, after all.

"Dream or not, I need warmth. Hopefully there's enough fluid in the lighter to make a fire so I'm not dreaming about frostbitten toes," she said to the trees in front of her.

The snow acted like an ice pack on her injured foot and the pain faded some. It still hurt, so she knew it hadn't gone numb. *It won't take long to get numb if I don't find warmth soon, though.*

After several minutes of trudging through ankle-high snow, Andrea found a small dead tree. She stopped next to it and reached for the dagger in her pocket. A sudden feeling of warmth moved up her arm and throughout her body as her fingers wrapped the handle. Courtney told her the dagger seemed to possess odd energy, but this was unexpected.

The snow melted at her feet, revealing brown pine needles underfoot, and the air warmed around her. Andrea held the dagger in front of her as sparks danced across it. The green patina flaked away from the blade.

Whoa, gnarly.

Andrea abandoned the small tree and turned to make the long walk up to the castle. Her hand stayed on the dagger as she tucked it back in her pocket, afraid if she let go her warmth would disappear. *I guess I can handle a barefoot walk in the forest if I'm warm.*

She stopped before the edge of the tree line. A pack of wolves blocked her path. One large black wolf, presumably the alpha male, stared with golden eyes. It wasn't a threatening stare; the wolf seemed more curious. It trotted over to her, maintaining eye contact. She held the dagger but kept it concealed, just in case she was misreading the wolf's intent. Her other hand grasped the pistol.

The wolf sat in front of her and continued to look deep into her eyes. Its gaze conveyed intelligence and a sense of security. Andrea gulped, then let go of the pistol and held out her hand for the wolf to sniff. It made a chuffing sound and licked her hand, then turned to the pack. They howled simultaneously before vanishing into thin air.

She ruffled the black wolf's ears and said, "I guess it's just you and me until I wake up."

Andrea took a step towards the castle, but the wolf held fast in front of her, blocking her. A rumbling growl emanated from the wolf as it looked at the castle. It looked deeper into the forest and back to her again, then chuffed.

"The castle is my best shot at finding people and getting warm without having to hold a damn dagger all the time," Andrea said to the wolf.

It shook its head like a person and pointed its snout back to the forest. The wolf walked off in that direction, then stopped a few yards away and looked back at her.

Andrea limped over. "If you insist."

The wolf moved deeper into the forest and Andrea followed. They weaved their way through the trees, which grew denser as they proceeded further. In some spots she had to crawl under pine branches to follow the wolf.

A red spot appeared on her coat's right sleeve. The rush to escape the hospital prevented her from attending to her wound, and blood seeped through the fabric. "Stop for a second."

The wolf obeyed and sat next to her as she leaned against a tree trunk. She took off the coat to examine her arm. The cut didn't look bad, and the bleeding had already stopped. Her tattoo was missing; Andrea discounted it as another oddity in a dream packed with strangeness. Aside from the initial shock of seeing blood, there wasn't anything worth worrying about.

She put the coat back on. "I'm okay, lead the way."

The wolf understood and resumed the journey, stopping sometimes to see if she still followed.

"Will you be here for me in the next weird nightmare?" Andrea asked as a pine cone dented her knee, but the wolf didn't answer. She scolded herself for expecting it to.

A clearing came into view, filling her with relief at the thought of standing again. Crawling through fallen pine needles was almost as unpleasant for her bare legs as walking through snow had been before she'd discovered the dagger's warming energy. Her legs were likely scraped to match her forehead from the parking lot battle.

The wolf waited at the edge of the clearing beside her while she brushed snow and dirt off her legs. There were a few scratches on both, but nothing deep enough to bleed. Her foot swelled, though the pain dulled.

Her furry friend nuzzled her hand and chuffed. Once the wolf had her attention it turned to look across the clearing. His snout pointed toward what she thought might be a cabin, but the snow came down harder than before and a breeze picked up. The blowing snow impaired her already poor vision.

"Cabin?" she asked the wolf.

She received a chuff in response.

"Are we headed there?"

The wolf chuffed again in the affirmative and sauntered through the deeper snow to the cabin. The wind picked up more, blowing snowflakes into Andrea's face and further hindering her vision. "I'm glad you're black, 'cause it'd be hard to see you otherwise," she said, shielding her eyes as tiny bits of ice joined the snowflakes smashing against her face.

The cabin became clearer as they approached, and once they were close the log structure blocked the snow so she could see better again. She stopped at the door and looked to the wolf. "Should I knock?"

The wolf shook its head and howled.

As the door to the cabin opened, so did her eyes. She looked up to see Luke shaking her awake.

"One of your cuts opened up." He pointed to her left arm. "I'll be back with some gauze and tape."

Andrea looked down as Luke exited the guest room. The cut from her dream greeted her, but on the opposite arm. Her tattoo was still there on the other shoulder, exposed by the tank top she wore since she'd planned just a quick nap on the guest bed.

Andrea threw aside the light blanket, grabbed her glasses, and pulled up the legs of her Hello Kitty pajama bottoms. Sure enough, the scratches were there. Her left foot looked fine, but then she thought of her dagger cut being on the opposite arm. She checked, and her right foot had bruising. Wiggling her toes shot pain through them. She stared for a moment in disbelief. It was a dream. How did wounds follow to the real world?

The medicine cabinet door shut in the bathroom, so Andrea covered her foot with the blanket. A chill ran down her spine as she thought of some of the close calls from her nightmares. How lucky she'd been to escape the gargoyles mostly uninjured. What kind of magic spell did the gargoyles use to allow her to receive real wounds from her nightmares, and why? Was it to get at Courtney? If a ring imbued with winged gargoyle blood could grant immortality, surely other sorcery existed. She needed to ask Ivan.

Luke walked back into the room with bandages. Andrea asked in a voice more frantic than she'd hoped, "Where are Ivan and Courtney?"

"They left a bit ago for a hunt. Why?"

"I need to ask something, that's all." She rubbed her eyes. "Maybe you could grab me some coffee so I can stay awake until they get back."

"Is something wrong?"

"Just nightmares. Thanks for waking me up. Plus the concussion, you know."

Luke nodded as he put the band-aid in place. "I get it. The gargoyles are damn terrifying," he said as he patted her shoulder. "Do you need anything else while you're awake?"

She shook her head. "I'd better pee, but you can go back to whatever you were doing. After coffee. Gawd, that nightmare was a bad one. No wonder I opened the cut. I must've been thrashing in my sleep."

"Yeah, I heard you say something about a wolf on my way by the room, and your voice was kind of strained so I came to check and found the cut. Hopefully they won't be out too long. Hang in there," Luke said as he left the guest room.

Andrea hobbled to the door, watching Luke go up the stairs. Once he was out of sight, Andrea hopped to the bathroom. She shoved her sweatpants down and stepped out of them. Her eyes followed the scratches on her knees and shins down to her foot, where the bruise looked clearer under the light.

"Bee happy." She snorted at the tattoo on her right ankle. "Gawd, how when I don't know what's going on? Were gargoyles really there? Could they have killed me?"

She took off her glasses, buried her face in her hands, and sobbed. "Please hurry home, Courtney."

21

Ivan parked between two large rock formations hidden from the roadway and coastal walking paths. Scott and Renee parked behind the Bentley. Mendoza pulled in last, blocking any chance of the other vehicles being seen with his Volkswagen Bus, its surfboard on top.

Courtney got out of the car. None of the members of the hunting party knew what to expect, since they were entering a rocky coastal area with intermittent radar coverage. Their only information was word from Petr about gargoyle concerns over an odd creature in the area. Everyone in the group stayed quiet and cautious.

"There's a veteran who lives near here we could ask about anything strange. He's a bit of a hermit since his fiancé disappeared," Renee suggested.

"I would be wary of a hermit with a missing fiancé. However, you should have mentioned that before we brought so much firepower. I would not wish to bring unnecessary attention to our efforts," Ivan said, aiming his thumb at Mendoza.

Courtney gaped at the big machine gun Mendoza carried, the giant ax on his back, and the bandages around one of his hands while Renee protested. "I did the investigation on Paolo myself. The guy was hiding something, but I felt him trustworthy otherwise. I told you about him before, how I thought the gargoyles might be involved in the case, but we couldn't find any evidence. He might know about our fight."

Ivan didn't acknowledge Renee's statement, watching Courtney and Mendoza instead.

Mendoza laughed. "Don't worry, kid. This M-60 is what I'm used to from my time in the Corps. I ain't a marksman; I spray and pray. Oh, and the band-aid is from a feisty pregnant feral cat someone brought to my vet practice."

Courtney nodded and looked back to Ivan as he opened the car door for Petr.

"Watch for any sign of a creature," Ivan said. "All we know is it is not a lycanthrope due to the new moon and it is not a gargoyle since they are wary of it. This could be something none of us have seen before and know nothing about how to kill, so stay close and be ready to retreat with haste. If you have locked your vehicle, unlock it now. The few seconds unlocking it could be life or death if we are overmatched. Petr has keener senses than ours, so he shall lead the way." Ivan secured a drum magazine to the top of his own large machine gun.

Courtney stared at the gun; its massive barrel and crude handmade wooden side grip intrigued her. She felt the pistol at her hip and thought it inadequate. *Hopefully whatever this is, it's vulnerable to my sword. Fuck bullets.*

Ivan followed Petr through a gap in the rocks tight enough to force the group to move sideways. Courtney went next, followed by Scott and Ray. Mendoza brought up the rear, his chest against one side while his ax scraped the rock at his back. The tight opening caused a Venturi effect, amplifying the sea breeze into a chilling wind, giving Courtney goosebumps.

The group emerged from the rocks at the edge of a secluded beach. Low fog rolled through the tall grass, obscuring all but the tips of Petr's ears. Ivan motioned everyone to keep low to take advantage of the cover. Petr moved slowly so the crouching party could keep up.

They stopped before reaching the crest of a dune. Courtney welcomed the break to focus on the ocean scent. The whispering breeze and the feel of fine beach sand beneath her palm made her reminisce about the last time she lounged on the beach with Andrea; she longed for another day like it. Her mind drifted back to when she was eight and nearly drowned after a jellyfish sting. She hadn't been swimming since, aside from her fall into the blood pit in the tunnels, but the Pacific still relaxed her and she couldn't imagine life away from it.

Painful thoughts of the sting and water filling her lungs forced her mind back to the present. Another scent crept into her nose, masked by the salty ocean smell. She couldn't place the scent, but found her eyes drawn to a pile of large rocks propped against the face of a cliff at the water's edge. Something seemed off about their positioning. Almost unnatural.

Geology was for dusty schoolbooks and dorks, not monster hunting. She dismissed the rocks and looked to Petr.

The gremlin's ears twitched as he whispered to Ivan, but she couldn't make out any words. Ivan nodded to the trembling gremlin and turned to the group. "Courtney, ready your sword. Two gargoyles approach. We will deal with them swiftly and silently. Lay down in the fog until they are nearly upon us."

She drew the sword and lay on her belly. "How do we know they'll come to us?"

"Did you not notice the prints in the sand all around? This is a well-patrolled path."

Courtney looked closer at the obscured dune. There were prints all right, but they were nearly imperceptible. Anyone with normal vision wouldn't see them, especially through the rolling fog.

The fog presented issues for her superior vision as well. She couldn't see more than a dark shape where Ivan lay. Her other senses would have to guide her until the fight began.

Courtney closed her eyes and focused on the wind. The wind itself didn't interest her, nor did the light rustling of the tall grass. Other sounds disrupting the peaceful breeze concerned her. As her focus tightened, so did her fingers around the handle of her sword.

Her heart hastened at a few grunts. Gargoyles, no doubt. Once this patrol was dealt with, the group could return to the unknown creature's trail. Courtney couldn't wait. Her lips curled into a grin at the idea of being the hunter for a change instead of defending herself.

She readied to pounce.

A fishy stench distracted her, thick with iodine, forcing itself up her nostrils, blocking out the smell of the approaching gargoyles. It had to be what concerned them. She frowned at the stink.

The distraction almost made her miss Ivan lunging at the first gargoyle. The second stopped as its partner fell. Courtney took full advantage, jumping up and swinging her sword into the gargoyle's throat. The blade stuck in its vertebrae for a moment. It took a couple of tugs to jerk it free. As the gargoyle dropped to its knees, another devious smile crossed Courtney's face. The dying beast covered its wound with one hand and reached out with the other as if begging for help. Courtney laughed as she lopped its hand off, then spun behind the gargoyle and slammed the sword through the back of its neck.

The severed head flopped upside down in the sand by Scott.

"Gotta admire that. He's keeping his chin up despite his loss," Courtney quipped.

Scott shook his head and stood, kicking the gargoyle head aside. "Any idea yet what we're after?" he asked Ivan.

Ivan wiped his blade on the fallen gargoyle's body and sheathed it. He raised the machine gun before answering. "We are here to discover if we need to cleanse our realm of another monster. These two gargoyles were simply a bonus."

Ivan whispered to Petr in Russian, who nodded and crept over the dune.

Courtney glanced between Mendoza and Ivan's guns again as she wiped her sword clean. Her fingers rubbed the pistol at her side and her confidence faded. She understood Mendoza's reasoning for a big gun, but what kind of creature did Ivan suspect to warrant his own? Might it be some sort of giant snapping turtle with an impregnable shell? A walking shark man? Maybe it was similar to one of the lobstrosity things Luke mentioned from the Stephen King book he was in the middle of reading. Her enthusiasm about meeting the mystery creature washed away thanks to those two big machine guns.

Scott leaned over. "Yeah, those guns make even my 12 gauge look like a pop gun. Try not to think on it too much; just focus on the gremlin."

Ivan heard them. "This weapon is intimidating? It is a Lewis gun, a relic by your standards. Your Glock is a bigger caliber. It looks larger because of the cooling sleeve around the barrel. I have a high level of comfort with this weapon because I have owned it since I found it in the back of an abandoned truck, deep within a forest near Novosibirsk in 1928. I can tell the story on our return trip. For now, we have a job to attend to."

Courtney drew her pistol. Ivan's reassurance didn't help as she looked over the pistol in her hand. The image entered her mind of a giant octopus oozing over the cliff ahead of them and wrapping her in one of its slimy tentacles as a snack.

Petr squealed and broke the horrid fantasy. Everyone dropped to the ground. Ivan whispered to the gremlin. It shook, but squeaked out an answer.

Ivan turned to the group. "Petr will go no further. We face a bipedal amphibious creature of a type I like to call a *lagoonie* due to the resemblance it shares with the titular creature in *The Creature from the Black Lagoon*. This will pose us little trouble, but we should still eliminate it. They are predatory, with voracious appetites, and our friend Petr would be a perfect meal for it. We will continue on while he hides here. I will bring up the rear to keep an eye on him. Courtney, take the lead. This is a good chance for you to gain tracking and hunting experience since lagoonies are rarely difficult for a skilled warrior."

Courtney nodded and stepped forward. She looked for odd tracks in the sand but mostly let her nose guide her. The stench strengthened as the group approached another pile of rocks, which Courtney thought looked purposefully stacked to form a wall. "Does that pile look weird to any of you?" she asked.

Ivan left the back of the group and stood beside her. "The curvature and positioning of the wall in relation to the coastline leads me to believe it was built to shelter someone or something from the wind blowing in off the ocean," he said, with a nasal tinge to his voice as he tried to pinch his nostrils shut.

"That's what I thought." Courtney smirked at the fact she wasn't alone in her misery with the awful fish smell. The smirk faded as she resumed her slow trek to the rock wall.

"Most lagoonies lack the intelligence to create such a shelter. We either have an exceptional example of the species here or this was constructed by human hands," Ivan said.

Courtney nodded, but instinct told her it was the creature's domain. Manmade or not, the shelter reeked. The smell was oppressive to the point she tried to hold her breath. She couldn't wait to waste the odiferous beast so she could go home and fill her nose with pleasant smells, even if she had to pour Luke's aftershave onto tissues and shove them in her nostrils.

Renee pointed to the bottom of the pile. "Careful, I think there's a tripwire there. Something shone for a moment."

Courtney didn't see anything until Renee pointed, focusing too hard on blocking out the smell. She stopped a few yards from the structure and looked down. There was definitely a tripwire. Fishing line was tied around a large rock across from the wall at one end and around a smaller rock at the base of the other.

"If that rock gets pulled out, it'll bring the wall down on us. It's not a shelter—it's a trap." Courtney growled. "This is way smarter than your average lagoonie. Didn't know the Black Lagoon had Rambo."

A shrill sound pierced the night. Courtney thought of a bat and shivered.

"Lagoonies have poor vision since it is unnecessary for hunting in the water. They use echolocation to hunt. I believe we should remotely trip this trap. It will be quite noisy and draw our quarry out into the open," Ivan suggested.

"Remotely? How?"

Renee picked up a rock. "I used to pitch on the baseball team in high school before I blew out my knee. I didn't plan to be a cop until one shot my big brother. Part of me wanted to be the first woman in the MLB, but after the knee, I figured the best way to fix what's wrong with policing was from inside. Didn't ever plan on getting dragged into fighting monsters, either, but here we are, and I can still throw precisely. That's talent; my aim ain't faded with age."

She winked at Courtney and chucked the rock. It nailed the precarious rock at the base of the wall and brought it tumbling down with a tremendous clatter.

The creature didn't pounce. A screech came from behind them, and its source moved away from the group.

"It's running away. It must be scared of us," Mendoza said.

"No," Courtney called. "Petr!" She ran past the others towards Petr's hiding spot.

A tall humanoid shape closed in on a smaller shape in the rolling fog. The lagoonie had outsmarted the hunters. Rage boiled in her over underestimating the beast as she raised her pistol and fired. Sand flew up behind the lagoonie, but it continued, unfazed.

Machine gun fire erupted behind her and bullets flew past her ear. Courtney lost her balance and fell, but squeezed off a couple of shots. Sand flew up in front of Petr. He skittered to a halt just as the lagoonie leapt for him. It sailed over his head and crashed into the dune.

Courtney spit dirt from her mouth and rose to her feet as the lagoonie did the same. She fired two more shots, which both hit the lagoonie and knocked it backwards. Its pained whimper brought a smile to her face and the thrill of the hunt took over. The stench faded from her thoughts, overridden by lust for blood as she tucked away the pistol and drew her sword.

Petr screamed what she assumed to be Russian obscenities at her as she walked past him. Courtney stared straight ahead at the lagoonie as she passed. "You're fucking welcome," she growled to the gremlin.

The lagoonie stared at her with inky black eyes. A thick mustache of squirming tentacles obscured its mouth, reminding Courtney of earthworms. It held one webbed hand over its scaly shoulder to put pressure on the gaping bullet wounds. Gills fluttered on its neck.

"I say this to most creatures before I kill them, but you're an uglier motherfucker than most. Holy fucknuggets do you stink, too."

It hissed back at her, exposing decaying serrated teeth. It took a step toward her.

She smiled at it. "Take one more step and I'll slice you into mini fish sticks."

The creature stopped, then took a step back. Courtney swung her sword through the lagoonie's knee. The monster flopped back to the sand, clutching at the stump.

"Too bad I didn't say which way to step. Sucks to be you. You seem kind of squishy, too, you know? Your leg came off easy," she taunted, sinking the sword's tip into a bullet wound.

Courtney twisted the sword and yanked it from the hole. The lagoonie whimpered, twitching as she poked and slashed random places with the sword. Maniacal giggling filled the air as she plunged the sword into the dying lagoonie's stomach. It gasped. Blood bubbled down its tentacle-festooned chin.

"What's the matter? Tummy ache? Aw, poor stinky baby," Courtney teased, wrenching the sword sideways and tearing open the creature's abdomen.

It raised its arm slightly and gurgled. Courtney sliced off the upraised arm. The lagoonie coughed, sputtered, and convulsed.

"You really thought you were going to outsmart me, didn't you?" Courtney said before jamming her sword into the lagoonie's forehead.

Courtney sighed as the lagoonie fell limp, disappointed her plaything lasted such a short time. She turned around, remembering the revulsion she felt not too long ago at the idea of having the gremlin as an ally.

Scott stood close behind, between her and Petr.

Damn, did I really lose all sense of what's going on around me while toying with this fucker, even with my senses so good?

Her blood thirst shattered as she looked over the shredded lagoonie corpse, wondering how she'd gotten so out of control. The aggression she'd felt when the symptoms from the winged gargoyle blood first manifested crossed her mind, especially how she'd wanted to kill the gremlin. This newfound desire for more bloodshed likely came from the blood of Mephallo.

Courtney shuddered at the thought and looked back to Scott, hoping he didn't see the fear and darkness fighting each other in her eyes.

"Remind me never to piss you off," he said.

"I'm sure you'll remember." Her voice sounded far calmer than she felt. Courtney stared down at the mutilated lagoonie, horrified by her delight in torturing it. It even had a poop emoji carved into its bleeding gut.

Renee joined them and whispered to Scott, "I'm glad she's on our side."

"Maybe. I don't get how she can go from cracking one liners to scared by Ivan's gun to Michael Madsen in *Reservoir Dogs*," Scott whispered back.

"She's female; of course you don't understand her," Renee joked.

"Fuck you," Scott said through a sideways grin. "That was a good one."

Ivan knelt to console Petr while Courtney stared at her handiwork.

"Could you tell him I'm sorry I almost shot him?" Courtney asked Ivan, choking back tears as she pondered her sanity.

"*Zuri govno i sdokhni!*" Petr yelled at her.

"What does that mean?"

"It means 'Thank you for saving my life. I am eternally grateful,' of course," Ivan said. He burst out laughing. "I am sorry. I would prefer not to translate something so vulgar. I must admit, I am quite entertained. I have not heard some of these words in decades."

Courtney blushed. "I guess my over-exuberance was good for something then," she said quietly.

"Over-exuberance. I had a different way to describe it in mind, but will not argue with the word you have chosen," Ivan said. He turned to the others. "Our work here is done. You three may leave. Courtney and I will be along momentarily with Petr. Do not wait on our accord."

The three nodded and headed back to their vehicles. Ivan placed his hand on Courtney's shoulder and sighed. "I understand what the winged gargoyle blood is doing to you. I struggled mightily with aggression for years after I acquired the ring and did many things of which I am not proud. Fortunately for me, the Great Patriotic War provided a release and perhaps some justification for the horrors I unleashed upon the German soldiers—as if they were their Führer himself. Unfortunately, you do not have the luxury of years to learn to control this. I implore you to snuff out these dark impulses the next time they try to take control, because you had an audience tonight who will likely try to take advantage of this weakness in the near future," Ivan advised.

"An audience?"

Ivan pointed up a nearby cliff. Courtney's heart skipped a beat when she saw Edthgar perched atop it, staring past her at the dismembered lagoonie. The winged gargoyle's red eyes fixed on her for a moment, and a disembodied grating laugh sounded in her head. Ivan didn't appear to hear it—at least, he gave no reaction.

Courtney looked away again and swallowed hard as she tugged Ivan's wrist. "We don't stand a chance against him now. Let's get the hell out of here before he decides to grab me and drag me to a bridal shop," Courtney said.

"Fear not. If he had any intention of attacking, he would have done so while you were wrapped up in slaughtering the lagoonie. He appears too busy scheming over what he has seen to get his hands dirty at the moment. However, Petr has had his cover blown and will be in danger if we leave him here. Let us all be on our way. I am sure our adversary is waiting to clean up the mess from his fallen minions so they are not discovered in the morning. I would recommend you clean your sword first," Ivan said, staying firmly in place as she tried to pull him away.

"Fuck," Courtney muttered, holding her sword over the shredded lagoonie.

Ivan laughed and tossed her the handkerchief from his suit pocket. "You may wish to leave some part of your foe unbloodied in the future," he snickered as she wiped the blade clean.

Courtney scowled at the lagoonie corpse and groaned. "Yeah, if I think of it."

She handed Ivan back the bloody rag, but he shook his head. "Lagoonie blood will not wash away so easily. Leave it with your handiwork."

Courtney took a deep breath, coughing from the smell, then knelt down and covered the poop emoji carved into its body.

"I had no idea you thought yourself the prodigy to both Zorro and da Vinci," Ivan joked.

"Shut the fuck up." Courtney giggled as she stood and ruffled Petr's ears.

"Bitch," the gremlin uttered in clear English as he swatted her hand.

Courtney gaped at Ivan.

"I did not teach him that. He is a good listener, and I suspect your conversation with Luke regarding coworkers the other day entertained him."

Courtney shook her head and headed down the beach toward the car. Her heart hammered as she glanced back at the lagoonie corpse, then to Edthgar's eyes following her.

I don't know which scares me more, that fucker or myself right now. Just let me get home without trouble and find a stiff drink. Please.

22

Andrea breathed a sigh of relief as the front door opened and she overheard Ivan whispering to Courtney. Everything must have gone well. Soon she'd ask for advice about her dreams. Even Luke's strong coffee couldn't keep her awake much longer, and she didn't want to sleep again without speaking to Ivan.

"Ivan?" Andrea whispered as he, Courtney and Petr walked by the great room.

"Go ahead. I'm stopping in the kitchen for a drink. I need it bad," Courtney grumbled.

Maybe things didn't go so smooth. It's weird the gremlin is still with them, too.

Ivan nodded and walked to the couch with Petr in tow. He sat beside Andrea, and his hand almost went to her knee. Petr hopped up on the couch and curled up on the cushion she'd propped her injured foot on earlier.

"You seem distressed," Ivan said.

Andrea nodded. "I've been having weird dreams lately. I didn't think anything of it until today." She stopped and gulped, unsure of how to continue. Ivan's facial expressions weren't visible in the dark living room. "Should I turn on a light so you can see?" she asked.

"I can see as clearly as on a sunny day. Turn on a light if you wish, however."

Andrea gulped again as she threw aside the blanket and rolled up the legs of her pajama bottoms so there'd be a visual aid as she started her story. Ivan stared at the dancing Hello Kitties printed on the pink pants, but said nothing as she reached for the switch to the light.

"The most recent dream started like the others. I was alone in the hospital running from the gargoyles. I tripped and hurt my left foot. I also got a cut on my right arm from the dagger Courtney took from the gargoyle in the parking lot. I don't know why it was lying in the hospital hallway, but it was."

Andrea stopped to collect her thoughts. The terror from the dream returned and her breath came in rapid, shallow pants as she remembered the gargoyle, plus how easy it was to pull the trigger. Her heart raced; she opened her mouth to speak, but no words emerged.

Ivan looked closely at her affected limbs. He rubbed the stubble on his chin and nodded, then patted her shin as he looked into her eyes. "The wounds appeared on the opposite limbs when you awakened. Interesting. Continue, please."

Andrea stayed silent for a moment, thinking over anything else from the dream of potential importance. What were the words Edthgar said? Were they Russian or any language Ivan might know? She couldn't remember, so she picked up the story at her escape.

"I finally found a stairway to get out of the halls and I walked through an empty office, where I found some clothes and a gun. The gargoyles were still coming and one saw me and I had to shoot. It was so easy, killing it. That kinda spooks me. I knew they'd all hear the gun and come after me, so I ran out into some snow.

"When I turned around to see where the gargoyles were, they were gone and so was the hospital. I was in a snowy field near a forest. Somehow the dagger kept me warm as I moved along since I was in a little dress and lab coat, looking for cover in the forest. I met a black wolf there and it led me crawling through all kinds of nasty pine needles that scraped up my legs. The wolf guided me to a cabin, but that's when Luke woke me up to tell me I was bleeding."

"I see. Did you discuss any of this with Luke?"

"No. He assumed the cut on my arm was from the parking lot, and I figured you'd know best."

"Next time, share details immediately. They will be fresher in your mind and something you may not remember could be key in deciphering your predicament."

Andrea thought of the gargoyle's speech, then realized what Ivan said. She swallowed hard. "Ne...ne...ne...next time?"

"I have an idea of what may be going on, but need confirmation. This will require you to dream again. If I am correct, you should begin right where you left off or in a similar situation." Ivan picked up the blanket from the floor.

"But what if something happens?" Andrea whined.

Her hand shook as she tried to take the blanket, and she dropped it.

Ivan reached down again as he answered. "I will watch over you while you sleep and awaken you at the first sign of distress. You will then share every detail."

Andrea trembled. "What if I get killed when the cabin door opens?"

"If my theory is correct, and I would say there is a ninety percent chance it is, you face no greater danger than having your ears talked off or your throat and mouth receiving minor burns from scalding hot tea," Ivan assured.

"Really?"

"I would not let you down, despite the wine you made me waste at our second meeting."

Andrea breathed easier as she pushed off her pajama bottoms and refused the blanket in his hands. "Wake me up if you see new wounds."

Ivan looked away, gesturing to her legs. "Is that truly necessary?"

"I'm not getting naked, don't worry," she said, hitting Petr in the face as she tossed aside her tank top. "Besides, I thought Russians had less concept of personal space than Americans."

"Who said I was your average Russian? I have lived in America longer now than I did in Russia, and much longer than you have been alive," he said, still looking away.

"You're ninety percent sure I won't get hurt, so you won't have to look all that close, or are you scared?" Andrea teased. She lay the back of her head in his lap with her legs dangling over the arm of the couch. "Wait, should I turn around so my legs are across your lap instead? You can't see my lower legs in this position."

Ivan looked down at her face and said, "You take more delight in annoying me than Courtney does in killing monsters."

"How about a quick goodnight kiss? It'll make me feel better, and since there's that ten percent chance you're wrong I could use a last kiss," Andrea joked as she handed him her glasses.

Ivan shook his head. She couldn't see his face but knew he was blushing. He brought his hand up to his mouth and kissed his fingertips, then placed them on her forehead. "If you insist, though it feels very silly since it will not be your last. Now goodnight."

"I'm glad you're so sure. It makes me feel much better. Goodnight," Andrea said, turning around so her legs lay across Ivan's lap.

Petr's fur brushed against Andrea's foot as he shifted his position to give her a bit more room. He quietly asked Ivan something in Russian.

"*Vy mozhete*," Ivan responded.

The gremlin curled up and fell asleep as quickly as Andrea wished she could.

Footsteps approached.

"Ninety percent, huh?" Courtney said as she handed Ivan a glass of wine. "You don't look like you believe that."

Andrea popped one eye open. Courtney put the wine bottle to her lips and chugged.

"I am not much of a risk taker, and I cannot say I am entirely comfortable despite the odds. She also does her best to make me uncomfortable." Ivan gestured to Andrea's legs as she snapped her eye back shut.

"She's never been shy," Courtney said. "I don't think I could've made it through school without her. I wasn't popular, but she was, and she's probably the only reason I didn't have every other kid leering at me and making my life more miserable than it already was."

Andrea smiled, and Courtney said, "Oh fuck. I thought you were asleep already. Dammit. Forget I said that stuff. Please?"

Andrea snickered. "It's okay; I love you too, like the sister I never had."

Ivan shook his head. "As touching as this is, we need you to sleep to confirm my suspicions and alleviate your fears. Courtney, go upstairs and try not to drown yourself with the contents of that bottle."

Courtney giggled as she walked out. "Okay, I'll grab another. This one is almost empty." She burped in the hallway.

When Andrea heard Courtney's steps on the metal stairs, she looked up at Ivan. "Bedtime story?" she chirped.

Ivan muttered in Russian, then said, "Perhaps a tale would bore you to sleep. Of what should we speak?"

"How about kid Ivan?"

"I cannot recount much of my childhood. My father, or so I thought he was at the time, was a factory worker. Our family was poor but we had our own little shack instead of one of the overcrowded worker apartments. He was involved in the revolution of 1917. I cannot recall which party he was a member of. Either way, he was killed. My mother smuggled me out of the city. We met up with her brother, and so began my life of adventure."

He paused, staring at the floor before continuing. "My uncle taught me to read and write, and he encouraged me to keep a journal of our adventures. For that reason, I can recall the 1920s onward much more easily. I also have several sketches in those journals. I suppose I may have become an artist had the allure of treasure hunting not been so strong."

He paused, and Andrea took the opportunity for a quick joke. "He didn't teach you about contractions, did he?"

"I believe contractions to be lazy. I like to be as precise as possible in all aspects of life, and speech is a part of that."

"So, um, did you have any pets as a kid?"

Ivan smiled. "Yes. When I was seven, the family next door had a pregnant dog and I was promised a puppy. He was a wonderful brown mutt, and my mother suggested the name Soboka, which simply means dog. I gave him a more noble name, Volkodav. It translates to wolfhound in English."

"So you named your company after your dog? That's pretty cool."

"Volkodav was my constant companion for eleven years, and my only company for his last three after my mother and uncle passed. I learned quite a bit from him."

"Like what?"

"He taught me to always be vigilant, the value of trust and friendship, and perhaps most importantly, how fragile life is."

Ivan sighed and shut his eyes. He took a deep breath, then met her gaze as he continued. "We were out hunting for food. He was aging, and failed to spot a bear trap. I tried everything I could to free him, but failed. I could not just leave him, so I sat beside him until he nuzzled my rifle. He decided the person he trusted most should end his life and move on. I could not let him starve to death, so I did as he wished.

"I could see in his eyes I was doing what he wanted, that I was forgiven, but pulling the trigger was the most difficult thing I have ever done in my life. I hugged his body and cried for hours afterward, then buried him and made the three-day trek back to civilization to drown my sorrows or kill myself by alcohol poisoning while trying."

"Oh gawd, I was hoping for something to bore me to sleep, not a tearjerker." Andrea dabbed her eyes with the blanket.

"Yes, it is a painful memory to revisit. Perhaps I should discuss legal paperwork instead? That may prove boring enough."

"Yeah. Courtroom drama stuff usually works."

"Then I shall regale you with the tale of my battle with the insurance company regarding the value of my burned Cadillac."

"Oh yeah, that oughta do the trick."

23

Andrea's eyes flew open, but Ivan was nowhere to be seen. Instead, a stained wood ceiling and walls greeted her. Dim, flickering light danced over the knotted wood. She looked around the room for more candles to go exploring, until a glowing orb in the center of the room made her sit up. It looked like a miniature sun, no larger than a ping pong ball, hovering near the ceiling.

She tossed aside the quilted wool blanket. The dress she'd found at the hospital was gone. Andrea wore her own underwear from the waking world in the Mays mansion. Come to think of it, how did she get inside the cabin? Where was the wolf? She expected the dream to start where the last left off.

Well, at least it's warm in here. Gawd, being out in the snow in my underwear would've sucked. I gotta figure out what's going on, and that mini sun is a good start, I guess.

The orb flared brightly as she looked at it. Andrea stepped onto the fine oriental rug and shivered, grabbing the blanket. Each step she took until she stood directly beneath the orb made it light up brighter. The ceiling was too far above her head to get a good look, so she scanned the area for a stool.

An older man stood in the doorway. Andrea stifled a scream and lost her grip on the blanket. It flopped open, but stayed draped over her shoulders.

"I see you still don't believe in warm clothing. I'm not complaining, mind you; it's a nice view," the man said.

Andrea wrapped the blanket around herself again and scowled.

The man chuckled, stroking his thick gray handlebar mustache. His turquoise eyes met her gaze as he spoke again. "If I wanted to do anything, I easily could have at any point from when you flopped at my doorstep to now. I prefer stimulating conversation."

Something about those eyes seemed familiar to Andrea, but she didn't know why. She'd never seen this man before. His fancy vest, suit, bowtie, and slicked-back hair made her think of an Old West businessman, but his deep raspy voice had a tinge of an Eastern European accent. His appearance wasn't solving any mysteries, so she figured she'd best indulge his desire for conversation.

"Who are you?"

He raised an eyebrow and said, "You show up at my cabin with a dagger and a gun, barely dressed yet somehow not freezing, guided by a huge wolf, and you want to know who I am? I don't know if you're trustworthy or a treacherous witch. I'll answer your question after you answer mine. Considering I provided you shelter with no knowledge, I think it's only fair for me to know who you are before providing any further charity. Well, aside from some tea, because it would be rude of me not to offer something to drink."

Andrea smiled at the mention of tea, remembering Ivan's advice. "Okay, deal," she said to the mystery man.

"Follow me into my study. We'll be comfortable there."

Andrea glanced around for clothes to put on first, but saw nothing. "Um, am I supposed to go around in my underwear? This is a little awkward."

"Apparently so. You were dressed when I tucked you in, so this is what you've decided to bring here this time around. Something can be figured out later, but please come along for now. I promise I won't take away your blanket."

Andrea gulped and limped along behind him down a short hallway lined with medieval tapestries. Another orb hovered near the ceiling to light the hallway. She wasn't sure what had her more curious: the snowy landscape, the small cabin being the size of a mansion inside, the burning orbs, or the man who seemed just as curious about her.

The man turned left into a massive library. Scores of shelves filled with old leather-bound books were arranged in two rows to either side of the room. In the central area stood massive stone pillars with hieroglyphics and other ancient writings carved into them. The pillars were set in a highly polished marble floor. Between the centermost pillars of the study sat a massive ornate wooden desk with a chair more like a throne. A few modern-looking leather office chairs surrounded the desk.

He sat on the throne and pointed to one of the leather chairs. Something clattered as he opened one of the desk's creaking drawers. "This desk may have some fine carving on it, but its maker knew squat about how to make a drawer work smoothly," the man joked as he set two ceramic saucers onto the desk. He placed a dainty teacup on each and nudged one over to Andrea. "How do you like your tea?"

"Strong and dark, with a little honey if it's not too much to ask."

"Of course not," he said. "Now hold up one finger."

She gave him a puzzled look, but did as he said. He grinned and held up a finger of his own. "Watch carefully how I make tea. I'm sure it's different from anything you've seen."

The air an inch above her finger glowed. Andrea watched with her mouth open as the glow formed into a tiny orb just like the ones lighting the cabin. It bathed her hand in light and pleasant warmth.

"Now look into your cup," he said.

Condensation formed in the bottom of the teacup. The droplets grew in number until they formed a puddle.

"Does Himalayan sound good to you, or perhaps something else?" he asked as the water level rose.

"Um, yeah, Himalayan sounds fine," Andrea said, too transfixed at the sight to look at him.

"That will take me a moment to summon, so in the meantime you should heat the water."

"How?"

"Dip your finger in it, of course," he said, chuckling.

"Huh?" Andrea waved her hand. The orb followed her finger. She smiled wide as she drew a figure eight in the air, marveling at the orb trailing her finger precisely. She pushed it slowly towards the cup. As soon as it hit the water the orb broke apart, so she spun her finger to stir it around. The water steamed as the orb fully dissolved. "Gawd, that's so cool," she whispered.

"Now for the leaves," the man said.

A hole appeared in the bottom of the cup and through the desk, but no water leaked out. Instead, tea leaves entered the cup through the hole and began to swirl. The water darkened and the leaves disappeared from sight.

"The honey went in the same way as the leaves. I know you can't see it so you'll just have to take a sip and see for yourself," the man said, beaming with pride.

Andrea took a cautious sip, in case the tea was scalding hot as Ivan had warned. It wasn't. If anything, the temperature was perfect.

"How do you like it?"

"Wonderful. Best tea I've ever had."

"Excellent. I'll make a note of that for the future. Now, what is your name so I can write down your blend?" He set a piece of paper on the desk, followed by a jar of ink and a quill pen.

"Andrea Browning," she said, amused by the antique writing utensils.

"Ah, there was an actress in the late 1930s named Andrea Leeds. She had darker hair though," the man said wistfully.

"I'm sorry, I don't know much about old films, but the tea is great."

"Bah! Old? How old are you?"

"I'm in my early twenties. 1930 was like sixty years before I was born."

"Hmm, yes, that would make her films seem old to you. One can never be sure in matters where magic may be involved. For all I know, you may be a shamaness who has stayed young for centuries, though your fascination with the tea trick would suggest not."

The man rubbed the stubble on his chin and met her gaze. Again, something seemed so familiar, but unlike the orb, she couldn't put a finger on it.

"Yeah, that'd be weird. I don't watch a lot of modern movies either. I listen to music more often in my free time," she said.

Classical music filled the study from nowhere and everywhere at the same time. The music was familiar to her much in the same way as the mystery man, but she still couldn't place either. Perhaps she was here in another dream and didn't remember? Andrea doubted that since the tea trick seemed memorable, but what other explanation could there be?

He resumed the questioning. "From where do you hail?"

"California."

The man shook his head and grumbled, "From the same state as Hollywood and doesn't know film history? *Tsk tsk.*"

"I'm at the other end of the state. Drake's Landing is north of San Francisco."

"Either way, you're far from home. How did you arrive in this remote part of Romania?"

"Romania? We're in Romania?"

"Someone snuck in without going through customs first, I see. So sad you didn't get your passport stamped either, because a Romania stamp would be quite the conversation starter. I'd skimp on details, though, if I were you; some might think you mad if you start talking about magic tea."

Andrea shook her head and looked at the cup. "I don't understand. I was being chased through the hospital back home, but when I escaped through the entrance I stepped into this snowy place. I turned around and the hospital was gone, so I tried to find cover until the wolf appeared. It insisted I follow it here. How does a Californian hospital open into Romania?"

The man rubbed his chin in contemplation again. "I see. I still can't help the thought that you're leaving out some details I might find very important. Who was chasing you? Why were you hospitalized in the first place? You might want to spill a few more beans if you're to convince me you're not a witch. Some witches are very good at acting."

"My friend Courtney and I were attacked in the parking lot at work. I got a concussion and some cuts. Since then I've been having nightmares about being chased, until the last one brought me here," she nervously explained, avoiding mention of the gargoyles unless the man made it absolutely necessary.

"So you're aware you're dreaming? Interesting. Do you know what this place is then, other than a Romania somehow directly accessible from California?"

"Besides a deceptively sized cabin owned by some sort of wizard, I haven't got a clue," Andrea said, her voice pitching ever higher as the man pried for knowledge she didn't have.

"I will tell you momentarily, but first I have to ask about something you arrived with." He placed the copper dagger on the desk in front of her. "The last I knew, this was in the possession of a pretty nasty creature's most trusted minion. For it to be with you would suggest you vanquished one of Edthgar's favorite underlings."

Andrea blinked rapidly at the knife. "You know about the gargoyles?" she squeaked.

"I've known about them for a very long time. No offense, but I have a difficult time imagining you taking down a seasoned warrior without wizardry more advanced than you seem to show even the slightest knowledge of."

Andrea sighed and explained. "I didn't. My friend Courtney did. The gargoyles were after her and I just happened to be there. I got knocked around. My glasses flew off and when I was feeling around for them I found the knife." She showed him her stitched palm and said, "The sharp part. That's generally my luck, like how in my last dream I fell on it in the hospital and cut my arm."

The man studied the cut. "That explains the magical energy I sense from you. Some of the dagger's power flowed into you through that slice. This blade has become connected to you, and it followed you into your dreams. This place is a dreamscape between dimensions. Few find their way here. When I sensed the energy of you and the dagger, I opened the path for you to come through. I believe your story, so I'll give you more information.

"First, my friend Fenrir would like to say hello." The black wolf peeked around the desk before trotting to Andrea.

"So your name is Fenrir?" she asked the wolf.

"*Yes,*" said a Scandinavian-accented voice in her head.

"You can talk?"

"*No, but I can communicate telepathically since your mind has opened to the possibilities of magic. 'Tis a wonderful thing, is it not?*"

"It sure is."

The man tapped the desk to regain her attention. "Fenrir helps guard doorways to the dreamscape. When I opened the portal for you, I asked him to scout. He didn't feel you were a threat, so he brought you here and told me of your arrival. Your story corroborates with it."

"So you knew I was trustworthy before questioning me?"

"Not necessarily. Trustworthy and threatening are two different things. I may have let you into my cabin, but I needed more information before I made my decision. Besides, what would complete strangers talk about besides trying to figure out who the other might be? I don't get many visitors anymore so I was eager to chat, though perhaps my social skills have faded."

"Yeah, considering you still haven't told me your name yet. I'm gonna wake up and not have anything to call you but Magic Tea Guy," Andrea teased.

"Which name? I have had several over the years, some flattering and some not so flattering," the man said. He chuckled. "The name I was given at birth is Ludari. Sadly, its Sumerian translation is *eternal man*, not *magic tea guy*."

"Sumerian? Who speaks that anymore?" Andrea joked.

"No one in most dimensions aside from archaeologists and the few who collect artifacts from ancient civilizations, such as myself," the man explained. "It is still prevalent in a few dimensions. There are infinite other dimensions, with infinite Earths only slightly different from each other or unrecognizable to others, and these dimensions connect through magic. All these planes of existence have dreamscapes like this one. It doesn't take great magic to visit the dreamscapes of alternate dimensions, but to travel between those dimensions in a physical form takes incredibly strong magic. To do so without side effects takes the most potent magic imaginable and a bit of luck.

"Thankfully, when I traveled to your dimension I was granted a beneficial side effect: immortality. If you doubt my story I can show you other dimensions through the dreamscape."

Andrea's smile threatened to split her face in half. "Absolutely. I'd love to have something to rub in Courtney's face that I've done and she hasn't."

"Very well then. Take my hand." He reached out with one hand and placed his other's pointer finger in the center of his forehead. "This is where the third eye is, that sees the invisible. Put your finger there and close your eyes," he instructed.

Andrea giggled and said, "We're off to Neverland." She felt a slight tingle in both hands, followed by a sharp jolt of electricity. Next came a breeze lightly blowing through her hair and the blanket.

"Open your eyes," Ludari said.

Andrea did, and was amazed to be standing in the parking lot at work. "Oh gawd, I'm at work in my underwear!" she protested.

"No, you're not. This is still dreamscape. No one will see you unless they are also in this realm," Ludari assured. "The Motherlode. That's quite an interesting name for a store, isn't it? Close your eyes again."

She did, and upon feeling another shock she opened them again. They stood in the same parking lot, but the store had changed. A green-and-orange sign shaped like a crown took the place of The Motherlode's golden circle. "Electronics Empire? That's different. I like the colors," Andrea said.

"Allow me to show you another," Ludari said eagerly.

Andrea closed her eyes, felt the shock, and looked around again. "Best Buy?" She stared at a sign sharing The Motherlode's blue and yellow color scheme in a sign shaped like a tag.

"Wait a moment," Ludari said. He let go of her hand and pulled a pocket watch out of his vest. He wound it backwards, and time did the same. Cars and people appeared and disappeared in a mad flurry, and the sun rose and fell numerous times in a matter of seconds.

Andrea stared at her Miata, intact, and parked next to Hank's Blazer instead of the Willys. "This is the same night I was attacked, just in a different dimension, isn't it?"

Ludari nodded.

Andrea moved closer where a copy of herself and Courtney leaned on the Miata and talked about their coworkers, Lizzie and Todd. However, in this dimension, both girls puffed away on cigarettes. Andrea felt a tinge of guilt, knowing her counterpart in this dimension was likely responsible for Courtney smoking. No gargoyles attacked in this world, so the workplace gossip continued until the two dropped their cigarettes and snuffed them out. They hugged, and Courtney gave Andrea her condolences on her breakup with Kristi before they got into their respective vehicles. Andrea cringed and hoped it wasn't the Kristi Courtney knew from her time in private school.

"Come back to me and I'll show you more if you wish," Ludari said.

She hobbled back to Ludari, eager to leave this dreamscape dimension with its oddly named stores and smoking version of Courtney. She definitely wasn't telling her about this dimension. If Courtney and Ivan could keep monsters secret from her, she could keep inter-dimensional gossip to herself.

"Hmm, that injury could use a little help," Ludari said. He knelt down and placed his hand on her foot. A tingling sensation passed through her toes and forced out a giggle. She backed away. No pain accompanied her steps.

"You healed me? Thank you! I thought you were trying to cop a feel for a second like my weird ex. Sorry."

Ludari snickered and beckoned her back to him. She took Ludari's hand and they were away again in the blink of an eye.

This time when she opened her eyes, they stood on the water of the Thames River and looked up at London Bridge, adorned with Nazi flags.

"In this world, the United States still viewed Britain as their greatest enemy, so they supported German efforts in World War IV. Yes, you heard me right: four. Too bad the Nazis had them invade Russia via the Aleutian Islands and the far east. The Soviets developed the atomic bomb first. There's nothing left of America to show you," Ludari told her.

Andrea shivered. "Can we go somewhere else now?"

"Certainly."

They blinked away and stood in a forest clearing. "In this world, Europeans never came to America. A mysterious contagion from the Incan Empire wiped out the native human population. No worries for us, though; the virus died out centuries ago," he explained in a glum tone.

Andrea shivered again and closed her eyes, picturing Ludari's study. She felt a stronger jolt of electricity throughout her body. Static electricity crackled in her ears.

When she opened her eyes, she was back in the study, sitting in one of the office chairs with Fenrir curled up by her feet. Dark purple mist appeared behind the desk. As it faded away, it revealed Ludari in his seat with a smug grin.

"Why did you show me so much bad?" Andrea asked.

"If I'd shown you the dimension where you're a world-renowned actress working under the name Angela Bronson you wouldn't have wanted to leave, and therefore wouldn't have taken it upon yourself to use your own magic for the first time."

Andrea thought for a moment and realized he was right. She'd willed herself back to the study. Sparks danced on her knuckles as she looked down. "Wow, my own magic, all thanks to a silly dagger and clumsy hands. Will I be able to use this in the real world?"

"Not much yet. You'll need training, but I can see you've got great potential. I will help you progress as you keep visiting in your sleep. Just promise me you'll put it to good use against the gargoyles. I wish I could help in the real world, but unfortunately I'm locked in a special dungeon one of my children built. He fears I'll be soft because I remember the gargoyles when they were human in my own dimension. I botched the spell that brought my servants here, and that's why they're the monsters they are now. I won't be soft; that's an unfounded belief. I want to end their misery. It's the greatest favor I can do for them," Ludari said.

"Wait a minute, you brought them? Ivan told me his father summoned his servants to this dimension but the spell was faulty and mutated them. You're Teuffelmann? I see it now, why you're so familiar. You two have the same eyes!"

"You're finally aware. I wish he'd let that awful name die out and call me by my real one, or even Magic Tea Guy. I quite like my new nickname; it's fanciful and makes me feel millennia younger," Ludari said.

"Teuffelmann is a pretty awful name," Andrea agreed.

"Could I ask you another favor? Once you leave, which I feel won't be long, please ask Ivan to visit more often. I know his Romanian mansion is a long trip from his business in California, but it gets awfully boring sometimes when your only company is one of his staff named Eryk. Not a bad fellow, but he is much too open when speaking of his health concerns and dating difficulties. It makes for some rather dreary chats."

"I will, but what makes you think I'm leaving soon? Wait, could you heal my concussion first?" Andrea said.

"There is a disturbance in your aura suggesting you're about to awaken due to influences on your physical body in the real world. The disturbance is growing stronger. Alas, there's no time left for healing."

Andrea concentrated for a moment and said, "I can feel it, too. I'll look forward to our next visit. Later, Magic Tea Guy. Later, Fenrir."

She closed her eyes and opened them again on the couch in Hank's mansion. Everything was as dark and silent as when she'd first drifted to sleep, right down to Ivan watching her.

"You seem troubled. Was the dream not as I had suspected?" Ivan asked.

"No, it's fine, but I sensed something back here—"

Before she could elaborate, glass broke upstairs, and a loud thump followed.

24

Courtney's eyes fluttered open. Everything around her spun like an amusement park ride and she couldn't tell where she was. The left side of her abdomen throbbed. Something cold pressed against her bare legs, arms, and midriff.

Okay, so I'm on the floor in a room without carpets. That tells me a whole fucking lot.

She tried to push herself up, but dizziness overwhelmed her and she flopped back down. The pain in her side pounded again, causing her to breathe in sharply. The air was thick with the scent of Luke's aftershave, but he wasn't there. Courtney normally liked the scent but this was too much—the entire bottle emptied in one fell swoop. Besides, if he was there he'd be helping and doting over her, whatever was wrong.

She burped. The taste of wine returned. Some of the haze over her thought process dissipated, and she remembered the second bottle she'd grabbed after Luke fell asleep. A little more liquid sleep aid was supposed to clear her mind of the horrific zeal of slaughtering the lagoonie. Apparently, "a little" didn't happen.

Recollection crept to mind of stumbling to the bathroom and looking in the mirror after relieving herself. Only the hazy thought of falling remained, but she surmised she'd knocked down Luke's aftershave when she either passed out or slipped. The broken bottle probably caused the pain in her side, too.

A small orange shape entered the doorway. It moved closer, and Courtney tensed. Something like a tiny piece of wet sandpaper rubbed her calf a few times. The tension dropped as she figured out what her blurry vision mistook for a threat.

"You're a good girl, Bea," Courtney slurred to the cat licking her leg.

Another larger shape appeared in the doorway. "Luke?" Courtney asked.

"Yeah, it's me. Ivan's down the hall with Andrea," Luke explained. He flipped on the lights and knelt down. "Shit. There's blood everywhere," he said in a feeble voice.

He stepped over Courtney and set something metal down on the sink, then scooped up the cat and stuck her in the shower for safe keeping. Courtney groaned as he checked where her wound might be, then lifted her up by the armpits to help her onto the toilet.

Courtney was still dizzy but stayed upright on the toilet while Luke examined her legs. He moved to the wound on her side. Her vision improved enough to see his facial expression change to confusion as he looked at the wound.

"What the hell?" he said as he touched something stuck there. He wiggled it slightly. Courtney winced and bit her lip when he yanked it out. Luke held in front of her face to see.

"A gremlin claw?" she muttered.

Luke nodded and looked over to where Courtney lay earlier. A gremlin corpse lay crumpled there. Blood leaked from its crushed skull.

Courtney looked at the dead gremlin and started crying. "Petr," she whined. "I almost shot him, he almost got eaten by the lagoonie, and now he dies like this?"

She sobbed as Luke examined the flattened body closer.

"No black stripes. That's not Petr."

"Huh?"

Luke grabbed her ankle and held the claw next to it. He stared for a moment.

"This little shit must've been on Edthgar's side," he said, pointing to the dead gremlin. "He got in here somehow and scratched you. In your condition, you lost your balance and fell on him. He probably held his hands up in fear and that's where the claw in your side came from."

A shriek from the tower sent a worse chill down Courtney's spine than Luke's theory. Several higher pitched sounds followed, forcing her to cover her ears and grimace.

"Ivan says there's lots, whatever they are," Andrea squeaked as she rushed into the bathroom, her hands shaking and her eyes wide behind her glasses.

Luke reached for the sink. "I'm glad I grabbed the gun. Something felt weird before I got here."

"I can't fight like this." Courtney groaned. "I wish I could help."

Andrea noticed the gremlin corpse and her footprints in the blood puddle. "Oh no, no, no," she whimpered as she slid down the shower door and curled into the fetal position.

"I don't think gremlin blood is like gargoyle blood," Luke reassured Andrea.

Courtney watched him look at his own hands, covered in the blood from helping her up. He swallowed hard, then took a deep breath and raised the revolver.

* * * * *

Luke aimed the revolver towards the stairs. The only light in the hall was from the bathroom, but it was enough to see gremlin eye shine if any managed to get past Ivan. He hoped he could hit a target so small and fast. The .45 only held six bullets.

He held the revolver steady, waiting for something to shoot and taking deep breaths as his eyes adjusted to the darkness. As Courtney said after the tunnel battle, anticipation gnawed at him more than the fight would.

A shrill yelp echoed through the stairwell. Another yelp followed, then a loud metallic clunk against the stairs. *Sounds like Ivan got one.*

A gremlin peeked out of the stairwell. Luke rewarded its efforts in escaping Ivan by beheading it with a .45 round. A couple short bursts of Thompson fire erupted from the third floor, along with several pained yips. How many gremlins were attacking and how many did Hank just kill? Luke thought he might prefer a gargoyle attack. Those were large, slow targets without agility or stealth on their side.

Three more darted into the hall. Two ate lead right away. The third jumped at Luke, surprising him with how high it could leap. He smacked it out of the air with the pistol and blasted it as it squirmed on the floor. Two bullets were left, and the spare cartridges were on the third floor where Thompson fire caused more gremlin death screeches.

"Ivan, please don't let any more by," Luke whispered.

Another rushed into the hallway in defiance of his pleas. Luke waited for it to leap so it couldn't dodge as he fired. The gremlin's head exploded when the slug hit, covering Luke and the walls in bloody gray matter.

Something rushed past while he was blinded by blood. *"Devushka!"* said an awful squealing voice behind him.

Andrea screamed before Luke could turn around. An odd buzzing sound poured from the bathroom.

When he reentered the bathroom, the dead gremlin twitched, smoke wafting from its blackened fur. Andrea sat with a dumbfounded look on her face and her hand extended in front of her, palm out.

"What the hell happened?" Luke asked, staring at the smoldering gremlin.

"But, but, but...." Andrea stammered.

As much as Luke wanted to know what happened to the roasted gremlin, the hallway still needed protection. He exited.

Ivan stood by the stairs. "It is over. You have done well," the Russian said in a weary tone as he wiped his sword's blade clean with a rag.

"Awesome."

Ivan approached and said, "Most were after Petr. Edthgar must have sent the entire tribe after seeing him help us hunt the lagoonie."

Luke didn't care about the reason. He had something else to ask. "Gremlin blood doesn't affect us like gargoyle blood, does it?"

"Not at all. They are as natural as your cat. Gargoyle blood has magic in it because of the sorcery involved in the arrival of the winged ones. You will be fine after a shower," Ivan answered as he sheathed his spotless blade.

Luke let out a sigh of relief. "Damn, I was hoping it'd be like a magical weight loss supplement. Drop fifteen pounds without dieting, exercise, or excessive bathroom visits like miracle supplements."

Ivan laughed. "No such luck, my friend. Though perhaps it will offer you further employment. I could use a resourceful monster hunter." He placed his hand on Luke's shoulder and looked in the bathroom. "What happened here?"

Andrea didn't look up or answer. She stared at her outstretched hand with a demented smile. Courtney attempted to stand but flopped back onto the toilet.

"I guess the first gremlin caught Court unaware because of how drunk she is, and she fell on it," Luke said. "I heard the crash and came to investigate. No clue what happened to the crispy critter."

Andrea spoke. "He said my magic wouldn't be strong in the real world yet, but I did it."

"Ah, this must be about your dream. Who told you of magic?"

Andrea looked up into Ivan's eyes and growled. "You know damn well who it was."

Luke raised an eyebrow as he stepped over the aftershave bottle to get to Courtney.

Ivan smiled and rubbed the stubble on his chin. "I see. Things transpired as I predicted. That is quite comforting. Let us clean up and head downstairs to discuss things."

"Why didn't you say I'd be meeting your father?"

"If I told you, you would have let your guard down, and if I had been wrong it could have proven disastrous for you."

"You think I'm a child and can't think for myself, don't you?"

"My mission is not to argue. It is to protect those in our group, yourself included, and to vanquish any who threaten our survival. Clean yourself off. I will be waiting downstairs for details about your dream. Do not think magical abilities entitle you to act on your own and ignore the best interests of the group."

He walked out of the bathroom before Andrea could respond. Sparks flickered in her eyes as she looked at Luke. He blinked and looked away to Courtney.

Andrea grumbled and yanked open the shower door, scaring the cat out of the bathroom. Luke swore Bea's hair stood on edge, like there was static electricity all around Andrea.

"I just need to get the blood off my legs and then I'll be out of your way to tell my life story to Mr. Personality," Andrea said in a contemptuous tone as she started the water.

"Okay." Luke grabbed the dustpan beneath the sink to clean up the glass and avoid further conversation with Andrea.

"I'm sorry I couldn't help," Courtney sniffled.

"It's okay. You said things went bad tonight, and everyone has moments of weakness."

"I could've gotten you, Andrea, or Bea killed," she said, tears rolling down her cheeks.

"Keep that in mind next time you think you need so much wine. But hey, if I die in this mess it'll be by your side, and that's how I'd want to go."

"You mean it?" Courtney said, wiping her eyes.

"Yes, because I love you."

"I love you too!" Courtney said, tears flowing again.

Luke dumped the broken glass into the trash and hugged her tight. He spoke into her ear. "I need to see about cleaning up all this blood and the dead gremlins. Sit there and sober up a bit, then when Andrea's done we'll both go in the shower and wash this mess off. After, I'll tell Ivan I'll take his job offer and learn monster hunting full-time. Since Goldman is closing anyway I won't feel too bad quitting."

"I wish he'd offer me, too, so I could get out of Motherlode."

"I'm sure he will someday," Luke said, hugging her again and looking forward to more than just a shower.

* * * * *

Upstairs, Petr wept at the sight of his dead tribe mates. He failed them. Edthgar surely killed the Elder if he sent the whole tribe to their doom. Petr was the only one left. He vowed to do everything possible to help his new human tribe slay Edthgar.

Petr sensed Andrea's earlier magic outburst, too. He realized she could be key to victory. His tribe might be gone, but he vowed to watch over Andrea and prevent her from twisting into something wicked. Magic could help them win, but could just as easily be turned against them....

25

Courtney expected to see Ivan waiting in the hall as she and Luke exited the bathroom. The spotless walls and carpet surprised her, however.

"Holy shit, what kind of cleaners did you use?"

Ivan smiled. "The true key is the paint on the walls having a similar compound to my car polish. In a matter of minutes the blood flowed into the carpet, which has hollow yet absorbent fibers. I merely borrowed the wet vac from the garage. I am not looking forward to cleaning it or the stairs, but those can both wait until after our discussion."

"Cool. Is that why there's no holes in the walls from bullets, either? Does your company make car mats using that fiber stuff?" Luke asked.

"Precisely. As for the mats, however, they would not be affordable for the masses. I do have the same material on the mats in my car," Ivan said, smirking.

"That's okay, I can't be bothered to vacuum my car anyway," Courtney said. She rubbed her forehead. "Andrea's magic thing is way more interesting than car mats, so maybe we can get to the point before you drive me to drink some more?"

"I will allow her to fill in the details when she feels ready, but I will take care of the most important bits somewhere more comfortable," Ivan suggested.

"The great room?" Courtney asked.

"No, your friend is there and I believe she wants time to herself at the moment, or at least time without my presence. She seems rather peeved at me. Your room will suffice."

Courtney led the way. She and Luke sat on the bed while Ivan straddled the desk chair, arms folded across the back of it.

"Do you have the dagger you liberated from the gargoyles handy?" Ivan asked Courtney.

She opened the top drawer of her nightstand with one hand and took the dagger out from under a stack of tank tops.

"Careful, Courtney. You do not want to cut yourself with that blade," Ivan warned as he stared at the dagger.

"I knew it was weird the first time I picked it up, but what's so wrong with it?"

"It is imbued with potent magic. Copper is not only highly conductive to electricity, but also to mana. When Andrea was cut by this dagger, magical energy flowed into her veins."

"So she has magical powers now?" Luke said. "That's how the gremlin turned to charcoal? It doesn't really sound bad."

Ivan shook his head and said in a somber tone, "Magic is nothing to be trifled with, and if you do not know what to expect it can be very dangerous. It happened to be beneficial in this instance. However, what if your cat scared Andrea?"

Luke looked over at Courtney's desk where Beatrix slept on the keyboard. "I see your point."

"I'm not eating Chinese for a while now," Courtney groaned.

"It is an odd time to be hungry," Ivan said, perplexed.

"There are jokes about—you know what, never mind," Luke said to Ivan.

"Good idea, I think," Ivan said. "Hide the dagger where Andrea cannot find it. She gained her magic from it, and as such it could amplify her abilities beyond her control. The mana flowing through it could prove difficult to resist. Until we know what capabilities she has and that she is in full control, we cannot risk it in her hands."

"You act like she's more dangerous than the gremlins were," Courtney said as she tucked the dagger away.

"The gremlins are all dead, aside from Petr. That is certain. We do not know how powerful Andrea is or what sort of magic flowed into her. Uncertainty is dangerous. I know she is your friend and you trust her. However, I do not trust magic under any circumstances. It can twist good people in terrible ways. It has a mind of its own and a way of manifesting far different from how the user intended," Ivan explained. His brow furrowed as if a painful memory stomped through his mind.

"Murphy's law," Luke said.

"Precisely."

"If you're so uncertain, why aren't you with her right now getting shit figured out?" Courtney asked.

Ivan had no immediate response. He looked down at his crossed arms, breathed deeply, and thought deeper. "I believe it would be best for you to do so. You know her better than I, and she will be more open with you. Magic is a fresh concept to you, so you may notice subtle changes I may dismiss due to my disdain for the arcane arts, aside from my ring.

"This is a predictable object, and I am a creature of habit. All this change of late makes me weary. I long for the day when things are stable enough here for me to feel comfortable heading to Romania while my mansion here is rebuilt exactly as it stood before," Ivan confessed.

He looked into Courtney's eyes. His gaze unnerved her because she saw something there she never saw before: doubt in himself.

"I'll go talk to her, but tell me what she told you so I'm not going into this shit blind. Like you said, I've got no clue about magic. I don't know what kind of shit I should be asking."

"I will let her do that. You already have all of the details from her prior dreams, and as I said, she will be more open with you. She was not in the mood to speak with me because she felt I withheld details from her, and I cannot be sure she has not withheld from me due to some trivial vendetta. I did not provide her with full information with the intent she would stay alert, but she did not approve. I seem to always misstep with her."

"Yeah, she's a bit different," Courtney said. She was glad the enhanced healing from the gargoyle blood also sped up sobriety's return. Andrea needed to talk about the dream while tonight's events danced vividly in her memory and emotions were still fresh, and Courtney couldn't play peacemaker drunk. The task would be difficult enough sober.

"I'll talk to her now, I guess." Courtney walked to the door. She paused just outside the room and listened to what was said on the other side. Ivan might say something giving her a hint what to ask Andrea.

"I do not think I will ever understand Miss Browning," Ivan said to Luke.

"Andrea doesn't understand Andrea."

Ivan chuckled, then sighed. "I suppose I should resume the cleanup. I do not envy you either, having to work in a few hours on so little sleep. I remember how I used to struggle before the ring rendered sleep unnecessary."

"I'm only going in today to quit so I can take your job offer. I'll nap all I want afterwards," Luke said.

Ivan's voice lightened. "Fantastic. Get some sleep now, for tomorrow will be too busy for naps. I will draw up the contract once the stairs are clean."

The desk chair creaked as Ivan stood, so she darted to the stairs. Andrea's situation worried her enough. She didn't need admonishment from Ivan adding to her addled thoughts.

Courtney paused at the end of the hall and looked down at the towel around her and the gremlin blood on the steps as Ivan exited her room. She glanced at her feet, shook her head, and headed back.

Ivan raised an eyebrow at her as she approached.

"I just took a shower. Those stairs are a mess. I think I'll be a little more comfortable talking to her if I'm dressed and not re-bloodified," she said.

Ivan nodded as she passed him. He hurried towards the staircase, and she giggled as she reentered her room.

Luke yawned, then grinned as Courtney dropped the towel.

"Be patient. I still have to talk to Andrea before we can do anything else," she said as she opened the drawer again and fished through it.

"I hope it doesn't take too long. I'd like to have a little more fun and still get a couple hours' sleep," he hinted.

"I think we can arrange that." Courtney quickly dressed and grabbed her flip-flops from under the bed.

26

Courtney stopped outside the great room doorway. "Hey AB, still awake?"

"It depends. Is Ivan with you?" Andrea answered in a sharp tone.

"No, just me."

"Come in, then," Andrea said, her voice back to its usual softness.

Courtney wandered into the unlit room and sat beside Andrea. "I'm surprised you don't have a light on."

"I know you don't need one and I want to try something in the dark while Ivan's out."

"Try something?"

Andrea held her hand out to Courtney with the palm facing up. "Watch."

The air around her hand crackled with weak electricity for a few seconds.

"Pretty sweet, eh?" Andrea wheezed.

Courtney studied Andrea's face. Sweat dripped down her forehead and her chest heaved. The mini light show took considerable effort. "Awesome, but get some rest. You look like you ran a marathon through Death Valley."

"Definitely, after that one. I've got to learn this, though; it's my chance to be special like you. I can defend myself and fight back. I don't feel helpless now."

Courtney saw the spark in her eyes, literally and figuratively. The blood vessels in those tired eyes flashed like lightning. Courtney shivered.

"Are you okay? You look like you saw a ghost."

"Just a little chill," Courtney lied. Andrea seemed unaware of the electrical currents in her bloodshot eyes, which scared Courtney more. She now understood Ivan's warning about magic.

"If I could control it enough to make it look like it was coming from an accessory to a costume it'd be a great trick for Halloween," Andrea lamented.

"Here we go again...." Courtney rolled her eyes. When she looked back at Andrea, the lightning's disjointed dance in her eyes ended and left normal emerald irises in its wake.

"Chris said his uncle Mark might let us do my party at the grill. Wouldn't that be awesome? It's not as cool as this place, but it's as good as it's gonna get."

"I suppose."

"Ivan's rubbing off on you. You've got a sour tone in your voice."

Courtney sighed and said, "When you deal with real monsters enough you get less thrills out of dressing up like one."

"Party pooper. I'll bet you haven't even figured out a costume," Andrea joked as she bumped Courtney's shoulder with a fist.

"Well, damn, you figured out what I'm doing. I'm dressing up as an ass that shits out confetti. *Boom*."

Andrea giggled as Courtney spread her hands to mime an explosion. "That sounds like something Luke would do. You should be a princess, or something feminine without a hint of warrior. Get your mind off things."

"But Luke already picked out his princess outfit! Not really. He's been practicing spinning his pistol lately so it's probably some dumbass cowboy shit."

"I'll bet Ivan goes in a suit and tie. Does he ever let go of business and boredom?"

"You're assuming he goes. He's not much for social gatherings. It's tough to be in the limelight when you don't age." Courtney eyed the empty wine glass on the table.

"Think Chris will be a pirate?"

"He already told Luke what he's doing, and Luke told me I can't tell. It's a surprise, but it's not a pirate."

"I'll tell you what I'm doing so we can coordinate," Andrea hinted.

"I know what I'm doing. I'm going to be a Viking warrior. Unc is making armor for me and I'll be able to have my sword."

"Viking warrior? But they're dudes!"

"When I was debating what to do that'd fit the armor Unc insisted on making, Luke showed me pictures Chris sent him of women at comic conventions dressed as male characters with their own feminine twists," Courtney explained. "I think I can get away with being a Viking. Haven't you heard of shield maidens, anyway?"

"I've seen cosplay before. Gawd, I wish I wasn't broke. It looks so fun, but armor is going to be heavy."

"Remember, I'm stronger because of the winged gargoyle blood. I can pick up Luke with one arm now, and he weighs more than a couple armor plates will."

"I still think it sounds stupid. It could go well with my sexy witch outfit," Andrea pondered, staring off into the corner of the room.

"You'll nail the witch part easy enough," Courtney joked.

Andrea snickered, but the sparks returned to her eyes and her hair blew around a little, despite the lack of airflow in the room. The air was ionized and ominous.

Courtney shivered again. Andrea ran her fingers through her hair, static electricity crackling faintly as the sparks in her eyes faded.

"There's so much static lately, isn't there?" Andrea said, failing to realize she was the source despite her performance earlier.

"Yeah, the air is kind of dry lately," Courtney fibbed. She yawned and took the opportunity to change the subject. "So, can you tell me about your dreams before I fall asleep here, or will they bore me to death instead?"

"Oh, you won't be bored. You'll tingle with excitement at the thought of me as a sorceress in the future," Andrea gloated.

Courtney suspected the only tingles she'd feel were from weak electrical currents rather than excitement, or perhaps from fear of a much more complicated future. Monsters could be predictable, as Ivan said. Andrea's magic promised chaos. Courtney was scared for her friend, and more than a little scared of her new abilities if they remained uncontrolled.

27

Hank looked up from his workbench as Courtney entered the workshop.

"Hi, Unc," Courtney said.

"Hello, Cricket. How was work?" He set down his metal-shaping hammer and wiped sweat from his forehead as she wandered over to peek at what he was working on.

Courtney made a fart noise. "A shitshow, as always."

"Well, this ought to make the day better. I've finished forming most of the armor." He handed her the partially formed steel shin guard.

"I love it," she said, examining the crude surface. "It brings back memories of the Caddy fenders."

"Yes, good memories indeed. I'll smooth everything after you've tried it on and I know it fits. No point perfecting it until I know it's right."

"I'm sure it will. Luke had a lot of fun taking those measurements three times, so I'm pretty sure they're accurate. Don't go too smooth, though. I like how it'll look a bit rougher. Seems solid, too. I wasn't expecting functional armor for a Halloween costume," she complimented, handing the guard back to Hank.

"Why make it just for show?" Hank said. "It could be useful anyway. Once I know it fits I'll coat it with winged gargoyle blood and spray some of Ivan's polish over it to seal that in. Then I'll paint over it, do some weathering, and seal with a clear coat. It'll be strong and hopefully the blood deters underling gargoyles from attacking in the first place.

"Your joints will still be vulnerable because I can't make functional armored joints like an old blacksmith and have it done in time for Halloween," Hank explained. "Your mobility would be hindered if I don't get it right, and I know how much you value dancing around whatever you're fighting."

"Yeah, agility is number one," Courtney said, looking towards the breastplate leaning against the Bugatti's wheel.

Her mind kept drifting back to Andrea's high-voltage abilities, and an idea struck her. She turned back to Hank. "Is there a way to make it resist electricity?"

"I suppose I could spray rubberized undercoating on the interior of each piece, though I'm not sure how effective that would be. Worried about Andrea?" Hank questioned.

"Yeah. She doesn't have a clue how little control she has, and I don't think I can tell her, either. She started sparking over a simple joke. I don't think she knew, but—"

Courtney stopped due to Hank's facial expression. His eyes were on the opening door behind her. The air felt ionized, as if a thunderstorm was approaching.

"Hey Andrea," Courtney said without turning around.

"How'd you know it was me?"

"The air feels more electric, but also because Luke and Ivan aren't home."

Andrea stood beside her. "You can feel changes in the air?"

Courtney showed Andrea the fine hairs standing up on her arm and said, "All my senses are enhanced, including touch."

"Must come in handy in bed," Andrea joked, winking at her.

Courtney blushed as Hank cleared his throat.

"Oh gawd, that must make you extra ticklish, too! Those tickle fights were so fun as kids, before you turned into a badass." Andrea wiggled her fingers as she approached.

"Don't you fucking dare."

"There must be some reason you're here with the satellite remote," Hank said, scowling.

"Oh, yeah. Do you, um, have magic-proof batteries? I thought a boring documentary might help me sleep, but when I grabbed the remote all the juice got sucked into me and left dead batteries," she explained.

Hank sighed. "I don't think even Ivan has such a thing."

Dejected, Andrea said, "Okay, so can you change the batteries and turn the TV on for me so I don't drain another set?"

"I'll do it," Courtney said. "Unc's got a lot of work he's doing here. I'll sit with you until you fall asleep."

Andrea's demeanor brightened as Courtney led her out of the garage and down the hall. "Sometimes I think this whole magic thing sucks," Andrea confessed.

"Yeah, you're going to have to be careful in public," Courtney said, searching the pantry for AAAs.

"I think if I can visit Ludari enough in the dreamscape he can help me control it better, but until then it's controlling me."

"So you're aware of it? Good. I hated sneakily talking to Unc about it," Courtney grabbed AAs, grumbling as she chucked them back.

"Yeah, I keep shocking myself awake before I can start dreaming. If I had control, I'd shut it off and sleep. It's pissing me off," Andrea complained. She pointed to a lower shelf. "They're down there behind the ravioli. I feel the voltage. I'm creeping myself out so bad."

Courtney moved the cans and pulled out the batteries. "It makes no sense how this is organized. The batteries should all be together."

THE DEN OF STONE

"Organized or not, I just wanna fall asleep in front of the TV. I need to see Ludari or I'm never gonna be my old self again. It's been a few days and I've only gotten a couple hours of training." Andrea pulled Courtney towards the great room.

"AB, I hate to say it, but you'll never be the same. Monsters change things forever. You learn to deal with it. I know from experience," Courtney advised as she fumbled with the remote and changed the batteries.

"Well something closer to normal. I have to learn soon since my medical leave is over on the first. I can't be zapping customers."

Courtney turned on the TV. "Well, fuck, give me the magic then. I'd love to electrocute some of the assholes."

Andrea giggled. "I don't think it works that way."

Courtney set the remote down, but Andrea grabbed her wrist. Light sparks shocked her at her friend's touch. Courtney couldn't help but jump.

"I'm so sorry," Andrea yelped. "I didn't mean to shock you. Um, could you change the channel before you go please? And weren't you going to sit with me?"

"Oh, yeah, I forgot about the channel. I was just grabbing some water and coming back." Courtney rubbed her wrist and retrieved the remote.

"Gawd, there's little burns there! I'm so so so so so sorry!"

Courtney shrugged and scrolled through the guide. "I don't see any documentaries. How about some basketball? That should do the trick," she said.

Andrea sighed. "I guess. It's probably more boring anyway. Sometimes I really get into the nature docs. Like, there was one a few weeks ago about hornets. I couldn't look away!"

Courtney nodded as she selected the basketball game, then set down the remote. "I'll be back. Want anything to drink?"

"Some water would be good," Andrea said, staring at Courtney's wrist.

"Don't worry about the burns. They'll be gone in a few minutes," Courtney said as she exited the great room.

Once in the kitchen, Courtney swore quietly and examined the redness on her wrist. "Damn. We're going to have to wear rubber suits around her if this keeps up," she muttered as she opened the fridge and grabbed a couple water bottles.

She headed back to the couch and handed a bottle to Andrea, holding the cap end so her fingers wouldn't get shocked as her friend grabbed the bottom.

"Wait, do you guys have sleep aids?" Andrea asked.

Courtney nodded. "There's a little melatonin Unc picked up so I wouldn't have to go so heavy on the wine." She winced as she remembered sitting helpless during the gremlin attack. Other memories from her school years lurked behind those, but she brushed them off and headed for the great room door.

"Thank you!" Andrea said to Courtney's back.

Courtney nodded to her and debated taking one of the pills a little later after Luke and Ivan got home.

28

Hank sat beside Courtney in the darkness on the front steps, looking at the stars as they waited for Ivan and Luke.

"How much performance driving can Ivan teach in the dark? Luke doesn't have our night vision," Courtney said, tossing a pebble into the sky.

"You'd be surprised. It's not all about driving, either. Ivan wants Luke to learn how to use other senses besides vision. He'll have to focus more and rely on feel while driving fast in the dark. Cars and driving are a shared interest between them, which makes it easier for Ivan to convey his message."

"Relying on feel in a car you're not used to seems like trouble. Luke didn't even tell me what Ivan bought him for the security job. I want to see it before it gets wrecked, dammit. I don't care if he wants to surprise me."

"You're being overly pessimistic lately. The fact that Luke isn't used to the new car is exactly why Ivan wanted to do this. Since he's not used to it, he'll be more cautious, which means focusing more," Hank tried to explain.

"That's what we would do, but we're warriors. Luke isn't yet. I don't want him getting hurt trying to be like us."

Hank put his finger over Courtney's mouth. "You underestimate him. True, he's not seasoned yet, but he's further along than you give him credit for. He stepped into this willingly, without the curse of gargoyle blood, and he's learning. He's shown greater poise than I thought possible of that jokester, never more than against the gremlins. You'd have seen if you hadn't been drunk as a skunk."

Courtney nudged her uncle's finger aside and joked, "I've never seen a skunk with a beer. Skunky beer yeah, but not skunks with beer. It might be cute to see one stumble-waddle."

"True," Hank said as Courtney took a sip from her water bottle.

The two sat quietly until the sound of a roaring engine approached. "That rumble has to be a V8," Courtney predicted. "Sounds mean, too."

"You'll like it," Hank teased. "Ivan has good taste, and I think he picked the perfect one."

"You know what it is? Why didn't you tell me?"

"Luke wanted to surprise you. I'm not one to spoil surprises and neither are you. I want to see your excitement, just like when I gave you the Willys."

"The librarian gives me the willies. You gave me your car," Courtney joked.

"Luke's puns are rubbing off on you a bit much. Besides, Alec isn't bad once you get to know him. He's a big part of our group, archiving and examining manuscripts related to the gargoyles. Once you chat with him as a fellow monster hunter, he'll see more than eye candy. I admit I've wanted to deck him before for some of the looks he's given your skimpier outfits."

"That's nice, but I hear downshifts. They're almost here."

Hank signed and accepted her end to the conversation.

Courtney closed her eyes, listened, and said, "Maserati?"

Hank said nothing.

Ivan entered the circle and parked the Bentley. A green Jaguar sedan pulled in behind it.

"Holy shit," Courtney said. "I half expected a rusty Volvo wagon with a Ferrari engine."

Hank elbowed her. "It's nothing custom. The hardest part was getting the right options to match Volkodav—"

Courtney dashed past Ivan to Luke's car. "Show me everything," she said as the window lowered.

Luke shot her a sly grin visible from the steps. "Get in."

She darted around and climbed in. Luke threw it into reverse, backed up a few feet, whipped around the Bentley, and blasted away down the driveway.

Hank watched small puffs of smoke from the tires waft skyward. "Ah, youth," he said fondly.

"I seem to remember you fogging mosquitoes quite often in your Riviera," Ivan said as he sat beside Hank.

Hank laughed. "Exactly what I was thinking about. I miss that car. Never should've sold it to pay for the shop."

"A minor regret compared to many we share. How is Andrea?"

"Sleeping again. Your father helped her a bit while she napped earlier, so she's not draining all our electronics anymore. She's even hoping to do a little target practice later if she's able to conjure the lightning bolts she did in the dreamscape."

"Well, I hope you are up to that," Ivan said, looking away towards the bushes.

"I think she wants your help. Besides, I've got to put the finishing touches on Courtney's armor. The straps aren't going to make themselves, and I'm slow working leather and sewing. I'd be doing it now, but the rubber coating inside has to dry," Hank said.

Ivan mumbled a Russian obscenity as he looked back to Hank, who swore he saw a little color enter the immortal's cheeks. "I will make the straps so you can help Andrea aim.

I would prefer to avoid dealing with magic. She would also revel in annoying me by flirting." Ivan fidgeted with his ring and looked back to the bushes.

"You're really holding quite the grudge over that one glass of wine."

Ivan snorted. "How about we recount our youths some more and ignore the current youthful denizens of this mansion?"

"How was Anatalia's aim?" Hank asked.

Ivan's hands clasped tightly as he answered. "She was quite the marksman. Yes, I taught her, as I told you. I fail to see the relevance to Andrea. Magic and firearms are entirely different mediums of destruction. You have formal military training you could adapt to teach her. Perhaps she will be more receptive to your training than Courtney was to mine."

"Maybe. You know Courtney. She's more stubborn than either of us."

"For good and for bad," Ivan muttered. "Oh, I have her pistol in my car. She tried to throw it away. I am debating how to scold her without having her rebel further."

Hank laughed. "Yeah, you make the straps for her armor. I'll have her and Andrea work on their aim together. Courtney's settled on the sword and it's final, I think, but if we make it a competition, she'll actually try to shoot better."

"Sound plan," Ivan said. He glanced to the bushes again for a moment before he stood. "I will head inside now so I can sneak past Andrea while she still sleeps."

Hank laughed again and looked where Ivan had. Nothing moved, but as he listened, no birds called out. No squirrels chirped. Only insects buzzed. Something smelled like stink bugs.

The thing in the bushes stayed absolutely still until Hank went inside.

29

"How many times are we going to check the same damn places before we accept there's no entrances here?" Scott asked Renee as he kicked a rock into the bushes.

"There has to be an entrance somewhere around here, unless gargoyles appear out of thin air. We just have to find signs they were here and follow them." Renee mopped her forehead and put her sunglasses back on before glaring up at the sun. They'd found a few footprints in loose dirt and broken branches on small trees, but all the remnants of gargoyle activity led in circles.

They know to be careful to hide any paths to entrances.

"Maybe they know where the radar blindspots are and the cave could be anywhere within a mile radius," Mendoza suggested. "Just because the radar recordings showed them popping up here doesn't mean it's where they came from."

Renee sighed and looked between the two other monster hunters. Mendoza's grip on his machine gun was loose, the barrel pointing to the ground. Scott's plain T-shirt was soaked through with sweat in several spots.

"We've been out here for three hours, and still have a couple more places to look," Scott said. "How about we head to the deeper forest for some better shade; save the open spaces for tomorrow morning when it's cooler?"

"You're probably right. Let's go. If nothing turns up anywhere else, we can come back and expand our search radius," Renee said.

She tread carefully as the trio headed back down the hill. Renee paused for a moment at a strange chittering sound and exchanged a look with Scott.

"That was weird," they chorused.

Renee glanced around and said, "Where did it come from?"

Mendoza pointed to the left. "Just a woodpecker calling. You're getting jumpy expecting something that's not here."

He kept going down the hill as Renee sniffed. *Stink bugs. No gargoyle scent. He's right—we're jumpy.*

Renee followed Mendoza back to the hidden clearing they'd all parked in. The feeling of being watched continued until she got in her interceptor. Renee kept glancing back at the hill as she drove away.

* * * * *

The trio split up and headed home after further fruitless searches. Renee's stomach rumbled over the sound of smooth jazz on the radio, so she changed her turn signal from left to right at the stop sign, heading towards the Mexican place on Golden Hind Way.

Renee pulled into the parking lot and parked next to a familiar rusty Ford Ranger. Paolo Fernandez. His fiancé disappeared about a year ago, and though she knew he wasn't involved, her gut told her the man knew more than he let on about the circumstances of Marissa's disappearance. *Maybe I'll pay him a visit after some grub.*

As she exited her car, a man in a dingy desert camo boonie hat limped out the door to the dilapidated restaurant. He tipped his hat to Renee as he approached his truck.

"Officer Nelson. I see you have good taste in food," Paolo said, rubbing the graying stubble on his chin.

"As do you," Renee said. "I was actually thinking about stopping by to talk a bit after dinner, if you don't mind."

"Not at all. Just give me a bit of time to get my grocery shopping done. That's all I had planned for tonight anyway, except maybe some reading."

"Sounds good. I doubt it'll take long. Don't worry, it's nothing legal. I know you didn't have anything to do with what happened, despite what the chief says."

Paolo's nervous smile perked up into a genuine grin. "If only all cops were so honest and perceptive. If I had to be questioned by that gringo Beauregard again I'd likely commit an actual crime," Paolo joked as he climbed in the truck.

"Trust me, we all want to deck that dumbass back to whatever Georgia backwater he came from. Good luck with your groceries," Renee said, doing her best to ignore Paolo's prosthetic leg visible between his sneaker and the elastic at the bottom of his sweatpants.

"Today was a good day metal detecting, so I'm treating myself to name brand ice cream. Since you're stopping by, do you have a favorite kind?"

"Free is the best kind, my dude," Renee said as she shut the truck door for Paolo.

"*Muy bueno*. See you soon," Paolo said through the open window.

Renee watched the old truck drive off before heading to the restaurant's door.

* * * * *

Renee swatted another mosquito and grumbled at the trees around her. She closed her eyes and thought back to the night before, when insects hadn't been out for her blood.

Paolo didn't have any information for her about unusual sights, but the black raspberry ice cream and good company meant the evening wasn't wasted. The former soldier had given her a few tips on tracking in the wilderness, and they'd already helped her spot a few gargoyle signs she'd missed on the hillside the day before. Thankfully, the temperatures were also back down to seasonal levels instead of the flashback to summer heat the day before.

A crackling sound a few yards away snapped Renee out of her reminiscence. Scott turned to face her, his breath fogging in front of his face. Mendoza aimed his machine gun to their right as he uttered Spanish obscenities. Renee raised her pistol at a large, dark shape just before it charged away, snapping twigs like crazy.

"What the fuck is that?" Scott yelled as Renee fired a couple of rounds.

The bullets ricocheted off the creature like it was made of stone. *Gargoyle?*

Renee ran after the tall beast, but a minion gargoyle stepped out from behind a tree and slashed at her. Its claws barely missed her arm as she leapt aside, slamming into the trunk of another tree. Mendoza fired a burst that tore through the gargoyle's face.

Another crackle sounded as Renee rose to pursue the coal black one, but it was gone. Instead, the ground and trees around where it had been were coated in ice and snow.

"What was that?" Renee whispered as Scott rushed past her. "Some sort of tougher minion gargoyle?"

A second minion gargoyle peeked out from frozen shrubbery. Renee squeezed off a couple of shots from her pistol and sent the gargoyle sprawling, clutching its face.

Mendoza smashed the wounded gargoyle's face in with his ax as Renee joined Scott at the frozen spot. In the chilly center were two large boot prints. Rippling ice radiated from them. Renee glanced back; the spot where the thing first appeared looked fresh out of mid-winter. Mendoza scratched his chin as he rejoined them.

"Whatever it was, I think it proves we're on the right track to finding an entrance. I'm calling Ivan to say what we saw here," Renee said as she reached for her phone with shivering fingers.

30

While the rest of the monster hunters made no headway finding entrances to the gargoyle lair, Andrea made immense progress under the combined tutelage of Ludari in the dreamscape and Hank in the real world. Courtney's frustration at shooting grew; she wound up throwing her pistol into the small pond on Halloween afternoon. She still couldn't hit a target with any consistency, while Andrea routinely blasted apart hay bales with lightning bolts from her fingertips.

With the day's training complete and the Halloween party imminent, Courtney and Andrea waited with Luke by his car. Andrea kept shifting her seated position on the steps, eager to see Chris in costume and uncomfortable in the knee-high boots of her witch costume.

Chris' little blue Mitsubishi blasted into the circle, tires screeching as it stopped. Chris exited the car in a plain blue bodysuit with white boots and gloves. His long hair was spiked upward with immense amounts of gel.

"What the hell? You're Vegetable guy from that damned Dragon Ball sequel? That was your big secret? I was hoping for Jack Sparrow, or maybe Yamcha," Andrea shouted.

"Silence! I am Vegeta, prince of all Saiyans," Chris yelled back in character.

Luke spun one of his revolvers as he laughed, making a point to look over his own Rick O'Connell costume from *The Mummy*.

"You dare mock me?" Chris said, still in character as he walked over to the waiting trio. "I'll show you what a true Saiyan warrior can do!"

"I'm used to shooting mummies, but I might make an exception for dudes in tight bodysuits that leave nothing to the imagination," Luke said.

Chris shook his head and turned to Courtney. "You look like a warrior, at least. Tell me where you got your armor. I must know."

"The helmet's from eBay, but Unc made the rest."

"May I see it?" Chris pointed to the horned helm under her arm.

Courtney handed it over by the horns. His eyes widened as she let go and the weight pulled his arm down. He handed it back, blinking at the ease with which Courtney handled it.

Chris turned to Andrea. "You're not my Bulma, but I don't need a scouter to see your sexy level is over nine thousand." He kissed her and finally broke character. "You weren't kidding when you said sexy witch. I'm digging the fishnets and boots."

Andrea readjusted her black wig and hat and tried to think of a compliment for his outfit. "I, um, like that blue. It goes well with the Mitsu."

Luke unlocked his car and said, "We should be going."

"This is the supercharged one, right? Can't wait to see what this baby can do." Chris held the rear passenger door open for Andrea.

"No, go slow! You don't have to race just because you dressed for an old action movie," Andrea protested.

"Old? Good movies are timeless," Luke said with a wink, closing the front passenger door behind Courtney. As Chris slouched and contorted to get his extra foot of height into the back seat, Luke added, "Watch your hair, prince."

Chris groaned as he tilted his head to fit the hair, which knocked off Andrea's hat.

Luke got in the car. "How'd you fit in the Mitsu?"

"I reclined the seat and pushed it forward so I could reach the wheel. My knees were scrunched tighter under the dash than passengers on budget airline flights."

"That image is the scariest thing I think could happen this Halloween." Courtney groaned and rubbed her forehead.

"Says the girl who put blankets over the seat to protect it from her armor. The sword looks real, too. It's a bit scary," Chris said.

Luke started the car and joked, "She needs it to scare away trick-or-treaters."

"Yeah, I was wrong. Kids are way scarier than cramped airplanes," Courtney said.

"You do know Mark isn't letting anyone under twenty-one into his place for the party, right?" Andrea pointed out.

"Good," Courtney said.

Luke put the car into drive and departed the Mays mansion for Mark's Bar & Grill.

* * * * *

The creature in the bushes watched the humans leaving in their metal travel capsule. It gleefully chirped at a pitch beyond human hearing.

Edthgar, on the other hand, not only perceived its cries, but returned them from his temporary hiding place beneath a massive pine a mile away.

The creature heard its new instructions. Oh yes, it heard them well. It twitched with glee at its master's new mission. Six legs scuttled along as it dashed from the bushes towards what the master called "the tower."

* * * * *

Beatrix caterwauled and scratched at the door to Hank's office. Hank set his tea down next to the photocopied manuscript Alec had brought him in the morning, before Courtney or Luke awakened. Luke's cat had acted strange for the past few days, but it hadn't gone through this much effort for attention yet. He opened the door to scold the cat. It darted right past him.

"Beatrix, you're not allowed in here. It's dangerous," he said as he closed the door.

The cat peered up at him from under the desk, huddled next to sleepy Petr.

"I know Luke just left, but you'll have to wait. I can't play right now. I'm busy reading this old scroll to see if it gives me any clues about what gargoyles need in order to take a queen. I need to try to protect my niece, your owner's lady."

The cat stared up at him, pupils wider than he'd expect in a well-lit room.

"Fine, you can stay there, but I'm reading." He sat down and picked up his tea, paying no mind to the cat's terror.

* * * * *

Luke parked next to Tadeo's car, where Tad sat on the fender wearing a cheap tuxedo.

"Your car goes with my costume, broski," Tad said to Luke as Courtney got out of the car. He pointed to the hood with a crowbar. "Where's the cat? Did someone jack your hood ornament already?"

"Jags don't come with them anymore. If they did, I'd be worried about the mafia guy with the insanely polished dome," Luke said.

Tad looked at Courtney as she tucked her fake glasses into her pocket—they would interfere with the helmet's nose guard once she put it on. "Nah, man, I'm outgunned. Any good mafia greeter knows when they need backup."

"Where is your backup, anyway?" Chris asked.

"Heidi couldn't wait for the bathroom, and it's taking a while because she's in a Dalmatian onesie and has to take everything off," Tad said, blushing. "She should've known not to have Guido's Pizza for lunch."

"Aw, how cute! The Dalmatian part, not the Hershey squirts," Andrea said. "I can't wait to see what Todd and Lizzie show up as."

"You invited those dipshits?" Courtney grabbed Andrea's arm and squeezed.

"Yeah, and a couple other coworkers. You know Todd and Lizzie are an item now?"

"I told you weeks ago. Who else did you invite?" Courtney asked, letting go of Andrea's arm to grip the handle of the sword for comfort.

"Easy, Killer. I invited Josie, Marcus, Devon, Enrique, and Melissa."

Courtney shook her head, pointing to the end of the lot. "Todd's Jetta is here already. Let's just get inside," she grunted as she put on the helmet.

Courtney led them to the entrance where Lacy greeted them dressed as Marilyn Monroe. "It's great to see you all again," Lacy said in a monotone voice. "Food is set up buffet style by the stage, and drinks are at the bar as always. The tables are all put away in the basement, so we encourage everyone to mingle and have a great time."

"Does everyone get the same spiel, cuz?" Chris teased.

Lacy blushed. "Does it show? I haven't been so nervous memorizing something since the preamble to the Constitution."

"You did fine, Marilyn. Just steer clear of fans," Chris said with a wink.

She returned it. "I stitched extra wheel weights from Daddy's motorcycle into the bottom of the dress just in case!"

The group laughed as they headed for the stage where Mark sat, strumming his guitar in shredded jeans, dusty boots, a faded bandana, and a worn leather vest that showed off his tattooed arms. His biker 'costume' was likely thrown together from his own clothes.

Stacy swapped an empty tray for one full of chips and dip. The red dress of her Jessica Rabbit costume sparkled under the stage lighting, but she struggled to keep her wig on straight. When she saw Chris, she stopped, letting the wig droop to one side. "My god, you must've used five pounds of gel to keep your hair up like that," she said.

He straightened her wig out for her. "I thought Lacy was going to dye your hair instead of using this lousy wig. What gives?"

She took off the wig and sighed. "I tried everything, but as you can see, it came out more pink than red."

"I love it."

Stacy stuck the wig back on. "I don't, so I'm hiding in the kitchen when I can."

As Stacy darted away, Chris returned to Andrea, Luke, Courtney, and Tad. "I think the pink looks great on her," Chris said.

Luke nodded while Courtney eyed the bar.

"I don't think she likes crazy anime-girl hair colors like you do," Andrea said. "Pink is better than blue—like the Bulma pic you've got for your phone wallpaper. Why you had to pick Vegetable instead of Yamcha. The OG Dragon Ball was so much better."

"I've donated to Melon Kallie for a couple of years. She's done pink hair too, but I love her Bulma. That's about the only thing sexier than that witch outfit on you. Or off...."

Courtney ignored Andrea's retort, watching the stage until she felt a tap on the breastplate covering her collar bone. She turned to see a small winged gargoyle. Courtney drew her sword and snarled.

The gargoyle spoke. "Whoa, easy, Courtney! It's me, Todd. From work? Lizzie's right over there in the surfer girl get-up. See?" her coworker protested.

Courtney slid the sword back into its sheath and apologized. "I'm sorry, the whole Brazo de Dios thing just has me really jumpy." She tapped the spray-painted cardboard wings taped to his gray hoodie and laughed, not so much at the sad attempt at a gargoyle costume but at herself.

"I understand. I should've said hi instead of the tap, but it's noisy in here, and I wanted to see if the plate on your shoulder was real metal," he said.

She looked into his brown eyes and saw sincerity. Still, she felt uneasy and had no idea why. Everything seemed fine at the party, but she couldn't shake the all-too-familiar feeling of impending doom.

* * * * *

The cat pawed at Hank's ankle. "What's gotten into you?" he said, looking down at the cat.

Beatrix faced the door, staring. She kicked Petr with a hind paw, trying to awaken him.

Hank realized the cat wasn't seeking attention. She was trying to deliver a warning.

Something flickered on the radar screen. Hank briefly saw a mass of green dots approaching the mansion.

Every dot disappeared, even the white dots representing the monster hunters.

Hank rose from the desk and watched the screen, waiting for it to display something, anything. Nothing appeared. "What are you up to, Edthgar?"

He walked over to the gun case and stared a moment, then unlocked it, grabbing a shotgun with a flashlight taped atop the barrel. The glass door rattled as he closed it and opened the fireproof cabinet next to it.

Hank's fingers shook as he took a deep breath and reached into a box of shells. Gargoyles never made him nervous anymore. Something else was out there. *Is it that dark thing the others saw a couple days ago, or something else?*

"Stay," he said to the cat as he loaded the gun, shoving extra shells into his pockets.

The cat meowed. Hank swore it sounded like, "Don't go!"

Hank switched on the flashlight as he approached the door. The only way to jam the monster radar was to block or damage the antenna in the tower, so he knew his destination.

He locked the door behind himself and walked to the stairs. Patrols in Vietnam came to mind, though there was no comparison. There he'd been in a hostile environment, shot at by other human beings while dodging booby traps. Here there were no punji sticks, stinging insects, or venomous snakes. This was familiar territory, but he was defending it from supernatural foes. He wasn't sure if he preferred the snakes or the unknown waiting above.

The chilly air in the stairwell helped settle his nerves. Colder air was another difference from the jungles he fought in decades ago. Sweat still beaded on his forehead, just like those anxiety-filled patrols decades ago.

No creature waited for him in the tower. He sighed as he lowered the shotgun. The overhead hatch to access the array of antennas was still locked and in place.

Something moved outside the window. Globs of a gelatinous substance oozed down the glass and dangled in the breeze.

Hank pulled his cell phone out of his pocket to call Ivan, but it went to voicemail. "As soon as you hear this, drop whatever you're doing and get back to the mansion. I've got a feeling something big is going on. The radar's gone out and something strange is on the dome."

He examined the ooze on the windows, trying to make sense of what it could be and what could have done it. It wasn't the work of a gargoyle, but Edthgar had to be behind it. Hopefully the stuff wasn't acid, eating away at the dome and eventually the antenna to put the radar out of commission for good.

Hank moved closer. Even through the sealed windows, the strong scent of stink bugs hit him. *Just like the other night on the steps.* Strands of something like spider silk drifted down as goo smeared the glass.

Whatever it was, he needed to get a hold of Courtney—to warn her to stay away. Even if Edthgar attacked the mansion, he couldn't get her if she stayed at the party around a crowd of people, too public for the gargoyles.

His thumb hovered over her contact info when something scraped the glass behind him.

31

The party died down after a few hours.

"Thank you so much for hosting; it really means a lot to me," Andrea said to Mark, shaking his hand.

"Don't mention it. It was nice to have a different sort of event here. Everyone seemed to have a great time. Hopefully I'll get some new repeat customers in the future."

Andrea laughed. "Hopefully. I love this place. It'd be great to see it do even better. Have a good night."

Chris, Luke, and Courtney said their goodnights to Mark and followed Andrea out to the parking lot.

Stacy leaned against Lacy's Mini Cooper, sans wig and heels but with a cigarette hanging from her mouth as she faced the stars with her eyes shut.

"When did you start that?" Chris scolded.

"It's not real, just a costume prop, and I'm just chewing on it to relieve stress while I wait for sis," Stacy answered.

"Good. Have a good night," Chris said.

"You too," Stacy replied.

Luke unlocked the Jaguar, which sat alone in the lot aside from Lacy's Mini and Mark's old van. Tadeo and Heidi departed earlier in the evening because of her continuing need for the porcelain throne.

"I can't wait to get back to the guest room and have a witch trial," Chris joked.

"Gawd yes. These boots are killing me. Next year I need a costume with sandals, or barefoot," Andrea groaned as she limped along.

Courtney stuffed her helmet into the foot well. "I must be weird because I feel totally comfortable with all this armor."

"Yeah, you're weird," Andrea said to Courtney. She turned to Chris. "So what's the penalty if I'm found guilty of witchcraft at this trial?"

"You'll be stripped naked and tied to a bed."

"Can I forego the trial and just plead guilty?"

"Of course."

"One condition. Get the gel out of your hair first. I am not letting you play Vegetable guy in bed," she teased, touching his hair and frowning.

Courtney leaned her head against the window as Luke steered toward the road. She pulled her phone out and saw six missed calls, all from her uncle, and a voicemail. The bad feeling she'd banished with a couple shots was back.

She played back the message, but only picked out a couple of words through odd static: "stay" and "big." The message played back a second time, and a third as her fingers rapped against the dash. The fourth playback made her slap the console.

"What's up?" Luke asked.

"I don't know; I couldn't get anything meaningful out of the static."

The message played over and over, but the only thing standing out more each time was a shrill chirping sound like a cicada. It was barely audible with her superior hearing, so she doubted anyone else in the car could hear it. Whatever it was, the word "trouble" flashed in her mind like a massive neon sign.

"Luke, step on it. Something feels really wrong about this message," she said before turning to Chris. "You might not be able to stay tonight, but we won't know until we get back."

"So much for the judgment," Chris said to Andrea.

Faint lightning appeared in Andrea's eyes behind the lenses of her glasses, and Courtney hoped Chris didn't notice. Her friend hadn't experienced a high-stress situation since the lessons with Ludari, which left questions about how she'd react. Courtney feared the potential of an electromagnetic pulse from her friend while in the car—possibly disabling it and preventing them from returning to the mansion to find out what was going on.

Courtney tried calling Hank, but got a busy signal. The home phone was dead when she tried that number. She tried Ivan, but got another busy signal. Hank had to be talking to Ivan on his cell. It didn't make her feel better, but at least it meant Hank lived.

"What's wrong?" Andrea asked.

"I don't know."

She tried Hank again, then Ivan. Still nothing.

Everyone sat in tense silence and looked out at the clouds rolling in to obstruct the stars as Luke hustled the car towards home. No cops sat with radar out, and no slow traffic hindered them as they arrived at the Mays driveway in good time.

Courtney's phone rang as Luke drove up the driveway. "Hello?"

"Stay away tonight. I think the gargoyles are making their move and I'd prefer you be far from the action," Hank said over the phone.

Courtney grabbed Luke's arm and yelled, "Turn around!"

"Yes, do that," Hank called from the phone.

"Brazo de Dios?" Chris asked.

No one answered.

Courtney hated the idea of running from a fight, but her uncle wouldn't tell her to unless he felt it truly necessary. She held onto the sword handle as Luke slid the car around the circle in a cloud of smoke.

At the bottom of the driveway, one of the statues fell over and blocked their way out. Luke slammed onto the brakes and put the car into reverse to back up the circle.

"They've got us trapped!" Courtney yelled at the phone.

"Get ready for the hardest fight you've ever seen. I'll bring down some guns," Hank instructed and hung up.

Luke parked the car and said to Chris, "I'm sorry we dragged you into this shit, too, bud."

"Into what?" Chris asked, bewildered.

Andrea looked over to him, eyes shimmering with electricity. "Monsters." She grinned.

"Monsters?" he squeaked. His frantic eyes darted around.

Courtney got out of the car, put her helmet on, and drew her sword. "Come and get me, you ugly motherfuckers!" she screamed.

Luke drew his pistol and moved to her side. Andrea walked to her other side, electricity crackling all around her body. The trio formed a circle around Chris.

"Who put drugs in my drink? This shit can't be real," Chris stammered.

The first gargoyle charged from the trees at Courtney, but she dropped it with a slash to the throat. A second whack finished beheading it. Her heart raced, yet time slowed down. Everything gained surreal clarity.

Three gargoyles ran across the circle, but they met Thompson fire from the mansion doorway.

"Chris, come to me!" Hank yelled.

Chris ran towards the house. Countless gargoyles swarmed all around. One nearly tackled Chris but was struck down by a lightning bolt from behind. Chris tripped and face-planted in the bushes by the house, then stared as Andrea smiled at him, sparking like a human Tesla coil. She winked as he scampered up the stairs.

"Can you use this?" Hank asked Chris, holding out a small submachine gun.

"I'll find out," he said shakily.

Gargoyles fell to Courtney's blade, Luke's bullets, and Andrea's lightning. Courtney laughed at Andrea's tongue stuck out at a convulsing gargoyle, its eyes burnt out by electricity.

Luke blasted a roaring gargoyle and yelled, "I'm out! Cover me while I reload."

Courtney tore apart gargoyle after gargoyle with her sword by the nose of the car. Andrea burned others to a crisp with high voltage by the trunk. Chris and Hank picked off a few incoming gargoyles before they could reach the embattled trio by the car.

Minion gargoyles hesitated to strike out at Courtney. "Your will to fight break? Bunch of fucking chickens," she said, her eyes moving from one minion to another until wings beat from above.

Edthgar swooped down, drilling Andrea in the side of the head on his way to tackle Courtney.

Her sword and helmet clattered to the asphalt.

A spider-like creature with a near-human torso and the head of a mantis skittered around the corner of the house, spewing globs of gelatinous matter at Hank and Chris.

"What the fuck is that?" Chris said, ducking to avoid the flying ooze.

Hank fired the Thompson, smiled, and said to Chris, "Dead. That's what it is."

Edthgar loomed over Courtney and seemed to laugh, ignoring Luke and the unconscious Andrea. The other gargoyles stopped and watched as Courtney spat in his face.

"Go ahead, try your worst. Fuckhead," she said with a growl.

Several gargoyles surrounded the landing as Hank noticed Edthgar over Courtney. One slapped Chris's gun out of his hands while another grabbed the barrel of the Thompson, but none advanced any further. They stared the duo down. The gargoyle flinched as Hank yanked the gun from its grasp. It growled, slashing his forearm with its claws, then waggled a finger until Hank set down the gun and spare drum.

Courtney's heart pounded as Edthgar lowered his face to within inches of hers. His tongue lolled out of his mouth and across her lips. He appeared to laugh again.

Her sword was out of reach, but she wrapped her fingertips around one of the horns on her helmet. She looked away from Edthgar's crimson glowing eyes and noticed the area above his right eye had burn marks around the base—and cracks in the horn. Did the Bentley's flamethrower weaken it?

Despite her disgust from the lick and the sickening feeling of fetid saliva on her face, she snickered. "Is that the best you can do? Pathetic. Gross, but doesn't scare me one bit." She stuck out her tongue at the beast above her.

His eyes glowed so bright they almost blinded her as his tongue shot out again and licked the tip of hers. Vomit threatened to rise if he licked her again, so she swung the helmet. It smashed into his fractured horn, spreading the cracks further.

Edthgar roared in pain and reared up, allowing Courtney to get back to her feet.

"Luke, shoot the horn, shoot the fucking horn!" she screamed.

Edthgar turned to Luke, his glowing eyes bathing everything around him in scarlet light as they widened. Luke fired at point-blank range. Edthgar's right horn shattered at the base and dropped to the pavement, smashing into several pieces.

Luke smiled as Edthgar wailed and stumbled backwards. He emptied the revolver into the other horn. Hairline fractures appeared.

Courtney retrieved her sword and swung at Edthgar. She missed the horn but left a deep, bloody gash above the winged one's brow.

A minion gargoyle threw itself between the two of them, taking the next blow from her sword across the chest, allowing Edthgar to escape toward the back of the house. Courtney finished off the minion with a couple whacks and ran after Edthgar.

Battle frenzy consumed her and Courtney welcomed the two gargoyles jumping out from the shrubbery. She beheaded the first with three chops while the other hesitated. It tried to back away from her advance. "You smell your shithead master's blood on my sword, don't you?" she yelled.

The gargoyle shook as it scrambled backward, until a bullet exploded the side of its face.

Up above, Edthgar struggled to fly away into the thickening dark clouds.

"We almost had him!" Courtney lamented.

"Next time we see him will be the last. We'll finish him off then," Luke said.

Courtney looked around and panicked. "Where's Andrea? Is she hurt?"

"Oh shit," Luke said, looking back to the car.

Courtney spotted Andrea's purse near the edge of the paved circle, along with the witch hat and bloodied wig. Drag marks in the grass led from the circle to the back of the house. Courtney snarled and stormed along the trail of rumpled grass into the clearing behind the mansion.

A solitary gargoyle stood near the trail's end, staring towards the pond through Andrea's broken glasses. It wobbled on legs streaked with blood from a bullet hole in its abdomen.

"Where is she?" Courtney screamed, pointing her sword at the beast.

The gargoyle pointed up at the sky and coughed. "With Edthgar."

Courtney stood a few feet from the gargoyle, fuming. She stared at the wounded thing as its shaking worsened.

"Do it. I am not afraid. I look forward to my freedom from tyrannical demands."

Courtney walked up to it and snatched Andrea's glasses from its face, then turned around and stalked back to where she stood before. *Control yourself. Keep it together. Don't let it taunt you.*

"That'd be merciful. Your kind doesn't deserve mercy," Courtney said, facing away from it. She jammed the tip of her bloody sword into the ground.

A thump sounded behind her as the gargoyle fell over. Courtney knelt by the sword, holding Andrea's glasses in one hand and the sword handle in the other. She ignored the gargoyle as it crawled to her.

It reached for her knee and spoke again. "This is the difference between our kinds. You have freedom to choose how to fight. We can only do as Edthgar demands, which is usually death. Our existence is spent in servitude until we are finally allowed freedom with our last breath."

Courtney brushed its hand off of her knee and pulled the copper dagger from her boot. She jammed it into the gargoyle's skull, granting its wish. "Shut the fuck up."

Her lip quivered as she returned her attention to Andrea's glasses. One lens was cracked, and the other had blood on it.

She jumped as Luke put his hand on her shoulder. Hank and Chris walked around the corner of the house as she swallowed hard and looked past them, towards the parking circle.

"They all just up and retreated. What happened?" Hank inquired.

"Where's Andrea?" Chris asked frantically.

Courtney whimpered. "They took her."

We were so close.

The glasses rattled as her hand trembled. A choked sob escaped her lips and the tears washed Edthgar's drool from her face.

32

Ivan waited in his car while Hank dragged the statue out of the driveway with the winch on his Blazer. Once through, Ivan maneuvered around gargoyle corpses while Hank unhooked the winch, allowing the broken statue to flop over in the bushes to the side of the entrance.

As he parked, Ivan saw Luke filling Chris in on all the details about gargoyles between vomit sessions into the shrubs. Andrea's boyfriend wasn't taking the revelations well.

He watched Courtney put her anger to good use by chopping apart gargoyle corpses. Forty-two gargoyles had died tonight, probably a significant chunk of their population. However, the loss of Andrea diminished any cheer the group could have taken over the number of dead gargoyles, and whatever the insect-like thing was.

Hank parked the Blazer and walked over to the giant bug carcass as he motioned for Ivan. Ivan sighed, got out of his car, and joined Hank. He wanted to ask about the bandages wrapped around his friend's arm, but Hank spoke before he could.

"I have no clue what it was. I've never seen anything like it—a sort of centaur with the body of a spider for the bottom half, a torso like a human on top, and some sort of bug head spitting out the goo."

Ivan squatted by the corpse, holding his breath due to the stench of the brown stew of internal matter spilled from the bullet-riddled carapace. In his century-plus of life, he had smelled few things as foul as this abomination's insides.

"I am also puzzled, but may have a theory. A story my father told in one of our conversations over the years has sprung to mind. He told me of a swamp on his world, populated by strange man-bugs he was unwilling to describe. If I remember correctly, he called this place *Anzillu Bit Tuklati,* and few of his people dared venture near the outermost regions of this swamp unless they absolutely had to. This creature seems to fit the bill. I believe it was summoned from the dimension where he and the gargoyles originated. I'm uncertain how, as that magic is complicated." Ivan moved away from the corpse to escape the smell.

"So now Edthgar is summoning things from other dimensions to send into battle? His minion gargoyles weren't bad enough?"

"No. Edthgar does not have that capability, but look around. He must be running low on minions with the sheer numbers we have killed recently, along with all of his gremlin spies. It takes time for hatched gargoyles to mature. He probably cannot wait long for fear we will find him and end this war before he can play his final card by taking a queen."

"So if Edthgar can't summon things, how do we explain that monstrosity?" Hank said, pointing to the bug.

Ivan sighed and looked to the thunderstorm in the distance. "I asked Renee to look over evidence collected from the fire at my mansion to see if one particular artifact was present. I had the Halgaard rune in my possession before the fire. It was not in the evidence locker. Fire would not have destroyed it, and it would have stuck out like a sore thumb to the team collecting evidence from the burned rubble.

"I think perhaps Edthgar somehow discovered I had the rune, stole it, and used the fire to cover his tracks. With the rune he can control Halgaard, since they are both of the same dimension. Halgaard would have the power to summon inter-dimensional beasts; word from my father is he retained his human intellect, which is why he eluded discovery for all these centuries.

"He did not want to fight humans once he remembered being one of us. He in fact helped the Sumerians stave off the other gargoyles. Until recently, there were occasional sightings of him in Europe as he offered advice to mercenary groups hunting monsters there. Gaining control of his brother would certainly make Edthgar more aggressive in his quest. Perhaps it was even his goal to make a human woman absorb blood the night of the attack here so he could take a queen. That is my theory."

"Lovely," Hank said with a scowl. "No wonder it knew to block out the radar with whatever crud is sprayed everywhere."

"My father often says Halgaard may even be smarter than he is, and if he'd sent Halgaard to this world first instead of coming himself he would not have needed to summon the others, avoiding the flawed runes which created the gargoyles in the first place."

"Hindsight is always 20/20. Your father is a royal fuckup, you know that?"

"Yes." Ivan cringed. Hank rarely swore; the defeat tonight must have hurt him immensely.

Ivan looked over to Courtney and said to Hank, "After I speak with your niece I will climb the tower and look at the substance. With any luck the incoming storm will wash it all away, along with the blood."

"Okay. I'll call to make sure Renee is on her way to make yet another fake police report," Hank grumbled.

Ivan walked over to Courtney. "I am deeply sorry I was unable to return in time to be of any help."

THE DEN OF STONE

"Where were you? I get Unc didn't want to go in the tunnels because he thought we could finish Edthgar out here, but still, where were you?" she said, quiet fury in her voice.

"I was at the library examining documents pertaining to the fault line running through this area, because I felt with enough research I may be able to find an entrance to the gargoyle lair. There were also a few accounts of ancient gargoyle activity to examine for clues about the strange beast witnessed by the others. I had my phone silenced and out of sight, so I did not notice it vibrating when your uncle first called. It is entirely my fault I was not here to help."

Courtney said nothing, taking another whack at the gargoyle corpse in front of her.

"When I was on my way here your uncle called me again. He said one of the gargoyles told you Edthgar took Andrea."

"Yeah, and?"

"How did it tell you this?"

"It opened its mouth and spoke, how the fuck else?" she snarled.

"It spoke English?"

"I understood what it said, didn't I? Are English-speaking gargoyles a big deal? Do they usually have to press *dos para Español?* The first one I killed spoke English."

"Is that so? Minions of Edthgar almost exclusively speak Gaelic, if they speak at all. Minions of Halgaard speak English."

Courtney stopped hacking but still didn't look at Ivan as she said, "So we're against two of the fuckers now?"

"I believe we have been since my mansion burned. The fire was most likely a ruse by Edthgar to hide the fact he took the rune, to cover his intent to force Halgaard to serve him. According to ancient accounts, Halgaard has a face like coal and uses magic based around cold. It appears he has been teleporting minion gargoyles to the places they've appeared on our radar. Little wonder we are no closer to finding the entrance to the lair."

Courtney looked over the bloodied blade of her sword and smiled. "I guess that means we get to kill two winged ones when we rescue her."

She turned and looked into his eyes. Ivan recognized exactly how she felt in that look. She would become an unstoppable force, gleefully killing anything in her way. It was the same cold-blooded rage he'd felt following Anatalia's death, the same fury he'd unleashed on hordes of Nazi soldiers when the German invasion of Russia halted his quest to slaughter every last gargoyle for what they'd taken from him.

Seeing this look in Courtney's eyes made him shudder. Because of him, she was drawn into the war against the gargoyles—also by extension Andrea, because she would not have been dragged in without Courtney's involvement. Because of him, this vibrant young woman was being hammered down into a ruthless killing machine, and her friend would no doubt face unfathomable horrors at Edthgar's hand. As much as Andrea annoyed him at first, she'd certainly grown on him, and he felt a crushing weight on his heart thinking of what may become of her before a rescue could be attempted, if the lair could ever be found.

"Let me help. I have to retrieve my sword from my car," he said, but she didn't respond as he walked away.

Ivan balled his fists as he thought of Andrea in Edthgar's grasp.

33

Her head throbbed and her vision blurred, but Andrea saw upon awakening she was no longer at Courtney's home. The chilly night was gone. Humid air plastered her costume to her damp skin. Unnatural dim orange light surrounded her, but the most damning evidence of her situation was the cold metal band around her wrist and thick chain attached to it.

As her eyes adjusted to the poor lighting as well as possible without her glasses, Andrea took in her surroundings. The chamber looked to have been carved out by claws from whatever type of faintly glowing rock made up the cave. Condensation clung to the stone and the rusty chain. Small patches of moss sprouted in several spots.

Most importantly, she was not alone. Another woman sat chained across the chamber—and it wasn't Courtney. She had dark hair, dark eyes, tanned skin, ragged red high-top sneakers, and a dingy dress, which at one time was probably white. Her captivity must have been lengthy, judging by that dress and her thin arms.

"You're awake now?" the woman asked in a soft, breathless voice, tinted by a Spanish accent.

"I guess so," Andrea answered, rubbing the side of her head. "What is this place?"

"We are prisoners in *el Diablo's* den of stone."

Confirmation of her suspicions hit like a punch to the gut, even though she expected it. Edthgar had taken her, and she feared her friends suffered worse fates. "Did Edthgar bring anyone else in?" she asked the woman.

"No, only you. What is your name?"

Andrea felt some relief knowing Courtney wasn't here. It meant all wasn't lost. Edthgar would never kill his future queen. She breathed easier and answered, "My name is Andrea."

"I am Marissa. How did you know Edthgar's name?"

"My friends are fighting against him. I suppose I'm here as bait to force their hand."

"I see. They gave him trouble tonight, I would say," Marissa said. A hint of satisfaction crept into her voice.

"Oh?"

"He has lost a horn and has a big cut on his face," Marissa answered, smiling.

"That must be why I was captured. He was about to lose otherwise."

"I cannot wait until he is defeated. It is an honor to meet one of those who will help bring about his end. May I ask what day it is? I cannot tell the passage of time down here."

"It's Halloween night—or early November first, I guess. I don't know how long I've been out. Too many concussions lately."

"Halloween again? I was taken days before Halloween, and I know I've been here more than a week. A whole year lost." Marissa began to weep.

The sight of Marissa's tears and the fact the gargoyles would keep someone over a year hit Andrea like a rock. "What do they feed us?" she asked Marissa in a panicky tone.

Marissa spoke between sobs. "They make my fiancé bring non-perishable foods. He also has to bring other supplies, but the food is just for me, and now you. There is also bottled water, because the water flowing deeper in the cave is full of nasty things. The gargoyles don't want me getting sick. They keep me alive to make Paolo help them."

"It'll be over soon. My friends won't wait long. They just have to find a way in here, then we'll both be free."

Marissa's dark eyes widened and her head snapped towards the dark opening to the chamber. She turned back to Andrea, huddling against the wall and hugging herself. "He's coming."

Andrea focused as the pounding steps grew closer. After nearly a minute, Edthgar entered the chamber. The gash on his face was clearly from a sword. Good for Courtney. She'd barely missed his eye. Andrea stifled a grin at the sight—Edthgar could be injured. Thoughts of lightning flashed through her mind, and how it could hurt Edthgar to facilitate her escape before Courtney and the others mustered a rescue.

Edthgar stopped at Andrea's feet and looked her over. His eyes ceased glowing crimson. They almost looked like hazel human eyes. After a few seconds, they glowed again in a soothing blue. Perhaps this thing could feel emotions, conveyed through those strange glowing eyes. She liked it better when she could think of Edthgar as some demented monster, though the idea he could probably feel fear encouraged her.

Wait, when did I start looking forward to a fight? Is this the magic talking?

Edthgar looked like he was sizing her up when she heard a man's voice in her head. *"I was human once, not always a disfigured beast,"* the voice said. It had an exotic accent almost like Irish, and she might have thought it sexy if it weren't Edthgar.

His eyes fell to her thighs and the fishnets. The glow shifted to a warming shade of purple, and he licked his lips.

Andrea froze. The thing looked like it found her attractive. The taste of salsa from the party returned as her stomach threatened to empty, but she also blushed. *Oh gawd, disgust and pride at the same time? Ew.*

"Like what you see? How about a closer look at my boots?" She drilled the spike heel of her boot into his eye below the missing horn. The glow ceased. Blood erupted from the socket. It squirted into her hair and face, blending with the dried blood from the wound he'd inflicted during the mansion battle.

"You wicked little wench!" Andrea heard screaming in her head as the gargoyle let loose a terrifying roar that echoed in the small chamber.

Edthgar looked straight at her with his one remaining eye, glowing brightly enough to illuminate the whole chamber a ruby red—making sure she saw deep into the empty socket gushing blood.

Andrea smiled. "Now if we painted you purple you'd be a one-eyed, one-horned, flying purple people eater!" She wished she hadn't said, "people eater;" she didn't want to give him any ideas.

He grabbed her leg and ran a claw down the boot laces, slicing them apart, then yanked at her boot. Its resistance only lasted a few tugs. Edthgar tucked it between his jaws, shredding it with his sharp teeth. When he snatched her other leg she tried to kick him in the eye with her socked foot, but he blocked it. His hands squeezed both ankles. Andrea didn't have enough strength to break free.

He spread her legs and she heard an evil laugh in her head. *"Maybe later. I want you to dwell on that."*

He pulled off her sock, then hooked a claw in the fishnet stocking and tore it apart. *"Take off the other one. I cannot allow you to have that spike as a weapon."*

"Fuck you! My boyfriend thought these boots were sexy as hell, even if they're uncomfortable. Are you going to buy me another pair after Courtney wastes your ass?"

Edthgar moved to Marissa, who sobbed as she curled up on the stone floor. He placed a claw at her throat, forcing her to look at Andrea, and pressed gently, drawing blood. Marissa stopped crying, paralyzed by fear.

"Take the boot off or I will shove this claw all the way through her spine, leaving you alone with your fear of what's to come."

A tear rolled down Andrea's cheek as she untied the boot and yanked it off, tossing it to Edthgar. He shredded it like the other.

The voice spoke again. *"Very good. Tears taste wonderful. Seeing that one makes me excited for more. Now, let's see some more skin."*

Andrea pulled off her sock and tore the other fishnet. "There, are you happy now?" she said, wiping the tear from her cheek.

"Why stop there? I have heard there is fancy lingerie in this day and age. Perhaps those legs of yours have me thirsty to see more."

"No. You'll have to work to see that," Andrea said with a hiss. She balled her fists as Edthgar studied her. One of her fake nails broke off as her hands shook. Hopefully she looked more defiant than scared.

The disembodied voice spoke again in an exasperated tone. *"Very well. Say goodbye to your only human contact for the foreseeable future."*

"No!" Andrea screamed. She pulled down her skirt.

Andrea heard a demented giggle in her head. *"Cat print? I love cats. Their cries are so satisfying as I bite their tails off. My brother Grigori is terrified of cats. At one time they were the only meal I could guarantee myself. Continue, my adorable prisoner. It surprises me to feel some of these human desires returning."*

Andrea swallowed the rising tide in the back of her throat and unbuttoned her shirt. She left it hanging by the sleeve on her chained arm. "Now are you happy?"

Edthgar stomped away from Marissa to Andrea's side. His eye faded to a pink glow as it traced her collar bone. Andrea's legs shook, but she stayed standing as the eye settled on her chest.

Please, no.

Edthgar placed his claw on her bra between her breasts. She held back a whimper as he tore it open, exposing her chest. He tore the straps on her shoulders as well, dropping the torn bra to the floor.

"Beautiful," the voice said in her head as his eye lingered on her chest.

The eye didn't stay there long enough, drifting over her belly to her hips. His curved claw reached down and hovered there for a second as a whimper escaped her lips. He laughed, withdrawing his hand and licking away her tears.

"I will let you keep that secret for a little while. I don't want to break you quite yet. I think I might enjoy your spunk and want more fun," the voice said in her head. *"Besides, terror tastes so much sweeter the longer it brews."*

Edthgar licked one of her nipples. *"Your sweat already tastes decadent from fear. It should be like ambrosia later."*

He turned around, grabbed the shredded boots, and walked out of the chamber. His deranged laughter cackled in her head for a few seconds after the spiked ball on the tip of his tail disappeared from view.

Andrea slid down the wall, staring through the empty entryway.

"Are you all right?" Marissa asked.

"Never better," Andrea lied. "Are you?"

"Never better," Marissa lied back.

They both forced a laugh.

"I'm a little jealous of your shape. The past year has turned me into little more than skin and bones, as you can see. Paulo would not recognize me," Marissa whispered. She looked down at a rip in her sneakers.

"I can't see well without my glasses, but I'm sorry for what these monsters did to you."

"Aren't you going to get dressed?" Marissa hinted, keeping her eyes on her sneakers.

"I don't know. I figure he's going to tear them off when he can't wait any longer, and I'd kind of like to have something to wear when I get out of here."

A tingling sensation fluttered against Andrea's bare back and legs. The orange glow of the rock pulsed where it touched her skin. Mana. The strange rocks had magic in them for her to absorb. She blinked a few times and grinned before Marissa spoke again.

"Deep thinking. You're making a plan, aren't you?"

"Maybe. It's crazy, dangerous, and unpleasant, but it's a start," Andrea said, looking at the glowing floor instead of Marissa.

She concentrated and felt the tingle as more energy flowed into her body through her bare skin. The drained remote batteries crossed her mind, and she realized a potent battery existed all around her. The earth itself was fuel for her magic.

"You do have a plan. I see you smiling," Marissa said.

Andrea put her skirt back on. She drew slightly less energy, but if she concentrated on her legs she found she could take in enough to make up for it.

You left this out of your lessons, Ludari. Whatever this rock is, it rocks.

Something dripped from her face, splattering on her chest. Drops of blood. It was Edthgar's blood—winged gargoyle blood. She must have absorbed some of it, too. Andrea thought back to Courtney telling her how it enhanced senses, including touch. She wondered if it might also enhance magic. Ludari was going to be answering so many questions in the dreamscape when she next slept.

Andrea put her shirt back on. Edthgar would be more suspicious if he found her naked when he next entered the chamber. Besides, the sick bastard was probably looking forward to tearing her shirt open. It would distract him as she enacted her plan. A smile crossed her face, thankful he shredded her boots. With bare legs, she could draw as much energy as she wanted without arousing suspicion.

Only one sock lay within reach, but it was covered in blood and had a tear where Edthgar's claw hooked through it. No matter. She could draw still more energy through her feet.

Static electricity crackled around her legs as she looked into Marissa's eyes. "Oh yeah, I've got a plan, and it's gonna be a shocker."

Andrea held up her hand. Sparks danced across her palm.

34

The next day, Courtney arrived home early and parked behind the Pontiac, which should have become Andrea's car. Luke's new Jaguar was gone. *So much for his humor to distract me from all these shitty thoughts.*

The sun peeked through the clouds for the first time since Halloween, illuminating Andrea's favorite spot to sit on the stairs. Courtney hated the sight. At least clouds and thunderstorms matched her dark mood.

Courtney scowled, looking away from the sun and shuffling towards the stairs. Her shoes weighed two hundred pounds as she tried to lift her feet.

Her fingers fumbled with her key. Courtney almost dropped it before she realized the door would still be unlocked. Hank and Ivan's cars were both in the circle. She squinted at the doorknob; focusing on something mundane might burn away the fog suffocating her mind.

The front door creaked open and she stepped into the foyer. As it closed, she thanked it for blocking out the sun. Sunshine was for normal happy people, not warriors of the night who couldn't protect their friends. The familiar battleship gray walls comforted her little, but at least they weren't a massive middle finger to her mood like those cheerful rays of sun.

Courtney chucked her fake glasses onto the top shelf above the hanging jackets, then threw her blue polo shirt to the floor. The belt hit the closet floor with a nice thud when she hurled it to the corner. Kicking off her sneakers didn't relieve how heavy her feet felt as she wandered towards the kitchen.

Her uncle wasn't in the kitchen. She sighed and walked to the great room, which was also empty. *I guess my room is next.*

The empty photo frame caught her eye on her way to the stairs. Its analog to the void left by Andrea punched her in the gut. She closed her eyes as she moved by, unable to bear the sight of it, even in her peripheral vision.

Courtney climbed the stairs to her room slowly and methodically, but her mind couldn't keep up. It continuously played through the battle to the moment she lost track of Andrea. The real world was like a video playing in the background while her imagination took the forefront.

Sun cascaded through a window in the hallway. "Fuck off," she muttered, pulling the curtains shut before continuing to her room.

Courtney chucked her keys, wallet, and phone at their usual spot on her computer desk. The phone bounced off the back of the chair and onto the bed beside her as she removed her work pants. "You just couldn't do me a fucking favor and break, could you?" Courtney hissed at the phone.

She eyed the mats for a moment, then shook her head to clear it. There was plenty of time to fit her workout in today, perhaps two workouts. Right now she didn't feel up to it. The tower called to her. Up there, she could stare out at the world without having to feel like a part of it.

Her thoughts wandered as she meandered down the hall and up to the tower, too numb to care about the cold steps and chilly air.

Courtney stared at the natural stone surrounding her in the stairwell. The mottled darker spots on one stone reminded her of the cloud Edthgar flew into as he escaped. His flight looked labored; she should have known he carried Andrea. She closed her eyes but the image remained, etched into her mind. Tears threatened to burst free to release the anguish over the replaying image.

"You are home quite early," Ivan said as she emerged from the stairwell.

"A little."

He held out a glass of wine and beckoned her to sit on the bench beside him. She sat and took the glass, but didn't drink.

"I see you have already dispensed with your workplace attire as well. You appear ready for your workout routine."

"Looks can be deceiving. The only thing I feel ready to do is curl up in a fucking ball and cry," she confessed.

"When should I draw up the paperwork for you to join Volkodav Securities? I assume you are available to start tomorrow."

"You're sharp. I hadn't even thought about unemployment yet—and you knew to expect me up here."

"I happened to be in the kitchen when I heard your vehicle in the distance, so I brought a few things up here with me. You took enough time to allow me to get here."

"Still, you knew what was going on."

"Sometimes it can be painful to be so perceptive. I often find myself wondering if I could have protected more people over the years if my mind was as honed then as it is now." A frown crossed Ivan's face.

"You're reading me like a book. The fight with Edthgar keeps playing through my mind. I can't stop wondering where I went wrong."

"Sometimes one can do everything right and still lose. I learned that lesson the hard way as well. When I look in your eyes, I see things reflected back I felt so many moons ago. In a way, it is like reading a revised edition of a book you have read countless times before."

Courtney looked down at the red wine in her glass, preferring not to think of Ivan as an emotional wreck. She opted to change the subject. "The personnel manager was at the door when I got there. We went straight to the conference room, where she went over all kinds of bullshit I barely heard. I knew what was coming. I didn't care about my poor attendance, or bad sales performance since customers were 'afraid of the girl at war with a gang.' I just wanted to get to the point and get out."

Courtney looked at her freshly painted fingernails. "She said the constant black polish added to my scare factor and recommended psychiatric help, because even though the gang member I accidentally killed was a despicable person, I showed no sign of remorse. I tried not to laugh and tell her she had no idea, that I repainted my nails to cover up the dried gargoyle blood I couldn't scrub away. I listened to her ramble on and wondered how much time she'd spend in the looney bin if she knew how the world really is."

Courtney's lips curled into a fake smile as she finished the story. "I looked her in the eyes and said, 'If I'm such a terrible person, why are you wasting our time telling me what we both already know? Give me my pink slip and let me be on my merry fucking way.' I couldn't help but laugh on my way out the door. I saw a customer staring at me as if I had a gun pointed at him, but it was just the look on my face and the way I laughed—laughing because it sure as hell beat crying. I hated that job, but it's one of the last things I had that reminded me of when I was still a normal person and not some freak who feels most alive when I'm killing. At least I won't have to worry about the fake glasses anymore if my old life is gone. I see Tad and Heidi rarely enough I can just say I got Lasik with whatever insurance Volkodav offers."

Courtney laughed as the floodgates opened and tears streamed down her face, surely smearing her excessive black eyeshadow. "I wish I'd said 'thank you' when she said I needed help," Courtney cackled.

"It sounds like you heard every word and cared more than you wish to admit."

"I didn't realize it until I saw Andrea's time card by the clock after I cleaned out my locker. Shit, my stuff is still in my car," she realized, snapping somewhat back to the present.

"Do not worry about it right now. Just sip your wine."

Courtney did as Ivan asked. She looked back at the glass, swished the remaining wine around, and gave him a genuine smile. "This is good stuff," she said, then took another sip.

"Cabernet Sauvignon. However, I must return the subject to perceptiveness. It should have been obvious to ensure the Halgaard rune be kept in the most secure part of my house, yet I tossed it in a kitchen drawer with various extra screws and rubber bands I could think of no other place to store. I thought if someone searched for it, they would automatically assume it was well protected and ignore simple hiding places. Thank goodness my study and wine cellar were in fireproof vaults. That helps our fight so very much right now, having wine bottles in every corner of my room here while the remnants of my home are demolished."

Courtney stared at the glass. "It's still good stuff." She wiped her cheeks and frowned at the smudge on the back of her hand.

Ivan handed her the unmarked bottle. "During the Great Patriotic War, World War II as you would call it, the Soviet regime learned of their immortal soldier wreaking havoc as I laid waste to Hitler's finest troops. I feared no bullet or conventional weapon. I quite enjoyed the riches of capitalism and my hunted treasures even then, so I was no communist. It was nevertheless a tremendous honor when Comrade Stalin insisted upon meeting me.

"We wound up meeting several times over the war years. I never particularly cared for the man, but he was still the leader of my country. We would play a game of billiards perhaps every couple of months or so once the war ended. Eventually his demeanor changed. He saw many party members indulging in luxuries he felt only the leader of the party should have—and realized they admired me more than him. He had them executed, but his solution was not so easy with an immortal. I was a threat, so I had to go.

"All my belongings were packed in large containers and placed on a ship to Sweden. As I stood on the dock that snowy day in St Petersburg, Leningrad as it was then, he sent an aide to ensure I got on the boat—and to give a final farewell. I no longer existed to Russia. I would be banned for as long as anyone who remembered lived. That order has not been rescinded by the bald weasel currently running the nation."

Courtney took another sip and said, "Damn, that's good and old."

Ivan continued. "The aide asked where I would ultimately go. I told him California. He scowled, thinking I would try to bring down Russia as vengeance for my banishment. I reminded him the war got in the way of my quest to rid the world of gargoyles, and California was where Edthgar fled while I fought to keep Russia safe. Destroying the gargoyles as the Nazis advanced would have meant little if my homeland had been taken from me. Though I have been away for so very long, it remains. I will always remember what Dimitri said next."

He took a sip, glanced to Courtney, then looked back to the bottle. "First you save Russia, then the world. When will you save yourself from your crushing sense of duty? You are but one man, tortured over a couple of deaths, and it takes an army. If you fail to let it go, you will never be happy even if you succeed. Stalin has been responsible for more deaths with less honorable reasons, yet sleeps well at night. I think I'll accompany you—do some good in the world.'

"We both got on the boat, but as it chugged away from shore, a bullet tore through Dimitri's forehead. It was another grim reminder of what my homeland was, and that perhaps I was better off away, fighting the gargoyles. Shortly following my arrival, I learned of Stalin's death. I felt sadness for a man I despised. I realized I would never be able to move on when I lost someone. Holding on to those we love, or at least their memory, is what constitutes a normal human in my eyes, not the ability to hold a job and hide your true nature. Loss never gets easier, but you learn to use it as fuel to carry on."

"You should grow a big-ass mustache," Courtney joked, to avoid delving deeper into life lessons.

"My hair and facial hair do not change. The ring prevents it. Otherwise, I can guarantee this annoying stubble would disappear."

"It was a thought," she said, finishing off her wine. Courtney handed over the empty glass and the bottle.

"Perhaps after I discuss something uncomfortable to me. I have been roped into a social gathering for Volkodav shareholders. I normally find a way out of such things to keep my profile low. Against my wishes I have been named a guest of honor along with some government officials with whom we are negotiating a rather sizable weapons contract. I have seen the seating arrangement, and it is set up for a guest and their date." Ivan blushed.

Courtney giggled. "So my first job with Volkodav Securities is pretending to be the billionaire's latest fling? Awkward."

"There will be no attempts at affection, I promise. I need you to be the eye candy and appear tremendously bored with the soirée so we may escape as soon as the business proceedings are complete. That way we can return to more important tasks, such as locating an entrance to the gargoyle lair," Ivan said. He looked out the window and wistfully added, "Anatalia would have found such a party immensely tedious. She would feign inebriation to escape and resume whatever adventure we sought next."

"I can do more than pretend to be bored or drunk. I'll do it for real," Courtney said, some cheer entering her voice for the first time in days. "Anatalia sounds like she was beyond special."

Ivan nodded and poured Courtney a second glass of wine. "Real boredom would be good. Genuine intoxication could make you sloppy."

"Too bad. I was thinking back to when Andrea made you spit out your drink. Good times. I miss her so much, but I know no matter how much I'm hurting, she's got it worse. I hope she's holding up okay. You know, she would've killed to be your date before she met Chris."

"She has grown on me since those dastardly initial impressions. Your friend has much more spirit than I gave her credit for. We will get her back and she will be annoying us again in no time," he said, patting Courtney's shoulder. Ivan blushed again as he looked out the tower window.

"What did Anatalia look like?"

Ivan sighed before he answered. "Tight blonde curls. Sparkling green eyes. A small scar through her left eyebrow. A constant mischievous grin, with freckled cheeks always ruddy from the cold."

"She sounds like she was lovely," Courtney said, thinking of Andrea's own wavy blonde hair and green eyes. *Yeah, annoying, you said. Andrea's grown on you, all right.*

35

Unlike Marissa, Andrea had the luxury of visits with Ludari to help track time. Three days passed without Edthgar following through on his threats. Until the dreaded moment arrived, Andrea stored energy to fuel her magic. Ludari confirmed her power would grow to immense levels once the winged gargoyle blood she'd absorbed kicked in.

Minions checked on them every couple of hours to empty the dishpan she and Marissa shared as a bathroom or to bring food and water. After six consecutive cans of beefaroni, Andrea was thrilled to see a box of Twinkies. She thought of Luke and wondered if he made it through the fight. Courtney would be delighted to see her eating beef, too, if that's what the meat in the can really was. Every bite brought Andrea to tears, thinking of whatever fuzzy creature perished to produce the cheap meat.

The next gargoyle to check in stopped to watch her. It stared with cold, reptilian eyes, and its malformed human-like mouth hung open. The thing's clawed fingers flexed as it watched. Finally it placed its hand on her knee and rubbed down her shin to the bee tattoo on her ankle. Its eyes never blinked and never left her face. The slimy beast made a chuffing sound as it caressed her shin upwards, back to her knee, before it got up and took the dishpan away.

"If that thing rubbed my leg again I probably would've fried it, even though it would've ruined my plan. I need to surprise Edthgar when he comes back," Andrea whispered to Marissa.

"Your magic is wonderful. It feels so luxurious to have a hot meal again instead of cold slop. These are a nice change, too," Marissa said. Her fingers shook as she struggled to unwrap one of the Twinkies.

Another gargoyle wandered into the room while they devoured the Twinkies. This one looked a bit more human, albeit with skin like lichen on stone. It was the first Andrea had seen with hair. Patches of gray fur sprouted from its forehead, chest, arms, and ankles like thin grass. Fur covered it completely from belly button to mid-thigh. The gargoyle met Andrea's gaze with its own perfectly human emerald eyes.

It spoke to her in a husky female voice. "I'm always told how human my eyes are, but I never believed it until I saw yours."

"I never thought I'd see a furry talking gargoyle," Andrea said, staring back.

It sat beside Andrea and said, "Not all of us are monsters, despite Edthgar's efforts to make us so. I am Halla, daughter of Halgaard. Before Edthgar enslaved us, my father worked to find a way to make us human, like he once was. Edthgar was always fearful, but the death of his last concubine is what made him seek the rune. There was only one female gargoyle left, and he wanted insurance until he could take a queen."

"It's not just Marissa and I? He's using his own kind like pawns?" Andrea asked.

"My father and brothers do not like to fight, but they asked me to tell you if the opportunity comes, we stand with you and your friends. We never wanted to be at war. If Edthgar feels it necessary to spoil everything good in this world, we will fight back now that we see hope for victory," Halla said.

"Thank you. Why did they send you? Why not your father?"

"Edthgar will not harm me since I am the last female, at least until he has his queen and can produce more young."

"I have a plan. I won't go into details, but you'll know when I set it in motion. Will you help Marissa, too?"

"Of course. May I ask something you may find strange or silly?"

"I'm talking to a furry gargoyle; what could be stranger?"

Halla laughed, exposing human teeth with elongated canines. "May I touch you? I want to feel human skin so I know what I hope to have someday."

Andrea blushed and nodded in affirmation. "Can I feel your fur?"

Halla giggled. "Yes."

Andrea brushed her fingers through the fur on Halla's forehead while Halla rubbed her cheek.

Halla pulled away. "You give me hope, but I must go. Edthgar is coming. I smell his malodor."

"Good luck, and be ready. It may be happening right now," Andrea called to Halla as she left the chamber.

Marissa said a prayer, eyes shut tight enough to give her crow's feet. "Let me know when I can open my eyes," her quiet voice said.

"Will do. Think you'll be able to run?"

"If I cannot, I will die trying."

Andrea's heart pounded. She suspected Marissa's did the same. Andrea held her breath for what seemed like hours, but must have been less than thirty seconds.

Edthgar entered the chamber without his loincloth. His remaining eye glowed pink.

"What took so long?" Andrea asked.

No voice spoke in her head, but Edthgar advanced and loomed over her. He extended his wings to steady himself against the chamber walls, leaving his hands free to caress her hips. His claws slid under the top of her skirt and gently pushed it down around her ankles. The gargoyle stared into her face, his glowing eye blazing neon pink like a sign on the Vegas strip as he pulled her skirt off the rest of the way. It hit the floor. He scooped it up with a claw and flung it across the chamber, where it landed in Marissa's lap.

Andrea wished he'd get it over with, but she supposed he wanted to go slow to build her terror. He carefully unbuttoned her shirt with more dexterity than she thought possible from his ragged dinosaur claws. His fingers felt like sandpaper as they rubbed across her skin and spread her shirt open so he could admire her chest again. She half expected that rotten slug of a tongue to come out and slather her in his swamp-water saliva, but instead he nudged the shirt from her shoulders.

Edthgar released her wrist from the shackle and finished removing her shirt. She blinked as she watched the rusty chain hit the floor. Not having to magically burn it apart made her escape plan easier than anticipated—if the first part worked.

Andrea focused on his eye as he pulled off her panties. All she wanted to see was the terror turned against him when he realized he'd played right into her trap.

The voice finally spoke in her head. *"No resistance? I am disappointed, yet pleased you realize submission is in your best interests."*

"I was waiting for some half-assed pillow talk." Andrea gulped as he spread her legs.

Edthgar held her against the rock wall. Andrea wanted to vomit in his face, but held it in. She had far more dreadful plans than bile. The timing needed to be right.

Every part of her body tingled as Andrea drew forth energy collected from the earth. Edthgar breathed heavily, filling her prickling nostrils with his rancid breath.

Andrea glanced down to see a very human appendage the size of a baseball bat mere inches away. She looked in his eye and smiled as she unleashed electricity into her captor's perfect lightning rod. Edthgar slammed into the ceiling, filling her head with squeals like the distant memories of pigs slaughtered at her aunt's farm. The dying pigs' pain was what first convinced her to become a vegetarian, but Edthgar's agony delighted her.

Andrea's back scraped the wall, and her tailbone dinged a protruding lump on the way down. A jagged bit of rock on the floor dug into her butt cheek. The pain was nothing compared to the ecstasy of Edthgar's cries.

She glared at the winged gargoyle and pointed, lightning striking from her eyes and fingertip. "Speaking of resistance, you don't have much to electricity, do you?"

Edthgar flailed against the ceiling until Andrea stopped shocking him. He dropped to the floor, twitching, while Andrea fetched her clothes and redressed.

She desperately wanted a shower to rid herself of Edthgar's insipid filth, but escape came first. Andrea buttoned her shirt enough to keep herself covered and squatted by Marissa's chain.

"You'll be free soon," Andrea said. Sparks formed in her palm, an orb of white hot fire to burn through the chain.

Marissa opened her eyes. "I can't say thank you enough for what you've done for me."

"Don't thank me yet; we still have to get out." Andrea kept looking over her shoulder at Edthgar while she burned through Marissa's chain. His spasms were intense, but fading. The damn chain needed to melt before the thing recovered.

Halla peeked into the room. "We must hurry. His followers are coming and my brothers cannot hold them off long."

Marissa's chain fell to the floor.

Andrea helped her up. "Lead the way," she told Halla.

Halla jogged down the cavern to the right. Andrea led Marissa in her wake. Veins of the odd luminous mineral poked through the stone, unlike the full wall of the chamber, darkening the pathway out of the lair.

Andrea couldn't see well enough to tread carefully. She cursed Edthgar every time something jagged dug into her feet, but at least they could draw in more energy as she ran. Another fight was sure to come. Andrea's heart jackhammered against her sternum, but a smile crossed her face at the thought of Edthgar's smoking, seizing body.

Is this the excitement before a battle Courtney talks about? Gawd, I'm looking forward to violence. What is happening to me? Is it the gargoyle blood or the magic?

Marissa stumbled, almost dragging Andrea down. Prayer after prayer left Marissa's lips as they charged onwards, as fast as her weakened legs would allow.

A roar echoed in the depths of the cave behind them. Edthgar was back to his old self. The roar compelled Marissa and Andrea into another gear, and they gained on Halla. The trio closed in on a dead end.

"I thought you were leading us out?" Andrea screamed.

Halla vanished into the rock ahead like a ghost. Marissa nearly stopped, but Andrea pulled her ahead towards the spot where Halla disappeared. They charged through the illusion of rock and emerged into open air.

Andrea dropped to her hands and knees under the starry night sky. Beach sand always felt wonderful, but never so sweet as now. The sound of the tide rolling in was the most beautiful sound she'd ever heard, until Marissa laughed.

"Thank you, Lord!" Marissa exclaimed, tears streaming down her face.

Andrea rose. Her legs throbbed, her lungs burned, her insides ached, and her feet were numb, but they had to get further than five feet from the lair. She ignored her pains and looked out at the Pacific. "We have to keep moving. They'll chase until they catch us or we reach safety, and I don't know where that is."

Halla helped Marissa up and said to Andrea, "I will help her this time. We go north along the shore. There's a small dock not so far away. We'll get away in a boat."

They ran down the beach, splashing through shallow tidal pools.

"Can't Edthgar still pick us off on a boat?" Andrea asked.

"You hurt his wings. It'll take time to heal since his magic is weakened by the missing horn. He cannot fly on one wing," Halla said.

Their pursuers emerged behind them. They were closer than Andrea liked.

Something moved in front of them—something like a giant bug. It spewed stringy strands at Halla, tripping her and Marissa. Andrea blasted the thing with a bolt of electricity before it could entangle her.

She stopped next to Halla and Marissa, blasting as many gargoyles as possible while trying to extricate her fellow escapees.

"Leave us. Get in the water and swim. My kind cannot follow," Halla pleaded.

"No," Andrea said.

"Go. At least one of us should be freed tonight," Marissa said. "God chose you, not me."

Andrea hesitated, then said, "Crawl away from the water. This is gonna be big." She ran out into the waves until they reached her waist. Even if the escape failed, at least she'd feel cleaner. Sparks crackled on the surface of the water around her.

Edthgar burst from the cave, roaring as he passed through the rock illusion. He pounded his charred chest and roared again.

His left wing extended partially, but the right one remained a crumpled and misshapen mess.

"I underestimated you," Andrea heard in her head.

She pictured a man sneering as Edthgar spoke. Her arms raised to the stars, and her electrical energy blasted skyward. It formed a small thundercloud. Lightning rained down on Edthgar's minions.

He roared again, and another bug creature dragged Halla and Marissa toward Edthgar.

"If you don't submit, I will skin the other human alive in front of you. Her life is in your hands," the voice said with a snarl.

Andrea paused. Another creature erupted from the water behind her. Something solid clubbed the back of her head. Salt water filled her nose and mouth. A giant lobster claw grabbed Andrea by the arm. It dragged her face through the sand as it hauled her back onto the beach.

The thundercloud dissipated. All Andrea could manage in her own defense was a weak jolt. Unfazed, the lobster-thing handed her over to Edthgar.

"If you so much as try to escape again, I will bathe you in the blood of your friend here," Edthgar promised.

Andrea couldn't muster a response. She dug deep and gave it everything she could.

Nothing happened.

If Edthgar's blood enhanced her abilities right away, maybe she could've done it. Ludari told her it could be weeks before changes manifested. Did they have long enough?

Andrea wept quietly as the outside world disappeared. Edthgar dragged her along, rocks bruising her knees and cutting her shins. Minions carried Halla, but hauled Marissa down the passage as roughly as Andrea.

"Courtney will come," Andrea said, wheezing.

"I'm counting on it. Soon I'll have what I need to end this conflict. First, I think we should pick up where we left off."

Edthgar stopped in a large cave and threw her against a stone column. Andrea pushed herself up, but he kicked her in the chin. The back of her head bounced off the rock. His clawed hands reached down and opened the buttons of her shirt.

Minion gargoyles gathered all around the cavern. They held Marissa and Halla in place facing Andrea.

Andrea screamed as her skirt came off.

36

ourtney and Luke sat in the tower, looking through the window at the stars. She wore her robe post-shower. Luke held her to keep her warm. She shivered frequently, but not from the temperature.

Andrea wasn't able to enjoy this beautiful clear night sky. Courtney reminisced back to so many nights when the two of them would chat in the parking lot after work, and how much Andrea enjoyed putting her Miata's top down to enjoy the stars on her commute home.

Courtney shivered again. Luke held her tighter as clouds formed suddenly in the distance. "I guess it's not such a clear night after all," she said.

Furious lightning spewed from the strange cloud.

Luke stood. "Remind you of anything?"

The two dashed down to Hank's office.

"Check the radar," Courtney yelled to her uncle.

Hank swiveled his chair to look at the screen. Courtney and Luke crowded behind him. A large cluster of blinking green dots swarmed the shore, along with a single white dot off in the water.

Luke hammered at the keyboard to zoom in on the swarm of activity. Green dots disappeared every second until a yellow dot popped up behind the white one. The yellow and white dots moved together towards a cluster of green. They stopped by the satellite image of a large rock, and all but the yellow dot disappeared. It made its solitary way back out to sea and vanished.

"What are yellow dots again?" Luke asked.

"Anything we don't see often enough to have a set color to represent," Hank answered.

"Could it be another one of those bug things?" Luke asked.

"No, the radar didn't pick those up. We need to examine one more closely to program the system to detect their brainwaves."

Courtney moved next to the screen and stared at the satellite image of the beach. "More importantly, who was out there?" she asked.

"No one in our group is unaccounted for. Ivan's at the library with Alec, Renee is off duty at home, Mendoza is working at his vet office, and Scott is at Mark's. You and I are the only other ones who have absorbed blood, and we're definitely not on the beach now. It makes no sense witnessing a battle on radar with none of our people involved," Hank said, puzzled. "How did you two know to come down here and look?"

Courtney smiled. "We saw a thunderstorm pop up out of nowhere on a perfectly clear night while we were in the tower."

"Andrea? She never absorbed blood, though, so it can't be her. She wouldn't show up as a white dot."

"I drew Edthgar's blood after we destroyed the horn. He flew off carrying her. He could've bled on her then. She could've absorbed a different gargoyle's blood down in their lair. If what we saw on radar was her trying to escape, she could've even touched their blood in the fight to get out. It makes perfect sense," Courtney theorized.

"I'm going back up to the tower to see if the storm is still there. That'll be a pretty clear answer," Luke said as he exited the office.

Hank grinned at Courtney. "Either way, I'll have Renee and Scott check it out tomorrow while you get ready for Ivan's party. It's the same area you fought the lagoonie. You know, a few nights ago that was a blind spot on the radar. Electrical activity could certainly boost the signal."

"No wonder gargoyles came out of nowhere. That's where the entrance is," Courtney exclaimed. She hugged her uncle. "I can't wait to get her back."

Luke reentered the office. Between heavy breaths, he announced, "The storm is gone, as quickly as it formed. It's got to be her."

Hank hugged Courtney tighter. "Even if Renee and Scott find the entrance, we'll need a plan of attack. It may be a couple of days before we can organize a proper rescue. It won't do her any good if we rush in and get trapped like Edthgar likely has planned."

Courtney looked into her uncle's eyes. "It's going to be so good to get her back. I can't wait to kill every last gargoyle for what they've done."

The end game neared, and she wouldn't stop until her sword dripped with the blood of every last monster in Edthgar's lair.

37

Police tape flapped in the breeze, blocking off the section of beach shown as a hub of radar activity the night before. Fog blanketed everything, making Renee and Scott's investigation more difficult.

Renee could barely make out the silhouette of a person standing beyond the edge of the tape. She doubted they'd seen anything, but it couldn't hurt to ask.

"I'm going to leave you on your own for a moment, okay? There's some guy standing over there watching us," Renee said to Scott.

"Are you sure it's a guy?" Scott asked.

"You think some pretty college girl is standing in the fog this early in the morning to look at your ass?" Renee joked.

Scott frowned and countered, "I meant it could be a gargoyle dressed up like a person, like Havardr did before we offed him."

"If it's a gargoyle I'll shoot it. I doubt crime scene tape would stop one of them from coming after us."

"Yeah, you're right."

Renee walked towards the tape where the watcher stood. Partway there she kicked something solid. Renee knelt to check it out. A large hunk of glass poked from the sand at the high tide line.

"Scott, get over here. I've got something interesting," Renee yelled as she brushed wet sand off the rough glass.

Scott ran over and took the massive chunk from Renee with both hands. "Shit, this is heavy. It's weird, but I don't get how it means anything.»

He dropped the pillow-sized glass and it plunged into the sand. Renee nudged it so it fell over flat.

"When sand is superheated, it forms glass. Lightning strikes can do that," Renee explained. She rubbed a fingernail along the streaks on the top of the chunk. "See this red stuff? It flakes off because it's dried gargoyle blood. Andrea was here last night, all right. I think she zapped a few bad guys before they dragged her back into the lair. See if you can find more glass blobs. If there's more, there may be a pattern and the central point should be the entrance."

"I'm glad you're here to provide some smarts. I sure as hell wouldn't have thought of that," Scott said.

"Of course not. You'd have to think first. I'm going back to interviewing the dude by the tape. He's far enough away I hope he didn't hear us talk about gargoyles," Renee said as she stood.

The breeze kicked up a notch as she headed for the caution tape. Renee zipped her police jacket as high as it would go. This was one of the chilliest mornings she could remember since moving to the Point Reyes area from Los Angeles, but at least it wasn't cold enough to snow. She'd seen enough of that fluffy white bullshit in her year in Chicago to convince her to head to the sunny sands of southern California.

The move to the smaller Drake's Landing Police Department had been to escape the endless shootings for a more mundane existence of breaking up the occasional bar fight. If she'd known what she'd be getting herself into, she probably would've gone back to New Orleans. Then again, voodoo scared her, too. At least Nadine Marsh was still there, from what she'd heard in phone chats with her dad.

"When will the beach be open again? I like walking here with my metal detector," the man by the tape yelled in a Spanish accent. The familiar sound snapped Renee back from her mind's quest to figure out where she'd gone wrong in life.

He sounded nervous, and when she got close enough to recognize the man's thin face, the beads of sweat on his forehead confirmed it. Paolo Fernandez. A backpack and his metal detector were slung over his shoulder.

"I can't say how long before it's opened again; there's an investigation going on," Renee answered.

"I see," Paolo said. He hung his head, and Renee swore his grip tightened on the backpack straps.

Strange. "Since you frequent this area, maybe you could help a little. Have you seen anything out of the ordinary lately, like a high number of footprints?" Renee asked.

"The thunderstorm last night was odd. I've never seen a five-minute storm before. The heavens thought fit to unleash their fury on some soul last night, but that wouldn't be criminal, it'd be divine," Paolo said. His eyes grew wide and he pointed behind Renee. "And now I see why."

Scott fired his shotgun and screamed as Renee spun. She ran back to Scott as a massive algae-covered bipedal lobster loomed over the private investigator. It clamped Scott's bleeding shoulder in one pincer and crushed his shotgun with the other.

Renee fired her pistol at the thing, but each round bounced off. She might as well have tried to take out a tank with a slingshot.

The creature threw the mangled shotgun at Renee, hitting her surgically repaired knee and knocking her over. Renee stood and raised the pistol, but the thing's pincer came down on

Scott's stomach. Her knee throbbed as she ran in closer, trying to find a soft spot on the crustacean from hell, blocking out Scott's screams.

Paolo ran past Renee to the pile of rocks the monster hunters collapsed during the lagoonie hunt. Renee barely noticed, focusing on the lobster. She fired at its stalk eyes, but again the bullets ricocheted away.

"Get down!" Paolo yelled. He stood beside the rocks holding an AK-47 with a grenade launcher mounted beneath the barrel.

So you're the one that built that, not the lagoonie. Hiding weapons? I knew something was off about you.

Renee dove as far away from the lobsterman as she could. Paolo fired the grenade launcher, and the top half of the lobsterman exploded.

Renee scrambled to check on Scott as the last chunks of lobster meat splattered the sand around her. Her stomach lurched at the sight. She forced away memories of her partner's body after the first gargoyle they'd encountered in her early days in Drake's Landing.

Scott's abdomen leaked across the ground beneath him, and severed sections of his intestines were strewn around, mixed with lobster parts. He still breathed, but not for long.

He looked up at Renee and coughed as he wheezed. "It's funny; I had lobster for dinner at Mark's last night."

Renee knelt by her fallen friend. "Hang in there. We'll have lobster together when you're out of the hospital."

"Can we watch Braveheart too? I can relate to the ending now." Scott sputtered, blood dribbling down his chin.

"Whatever movie you want," Renee said.

She squeezed Scott's hand in hers as he trembled and looked down at his belly. "I think I'll have to take a raincheck."

Scott coughed up another stream of blood, mumbled incoherently, and stopped breathing.

Renee bowed her head as she closed her friend's eyes, then pounded her fist into the sand. "Eight years fighting gargoyles and a fucking lobster gets him," Renee said, staring ahead but seeing nothing.

Paolo bowed his head and held his boonie hat over his heart.

Renee growled at him. "Hiding a grenade launcher on a beach? Maybe the other officers were right about you."

She raised her pistol, but Paolo kept his rifle by his side. He rubbed below his eyes with the back of his hand, then knelt beside Renee.

"I lost friends in Afghanistan, too. I know how you feel. Take it out on me if you wish, but it won't bring him back. Killing the monsters lurking here will."

Renee grabbed Paolo's collar and shoved him down, screaming. "And what the hell do you know about monsters that you never mentioned in any of the interrogations?"

Paolo looked to Scott's body, and he swallowed hard as he answered. "I thought talking about the demons in their den would make you think I was crazy, and I'd never get the chance to rescue Marissa."

Renee let go of Paolo's collar. "Rescue?"

"She and I walked along this beach constantly when I was getting used to my prosthetic. One day, demons jumped us and took her. They forced me to bring them supplies in exchange for not killing her. It's taken a while, but I've scraped together weapons so I could go in their cave and bring her back, along with the other one they just took. They had me double the food I bring, so I can only assume another is there."

Renee glanced to the soup can beside Paolo, then back to Scott. "If you're fighting gargoyles, I'll ignore the black market guns. Scott and I came here to find the entrance, but now...." Renee's voice cracked as she stared at her dead friend.

Paolo sat up and pointed to a large rock nearby. "That's it. They have an illusion in place to hide it." He grabbed a pebble and threw it at the rock. It disappeared without a sound.

Renee shivered and closed her eyes. "Ever been in there?"

"Only to a certain point to drop off what they request."

"Could you map it out?"

"Yes. I could do so blind. It's burned into my memory."

Renee put her hand on Scott's motionless shoulder. "We'll get you out of here soon. Once we make a plan, we'll finish this shit for you."

She pulled out her cell phone to call Hank. After he received the situation report, she got on the radio to the police station. As she choked out the last instruction, Renee rested her forehead against Scott's and let the floodgates open while Paolo kept watch between the rocks and sea for any threats.

38

Andrea sat with Ludari in his study in the dreamscape. Both sipped their tea in silence until Ludari spoke.

"You're spending a lot of time here lately."

"Are you tired of seeing me? I'd rather not be present there while Edthgar...I don't want to say it," Andrea said, hugging herself and shaking. "They cast a spell so I can't fuel my magic, so there's nothing I can do. At least here I have clothes. Edthgar took what little I have left and laid it just out of reach. Now that I know I can get here without needing to sleep, I'll take this escape as much as I can."

Ludari stroked his chin. "I may know a counter spell. I simply have to remember where the scroll is. I haven't seen anyone who could challenge my magic in ages, so I've had no reason to use it."

"If your magic is all powerful, how come you're locked up? I'd kill to be free, if I could. I feel so helpless," Andrea whispered, nearly dropping her cup from her trembling hand as she set it on the desk.

"I could escape easily, but I don't want to. I have a wonderful collection of artwork and would worry terribly about what kind of trouble Eryk is getting himself into without a voice of reason. Most importantly, I would break a promise to Ivan that I'd lay low until Edthgar was vanquished so I couldn't be captured and used against him, as you are being used now."

A scroll floated out of one of the rows of shelves and made its way to the desk. It unfurled as it lay before Ludari. One line of symbols glowed. Ludari pointed to them. "I don't suppose you can read Sumerian?"

Andrea peered at the words. "*Klaatu barada necktie?*»

"Interesting guess, but wrong."

"Movie quote."

"I don't know that one, but I'll teach you Sumerian. They created several spells to counteract old elven ones. Open your mind.» He placed his hand over her eyes.

She squirmed at a jolt of electricity in her head. The symbols on the scroll rearranged into something she could read. Her eyes scanned the words before her, and she read them aloud. *«Peta babkama luruba anaku. Tanadassi duru."*

"Very good. When you leave the dreamscape, concentrate all your energy on those words as you say them. It's potent spell-based magic, and should overcome anything Edthgar could muster," Ludari explained.

"What if it's Halgaard's spell?"

"It should still work, but if not, hope for a swift rescue party."

"How comforting."

"You're powerful enough to visit the dreamscape at will. I would be fairly confident if I were you. The only step above that is to have your consciousness in both the dreamscape and the real world at once, as I do."

"I'm so powerful I can't even keep my clothes," Andrea said, shuddering harder.

"You simply need training to hone your skills. You're far beyond the average pupil. You're ahead of many veteran mages back when magic was prevalent, in fact. Now go and believe in yourself. Find out what you're truly capable of."

Andrea scratched Fenrir's ears. "Wish me luck."

"Good luck," Ludari said.

"*Good luck,*" Fenrir's voice said in her head.

She closed her eyes. When they reopened she was back in the cave.

Marissa and Halla both slept, so she'd have to take care to avoid awakening them before she was free. She didn't want to give them false hope in case the incantation failed.

Andrea focused her mind and said the words. Nothing happened at first, but after a few minutes the glowing rock around her pulsed with brighter light. Her bruised skin tingled as the energy of the earth flowed into her body again.

"It worked," she whispered.

Pain shot through her head, like her brain tearing in half inside her skull. Something was wrong. She couldn't focus her mind to go back to the dreamscape to ask Ludari. Andrea squeezed her eyes shut, but the light of the rocks shone through her eyelids. Everything around her hummed malevolently, like poorly meshed gears.

Andrea screamed and fainted.

39

Courtney sat at the bar as colored lights reflected off the ice in her glass of water and the sequins in her black dress. She scowled at the TV, talking about a local private investigator killed due to gang-related activity.

I should be cutting my fucking way through that lair right now, but no, here I am, pretending to be from Odesa and doing a fake accent so I can play Ivan's date. Bullshit. Some things are more important than a fucking business deal: Andrea's freedom. Scott's life.

The glass shook in her death grip as a nasal British voice came from close behind. "Wow, I don't think I've ever seen anything more beautiful in my life."

She didn't turn around, instead looking at the Caribbean vacation ad on the TV as she prepared what she'd say in the fake Ukrainian accent. Ivan had suggested she pose as Ukrainian since she couldn't get the accent heavy enough to be Russian.

"Ukraine has a high rate of education, so less accent would be feasible. Plus, when someone asks if you are Russian, you would have an excuse to be angered and say you are Ukrainian. That fire should make most fops who may hit on you back off while I meet with Senator MacDougal," Ivan had said.

Courtney grunted and faced the Brit behind her, with his messy blonde hair and suit wrinkled over a portly frame. "So why don't you go there and leave me the fuck alone?" she said, aiming her thumb at the TV.

"I much prefer the view in front of me to the feeling of sand." He exposed crooked teeth in what Courtney presumed was supposed to be a smile.

"Fuck off and let me finish my drink," she said with a growl.

"Hmm, such lovely manners for a Russian lady. My name is Boris—"

She cut him off as she bellowed, "Ukrainian! I'm no fucking Russian!"

Every eye in the room turned to her as she stood, looming over the man due to the height of her heels.

"Perhaps you should have a few less drinks?" he suggested quietly.

She slipped off a shoe and held the pointy heel up as she said, "Maybe I should bury this in your fucking eye so I can have another drink in peace."

Someone grabbed her arm. As Ivan pulled her away, he said in her ear, "Save that feeling for tomorrow. We are leaving early as I have received grave news from my New England operations. Edthgar knows we are closing in on him. He had Grigori strike across the country. I will discuss more at the meeting we already scheduled tonight with the other hunters. It does not change our plan for tomorrow."

"Better fucking not. If you think I'm not slaughtering that motherfucker ASAP you're mad," Courtney said, yanking herself from Ivan's grip.

"Please, the crowd thinks you are referring to the mayor of London you just threatened with your shoe. We need to leave."

Courtney brushed off her stocking and put the shoe back on. "Well, yeah, I'm going, but it's hard storming off in one heel."

Ivan's grim expression broke into a slight grin. He nodded as she followed him out the door. "Perhaps the others will be able to arrive early so we can get the meeting over sooner, allowing you to go to bed so we can move up the attack a few hours. I want you well-rested, since it will be a hard fight going into gargoyle territory," Ivan said as they approached Luke by the Bentley.

If you think I'm sleeping well tonight while Andrea sits in that fucking cave, you're sorely mistaken. My sword is getting a good sharpening. "Of course," she lied.

Ivan glanced back. "Also, please try not to dream of skewering the mayor of London. I am not fond of the man, but unfortunately he looks to be someone who could ascend in power in Britain, with whom Volkodav will likely have dealings in the future."

"An asshole's an asshole, whether they have wings or a fucking mop on their head."

"You listened to my story about Stalin too well. I will be a moment while you wait in the car. I must speak with Chief Dooley from the New England warehouse security department."

* * * * *

Once the unarmed trio arrived at the mansion, they hurried inside to avoid the gargoyle spying in the bushes. It made no move to attack anyone who arrived, and Ivan deemed it unnecessary to dispatch the beast. "Let it warn Edthgar that the Grigori diversion did not work, and that he dies tomorrow," Ivan said.

The meeting went off at the scheduled time since Alec still had commitments at the library and couldn't leave early. To fill the time beforehand, Courtney kicked out her frustrations with a vigorous workout routine while Luke helped Hank prepare the arsenal for the assault. Once the meeting time closed in, Hank went over the weapons with all participants except Luke, Courtney, and Ivan.

Luke joined Ivan in the kitchen while Courtney showered.

"I should have asked what you wanted earlier so I would not have had to wait for you to come in." Ivan pointed to a tray of empty glasses.

"You're antsy too, eh?" Luke said.

"One could say so. I have waited eighty years to kill Edthgar, and it seems the day is near. Once we eliminate Grigori, Halgaard is no threat, so the war is over. It has occurred to me that I have no plan for what comes afterwards," Ivan replied. "And you have not answered my question."

"Beer. If I were you, I'd probably travel, see the world for the good in it instead of to fight monsters or find treasures."

"I quite like your idea. I can also revisit and pay tribute to friends lost long ago. However, once that is done, what do I do? It will take years, but I have an eternity to fill with purpose," Ivan said, grabbing a bottle from the refrigerator.

"Write a book? That's what I'd do if I had detailed diaries like you. It could make a great series, you know. Change some names and details and you could have bestselling fiction, as long as the public doesn't find out about the gargoyles before we're done."

"You may be on to something."

"What are you giving Courtney to drink?"

"I will pour her a glass of wine I received when exiled from Russia. She seemed to savor that rather than guzzle it. It appears she views alcohol much as I did before Anatalia gave me a reason to see life through sober eyes, as a crutch to wash away the worst thoughts caused by the deeds we must do to effectively fight monsters."

"Can I cancel the beer? That wine wine sounds kind of interesting."

"Very well," Ivan answered, putting the beer back in the refrigerator. He grabbed the unmarked wine bottle from the counter and started pouring drinks.

Courtney stopped in the doorway. "That stuff is unreal. It's like you can taste the history with each sip," she said to Luke.

He smiled when he saw Courtney's new outfit. She wore baggy sweatpants and wooly socks, but most importantly, the new hockey jersey he'd bought with a small portion of his first check from Volkodav Sekurities. "Wow, that's huge on you, but you look great in it. I'm worried I might not get it back."

Courtney adjusted the wide collar to hide her bra strap. "Damn, I was trying to look as unsexy as I could."

Ivan poured scotch into the final glass. "I will let everyone know we are ready." He pulled out his cell phone to call Hank.

"And you call contractions lazy?" Courtney joked.

"Hello, Hank. We will be ready for the meeting shortly. We are waiting for everyone in the great room," Ivan said. He hung up and said to Courtney, "I would call this efficiency rather than laziness."

Ivan walked past Luke and Courtney, carrying the tray of drinks into the great room. They followed him in and sat on the couch, leaving a space on one end for Hank. Ivan set the drinks down on the coffee table, then returned to the doorway with his glass of wine and phone in hand. He brought up a map on the phone while Luke and Courtney grabbed their drinks.

A minute later, Alec yelled from the stairs in his booming British voice, "Did you pour my scotch, you Communist bastard?"

"It is waiting here for you, ignorant Limey," Ivan yelled back.

A hearty laugh emanated from the hall. Shortly thereafter, Ivan and the heavyset Brit embraced in the doorway. Alec wandered into the room, fetched his scotch, and sat in the recliner furthest from Courtney.

Hank walked in, grabbed his glass of whiskey, and sat next to Courtney.

A man Luke didn't recognize took the glass of water and sat in the remaining recliner nearest Courtney. Chris and Ivan leaned on opposite sides of the great room entryway.

"We've never had a proper introduction," Alec said to Courtney. "Alec Winfield. I'm happy to see you know what trousers are."

Courtney smiled, nodding at him. "Careful. You're the second Brit I've wanted to stab today."

Ivan cleared his throat as Alec laughed and said, "I thought you wanted to stab everyone every day anyway?"

Courtney rolled her eyes and looked over to Luke, ignoring Alec.

Alec said to Luke, "I haven't the foggiest idea who you are."

"Luke Stillman. Courtney's boyfriend, and also sorely tempted to stab someone. Just with a plastic fork, because I'm not as murderous."

Alec roared out laughing. "I like this one, someone with a bloody sense of humor."

"I am Paolo Fernandez, former Eighty-Second Airborne," the unknown man said. He pulled up his pant leg to show the prosthetic limb and continued. "The gargoyles took my fiancé Marissa long before your friend. I have been inside their lair to a certain point to deliver food and supplies they demanded. Your uncle told me all about you and your friend Andrea. I have waited for the day I could rescue Marissa for so long. Now we get to do so together."

Luke gave his introduction, then Chris unfolded a large sheet of construction paper to tape over the television screen.

He aligned a second sheet carefully alongside it, completing the hand-drawn diagram of the lair as far as Paolo had been inside.

Chris spoke with little emotion in his voice. "Ivan gave me parts to build a portable detector, but it won't be ready in time so you'll be blind inside. I'll be manning the radar here to watch for pop-ups outside the lair in case there's any hidden veins leading out that Paolo never saw or are further inside. I'll be able to direct those outside with guns." He grabbed the mug of rum off of the tray and walked back to the doorway.

Courtney's hand closed tightly on Luke's. Her fake nails for the gala dug in his skin. "If Chris is watching the radar, does that mean you and Unc are going in the cave?" she whispered, her voice high.

Luke shrugged and didn't answer.

Ivan moved to the map and pointed at three spots in the cliffs around the entrance. "Alec, Mark from the grill, and Dr. O'Rourke will be on the cliffs so that they may pick off any gargoyles outside the lair. I would have had Luke out here as well; however, we will need him inside. We are shorthanded when it comes to capable personnel due to the death of Scott today. Renee was only able to convince the police chief to send two additional officers."

Paolo signed a cross over his chest at the mention of Scott.

Courtney swallowed hard as she looked in Luke's eyes. He shrugged again, but it didn't soothe her any. Her teeth dug into her lip as she turned to her uncle.

Ivan continued, "The rest of us will head into the large chamber used for storage."

"But we'll be trapped in there," Courtney protested.

Alec hushed her and said, "Let the man finish. He's not quite so daft as Prince Charles on a horse."

"We want Edthgar to think so," Ivan countered. "We are going there to lure him in, make him think he can waltz in and take Courtney as his queen. He believes the time for his ultimate victory is at hand, and if I know the way he thinks, he will be arrogant and overconfident as he rushes headlong into our trap. Hank and Renee will be hidden in the corners by the entrance, at the ready with the net guns my company developed when we fought Mephallo. Those barbed nets will wound and restrain Edthgar all at once. Luke, Hank, Mendoza, and Renee will spring into action to remove his horn and finish him off.

"While that happens, Petr will lead myself, Paolo, the other officers, and Courtney into the depths of the den to rescue Andrea and Marissa. Petr has a sharp sense of smell, so he should lead us right to where they are being held. Courtney, you will follow Petr closely and Paolo will be behind you. The other officers and I will have your back so you will only have to be concerned with gargoyles ahead of you.

"If Edthgar falls before we find them," Ivan continued, "we will no longer have to worry about his minions. Whenever a winged gargoyle is vanquished, his underlings turn to stone, which is why you see so many gargoyle statues in Europe. If this happens, our path out will be easy. If not, I will carry both Andrea and Marissa if they are too weak to run on their own. Courtney will lead the escape, and Paolo will watch my back. This is the basic plan. We will all have headsets on as well, so we can communicate on the fly as the situation changes."

Courtney nodded and said, "So I get to kill every last gargoyle I see, except Edthgar."

"That is my hope. I do not want to imagine Edthgar surviving long enough for you to finish him, because it will most likely mean that everyone attacking him in that room has perished."

Courtney nodded again, gulped, and looked at Luke and her uncle.

"You and Luke may leave," Ivan said. "I am aware you two have had a long day. I will give you both details tomorrow when we pick up the net guns from my San Rafael warehouse. You need your rest."

Luke and Courtney both stood and exited with their drinks.

On their way up the stairs, Courtney took a large sip of wine and said, "I'm scared of losing you. You don't heal like the rest of us, except that Paolo guy. I really don't like the idea of you being inside, especially with Edthgar."

"I'll be fine. It lets me finish what we were about to accomplish the other night. Don't forget, the two of us almost took him down without the help of nets. There'll be four of us this time, better prepared because we're expecting him. Piece of cake."

"It's not going to help my fighting if I'm worried sick about you."

Luke stopped by the door. "If I don't get hurt I don't need to heal fast. Don't underestimate my desire to avoid pain. Being a wuss could come in handy."

"You're not a wuss. You'll be stubborn and do anything to keep Edthgar from me, I know it," Courtney said, walking to the bathroom.

"Either way, I'm in the fight. I'm seeing it through to the end, just like you. Don't think I'm not worried about you, too, going deeper in the cave than we have mapped. There's no telling what's down there," Luke said. He pushed the door all the way open and walked into the bedroom to end the discussion as she stared back at him.

I know how to make you stop worrying. Luke looked out the window towards the trees at the edge of the parking circle. His fingers darted under the pillow and rubbed the handle of Courtney's sword.

40

Courtney awakened from a vivid nightmare about the rescue failing. She blinked away sweat from her eyes and reached out to Luke for a hug, but he wasn't there. He must have gone to the bathroom. Some noise from there probably woke her from the nightmare.

She set her head back down on the pillow. Something didn't feel right.

The sword wasn't there. Did she not put it back after sharpening it? No, she distinctly remembered patting it before bed. Her gaze turned to the window. The outside lights were on. Her heart rate doubled and she felt as if it would hammer its way out.

"What the fuck is going on?"

Courtney threw the sweaty sheets aside and bounded out of the room to find Luke. The bathroom was unoccupied. From there she darted down the hall towards the stairs. Light shone into the stairwell from below, so she didn't bother heading to the tower. Courtney ran down to the first floor, skipping steps as her heart skipped beats.

A single gunshot pierced the night as she emerged into the first floor hallway. Luke's revolver, without a doubt. Courtney sprinted to the foyer. The front door was open.

Out in the circle, Luke smashed her sword into the throat of a gargoyle on the ground. Blood gushed from the wound like a geyser. Luke bent down over the dying beast.

"No," Courtney yelled from the landing.

He didn't turn, reaching down to the gargoyle's body, then to his own face.

Courtney dropped to her knees on the landing, gasping for breath.

Luke finally turned to her with a line painted on each cheek in gargoyle blood like war paint. She wanted to cry as she watched it absorb into his skin, but found she couldn't.

His lack of worry before made perfect sense now. He'd decided during their chat what he would do. The gargoyle waiting outside gave him the perfect source to attain faster healing. Her fear made him do it. It was her fault for drawing him into the fight in the first place, and now he'd ensured a deeper role in the fight as long as it lasted. All because of her.

"Let's get back inside. If you didn't catch a cold in that dress before, you'll definitely catch one standing out here naked," Luke said as he walked back up to the house.

"But why?" Courtney muttered as she moved an arm over her chest and her other hand below her waist for coverage.

"Now you don't have to worry about me not healing faster. As soon as you said how worried you were, I remembered Ivan's warning about this gargoyle and made up my mind to do it. I'm tired of being thought a liability because I don't heal fast like you despite how many times I've fought right by your side, or without you against the damn gremlins when you were too sloshed to stand up. Maybe now you'll accept I want the gargoyles gone just as much as you do and I'm just as capable as you are," he said, standing over her.

She looked up at him. "It's going to be a curse as long as we live."

"That might not be beyond tomorrow for all we know. This can only be beneficial right now, because once we kill Edthgar and Grigori, it's over. No more gargoyles to hunt us. If I get hurt, this helps me. It can't hurt anything at this point."

Luke pulled her up by her armpit and added, "It's done either way; let's get inside and go back to bed."

Ivan stood in the doorway, his gaze focused on the corpse bleeding out on the asphalt, avoiding Courtney. "I will clean up the body. Please go inside; it is only forty degrees. I do not think your uncle needs to see your choice of outfit, either," he said.

Courtney looked back at the gargoyle, then at Luke, and shivered. *I'm so fucking sorry. You shouldn't have had to resort to this. I should've been better. Fuck. Why would you choose to become a murderous freak like me? Why? You had a chance to stay normal.*

41

Ivan's Bentley led a convoy of vehicles to the same clearing by the beach where they'd hunted the lagoonie. The members of the attacking group all exited the different vehicles and fetched their weapons and gear for the fight to come.

Luke helped Courtney put on her armor, tightening all the straps for her. He slung a rifle over his shoulder and grabbed his new katana from the back of the Willys.

In turn, Courtney helped him strap the scabbard to his belt. "I wish I'd had more time to show you how to use that," she said.

Luke held the green fabric-wrapped handle of the sword. "Gargoyles don't use them, so all I really need to know is to hit them with the sharp part before they get me with their claws. Besides, it's just a backup if I run out of ammo." He checked the revolver at his other hip and the extra magazines of rifle ammo stuffed into his cargo pockets.

Courtney rolled her eyes. "Basically, but there's a lot more to it. Who knows what else is in there? Halgaard could've summoned more than those bug things."

"We'll find out, I guess, right?"

Paolo walked up in full combat gear, carrying his rifle. He also had a machete at his waist. An extra helmet hung from his stuffed pack. He nodded at them, pointing to the helmet. "For Marissa," he said.

Ivan and Petr made their way over next. Ivan wore his usual suit, but he carried a smaller submachine gun with a drum magazine in addition to his ever-present Russian naval sword. "I have taught Petr more English so he can communicate with you since you will be leading the search for Andrea," Ivan said to Courtney.

"Hi, bitch!" Petr said.

"As you can tell, he is still quite fond of the colorful language he learned from you," Ivan said, blushing.

Courtney ruffled the fur on the gremlin's head and joked, "When we get home, I'm going to shit in your litter box, you little asshole."

Petr giggled and said, "Hank scoops anyway."

Hank walked over, claymore strapped to his back and Thompson in hand. "Use his box and I'll make it your duty to scoop it from here on out."

Courtney sighed and looked over to Renee and Mendoza. The veterinarian had his ax on his back and the same machine gun, but also had a couple of dark green metal totes hanging from his hips. The faded yellow text said they contained ammunition.

The other two police officers eyed the group. The skinny one, Wang, glanced at the machine guns and back to his pistol. Courtney smirked at the frown on his face, remembering how she'd done the same thing before she swore off guns for good. The heavy one with greasy hair, Beauregard, carried a shotgun and wore a thick bulletproof vest that Ivan tapped.

"That may not fit through the gap in the rocks. Leave it behind if necessary," Ivan said. He looked back to Courtney and rolled his eyes as Beauregard pointed to her armor. "Your gut alone is wider than her armor. Remove it temporarily and put it back on once we are through if you must. I will say, however, that our opponents do not use projectiles and the vest is useless against claws and teeth."

"Claws and teeth? The hell are we doing, gator hunting?" Beauregard drawled.

He spotted Petr and swallowed hard as Ivan said, "You were selected because you know about the gargoyles. That is what we hunt today."

Mark's old van pulled into the clearing. He got out along with Dr. O'Rourke. Both carried hunting rifles with scopes.

Alec shuffled over last with a massive machine gun. "I haven't gotten to fire this wench in anger in God knows how long. This ought to be a smashing good time," he said to the group. He turned to Ivan. "No Lewis gun?"

"No, it may be unwieldy if the cave gets narrow in the deeper sections. The PPSh will be much more manageable in tight quarters."

Hank said to Alec, "Don't get overeager with that Bren. I don't want to get shot again."

Alec laughed. "Take care of your business in the cave and I won't have to go in there. The air raid shelters I hid in as a wee lad because of those Nazi wankers were bloody claustrophobic, and I'd sure get overeager if I had to deal with that rubbish again."

Ivan held a bag full of earpieces and handed them to everyone aside from Petr, since an earpiece would not fit in the gremlin's larger ears.

"Chris, can you hear me?" Ivan said.

"Loud and clear, Ivan," Chris said into the microphone back in Hank's office.

"Did everyone hear Chris?" Ivan asked.

Renee shook her head, so Ivan gave her a new earpiece and dropped the other to the sand.

"Chris, speak up again," Ivan said.

"Can you hear me?" Chris replied.

Renee nodded and gave a thumbs up.

"Okay, now we will all speak one at a time to ensure everyone has a working microphone, beginning with Alec," Ivan instructed.

Each group member obeyed, and Chris confirmed he heard each of them.

"Very well. Let us begin," Ivan said to the group.

Courtney spun her sword and sheathed it again, then shot Wang and Beauregard a wink.

Beauregard turned to Renee and said, "What in blazes have you gotten me into?"

"Something honorable, for once." Renee turned sideways to slide between the rocks. "If you don't fit through here, we could always have Courtney make you skinnier."

As Courtney grinned and stroked her sword's handle, Beauregard sucked in his gut and said a prayer.

That's right, pray you don't hold me up in there. Nothing is keeping me from Andrea. Not you, not any gargoyles, not any fake gods. I'll drown this fucking cave in as much blood as I have to.

42

Courtney stopped with the rest of the assault team at the rock illusion. She tried not to smile as her fingers tightened on her sword. *Soon, Andrea. We'll have you back.*

Ivan looked up at each person positioned on the cliffs with their guns. They all gave him a thumbs up. He nodded, then said, "Paolo, lead us in."

Paolo raised his rifle and passed through the stone.

"I could feel this rock was weird when we hunted the lagoonie," Courtney said to Ivan. "I should've said something then, but I got too...distracted. Scott might still be alive if I'd stayed in control."

"Remember that next time something feels wrong," Ivan said before entering the cave.

She followed him in. Static electricity tingled on her face and hands as she walked through the false rock. The air inside was damp and reeked of mold. Patches of moss grew on wetter parts of the stone around her.

Static crackled briefly in her ear, then the earpiece went dead silent. She looked over at Luke wiggling his earpiece. He returned her look and shrugged.

The group advanced in silence toward the storage room. Nothing opposed them but darkness as they descended, though the sulfur and cucumber gargoyle stench was everywhere.

One of the bug creatures scuttled out from an alcove in front of the group. Its mandibles clicked without a sound human ears could hear, but Petr covered his ears and groaned in pain.

The bug turned to run. Paolo fired a quick burst. Its head exploded, and the rest of the body flopped over. One of the spidery limbs twitched sporadically until Paolo blasted it off with another short burst of fire.

"We must make haste to the storage room, for they surely heard that. Hurry before Edthgar can cut us off," Ivan ordered.

He led the mad dash onwards. Several more bugs emerged from hiding. All met their ends via gunfire from the monster hunters. One crawled along the ceiling of the cavern, and Courtney ducked aside to avoid its falling corpse after Luke blew it away.

They rounded a corner and encountered the first batch of gargoyles.

Courtney charged ahead to challenge the three monsters, sword drawn. She swung as the first gargoyle lunged at her. Her blade sliced deeply into the softer part of the gargoyle's abdomen while its claws glanced off her breastplate.

She whirled around and lopped the head off the second gargoyle before the first hit the ground. Ivan's sword burst through the third gargoyle's back, and Courtney grumbled as she wiped her blade on the second's twitching corpse. "I guess you can have one kill."

Renee shot the wounded gargoyle in the head with her pistol as Ivan pointed ahead. "This is no time for competition. Move," he said.

"The room is just ahead on the left," Paolo yelled.

The group ran ahead, unopposed. Ivan signaled for them to stop by the doorway. "Mendoza, you go first with the M60. I have a feeling they may be waiting for us in there," Ivan instructed.

"With pleasure," the veterinarian said.

He entered the large arched entrance to the store room and opened fire, lighting the cavern with bright muzzle flashes. Empty shell casings spewed from the machine gun and clattered to the rock floor. Gargoyle howls joined the cacophony of gunfire and falling brass.

"Clear," Mendoza said as he lowered the gun and beckoned everyone into the room.

Water dripped from stalactites hanging from the tall ceiling and onto stalagmites, aside from one rocky spike with a shredded gargoyle corpse draped over it. Three natural rock columns held up the ceiling of the cave. One was cracked in several places. A fourth column lay shattered on the floor, and the moss growing on the fractured sections suggested it fell decades or centuries ago.

Courtney's gaze drifted to glowing veins of stone visible through cracks in the walls. The strange mineral poked through at the backs of shelves carved from the stone. Stone tablets lined the shelves, and the tablets were covered in runes similar to those on her sword. A wooden pallet sat beside the shelving, plastic water bottles and cans of cheap pasta stacked on it.

Courtney's heart sank when she spotted a mangled boot coated in blood beside the pallet. She stepped over dead gargoyles to get a closer look. It was definitely Andrea's, but as she touched the boot, some of the blood absorbed into her skin. Her fingertip tingled like when she absorbed Mephallo's blood in the tunnels.

Edthgar's blood. You did good, AB.

"Ivan, get over here."

He stomped on the head of a gargoyle as he approached Courtney. "That boot—is it one of the ones Andrea wore when she was taken?"

"Yes, but it's Edthgar's blood. I can smell his stench, and it absorbed when I touched it."

"Your theory about her absorbing gargoyle blood seems to have merit. I do not believe she has been kept in this room, though. Her shoes were most likely taken as punishment or torture, perhaps for that escape attempt," Ivan said, his fist clenching.

Courtney noticed his fist and the twitching muscle in his neck, but chose not to say anything about either. Behind him, Beauregard shook, and his pants were wet. Courtney narrowly avoided laughing.

Instead, she asked Ivan, "What's this glowing rock?"

"It is called *quodpetram*, which is Latin for *mana rock*. It is quite conductive to several forms of energy, especially magic. It is difficult to harness this without using magic, which is why it is largely ignored in science. It would, however, explain the powerful illusions keeping the cavern entrance hidden for so long."

Edthgar roared deeper within the lair.

"Everyone to your positions!" Ivan yelled. He turned to Courtney. "We can examine all of this room more closely after the battle is done. Those scrolls and tomes could prove useful."

Hank and Renee removed the harpoon-like net-firing guns from Paolo's pack and headed to the corners of the room beside the entrance. Courtney, Ivan, Paolo, Wang, and Petr took their positions in the center. Mendoza and Luke stood behind and to either side, while Beauregard slunk behind Courtney. Everyone raised their guns, ready to unleash hell upon Edthgar as soon as he entered the room—aside from Courtney and the unarmed Petr.

Courtney had an idea. "Ivan, why don't we all fight to kill Edthgar first, then get Andrea back easier after?'

"Edthgar wants you to be his queen. If you stay here, he could grab you and take you away without retaliation, because we would risk shooting you. It is better to divert his attention, for the moment of indecision could hasten his demise. I also want his spirits crushed as you slip through his hands again. He will consider being killed by anyone other than you or I a terrible indignity, and I will take great satisfaction in knowing he dies feeling pathetic," Ivan answered.

Courtney understood. She humiliated the lagoonie when she killed it, and Ivan wanting Edthgar to suffer a similarly demeaning demise was poetic.

Edthgar roared again, closer.

Courtney turned to Luke and said, "I love you."

He winked. "I love you too."

Both wondered if the anticipation of the fight would kill them before any gargoyle could.

43

Heavy gunfire came from within the cave, but stopped quickly.

"Bloody hell, I wish we knew what was going on in there," Alec muttered as he stretched out his legs. "I'm too old to squat this long."

Back at the mansion, Chris burped. "I've got no communication with them or signs on the radar here except your white dot. Believe me, I'm worried too. All I can do is pound back energy drinks."

"Careful with that shite, lad. You'll rot your teeth out and look like me," Alec said.

A gunshot came from across the way.

"Gargoyles coming up from below!" Mark yelled.

"Shit, still nothing on the radar. What do you see?" Chris asked.

"Not a whole bloody lot. Aim a light down there, someone," Alec bellowed.

O'Rourke whipped out his cell phone and aimed its flashlight at the rocks below, showing several gargoyles climbing straight out of the ground.

"Another bloody illusion hiding their entries, eh? Tough shite, you bastards," Alec said as he opened fire.

* * * * *

The rock vibrated underfoot as Edthgar approached. He howled again yards from the doorway. Courtney thought she heard gunshots outside over the sound.

"Shield your eyes when he enters," Paolo said to everyone. His finger moved to the grenade launcher's trigger.

Edthgar barreled into the room, roaring until the grenade fired from Paolo's gun. He tried to dodge, but the grenade blasted his shoulder. The explosion knocked him from his feet and slammed him to the ground.

"Rats, I wanted to hit the horn," Paolo cried out.

Edthgar pushed himself up with one arm while the other hung limp. His cratered shoulder oozed blood, dyeing his stone skin crimson. He looked at the wound, then glared at Courtney with his lone eye. Scarlet light from the eye drenched everything in the room.

Renee and Hank fired their net guns. Both nets wrapped around Edthgar. He flailed against the netting, but the more he struggled, the deeper the barbs on the nets dug into him.

"We must go now!" Ivan yelled. "Leave Edthgar to the others!"

Courtney swallowed hard and gave Luke a nod as the rescue party ran past their entangled nemesis and out of the storeroom. She swiped at Edthgar with her sword on the way out, slicing into his cratered shoulder.

"So long, shitstick," she said.

Edthgar bellowed behind them as Luke and Mendoza opened fire.

"Did you see his eye?" Courtney asked.

"Yes," Ivan said.

"Think that's where the blood on the boot came from? Those heels could've done a job on an eye."

"I would bet on that."

Petr sniffed the air as he led them deeper into the lair. "Gargoyles ahead soon," he said.

"Good. I want to kill more," Courtney said.

"Crazy bitch." Petr giggled as they approached a corner.

More glowing quodpetram veins poked through the rock ahead, illuminating a cluster of man-bugs. Ivan showered the walls in bug parts with a prolonged burst of fire from his gun.

The group clambered over the foul-smelling pile of insect parts only to be greeted by the incoming gargoyles Petr warned them about. Paolo mowed down a couple and Ivan dropped three before Courtney engaged the remaining attackers.

One leapt at her, but the other froze in panic. She ducked under the leaping gargoyle and thrust her sword upward, piercing its chest and slicing open its abdomen. Blood spilled out and covered her in macabre war paint. The gargoyle flopped onto the pile of bugs, impaled by a sharp chunk of carapace.

The other gargoyle hadn't moved. Courtney twirled her sword, staring into the scared gargoyle's golden eyes. "Boo!" she yelled.

It stumbled backwards, falling over. Courtney laughed and walked over to where it tried to scoot away from her. Still laughing, she shoved her blade deep into the gargoyle's thigh. It whimpered as it stared up at her.

She pulled the copper dagger from her boot and spun it inches from the gargoyle's face. "I don't like that look you're giving me." She jabbed the tip of the dagger into both eyes, blinding the gargoyle. "Now you match your master. Should I cut apart your shoulder next?"

"Courtney, now is not the time," Ivan said.

She wiped the dagger off on the gargoyle's calf, then tucked it back in her boot and tore the gargoyle's leg open with her sword.

"I'll let you bleed to death in darkness," she whispered in its ear.

Before she stood, Beauregard screamed. Some sort of large serpent coiled in waiting around a stalactite descended, plunging its clawed fingers through his chest. The creature's jaws spread apart to welcome the portly cop as a meal. Beauregard thrashed against it, blood spurting as his flails weakened.

Wang fired at the creature, shrieking as each round barely sank into the serpent's iridescent brown scales. Its tail swung down from the ceiling, but Wang leapt out of the way, avoiding the bladed tip. Courtney blocked the tail with her sword as she stepped up to the serpent.

"Let the dumb fuck go and I'll make your death quick," she said to it.

The serpent hissed and threw Beauregard against the cave wall as it struck out at Courtney. It moved at lighting speed, but the claws clanged against her breastplate as her sword plunged into the roof of its mouth. The fangs paused inches from her head, waving back and forth. The beast's tremendous strength had Courtney hanging onto her sword for the ride. She banged into the rock wall but held on, placing her boots against the serpent's bottom jaw to hold the mouth open. "A little help, Ivan?"

The Russian pounded his sword into the serpent's neck repeatedly, but he made little progress cutting further. "Pull your sword free and let Paolo handle this one!"

Courtney yanked out the sword and jumped away as the serpent's jaws slammed shut. It dropped from the ceiling, sending reverberations through the floor as it landed. Small bits of stone fell and pelted Courtney's armor. She held her sword ready in case it struck as she backed away.

The snake's jaws gaped wide when it coiled to strike, and Paolo fired a grenade into the gaping reptilian mouth. A muffled explosion followed. The serpent trembled before collapsing to the ground. Dark blood seeped from between its scales.

Wang ran to where Beauregard lay against the rock wall. The man's vest was torn wide open and one of his ribs poked through the hole. A sucking noise came from his chest as he wheezed, blood dribbling from the wound and his lips.

"Hang in there; we'll get you out of here soon," Wang said.

Ivan stood beside him. "No, we will not. He will not last long. I believe he knows it as well."

Beauregard nodded shakily and coughed out, "Put me out of my misery."

"What?" Wang said, wiping his cheeks.

Courtney strode forward. "I told you not to slow me down." She plunged her sword into the wound.

Beauregard's back arched for a moment as he gasped, then fell back to the stone as Courtney tugged her sword free. Wang stared up at her as she walked away.

"Close his eyes and come along. We're getting Andrea out of this shithole." Courtney didn't look back as she patted Petr's head and said, "Lead the way, runt."

The gremlin took a few steps forward before a grating symphony of roars sounded ahead. A group of gargoyles burst through another illusory stone wall and charged straight at Courtney. She and Ivan rushed forward with swords swinging, cutting through knees to drop a couple gargoyles while Paolo knocked several away from them with a quick burst of gunfire.

Courtney giggled manically as she spun around, sword slicing into the three gargoyles surrounding her. She ignored the rest of the world, dancing between clawed assaults that bounced off her armor as the sword rent pieces of gargoyle flesh free. One lunged at her with its mouth wide open and venom on its fangs, but her blade swished past the jagged teeth and cut the gargoyle's head off at the jaw joints.

Something tugged at the bottom of her pant leg, and she raised the sword to plunge into whatever gargoyle still lived. It was only Petr. He pointed to where two gargoyles surrounded Paolo. The machete was stuck in one's shoulder, and Paolo swung his gun to fend off the pair of monsters.

Courtney ran forward and hacked into the side of the closer gargoyle's neck. The other turned to her with its golden eyes wide. She grabbed the machete handle and tugged it free, then swung her sword in one hand, the machete in the other, into each side of its neck. The gargoyle crumpled to the floor, holding its wounds. Courtney handed Paolo his machete, then brought her sword down in both hands to behead the fallen beast.

A couple of gargoyles tried to crawl away, trailing blood from various wounds. Courtney pounced from gargoyle to gargoyle, jamming the sword down into their bodies repeatedly until each stilled. Her tongue ran across her lips, and she gagged for a second before spitting. "Fuck, that was a bad idea. Petr, lead the way again."

The tunnel warmed and brightened the deeper they ran. Little gargoyle resistance jumped out at them, but when any did, Courtney finished them off quickly. Paolo and Wang didn't have a chance to fire at any before she hacked the beasts to pieces, laughing as she swung.

A solitary gargoyle stepped out of an alcove in front of them. It squeaked and turned to run until Paolo put a few bullets between its shoulder blades. Courtney stomped its face into the ground as she ran over it, and Wang put a bullet in its head on the way by.

The group ran ahead toward a sharp corner leading down. The heat and glow reaching around the corner had Courtney expecting to see a three-headed dog and a boat on a river of lava. All the turn revealed was another corridor with several veins of the glowing stone in both walls.

"I smell two humans and one gargoyle. Close now," Petr informed the group.

Brighter orange light poured from an opening in the side of the wall ahead.

"That must be the room," Ivan said.

"It is. I smell them, but something smell odd. Something else with them," Petr warned. He stopped a few yards from the doorway, and the others halted next to him. They all stood with their backs against the wall, feeling vibrations from the rock.

"I'll go first," Courtney said quietly.

Ivan nodded.

Courtney slid along the wall until she was just outside the entrance. Her heart raced in her chest, and her sweaty palms gripped the handle of her sword. Whatever creature awaited her in the room didn't scare her, but she couldn't help reminiscing to the night she first absorbed gargoyle blood. She thought of her debate over what to do while she stood outside the kitchen holding her flashlight as a club.

Courtney looked at the blood-drenched blade of her sword. On this night, no option existed but to press forward. The grin on her face split wider and she cackled as she spun into the doorway, eager to end the life of whatever inhuman beast waited inside.

44

Luke and Mendoza reloaded while Hank peppered Edthgar with his Thompson. Renee fired the shotgun at point-blank range into the cracked horn. Edthgar moaned under the netting and lay still. The red glow of his eye dimmed like a flashlight with dying batteries.

"Don't waste any more ammo on him. It's time to chop off that horn," Hank said.

Mendoza set down the machine gun and unbuckled the straps on his back to release his ax. He gripped the weapon and grinned at Edthgar as he approached. The wounded winged one didn't budge, seeming resigned to his fate.

Luke, Renee, and Hank all watched as Mendoza swung the ax. It made contact with the horn, spreading the cracks further. He swung again and again, with no struggle from Edthgar. On the seventh swing, the horn came off and shattered on the stone floor.

The netting snapped near where Courtney's sword had sliced into Edthgar when she ran by. The winged gargoyle's eye glowed bright crimson again. He stood and tore the netting the rest of the way, then swung it around over his head.

Mendoza moved back a couple steps before Edthgar swatted him aside like a bug.

They heard an Irish-accented male voice in their heads. *"You thought it would be so easy? Maggot humans, I will feast on you soon!"*

Luke shuddered, feeling as if something unclean wriggled through his ear and took up residence inside his head. He fired his gun until it was empty. Hank and Renee emptied their weapons, too.

Mendoza crawled over to the M-60, unable to put weight on his twisted leg.

Every bullet sunk into Edthgar, but he stayed on his feet. His tail swung around and smacked Renee in the face, though the spiked ball on the end missed her. She slammed into the stone shelving and crumpled on the floor as scrolls and tomes fell around her.

Luke raised the revolver and emptied it into Edthgar's chest, but the disembodied voice taunted as the gargoyle snarled. *"Like mosquito bites."*

Luke holstered the revolver and grasped the handle of his katana.

"Pathetic human. I will use your corpse like a club when the Russian comes back here."

Hank jumped on Edthgar's back between the crumpled wings and stabbed at his neck with a pocket knife. Edthgar bellowed and tried to claw at Hank, but couldn't reach him with his functioning arm.

Luke pulled out the sword and said to himself, "Sharp end goes in gargoyle. Sharp end goes in gargoyle." He charged at Edthgar as the winged beast flailed to shake Hank off of his back. Luke swung the katana and sliced into Edthgar's thigh, but the cut was shallow.

Edthgar jumped backwards, slamming Hank into the wall. Hank groaned and coughed as he let go, flopping to the floor.

Luke charged and slashed at Edthgar. The gargoyle spun using his limp arm like a shield. Luke's blade stuck in the bone, and when Edthgar turned again, the sword yanked out of Luke's hands.

Edthgar grabbed the collar of Luke's shirt and lifted him. He held Luke so they were face to face, then roared.

"Dude, breath mints. It smells like you gargled sewage."

Edthgar roared again and threw Luke across the room. Luke landed on the pallet of water bottles. The flimsy plastic bottles cushioned the blow.

Mendoza fired his machine gun at Edthgar once Luke was out of the way. Edthgar spun around and hammered Mendoza's face with the spiked ball on his tail.

Luke crawled to where Renee lay, hoping to grab her pistol. Edthgar stomped over slowly, some effect finally showing from the hundreds of bullets residing in his flesh.

Edthgar stood over Luke and raised one foot, holding it over Luke's head. *So long, insect.*

Thompson fire erupted from the corner of the cave. Edthgar staggered back and turned around.

Hank struggled to hold the gun steady, but he managed another burst of fire. "Luke! Grab the sword!"

Luke stood and wrenched his katana from Edthgar's arm. Edthgar picked up Mendoza's ax and lumbered towards the corner of the room with Luke in pursuit, hacking at him with the sword.

Hank changed the magazine on the Thompson as quickly as he could with his trembling hands. He fired again. Edthgar stumbled. His tail tripped Luke, who bounced off of a crumbling stalagmite as he fell to the ground. Luke lightly tossed the sword away so he wouldn't land on it.

Edthgar staggered towards Hank, his movements labored as more bullets sank into him.

Hank's ammunition ran out as Edthgar loomed over him. He looked up at the winged gargoyle, squinting from the intensity of the red light from Edthgar's eye.

Edthgar swung the ax and buried the blade in Hank's stomach. *"You have been a valiant foe for many years. I cannot help feeling some sadness now, knowing you will not see my victory. Farewell."*

Hank coughed as Edthgar yanked the ax from his gut. He raised a middle finger to Edthgar and sputtered, "You won't get out of this room. Luke will finish you."

"No. I will let you watch his demise before I bring this blade down upon your head."

Edthgar turned to face Luke. He held the ax ready while Luke retrieved his sword. Both blades dripped blood already, and more would coat at least one of them soon.

* * * * *

Courtney entered the room and saw three prisoners. The furry gargoyle chained on one wall confused her, but the thin woman had to be Paolo's fiancé.

The remains of Andrea's Halloween costume lay in the center of the room. Instead, Andrea wore a black robe with red piping. A hood covered Andrea's face, but the tattoo on her dirty ankle identified her.

Andrea looked up, but something was wrong. Her eyes weren't vibrant and green. They glowed orange, like the veins of minerals in the walls. The hood fell back to reveal faintly glowing orange hair. She allowed the robe to open and showed off black chainmail, along with tattooed runes glowing on her stomach.

"Andrea?" Courtney said in a hushed tone.

"No more." Andrea's voice was huskier than normal with an ethereal echo.

"What happened to you?"

"I am Sarrat Irkali. Your friend is no more, as will be the fate of any who oppose my king. Starting with you."

"Your king?" Courtney said in disbelief.

"King Edthgar, of course. He who shall abolish mankind. We shall rule together, king and queen," Andrea said.

Courtney breathed in sharply and tightened her grip on the sword as she heard Ivan's gun drop to the floor outside the room.

"I have been such a fool," Ivan said. "How could I not see Edthgar may take a budding sorceress as queen instead of Courtney? The world will burn, and I will be responsible."

Courtney stood motionless, staring at Andrea or Queen whatever she said she was. Courtney's fingers loosened on her sword for a second, but she swallowed hard and adjusted her grip.

The queen's hair blew about and glowed brighter until she appeared to have flickering flames for hair. She held out her hands, revealing more glowing rune tattoos on her palms, along with the scar from where the copper dagger cut her. "You have something of mine, and the time has come for me to reclaim it," the queen hissed, staring at Courtney's calf.

The dagger slid out of Courtney's boot, slicing her skin. She dropped to one knee and grit her teeth. Courtney's skin burned around the cut as if the blade were on fire, and for a moment she expected to see flames shooting from the boot as she glanced down.

The queen grinned at Courtney as the dagger floated into her hand. "Welcome home, *Am Eilimh*. The name is what you call Gaelic, though that derived from a much older language. It means 'of claim.' Your friend was claimed by my king as the vessel for my rebirth the moment she was first cut by it. You have also been cut now, but I do not claim you. You are but a lowly warrior. This body has potential as a mage beyond any I have inhabited before."

Courtney glared at the queen and spat. "You fucking shut my friend's mouth right now, bitch. You'll be queen of shit when your damned king falls." She stood, blocked out the pain in her leg, raised her sword overhead, and set her feet to swing.

The dagger released from the queen's hand and rotated in the air so the point faced Courtney. The queen laughed. "How fitting the first human I kill in my new body is its former best friend?"

45

E dthgar swung the ax. Luke dodged Edthgar's sluggish movements easily. He moved in close and slashed Edthgar's abdomen between dodges.

"*Stand still, maggot!*"

Luke kept moving and got behind Edthgar. He hacked off the remains of one the wings before the tail tripped him again.

Edthgar swung the ax down at Luke, grazing his cheek. Luke thrust the katana upward through Edthgar's jaws. Edthgar jerked his head back, taking the sword with him and leaving Luke swearing.

Luke rolled away towards Mendoza's machine gun. He stopped with his hand on the gun as his eyes drifted to the corner of the cavern.

Hank staggered towards Edthgar, one hand keeping pressure on his stomach and the other dragging his claymore.

Edthgar's gaze fixated on Luke, snarling through jaws rendered immobile by the sword as he tried to pull at it.

"What's the matter, katana got your tongue?"

Edthgar picked the ax back up and threw it at Luke, but missed.

Luke grabbed the machine gun and aimed it at Edthgar, but didn't fire.

Hank stood at Edthgar's blind side and released his stomach to grip his claymore with both hands. He shook as he raised the claymore overhead, but found the strength to swing the massive sword. The blade sank deep into Edthgar's neck.

Hank pulled the sword free and fell forward as it slipped from his fingers. A smile replaced the grimace on Hank's face as he hit the ground.

Edthgar grasped at his throat with his functional hand and fell to his knees.

Luke dropped the gun and stepped forward, then yanked the katana free from Edthgar's jaws.

His single glowing eye flickered as it watched Luke. "*No witty remarks?*"

Luke stayed silent as he swung the sword repeatedly, sinking it deeper into Edthgar's neck each time until the winged creature fell limp to the floor and the eye stopped glowing. Edthgar blinked, and Luke plunged the sword through that awful watchful eye.

Edthgar's chest rose and fell one final time. The winged gargoyle died, but Luke needed to be sure. He hacked away at Edthgar's neck until the head was severed, blood pouring from the wound to mingle with the puddle beneath Hank.

Hank rolled over and propped himself up against Edthgar's body. He looked at Luke, shaking. His lips parted and the barest whisper escaped. "You did well."

"We did well," Luke corrected as he sat beside Hank.

Hank grabbed Luke's hand and said in a stronger voice, "Take care of Courtney for me. Tell her goodbye and that I love her."

Luke squeezed Hank's hand and answered, "Don't worry, we'll both tell her. Just hang on, please."

Hank blinked rapidly and mumbled, "The picture frame. It's still empty. I never...."

His hand let go of Luke's and his head lolled over.

Luke hugged him tight, then closed his eyes and trudged off to check on Renee and Mendoza.

* * * * *

The dagger flew at Courtney, but she knocked it out of the air with her sword. "You'll have to try harder," Courtney said.

Paolo fired at the queen. The bullets stopped in midair.

"I can do that, too, but I can do so much more," the queen boasted. The bullets turned around and pointed at Courtney.

"Well, fuck me sideways."

The bullets zipped towards Courtney but clanged off of her breastplate. She breathed a sigh of relief despite the impact transferring through the armor. "I guess your magic can't do two thousand feet per second," Courtney said, raising her middle finger at the queen.

The queen frowned and replied, "I simply need more energy."

The glowing walls pulsed. Sparks shot up the queen's legs from the floor. She smiled at Courtney and pointed at her. A lightning bolt shot from her fingertip into Courtney's chest.

It had no effect. "Guess who has rubber inside their armor?"

Courtney stepped forward and stomped on the queen's toes, then delivered an uppercut to her chin. The queen slammed into the wall and shrieked at an inhuman pitch. Courtney blinked, grunting as her ears rang.

The queen snarled at Courtney, driving away any revulsion she felt at striking her friend. It wasn't Andrea anymore, just another enemy. Courtney swallowed hard as she watched Andrea's face grimace. "I'm sorry." Courtney raised her sword.

"No! She's still in there," Marissa yelled behind Courtney.

The queen blinked repeatedly and shook her head as she pushed herself back to her feet. "My king, I will help you shortly. I must finish here first."

The dagger flew through the air again and lodged itself firmly in Courtney's unarmored right shoulder.

Courtney grunted but tripped the queen. She knelt down and picked up a broken chain from the ground to wrap around the queen's ankles, then pulled the dagger from her own shoulder. After shoving the blade between chain links, Courtney wrapped the chain around the handle.

The queen struggled for a moment, flailing with bound legs and screaming while electricity crackled all around her body.

She stopped fighting. Her jaw fell.

"No, my king. My king," the queen whimpered. Glowing red tears fell as she drew her knees up to her chest.

Courtney was confused for a moment, until realization dawned. She turned to Paolo and said, "They did it. They killed Edthgar."

"Thank you, Lord," Paolo yelled.

Ivan stumbled into the room and looked down at the queen. "It is not over yet. We cannot leave the queen. Given time, she could find a way to revive Edthgar. That must not happen."

He looked ill, as if the words turned his stomach. His sword dragged against the stone as he stepped closer.

Marissa pleaded with Ivan. "Andrea is still in there. The queen isn't always in control. Please don't kill her. She can overcome the queen if you just let her live."

Ivan stood still, sword raised, but made no attempt to finish off the queen.

Paolo turned to the captive gargoyle and aimed at it. "I thought you said all minions would turn to stone when Edthgar died? He must not be dead yet, and we'll have a fight to escape," he said to Ivan.

"Minions of Edthgar, yes. This one looks different. It must be a minion of Halgaard, which is why it is chained in here. Halgaard did not help Edthgar willingly, and I am sure his minions felt the same way."

"It's true, my love," Marissa said. "Halla helped us try to escape. She says Halgaard and his followers hated Edthgar, and they were willing to fight to help us."

Paolo lowered the gun.

The queen's hair settled down and faded back to blonde. Her glowing tattoos disappeared without a trace. When she looked up at Courtney again, she did so with green eyes.

"Courtney?"

Courtney laughed and hugged her friend. "We did it. We did it!" she said to Andrea.

"Be careful, the queen is still in my head. She's settled down to grieve, but she's not gone. I've got to figure out how to get rid of her. We haven't won until she's gone."

"We'll find a way. There has to be a way," Courtney said as she freed Andrea's scraped legs from the chains.

"Can we get out of here first? I don't want her fueling her own magic with these rocks to try to overpower me, and I've seen enough of this fucking room to last a lifetime."

Courtney helped her up, then eyed Halla. "What about that one? I don't trust myself to let a gargoyle live if it's anywhere near me."

Halla looked to Courtney. "I will stay with Halgaard. He is held deeper within the cave since our escape attempt. All we want is to be human, and the magic in the walls here may be our best chance. Cut my chain so I can go to him; that is all I ask. You have already helped us so much by freeing us from Edthgar."

Andrea looked into Courtney's eyes. An orb of crackling electricity formed in her hand, igniting into a ball of flames. She moved over to Halla and burned through the chain.

"Thank you for helping us. Good luck, and hopefully when we meet again we'll both be fully human," Andrea said to Halla.

The two embraced. Courtney could hardly believe the sight of tears in a gargoyle's eyes as Halla let go of Andrea and walked from the room.

Andrea wiped her own eyes and freed Marissa. Paolo scooped up his fiancé and kissed her. "It has been too long, my love," he said to her.

"I never lost faith this day would come."

Paolo supported her as they left the chamber.

Andrea paused for a second and scowled as she grasped the robe. "I've got to get rid of this awful thing." She tossed the robe into the corner of the room and sent a fiery orb after it. Courtney watched sparks crackle in Andrea's wet eyes as the robe ignited. Her friend hugged herself and shook, and the sparks faded away.

Andrea whimpered, clawing off the armored garments. She tossed them on the pile, and her hands trembled as she picked up her skirt and shirt to redress. Courtney looked away from the scarred claw marks on her friend's back until Andrea spoke in a breathless voice. "I feel more human. For now."

Courtney reached for Andrea's hand. "Come on, let's get out of here. We've got a celebration before we figure out how to get the bitch out of you."

Andrea looked down at Courtney's hand around hers. She flinched, blinked, then squeezed back and looked in Courtney's eyes.

"Yeah, let's go."

* * * * *

Alec's finger left the trigger as the gargoyle in his sights twitched. It howled as crackling orange light moved from its feet upwards along its ugly skin, leaving solid stone behind. The Brit's knees popped as he stood to get a better view of the area below. Another gargoyle writhed on the ground until a bullet lodged in its forehead.

"Save your bloody ammo. They're dying on their own. The lads did it. Edthgar is dead."

Mark stood and yelled. "So should we join them inside?"

"You can if you want to. I'm not going in that miserable cave. I'll wait outside for you lot to come back out to celebrate."

Mark ran off to where the other hunters had entered the lair. Dr. O'Rourke nodded to Alec and said, "I guess I should follow in case they need me."

Alec nodded and hobbled along after the doctor.

We may have won, but why do I have this pit in my stomach? What was that shriek in there? I don't think we're out of the woods yet.

46

ourtney stepped over the stone remains of the gargoyle she blinded earlier. Seeing the stone gargoyles left her with no doubts. Edthgar was dead.

Wang dragged Beauregard's body behind the group, and Andrea moved along gingerly beside Courtney.

"Did you have to stomp on my poor foot? All the cuts from trying to get out of here were already sore enough. The queen blocked the healing I should've had from the blood I absorbed," she complained to Courtney.

"It was the best opening the queen left. If I went straight for the punch, she would've seen it coming."

Andrea rubbed her chin. "I hope she behaves so it doesn't happen again."

"That is up to you, is it not?" Ivan said.

"Yeah, but my abilities have limits, and I have to sleep. She's sure to take over then, just like I do when she sleeps. I'll need to keep covered, too, because I draw in magic energy most effectively through bare skin."

Andrea's free hand drifted down past her waist, and she shuddered. She stopped walking, though Courtney tried to pull her forward.

"Is that why Edthgar took your boots?" Courtney asked, shaking her hand.

Andrea blinked away tears, shook her head, and looked at Courtney. "No, I poked his eye out with a kick. He thought he was punishing me, but that's when I learned how easy it is to get energy from those glowing rocks. All the mana fueled my attempt to get away."

"I told you I would bet on that theory," Ivan chimed in.

"So the missing eye, crumpled wings, and charred skin were all your doing? Nice," Courtney complimented.

"Yeah, but he had worse for me. He had Halgaard put up a spell that blocked my magic. Then he...." Andrea paused and shivered. "He did...things. Bad things. A lot. There were incantations every time."

Andrea's hand rested between her legs and she looked away from Courtney.

Ivan's fist clenched again as Andrea continued. "I learned a counter-spell from Ivan's father in the dreamscape. I didn't know Edthgar's incantations were to summon the spirit of his queen from the necklace her essence was trapped in. When I broke through the wall stopping my magic, it also let her in. The wall was a setup from the start."

Ivan's tight fist shook. Andrea didn't notice, though her eyes were on Ivan's back. Courtney figured they saw Edthgar and the horrors he'd put her through. She pulled Andrea close to give her a hug, and though she flinched away at first, she let Courtney hug her until she stopped shaking. A strained moan escaped her lips as she rested her head on Courtney's shoulder.

"I'm sure you'll figure out a way to get rid of Queen Bitch," Courtney assured.

"If I can't do it myself, I know Ludari should be able to find a way to. I need to try on my own first. I'll feel like a real mage if I can do it."

Courtney released Andrea from the hug and pulled her forward again. Andrea didn't resist, but she also said nothing more. The only sounds in the tunnel were the shuffling of their feet, the grunting of Wang behind, the dripping moisture from the ceiling, and Paolo and Marissa's whispers to each other.

The store room was a short distance ahead as they rounded a bend. "Is it bad I want to point and laugh at Edthgar's corpse?" Courtney joked.

Petr piped in, "No, I piss on it."

"When everyone is done I'm burning the freak," Andrea added as sparks reappeared in her eyes.

Ivan stopped in the doorway and stared. He reached out to the rock wall to steady himself.

"What's wrong?" Courtney asked.

Ivan looked into her eyes but said nothing. Courtney knew right away no celebration would happen. She released Andrea's hand and rushed to the doorway. Andrea followed freely as they passed Ivan and entered the room.

Luke sat by Hank, hanging his head. His bloody katana sat across his lap, under his shaky hands.

"Luke?" Courtney said.

He looked up at her with a distant gaze. Aside from the haunted expression and a nasty gash on his cheek, he appeared uninjured.

Her uncle hadn't been so lucky.

"Oh no. I'm so sorry," Andrea said. Her tears resumed as she hugged Courtney.

Courtney's eyebrow twitched as her smile twisted into a snarl. She drew her sword, and it shook in her hand as she pushed Andrea aside to stalk towards Edthgar's corpse. Her gaze lingered on Hank's body, then turned to Luke.

"Move him," she said.

Luke nodded, waving Ivan over to help. They carefully lifted Hank and carried him away from Edthgar. Courtney didn't watch. She stared at Edthgar's severed head in silence, perfectly still aside from her left hand. Her knuckles whitened as she squeezed the sword's handle.

Courtney screamed, and the sword lashed out into Edthgar's snout. His head careened through the crumbling stone shelving and cracked the glowing rock behind it.

"You motherfucker! I'd revive you if I could just to fucking slaughter you over and over again!" she bellowed at the bleeding body, her voice echoing through the chamber.

Courtney hacked and slashed at Edthgar's corpse, screaming with each swing. Chunks of gargoyle flesh splattered the floor around the body until she stopped, gasping for breath. Her entire body shook as she plunged the sword into the gaping cuts in the dead gargoyle.

A pained groan wheezed out as she dropped to her knees, but she kept her hands on the sword's cross guard. Courtney lowered her head to rest against the pommel, then didn't move.

After a few minutes, Courtney stood. She swayed as she pulled the sword free. Held in one hand, the tip scraped against the bloodied stone as she turned to face the survivors. Clean streaks appeared in the gore on her face, washed away by tears.

Courtney pulled a rag from inside her breastplate to wipe her sword clean again, but she tossed it aside since it was streaked with her own blood from her shoulder. Her head turned to where Hank's body sat propped up against the water bottle pallet. Mark had arrived, and the doctor examined Hank, shaking his head.

"He...he told me to tell you goodbye, and that he loved you," Luke said in the barest whisper as he walked over and held out his hat for her to clean her sword.

"How did it happen?" Courtney asked as she took the hat.

"He saved my ass so many times. He diverted Edthgar's attention while I was down and wound up with the ax in his belly. Somehow he still found the strength to swing his William Wallace sword. He got Edthgar; I just finished it." That distant feeling never left Luke's voice.

Luke looked past her at the claymore on the floor, though she doubted he saw it. The skin of his cheek flapped to the side; he didn't seem to notice. She sheathed her sword and hugged him.

"It's not your fault, it was all the fucking gargoyles," Courtney said. She rested her head against his and added, "We've got a long road ahead of us still. If you want out, I understand."

Some grit entered his voice as he answered. "I'll be by your side, no matter where this takes us. Your uncle didn't save me so I could abandon you. Life without you would be more terrifying than any gargoyle."

Courtney swallowed hard and backed away as he finally looked in her eyes. No tears flowed. Instead, strength radiated from him. She sighed, thinking of how the gargoyles twisted her jokester into another battler with a thirst for vengeance.

No more tears for now. Andrea needs you to figure out what to do. She's as close to family as it gets without Unc.

Courtney turned back to Edthgar's corpse. "Andrea, you gave Edthgar some good burns before. Think you can light up what's left of the fucker?"

Andrea formed an orb of crackling electricity between her hands without a word. The orb grew and moved in front of her until it was twice the size of a beach ball. Her sparks ignited the air around them into a massive ball of fire. The ball collapsed as it hit Edthgar, lighting his remains up in flames. Andrea said an incantation, and the odor of burning flesh disappeared.

Renee limped over, dragging Edthgar's head with her. "I'm sorry I was out cold. I could've helped. It should've been me. I..." Renee said until Courtney put a finger to her lips.

"It's done. All we can do is make sure no one else dies. I'll kill anything that threatens us," Courtney said as she reached for Edthgar's head.

Luke took the other side, and together they tossed the head into the flames. Courtney glanced around at the other survivors watching the winged gargoyle burn. Her gaze turned to the fire rising from Edthgar to the cavern ceiling, and she wrapped her arms around Luke again. One hand drifted to her sword as the flames danced between the teeth in Edthgar's severed head.

How many more fires do we have to set before this nightmare is over?

ACKNOWLEDGEMENTS

There are far too many people who helped *The Den of Stone* become the tale in the preceding pages to name them all, but I'll try—and hopefully not get as long-winded as Ivan.

First up has to be Lorraine Jonsson. Without you wanting to know how the awful original version of this tale ended, I never would've taken pencil to paper on Courtney's tale again. Love you, Rainny.

Charlotte Ferguson, Heather Carman, and my parents: I want to say thank you for encouraging me to keep going and apologize for subjecting you to the messy first draft. Your feedback and the early edits by Anthony Monroe kept me motivated while I figured out what I was doing through the editing process.

Discovering the writing community on Instagram has been the biggest aid to figuring out what I was doing with this whole writing thing. There's been so much advice and encouragement, which has made this story better and pumped me up to deliver even more craziness in future installments of The Blood Key series.

I need to give a shoutout to my beta readers for helping pare this story down from the banter-y and overly-descriptive monstrosity they all saw. Luke Courtney, Sean Donovan, Weslyn Amory, Ciara Hartford, Eric Bronley, Jennifer Ascienzo, Maria Patenaude, Rachel Riendeau Hayes, Selena Martinez, and JE Smith: thank you.

River Ari and Lessa Dayne also need a special shoutout for all the extra aid given with editing and advice as my critique partner, respectively. Tony Paz and Giulietta Zawadzki have done some amazing art for this book series, too. Check out their portfolios and throw some extra business their way. The team at MiblArt created an exceptional cover under incredible duress in Ukraine and I couldn't be happier. Slava Ukraini.

Finally, I thank you, dear reader. My main goal with this story was to entertain you, and hopefully I've succeeded enough for you to pick up book two, *The Nightmare Path*, once I'm able to sort through that nightmare of a manuscript and whip it into something worthy of reading.

T h a n k   y o u .

AUTHOR BIO

Roger Sandri writes his first drafts by pencil and paper in beautiful southern New England because too much screen time strains his eyes, unless he's procrastinating on Instagram as @roger_sandri_wordslinger. He does warehouse work by day and writes (sometimes) by night. Feel free to shoot him a DM on his page and quote his muse Lorraine by saying, "Write faster, dammit," to motivate the lazy bugger.

Roger would rather read fantasy or horror novels, watch hockey, play Diablo II for the ninetieth time, or build model airplanes than have his picture taken for an author bio. Some theorize he may be part-Sasquatch, but honestly, he doesn't want to scare readers with his appearance—only his writing. If one should encounter him in the wild, approach slowly and bring up the aforementioned subjects. Otherwise, he generally speaks an odd assortment of grunts and is attempting to learn German as part of his desire to see Austria.

His writing supervisor, pictured here, is Camilla. He has one other cat named Bella. Together, they ensure any feline characters in his writing stay safe. The many tales Roger plans to write all blend in elements of horror, no matter the main genre, so the cats' diligence in ensuring their writer's pencil doesn't create too many character deaths is hopefully appreciated by you, dear reader.

Ingram Content Group UK Ltd.
Milton Keynes UK
UKHW041034080623
423097UK00002B/29

9 781087 959467